DECEIT

KERRY BARNES

H | **Q**

ONE PLACE. MANY STORIES

HQ
An imprint of HarperCollins*Publishers* Ltd
1 London Bridge Street
London SE1 9GF

This paperback edition 2018

First published in Great Britain by
HQ, an imprint of HarperCollins*Publishers* Ltd 2018

ISBN: 9780008318444

Typeset by Palimpsest Book Production Ltd, Falkirk, Stirlingshire
Printed and bound in Great Britain by
CPI Group (UK) Ltd, Melksham, SN12 6TR

Carly and Perry, you make me so proud.

Prologue

With her eyes shut tight and the cover over her face, she held her breath and listened to the creaking, as the door to her bedroom slowly opened. She could smell his aftershave, that intoxicating smell that lingered after he would leave. A smell she had learned to detest. Each slow, deliberate footstep was like death itself creeping up on her. Small beads of sweat peppered her brow as she lay there, desperate for the nightmare to be over. Yet, as she felt the bed sink, she knew then it had only just begun. Another night of terror.

His slimy words and hot breath made her shudder, as he pulled back the covers and brushed his bristly chin against her cheek. She kept her eyes tightly closed and gripped the quilt in a vain attempt to prevent revealing her body that was barely covered by the thin nightdress she was wearing. She was conscious of her breasts. They had just started to develop, not big enough for a bra but not small enough for a vest. Still, she was aware that they were there, and so was he, as he ran his large calloused hands over her.

She winced and wanted to yell, but the fear of death was more frightening. He whispered those dark, cold words, 'Scream and you will die. No one will believe you; no one cares, but me. I love you, my little darling. No one will love you as much as me. Now, let me show you how much I love you.'

She pushed her head deeper into the pillow, unable to look at his ruddy face and those narrow, brown, lifeless eyes. Over and over in her mind, she said, 'Please go away, please go away.'

The wind banged the open window, and for a second, she was back in the room, and his heavy body, like a devouring octopus, lay across her. She fought to drift off to another place, deep into a storybook she'd once read, but the loud bang made her jump again.

As she tried to turn her tear-stained face to the side, she suddenly saw an eye, staring in through a partially opened door. She recognised those eyes, and begged and pleaded, with the terror on her face, for the person behind that door to rescue her. But that figure with its sorrowful look disappeared as quickly as it arrived and only intensified her fear. She was all alone, and she was powerless to prevent this and other sordid acts from continuing. Why? Because she was a child, and he was an adult … a monster.

Chapter 1

The cold wind ripped at her face and through her thick Ralph Lauren camel coat. Kara quickened her pace, cursing under her breath, 'Damn the fucking car.' She rarely swore in public, but this freezing cold morning, she felt like screaming obscenities. The bus stop was a short distance and rather than wait for the AA man, she headed off, determined not to be late for work.

Just as she reached the end of her close, she noticed a woman, the same one she'd seen staring at her in Tesco yesterday. Dressed in a long black coat and black gloves, the tall fair-haired lady grinned. Kara was about to say good morning when the woman curled her lip and smirked. Baffled by the odd interaction, Kara looked away. She put her head down and continued.

As she hurried along the main road that separated the private development from the council estate, she pulled her hat down below her ears to stop the wind biting and giving her an earache. The bus shot past her, and her heart sank. She felt like crying. First, the car wouldn't start, and now she'd missed the bus. She contemplated going home and calling in sick, but she'd had two days off last week with that excuse and it wasn't going down too well with her manager.

The only other option was to cut through the estate and catch another bus; they were more frequent from the other side. She had only ever done this twice before and both times had been a nightmare. On the first occasion, she was almost in the middle of a war between two families hurling bricks at each other, and on the second one, she was chased by a pit bull. Luckily, the owner managed to stop the dog in its tracks before it sunk its teeth into her. Even so, it frightened the life out of her.

She stopped at the kerb and faltered for a second before crossing the road. None of the winos would be out this early, the teenagers would still be asleep, and so she made a decision to go for it. Besides, she was frozen to the bone, and waiting another half an hour would really cause her to spin on her heels and return to the warmth of her home. She stepped off the pavement, making her way through the estate. It was so gloomy and dingy, she felt as though she had entered a *Mad Max* film.

Why the council couldn't help these people by adding a play area or fixing the broken windows was beyond her. It saddened her to think that the poorer members of society were shoved into homes like these. It reminded her every day that they had nothing.

She passed the first block and was almost knocked down. A woman pushing a buggy wasn't looking where she was going because she had her neck craning over her shoulder, shouting up at the top maisonette, which was three storeys high. Kara looked at the baby in the buggy and smiled.

'You're a right no-good, a fucking wrong 'un, Billy Big Balls. I swear on me muvver's eyesight, you'll not fucking see me or the baby again, ya dirty cunt!' screamed the woman. Then, she turned to march on and glared at Kara, looking her up and down and making no bones about it. 'What are you fucking gawping at? Ya fucking snob!'

Kara was stunned. Before she could answer, the woman pushed past her, still shouting foul-mouthed insults. Glancing down at her expensive coat, long real leather boots, and Louis Vuitton

4

handbag, she felt self-conscious and out of place. Again, she felt near to tears because she wasn't a snob.

She looked up at the man hanging over the balcony with a white vest and his arms covered in tattoos. 'Julie, get back 'ere, ya fucking stupid bitch. I ain't gone anywhere near ya fucking sister!'

'Go and fucking hug a landmine, ya rotten dirty scrot.'

Kara looked away and carried on ahead. The main road was now in sight, as she hurried her way through the rubbish, dirt, and debris. Luckily, the bus arrived a minute or two later. The heat hit her, as she stepped on the bus and paid the driver. Instantly, the warm air made her nose run and her cheeks tingle. She got herself comfortable and waited for the driver to pull away.

But there was a hold-up. Kara looked out of the front window to see the mother with the buggy running down the road waving her hands to stop the vehicle. Kara smiled to herself. The woman had so much nerve to run down the middle of the road, swearing at the drivers of the two cars that hooted at her. The doors flew open and she hopped on, dragging the buggy behind her. 'Cheers, mate. Cor, it's fucking taters out there,' she said, out of breath.

The bus driver obviously knew who she was. 'Off back to ya muvver's, Julie?' he asked half-laughing.

Still struggling to find her purse, she replied, 'Yeah, that fat cunt has been sniffing around our Sharon again. I'm off up there to give her a fucking thump. Er, Tom, I think I've left me purse at home.'

Kara felt in her pocket for change, ready to offer the woman's fare, but the driver replied to the woman, 'Just get on, Julie.'

Kara watched as the skinny woman, dressed in a tight tracksuit and a body warmer, tugged the buggy and plonked herself onto the side seat. On the back of the buggy was a big bag that she dived into; she retrieved a dummy, sucked it clean, and stuffed it in the baby's mouth. Kara noticed the woman's hands were shaking and discerned the sores around her mouth. Her hair, tightly pulled back in a scruffy bun against her pale skin, did her no favours whatsoever. Two huge loop earrings dangled from her ears and a stud had been inserted through her eyebrow.

The woman noticed her staring and glared back. 'Do you know me or what? Ya keep staring, ya nosy prat!'

Kara looked away and stared out of the side window. Her intention wasn't to be nosy; she actually felt sorry for the girl.

As they approached the next stop, another young woman was waiting; she was so much like Julie, they could have been sisters. As soon as she hopped on, she plonked herself next to Julie. 'All right, Jue, where ya off to, then?'

Julie was searching through her tatty-looking fake Prada bag. 'Me muvver's, to see that skanky sister of mine. I found fat boy's phone with text messages on it, and I swear, it's her again. Well, she's gonna get it this time.'

The other girl was chewing gum and smiling at the baby. 'Jue, why don't ya just leave him? I mean, if it ain't ya sister, it's some other slag.'

Julie sighed and looked at her friend. 'Diane, where the fuck am I gonna go, eh? I can't live at me ol' gal's. My flat is all I 'ave, and that fat cunt won't get out. I wish he would get so pissed, he falls over the balcony and kills himself, or, I swear, one day, I'll give him a helping hand.'

Kara couldn't look at the girls; instead, she stared out of the window and listened to them talking about a world far removed from her own. She counted herself lucky that she had a job and money. Her life could have been so much worse. She had worked so hard though to get to where she was. Constantly studying – while everyone else her age was having fun enjoying parties, clubbing, and sports – had been a huge personal commitment but a necessary one to have the options in life she both wanted and needed.

Fortunately for her, the next stop was just ahead. So, as soon as the bus came to a halt and the doors flung open, she jumped the two steps and instantly threw up, luckily missing her coat. *Where had the time gone?* she wondered. She should have waited for the AA man.

Eventually, she was through a security gate and inside her lab, ready to get to work. Her lab was the biggest in the building and situated at the end of the corridor; opposite was the office that her manager occupied. She knocked and entered, as she always did, but was surprised to see two men dressed in dark suits in the middle of a conversation with Professor Roger Luken.

'Ahh and here is Kara Bannon,' said Roger, swinging on his swivel chair that had almost worn down to the sponge cushioning. His ruddy complexion was stark against his pure white mop of thick hair. He was a fit-looking man for fifty-eight, and yet, with his white lab coat and red spotted bow tie, he did appear to be every bit the mad professor.

Kara smiled nervously, not aware of who the visitors were.

'Kara, this is Dr Chan and Professor Naughton. They flew in early this morning. They are here to discuss moving the research project over to Denmark. I have told them all about your work and they are eager to see the set-up.'

Nervously, she smiled again and her hands felt clammy. She wasn't used to working alongside strangers or being unprepared. Roger knew what she was like: she was meticulous, well planned, and organised. Her boss must have known weeks ago. Under normal circumstances, he would have given her plenty of notice, but after the horrendous blunder she caused a few months ago, their relationship had changed. He wasn't so accommodating or friendly. She missed the banter and how he used to treat her with care and father-like kindness.

'Oh, I wasn't expecting … er … I mean, I haven't prepared.'

Roger waved his hand. 'Oh, don't be silly. They just want to see a dummy run. Besides, you will be leading the project in Denmark yourself.'

Kara raised her eyebrows and forgot herself. 'What do you

mean, Roger?' Her eyes darted from the visitors back to the professor.

It was Dr Chan who spoke up first. He could see how uncomfortable she was. 'It's lovely to meet you, Kara.' He put his hand out to shake hers. Flat and subdued, she returned the gesture.

'We think the assay that you have designed will fit in very well with our research and we would be honoured if you would work with my team to ensure we have the system operating at its maximum potential. There are always teething issues, and so, it would save us time if you were to initiate the project.'

Kara tried to take it all in, but her sickness was back again, and the waves of nausea were washing over her and filling her with dread.

Roger firmly got up from his chair and turned to face the two men. 'Would you excuse us, gentlemen?' He guided Kara out of the room and into her lab. 'What's the matter with you? You look as if I have asked you to go to the gas chamber.'

Kara studied his concerned face and felt a twinge of guilt. She let out a weary sigh, as her eyes fell to the floor.

'I'm sorry, Roger, I didn't mean to appear so ungrateful. I just don't like surprises. You know me, Miss Fussy Pants.' She attempted to laugh it off.

For the first time, she saw the annoyance spread across his face. 'Kara, if you turn this down, then I am afraid you won't be able to continue with your research, including your own project.'

Those words were enough to wake her up and bring her back down to earth. 'Of course, I'm happy to go to Denmark and help set the project up. I was just shocked, that's all,' she replied, with forced cheerfulness.

Roger gave her a cold stare. 'Kara, you know how this works. You must be ready to work overseas at a minute's notice. These projects are not for us to run. You know they are designed here and used at the company's other sites. You are in a very privileged position. Many others would chew my right hand off to have the opportunities you've been given. Now, don't mess it up.' He shot her a warning glare that sent a shiver down her spine.

Kara was upset that he was teetering on being angry with her. She felt the burning vomit rising again, and without a word, she fled to the toilets and threw up. Ten minutes later, she returned to the lab to find Roger, with a pipette in his hand, already setting up the assay. He glanced over his shoulder with a look of disdain and she felt gutted to have disappointed him. The only thing she could do was put a smile on her face and take over.

'Right, where have we got to?' She squeezed past Roger and the two visiting researchers, before pulling on a pair of rubber gloves.

'I have just coated the bottles with T12 cells. Are you happy to take over?' He gave her a false smile.

Kara nodded and mouthed the word 'Sorry'.

By lunchtime, she felt exhausted and was glad Dr Chan and Professor Naughton were ready to head back to the airport. She much preferred to work alone. It was even harder making polite conversation with two strangers. She loved her job but liked peace and quiet to concentrate. Part of her work involved designing routine tests to identify various strains of viruses that may have mutated. She used tissue culture, a layer of human cells, to coat the flat-bottomed bottle, and then she added the viral samples, before further contaminating the bottle with various bacteria.

The results were promising, as they demonstrated whether the virus had the capability to infect the specific bacteria or attack the human cells. This determined the level of mutation. As the most senior bacteriologist in the team, with the exception of course of Professor Luken, it was also her job to test random samples of vaccine batches. Holding a position of great responsibility, she was also allowed to do her own research, which was funded by the company. It was a project that would hold her in high esteem among the top scientists.

The tearoom at the other end of the corridor was quiet. Most of the staff had gone to the main canteen. Kara pulled sandwiches from her bag and examined the limp cheese and bread, which had been made soggy by the overripe tomatoes. She threw them back into the box and pulled out an apple. Kara was startled by her mobile phone, which vibrated in her back pocket. She'd forgotten she'd had it on silent. As she struggled to answer it before it rang off, she didn't look at the number, assuming it was Justin, her boyfriend. 'Hello?' She tried to sound upbeat.

However, the voice that greeted her was anything but upbeat. In fact, it was chilling. 'Kara, Kara, perfect Kara, how's dearest Justin?' A cold, sickly chuckle ended the call.

The apple fell out of her hand and rolled under the table, as Kara stared at the number. The voice was unrecognisable but the call had come from her mother's phone.

Before she had a chance to call back, Roger popped his head around the door, and as soon as he saw her there alone, he came inside and sat opposite. 'So, what's going on, Kara? You have been offish for weeks now.'

Her face was blank. She seemed to be staring aimlessly.

'Kara, are you listening to me?' he growled.

His raised voice snapped her out of her daze. 'Weeks?' she mustered.

He ran a hand through his long wiry hair and nodded. 'Yes, Kara, weeks. You have messed up three tests. Luckily, I realised and corrected your mistakes before the results went out. And I haven't forgotten the serious cock-up with the pigbel drugs.'

She bowed her head in embarrassment. That really was a huge mistake and one she would never repeat.

'It's not like you. Usually, you are meticulous, and to be perfectly frank, you're faultless, but you cannot afford to mess up. These are safety class four bugs and you are trained in this area because you are so good at your job. If this keeps happening, Kara, you will have to go back to quality control.'

'I am really sorry. Look, I will go to Denmark and sort myself out. I've just been feeling unwell. It's some dodgy virus I picked up from Papua New Guinea. When do I go?'

Roger stood up to leave. 'Tomorrow night. The flights are booked. A car will pick you up at seven o'clock, and you will be away for two weeks or longer, if need be.' His words were flat and not his usual endearing tone. Kara then heard him outside laughing with Sam James, the lab technician. Her heart sank. Roger usually laughed with her, but not today, and in fact not for a while now. She couldn't really blame him. It was her own fault – she was the one being distant. However, her pride wouldn't let her confide in him the reasons why she was not herself.

After making a cup of tea, she sat back on one of the mismatched chairs and sniffed away the tears that were ready to tumble down her face. The thought of going to Denmark for two weeks left her desolate. How could she sort things out with Justin, if she was away in another country?

But there was also something else bothering her – that weird phone call. The only other person who ever answered her mother's phone was Lucille, the carer. But the caller's voice, although somewhat similar, had such an unearthly tone to it.

Chapter 2

The journey home was mind-numbing. The bus was full, with only standing room, and Kara found herself hanging on to the pole for dear life. The bug was making her weak and the constant nauseous feeling was wearing her down. The bus arrived at her stop just in time before she collapsed and that was enough to force her to take a seat on the nearest wall.

The icy air from this morning had gone, yet the sky was still dark and gloomy, and it was only six o'clock. It just about summed up her own mood. After a few deep breaths, she headed home along the cherry-tree-lined road into her close. Mr Langley was retrieving his groceries from the boot of his car and only nodded out of politeness when she said 'hello'. Still, the Langleys were nice enough, keeping themselves to themselves, like the others in the close.

As soon as she noticed only her car was in the drive and not Justin's, she felt a sudden emptiness because he was working late at his car dealership business. *Again.*

They had met at her twenty-first birthday party lavishly laid on by her mother, Joan. Justin had turned up with Lucas Lane, her mother's friend's son, whom she'd known for years. She remembered feeling butterflies as soon as she laid eyes on him.

His mousy waves with streaks of blond tumbled neatly around his ears, framing his carefully sculptured face. He was tall with a perfectly proportioned physique. She guessed he was into sports from his muscular broad shoulders, probably a rugby player, she mused, but then his face was flawless, without the cauliflower ears, which suggested maybe he was into football instead.

That summer it was hot, and his golden tan set off his light blue eyes. When the party was in full swing, all she remembered was him and his shy glances. Lottie, her friend from her boarding school days, nudged her arm. 'Cor, he is real hot totty.' She chuckled. Yet Kara didn't need to be told – it was obvious – and she wasn't the only one eyeing him up. There was an enchanting awkwardness about him; he was confident, laughing with the lads, but when his eyes diverted to her, he seemed almost coy.

Lucas Lane was eager to show him off; it was obvious he was a popular lad among his male friends. A couple of the other boys were patting his back and clinking glasses, whilst listening to him telling a story. They seemed to be hanging on his every word. She could only assume he was pretty outgoing and possibly adventurous with wild tales of trekking through the Himalayas. Her heart did a backflip when he approached her to wish her a happy birthday, and to her surprise, he even brought along a gift: a small teddy, with twenty-one embroidered on it. That teddy still sat on her bedside table.

Kara hurried inside, hung her coat up on the coatstand, and went straight to the kitchen. She would cook him a nice meal, his favourite – chilli con carne – and hopefully he would sit at the table and talk. That's all she wanted – for him to talk to her. A few weeks ago, when she called Justin at work and said, 'I have chilli on the stove,' he'd replied, 'Something hot in the kitchen and something hot on the stove, eh? I'll be home in a jiffy.'

His deep husky voice, to her, just oozed sex, and she could listen to him all night; it was as good as any foreplay. Her eyes swam with tears. The onions weren't even out of the fridge when the torrent of tears flowed like Angel Falls. She'd been on the verge of crying for weeks. Justin hadn't actually done or said anything wrong; it was the distance that had come between them and it had happened almost overnight. She thought at first it was her, but then, as the days went on, he seemed miles away, quiet and aloof.

She asked him a few times if he was okay, but he snapped back at her, telling her to stop fussing. She told herself it would blow over and their relationship – perfect in her eyes – would get back to normal. Romantic meals for two, bubble baths together, and a shared bottle of wine in front of the open fire would all return. Yet, the days were now turning into weeks, and she felt her heart being ripped away from her.

Kara sighed and continued preparing the food. Once the chilli was simmering, she went upstairs to have a quick shower and redo her make-up; perhaps she had become a little dowdy and unattractive. The main bathroom was huge with a bath that would easily accommodate two people and a walk-in shower area much like a wet room. The full-length mirror screwed to the far end was surrounded by spotlights, so even a stray hair or a tiny spot could be seen.

Kara stepped out of her clothes, and for a second, she didn't recognise herself. Perhaps she'd let herself go. Her clothes were certainly tighter; she would have to renew her gym membership and spruce herself up. Justin was fit and his body was rippled with muscles. Another tear fell. She took a step closer and peered at her face. Her blonde hair needed a trim or a restyle; it was just long and flat. The usual shine had disappeared, and she had to admit to herself, she didn't look in the best shape at all. Her skin was not smooth and glowing; her face appeared pale and spiteful.

Perhaps that was it; maybe he wasn't attracted to her like before. At only twenty-six years old, she should look fresh and vibrant. Maybe it was her secret tears and all the worry that were souring her face, or the virus bringing her down. The bed sheets had been dry for over a month now, and he hadn't so much as touched her. She swallowed the hard lump in her throat. The shower was hot, and she had to turn it down a notch, submersing herself under the champagne-setting flow. Standing for a while, she allowed the water to tickle her back and massage her throbbing head.

She must get back to how she was before: toned, fresh, and attractive. Not that she fancied herself as anything special, but Justin did. He told her she was an even prettier version of Jennifer Aniston, and he wasn't the only one: a few people had said she was a lookalike. He always complimented her; in fact, he treated her as if she were the only woman alive. The problem was he hadn't lately, though.

Hearing the sound of the front door shutting loudly, her heart fluttered; he was home. She almost slipped over in the shower, trying to get out. She wanted to get dressed and apply a few layers of make-up, add her expensive perfume, and slip on her new floral print dress. He had bought it for her when they went to Harrods. She had to win him back. It was absurd that she was thinking she had lost him, but it was how she was beginning to feel, and if she dared even to think for a moment he was seeing someone else, she would feel sick. That notion was unbearable.

He didn't call up to her with one of his captivating comments like, 'Do you need a back scrubber?' or 'Do you need company in that bath?' She shook, putting her mascara on, knowing this was the time she would demand to know what was going on. She planned the words over and over in her head. She even thought of lowering her pride by begging him to go back to the way things were, with a holiday, or perhaps spicing up their sex life.

He wasn't in the kitchen, when she eventually wandered downstairs. He was in the snug, the smallest room where they went to read, where the bookshelves displayed an array of books from fiction to medical publications. In the corner was a desk and a computer to catch up on work at home. A three-piece suite softened the room and made it more homely than an office.

She peered in with a false smile on her face, when inside she was dying. 'Well, hello, sexy.' She tried to sound upbeat, but it was not reciprocated with his usual smile that lit up his face. He was staring down at his phone, and then he peered up with an expression she'd never seen before. It resembled a deep sorrow that dragged his eyes down.

She tilted her head to the side. 'Please, Justin, tell me what's wrong? I can't bear this tension, this … I don't even know what it is, but it's hurting me. You have changed so much towards me. I mean, I hardly recognise you … Look, if I've done something wrong, please tell me. Put me out of this misery.' Her eyes filled with salty tears and she let them hang there and build up, before they finally fell in streams. She made no sound but just stared, longing for him to run to her, throw his arms around her, and tell her he loved her.

He didn't; instead, he looked away, and in a meek voice, he said, 'I'm just tired and overworked. Please, stop fussing.'

She turned to walk away and hesitated, glancing one more time over her shoulder, to find him still staring at his phone. Her pain was tainted by so much frustration that she wanted to run back and shake him. *Couldn't he see how much it was killing her?*

With a heavy heart, she dished up the chilli con carne and carried the two plates into the dining room. Her hands were shaking as she lit the candle. He joined her, sitting opposite, but really, he wasn't himself. She watched him struggling to force the food down. Then, exasperation got the better of her. She slammed her knife and fork down on the solid oak table, making him jump. 'Justin, I can't take this anymore. What the hell's going on? You won't talk, and now you can't even eat. This isn't fair. Tell me now! What is wrong?' she shrieked.

Justin pushed his plate forward, clasped his hands together, and leaned his elbows on the table. She searched his eyes for answers, all the while feeling overanxious and thwarted with pending grief. Her heart was racing and her breathing shallow, as if she were awaiting the death penalty. This wasn't Justin, not her Justin, with the beaming white-teeth smiles and a face full of fun, spouting his jokes at every opportunity. The easy-going, sweet man who worked hard, loved hard, and cared for everyone, most of all her, seemed to be inwardly broken. She didn't recognise his sober expression or the dull look in his otherwise vibrant ocean-coloured eyes that once danced like the waves.

'I, er, I don't know how to tell you this, but I can't carry on deceiving you. Kara, I'm so sorry …' he replied, choking on his words.

'What, tell me what's going on? Please, we can work things out. Nothing is ever that bad.' Her voice was on the point of hysteria.

He shook his head and looked down in shame. 'Oh Jesus, Kara, there's no easy way to say it … I'm leaving you.'

The words took a few seconds to digest. She couldn't believe he'd just said them. Now stunned, she stared, shaking her head. 'No, no, Justin, please don't tell me you're leaving me! Why? Why?' She pleaded with him for an answer.

He looked up, his face drenched in guilt. 'Oh, Kara, you deserve the truth, but I know it will hurt you so much. I'm so sorry. I don't know how to tell you, but I can't put it off any longer … I never meant to hurt you, I swear, and for the record, I do love you, I always have, more than anyone, but I have to end our relationship … I did something stupid …'

Kara guessed he had met someone else and couldn't stand to hear those words, knowing it would destroy her. No one was more important in her life than Justin. He was her world, her rock, and her love. 'Please, Justin, it doesn't matter, don't tell me. We can work it out. I'll forgive you. Just don't leave me. Please, don't leave me.' Her mouth felt like it was chewing a hundred cotton-wool balls and her legs were like mushy peas.

Justin's bottom lip quivered, and then he placed his face in his hands. Kara was by his side with her arms around him. 'It's okay, we'll be fine, we can work this out, I'll forgive you. Just don't say any more. We can put whatever it is behind us … Come on, don't get upset. It's okay, I promise.' She'd never seen him cry before. It was guilt, she thought, but it didn't matter. They would sort it out. She would forgive him for anything right now, as long as he didn't leave her.

To her surprise, he pushed her away. 'Stop it, Kara! Just stop it, will you! I can't stay, I won't stay, and you have to let me go!'

Stunned, Kara stepped back, and looked at the love of her life, with his wet red cheeks. It was strange. All she could say, in a whisper, was 'Why?'

He grabbed the serviette from the table and wiped his face, before he took a deep breath. 'I've got a woman pregnant, so I have no choice.'

Kara threw her hands to her mouth in horror. *No, he can't have. He wouldn't do that. This was a nightmare … She would wake up and it would all be a bad dream.*

'Look, tell her to get an abortion, tell her … I don't know, Justin, but please don't leave me. I can't live without you.'

Kara was dancing on his conscience and he couldn't deal with it. 'Shut up! Just shut up. I'm leaving and that's it. Please stop, Kara. I've made my decision and it's final.'

Kara ran back to him, throwing her arms around his neck. 'Please don't, Justin, I'm begging you!' She could feel her heart being ripped to shreds, not in half so that she could fix it together, but in strands of lonely pieces that could never be whole again. Staring with begging eyes at the only man she'd ever loved, and for him to coldly look away, hurt like nothing on earth.

She slumped to the floor in agonising grief. In that single moment, her chest was crushed by heartache, knowing that this battle to hold on to their relationship would be fought alone. His cold eyes told her everything she needed to know – he didn't want her anymore, he wanted someone else. She curled in a ball and rocked, too distraught even to make a crying sound. Unable to ease her pain for fear of giving her false hope, he left the room and headed upstairs to pack.

The avalanche of grief mixed with furious frustration turned her self-pity to a burning anger. She gasped as the cold realisation hit her: he didn't even care enough to stay and work things out. Every nerve in her body was now on fire. She jumped up, screaming, as she snatched the plates and hurled them at the wall. The beautiful cream plaster mouldings were now covered in chilli, which was sliding down the Italian fresco wallpaper.

Her temper increased, and she ran up the stairs after him, shrieking, 'How could you do this to me? How could you be so cold and heartless? You fucking two-timing bastard!' Shocked by her own actions and even by the pitch in her voice, she threw her hands to her mouth and glared wide-eyed.

The suitcase was open, and he was carefully filling it with freshly ironed shirts and trousers. He wouldn't even look at her; it was as if she were a ghost. In a fit of fury, she grabbed the case and tossed it on the floor. 'How could you, how could you?' she cried.

Without a word, he held both her arms, before she tore into anything else, and gently pushed her out of the room and closed the door behind her. She had never shown such heartbreaking emotion. Her pleading, distraught expression mixed with that vile anger in her voice had turned her into an unrecognisable stranger.

Kara knew then that no matter how much she screamed, cried, or even begged, he was still going to leave. And he did – half an hour later.

The emptiness was like hell on earth, left with just thoughts of him and another woman. The misguided notion that he was totally besotted with her, only to find out he was sleeping with someone else, was the ultimate in deceit. He had taken away her perfect world in one fell swoop. The house that was once alive with love and passion was now a cold shell filled with memories that had ripped her heart out.

Every time she looked at a photo, a piece of jewellery, the furniture, the clothes – everything that was in the house, in fact – it all reminded her of him. How was she going to cope? The gut-wrenching pain was worse than anything she'd ever experienced. What did she have now, but a big empty void and a bleak future?

Sitting in the dining room for hours in a daze, she finally heard a bird tweeting. As she pulled back the curtains, the sun almost blinded her. She hadn't been to sleep at all. Every muscle ached, and her legs were numb from sitting. She clung on to the idea that maybe once he was away, he would realise what he was missing, and would return soon with a bag of apologies.

Too grieved to talk to anyone, she pulled the phone from the socket and struggled to the bedroom. As she opened the door and saw the small teddy on the bedside table, she retreated to a spare room and drew the curtains. Too exhausted to do anything but sleep, she lay on the bed and dragged the purple quilted throw over her legs. But as she closed her eyes to blot out the world, his face was there, with that sorrowful look.

Eventually, she drifted off and was tossing and turning, only to wake up with nightmares before drifting off again. At four o'clock in the afternoon, she sat bolt upright remembering the trip to Denmark. She would have to get her bags packed, but unexpectedly, her stomach was burning, ready to expel its contents. Crouched on the cold tiled floor and hanging on to the toilet, the vomit rose once more, and she almost choked. Her throat was alight with acid and her lips burned. All she brought up was bile because her stomach was empty.

After she washed her face and forced herself to clean her teeth, she wandered still in a daze back to the bedroom to get dressed. Her skin felt sensitive, and so she slipped into one of her soft lined tracksuits that hung sloppily off her shoulder. Justin liked her in her Sloppy Joes, as he called them; he said she could wear a black sack and still look gorgeous, but maybe it had all been a lie. She looked once more in the bathroom mirror and noticed the dark circles under her eyes, the red eyelids, and sallow skin. No wonder he ran to the arms of someone else. She looked a mess, and yet he didn't; his boyish broad smile and the twinkle in his round eyes were just the same – ageless.

The dining table had been cleaned and the crap that was up the wall was all washed down. Her heart skipped a beat. He was back. Perhaps he'd made a mistake. Quickly, she ran to the kitchen, expecting to find him, but only to have her heart ripped away from her again. A slim woman, with dark hair scraped back into a ponytail, wearing no make-up and sporting a piercing through her nose, stood with her rubber gloves on ready to start on the cleaning.

It was Angie, her cleaner of three years, who, in all honesty, Kara knew nothing about, except she worked hard, was reliable and trustworthy, and lived on the estate. Justin had taken her on when he read an ad in the local newsagent's window. Angie was eager to earn money on the side, just to have decent food in the cupboard. Her rent had gone up and she could barely cover the cost of living. If it wasn't for her brother Rocky, bunging her a few quid each week, she would have starved to death, but the cash-in-hand cleaning job paid the heating bill and allowed her to get her nails done or to have a night out once a month with the girls.

'Hey, are you okay, Kara? I saw you asleep in one of the spare rooms. I tried to be quiet … Had a row, did ya?' she asked, totally lacking any sensitivity.

Kara wasn't expecting to see Angie and was not in the mood to talk. She needed time and space to figure it all out for herself. 'No, I'm not well. Sorry, Angie, would you excuse me, please?'

Angie nodded. 'Yeah, sure.' She waited for Kara to leave, before she mumbled under her breath, 'Snotty bitch.'

Angie didn't really care one way or the other. As far as she was concerned, Kara and Justin were a professional working couple too busy to clean up their own shit, so they paid her to do it. They also paid well, so that was that. As she saw it, Kara was just a geek with her nose constantly in a book, too aloof to sit and have a cup of tea and a chat with her.

She cleaned two houses in the close and the owners were all the same – too preoccupied with their own lives to stop and share a piece of cake or even notice her there. She could not wait to get back home on the estate where at least there was friendly banter.

Angie was still washing down the kitchen, when Kara returned, in need of a cold glass of water, fighting off another wave of sickness that had engulfed her. If she didn't get her act together soon, she would miss the taxi.

'Kara, tell me to mind me own business, but do you need a doctor? 'Cos, I swear, you look bleedin' rough, girl.'

'No, I've just caught a bug, that's all,' she replied, holding back tears.

Angie didn't ask any more questions. She removed her rubber gloves and sighed. 'All done, I'll be back tomorrow, for me wages.' Her fake smile faded, and she hurried out of the room, finally slamming the door behind her, making Kara jump.

Shaking with pain and fear, Kara opened a drawer and pulled out two twenty-pound notes and placed them on the side. She knew she wouldn't be able to have a conversation with anyone without bursting into tears. When Angie returned, her money would be there, ready. She had to pull herself together somehow.

How could she go to Denmark in this state? She stared at the phone. She had to call in sick, but she could not bring herself to make the call straightaway. She was at the point where she couldn't handle another argument. In fact, she couldn't cope with anything, all her thoughts now consumed with grief over Justin leaving, and there was no way this wretched feeling of despair would leave her any time soon.

She pulled down the white case with the red cross and flipped open the lid; there, at the back, was a packet of cigarettes. She'd given up two years ago but now had an urge to smoke the lot followed by a bottle of brandy. Then she spotted the bottle of sleeping tablets. She grabbed it and nervously popped four pills into her hand. That would do it. Like a horse tranquilizer, that should knock her out. At least those tiny tablets would ensure some respite from the emotional pain.

She threw them to the back of her throat, filled a glass with iced water from the fridge, and gulped them down, gagging at the bitter taste. Almost instantaneously, she felt overcome with fatigue and staggered off to the bedroom. Her mind went back to her work and the trip. *Five minutes' rest and I will call Roger and let him know I can't make it.*

She had not realised he would have left the labs by now.

In the distance, she could hear the faint sound of a car hooting outside, but her vision was blurred, and her body wouldn't move. She ignored it, sank back into a deeper slumber, and slept for what she thought was just eight hours.

By the time she'd woken up, it was early in the morning, but she had absolutely no idea of the actual time or even which day it was. She strolled into the bedroom and looked inside Justin's wardrobe for a reality check. Sure enough, this was no nightmare – all his clothes were gone, with just a neat row of coat hangers, the only tangible reminder of his former presence.

She wandered from room to room, beside herself with heartache. Her mind just couldn't focus. Eventually, she made a coffee, lit up a cigarette, and sat in front of the television set, hoping something would take her mind off everything. But as soon as the screen lit up, she saw the date and almost gasped in horror – she had lost three days and had no idea why. The sleeping tablets had left her heady, but really, she should have known the date.

'*Oh shit!*' she muttered, her mind on the trip to Denmark. Her hands were shaking, as she plugged the phone back into the

23

socket. A cold shiver ran through her. Roger would be angry and humiliated. She'd let him down again and now she felt guilty. Without even thinking through how she would explain her absence from work, she called the office number. Roger answered within two rings. 'Professor Luken.'

Kara stared into space, holding the phone to her ear. 'It's me, Kara.' Her voice was a mere whisper.

There was silence, and she could sense his upbeat tone plummeting. 'Oh, so you are alive, then? Well, Kara, I think it's best that you contact Human Resources. This situation is completely out of my hands ... unless, of course, you are in hospital and couldn't get to a bloody phone.'

'Er ... no, I fell asleep. I mean, I was sick, I, um ...'

'Enough, Kara, I am too busy cleaning up your mess to talk. Call HR. I think they will need to see you. As far as I am concerned, you no longer work with me.' The phone went dead. Kara continued to stare into the distance. It was an unwelcome, life-changing moment: her career was over, and she now had nothing. Her boyfriend and her job were the two most important things in her life. Now, each was flushed down the toilet.

The only solace she had was there in that medicine box. She swallowed hard, again to force the nauseous feeling away, and shuffled on unsteady feet to the kitchen. As she lifted the lid to the medicine box, she got a whiff of stale sweat. Normally, that would have had her tearing up the stairs to the shower, but not today. All she wanted was to be rid of the torturous thoughts weaving in and out of her subconscious.

She swallowed another four tablets and reached for the bottle of brandy that she kept for cooking. The taste was harsh and ripped at her already sore throat. Squeezing her eyes tightly, she gulped back mouthfuls, gasped for breath, and then filled her mouth with more amber nectar. A sudden warm feeling softened her tense muscles and she stared at the drugs in the box. If she took all of them, she would be over this pain for good.

She shook her head, remembering a time when she'd stared at a bottle of tablets but didn't have the guts back then. She gulped more of the brandy, but as she was about to snap open the first pot of pills, she felt weak and overcome with tiredness. She made her way into the living room and flopped onto the four-seater leather sofa. Within seconds, she was out cold in body, yet her mind was awash with vivid nightmares of the past.

A noise in the distant recesses of her mind rendered her half-awake. For a moment, she was unsure where she was until she saw the huge inglenook fireplace and the antique trunk she and Justin used as a coffee table. Slowly, she pulled her aching body to an upright position and took large breaths of air. It was all coming back to her and her face crumpled in pain. After pushing the quilt from her legs, she frowned. She didn't want to get her hopes up, but who had covered her over?

Like a fragile child, she got to her feet and gingerly made her way to the kitchen. The money was gone, and the medicine box was put away. Angie! It must have been Angie who covered her over. A deep sadness enveloped her because she knew then that she had to get herself together and deal with the mental anguish of being alone. The date on the kitchen clock was flashing, and yet Kara could not comprehend it. She'd lost six days. *How the hell did that happen?*

Snapping out of her daze, and in a rush to pull herself together, she made breakfast, and just as she finished the last mouthful, she heard what she assumed was the postman, as he shoved the mail through the letterbox. She looked down at the floor and saw a letter from Lucas Lane and Partners, Solicitor, their solicitor and long-term friend. With no stamp, she surmised it had been hand-delivered.

She fingered her way around the seal and then ripped the envelope open. She had to read the words twice in disbelief. Discounting all the legal jargon for the moment, the solicitor said she was to move out by the end of the week. *What?* She fell to her knees and screamed like a wild animal. 'You bastard, you FUCKING BASTARD!' Gagging in between sobs, Kara punched the door repeatedly. *How could he be so cruel?* This wasn't her man; this was not him at all. He would never have thrown her out on her ear. She reread the letter, hoping she'd misread it, but the instruction was there in black and white.

Justin owned the house. It was his before they met, and now he was turfing her out to move in his girlfriend. *How could he?* This was their home, albeit in his name, but it was *theirs*. They'd shared and decorated it and made it their own.

Falling to her knees, she clenched her stomach, as if her insides were being pulled away from her. She gasped for air, as though her lungs wouldn't work. Unexpectedly, she was fraught with an uncontrollable rage. Her otherwise disciplined persona was somehow switched off, as if the devil himself had taken control of her senses. Tidal waves of incensed fury pushed her to act so out of character, that she wasn't fully aware of her actions. A sudden red mist descended and blinded her.

The sleeping tablets, the drink, and the feeling of utter betrayal pushed her to search the cupboards for something to destroy their love nest. If he wanted the house, then he could fucking have it. Yet, she was going to make dead sure he would never live in it again. She headed straight for the garage – his garage that housed every tool imaginable. There, by the garage doors, were the lawnmower and strimmer, which had stood unused because they employed a gardener, but Justin, being Justin, liked his man tools and toys.

By the side were two petrol cans, in case he ever needed to mow the lawn himself or fill up his car. In a fit of anger, she grabbed the cans and returned to the kitchen, intent on a mission. She would destroy their home – his home.

Her anger now reaching to a new level, she could only imagine Justin and some bimbo enjoying a house that she and Justin had painstakingly decorated and furnished. She splashed the petrol up the walls, over the sofas, up the stairs, and on the bed. Then, almost falling down the stairs breathless and seething, she ran into the kitchen, where she splashed the rest of the fuel over the worktops before throwing the can at the French doors, smashing the glass.

The sound made her rage heighten, as she pulled open a drawer, snatched the sharp carving knife, and began stabbing the highly polished cabinets, imagining it was his body she was desecrating. With one swift movement of her arm, she cleared the worktop of everything: the cups, the toaster, the kettle, and the antique vases belonging to his great-grandmother. They all crashed to the floor. Then, taking a deep breath, she reached for her lighter.

She backed away from the kitchen and towards the French doors. The broken glass on the floor pricked the heel of her foot and she winced in pain. Then, grabbing the newspaper that had been left on the kitchen table by the door, she set it alight.

Instantly, the flames grew at speed. Without a second thought, she threw the burning newspaper onto the kitchen worktop and retreated into the rear garden. Wearing only a thin tracksuit, the cold night air caused her to shiver. As she turned to walk away, an enormous explosion knocked her to the ground. The gas boiler had caught alight and had blown the side window clean away from its frame.

Kara lay on the cold damp grass, unable to move. The blast had also shot a heavy piece of the doorframe across the garden, striking her across the back. But all she could do was stare and watch as the brilliant-white detached house became steadily consumed with grey choking smoke. The growing flames flared up and out of the broken windows, licking the walls and turning them black. Everyone in the close could hear the loud bangs and whistles. As she lay there winded, a horrific high-pitched scream belted out from next door – it was not a woman's scream.

It hit her all at once like a bat across the head. Her eyes widened at the destruction in front of her, and voices in her head were pummelling her with fury for her irresponsible actions.

'Oh my God! Have I done this?'

Mr Langley was cradling his wife on the drive. Her head was bleeding profusely, and she lay there unconscious. The blast from the side window had shot shards of glass and debris just as Jenny Langley was taking the shopping from the boot of her car, resulting in her being hit hard around the head.

The neighbours ran from their homes to see Justin's house billowing smoke from the flames. One man called the fire brigade and another called an ambulance. Hearing Mr Langley's screams, they ran to his aid. Mr Johnson, a retired police officer, helped carry Jenny Langley away from the burning building and onto the grass where he rolled his jacket and laid it under her head. Mr Langley was in a blind panic. All he could do was hold his wife and offer up a prayer that she wouldn't die.

'Is anyone in there?' asked Mr Johnson.

Mr Langley was too traumatised to answer. The rest of the neighbours couldn't or wouldn't help. They gathered in the close, watching the once beautiful house being destroyed and seeing yet more devastation as the windows blew out from the blasts.

Slowly, but surely, Kara got to her feet and tried to register the devastation she'd caused. Reality hit her; she had just burned down Justin's house.

She heard the fire engine in the distance and knew then that she was in shit up to her neck. It was too late to turn back now though – actions have consequences.

28

Chapter 3

Kara looked around the room. It was soulless, with just the one table, four chairs, and a recording machine for company. She cupped her hands around the hot tea, hoping it would control the shakes. *Was it the cold or shock?* She didn't care, either way; all she felt was a deep head-banging numbness.

The chief superintendent marched into the room, with files under her arm, and sat pertly on the chair. Stony-faced and with eyes that were open but glazed over, Kara slowly peered up to see the middle-aged woman, with cold, spiteful eyes and wrinkles around her eyes and mouth, probably from too many cigarettes. With lank, lifeless, and short hair, with a few stands of grey, the policewoman was hardly a looker in the feminine stakes.

Cynthia Lipton, the chief superintendent at Bromley Police Station had been called on to interview the woman because the victim, Jenny Langley, was in the hospital on a life-support machine, and if she died, which was probable, then the person now in custody was looking at an accidental manslaughter charge with arson, which would carry a hefty sentence.

She sharply placed the folder on the table and clicked her pen. Then, having given the young woman the once-over, she concluded fairly quickly from her pale-as-the-moon complexion that Kara Bannon was in shock. This was going to be either like pulling teeth or watching paint dry. She introduced herself and quickly ran through the formalities.

She nodded to the young smartly dressed duty solicitor. 'Well, are we ready to take a statement?' she snapped.

Paul Reeves was fresh out of law school and ready to take over at his father's law firm. Lipton knew he was green around the ears and assumed he would be overly eager to get stuck in. However, she was taken aback when he replied, 'She wants to give a statement and is not interested in being represented, so I'll sit in, but to be frank, she's all yours.'

It wasn't like him. Lipton frowned. Usually, he was a pain in the arse, meticulous at putting her sort in their place.

'So, for the recording, please tell me your name, age, and occupation.'

Kara reeled off: 'Kara Bannon. Twenty-six. Epidemiologist.'

Lipton glanced at Reeves with a questioning expression.

'It means she studies diseases, how they originate, and how they affect the population,' responded Reeves, smugly. He loved it when he got one over the police.

Kara remained focused on a tiny spider crawling up the wall just above Lipton's head. 'Actually, I am a tropical epidemiologist. I study rare diseases of a class four nature that appear in Third World countries.'

Her well-spoken accent and precise tones stirred unease in Lipton because Kara appeared to be in a trance, yet she was able to answer clearly and precisely. 'Okay, Miss Bannon, tell me what happened.'

'I took two cans of petrol from the garage, doused the whole house, and then I set it alight.'

Now, Lipton had to ascertain whether or not Miss Bannon did it alone and whether it was an act of revenge.

'Miss Bannon, was anyone with you? Were you made to do this? I need to know *why* you did it?'

Lowering her gaze, she replied, 'No one told me to do it. I had to burn the house down. I couldn't let Justin and his new girl-friend move in. It was my home too.'

That was it. Lipton had a reason to charge the young woman with criminal damage, an arson attack, and a possible death by recklessness. She called in the custody sergeant who formerly charged Kara. Still in a stupor, she asked innocently, 'Is Justin here yet to take me home?'

As the detective looked down at Kara, she realised then that the woman was unaware of the seriousness of what she'd done. Lipton's mouth formed a smile, but she knew it didn't reach her eyes. She wasn't going to question her anymore; she had all she needed to charge and have the defendant remain in custody. As far as the chief superintendent was concerned, she had done her job – it was yet another notch on her arresting record.

* * *

The sergeant took Kara to a cell and placed a thick red blanket around her shoulders. Robert Wise, the custody sergeant, a big middle-aged man, with a salt-and-pepper-coloured moustache and grey hair, felt sorry for the woman. She wasn't the normal scallywag who came and went. She had class and was polite. He organised another hot tea and a sandwich and brought them to her. 'You will appear in court first thing tomorrow morning.'

With grief clouding her face, she took the drink and machine-wrapped sandwich.

Kara wondered if there was anyone out there who even cared that she was locked in a police cell. She had no family except Justin and his mother. Her own mother lived abroad now, and their only real communication was the odd phone call. 'Is it all right for me to go home now?'

Wise gave her a regretful sigh. 'No, Miss Bannon, I'm afraid you will be held until the court appearance tomorrow, and there, they will decide if they will let you out on bail, but I wouldn't bank on it. This is a very serious charge over your head … Look, eat that, and try to get some rest.'

As the heavy metal door banged shut and she heard the rattle of keys, the silent cold truth slapped her in the face. This was it now. She was all alone. Not only had she lost her job, she also had to accept her relationship with Justin was over, and now her liberty was at an end. Everything had been destroyed in a single, petulant, and hostile act of revenge. She could not even begin to imagine what her future looked like.

Her hands trembled so much that she dropped the plastic cup, spilling some of the hot tea on her legs. The liquid quickly made its way through her thin tracksuit and burned her shins. She winced and curled herself into a foetal position, holding her knees close to her chest. She tried to sleep, as it was the only way to relieve herself of her haunting thoughts.

* * *

The next day, the door was opened, and the sergeant studied the frail-looking woman curled up like a baby. His heart went out to her. His own daughter wasn't much older than this young lady. 'Miss Bannon, do you need the ladies' room? Are you hungry?'

Kara uncurled herself, temporarily released from the solitude and heavy weight of her sadness. With red-rimmed eyes hosting pools of deep sorrow, she shook her head.

They wasted no time in bundling her into the police van and hurrying her off to the courts. As soon as she arrived, she was sick, and this time there was no warning. Luckily, she missed her clothes but made a mess on the floor. The officer handcuffed to her was almost sick himself and tutted loudly, demonstrating how disgusted he was.

She was then led into the witness box, but she was barely able

32

to comprehend what the judge was saying. The courtroom itself was daunting enough, let alone being there with no one she knew. Urged on by the duty solicitor to answer the questions, she obliged, and within minutes, she was taken away back to the holding room.

It all happened so fast that Kara was not really aware of her surroundings. The only person she hoped to see was Justin – but he wasn't there. After spending the whole day in the holding cell, she was finally hustled into a sweatbox, as prisoners and prison staff called it, and was off to meet her new home for the foreseeable future.

* * *

Justin sat at the small dining table. Staring down at the spaghetti bolognese his girlfriend had made, he struggled to let the fork pass his lips. He was shocked to the core and his mind was a stifled mix of emotions.

'Justin, sweetheart, it's gonna be okay. The house was insured, right?'

Her voice was a little higher-pitched than Kara's, and at times it was quite shrill. He glanced up and smiled awkwardly. 'Yes, but …'

'Oh, come on, Justin, once we get the insurance money, we can have the house rebuilt in no time and just how we want it. It will be perfect for our new baby.'

'It's not the house … it's Kara I'm concerned about.'

Lucy's eyes, carefully defined by heavy make-up, narrowed. Her lips tightened and pursed, but she reluctantly remained controlled. 'Darling, people break up all the time, but they don't go burning down a house and practically killing the neighbour. That poor woman will be lucky if she is able to ever walk or talk again … I mean, who does that? Jeez, I think you were lucky to get out when you did, because, sweetheart, sooner or later, her madness would have surfaced, and God knows what may have happened to you.'

Justin made a sad attempt at a smile, but underneath, he was racked with guilt. 'I feel bad for her.'

Lucy flared her nostrils this time, unable to contain herself. 'Look, listen to me: you need to put your energy into thinking about our baby, instead of worrying about some nutjob!'

Justin was in over his head. Lucy wasn't anything like Kara and he had no idea why he'd shagged her. In fact, he couldn't remember it at all. Two months ago, he was out with a group of friends from the workshop, Dave's stag do. They did drink far too many shots and he recalled Lucy chatting him up, and if he was honest, he enjoyed the attention. Kara had been away for two months in Papua New Guinea on one of her expeditions, and he was lonely.

Then, he remembered nothing except calling for a cab the very next morning from Lucy's flat. He'd felt guilty at the time but still decided not to come clean; after all, Kara would never know. How could she? They never went to that particular pub together.

When Kara returned home for a week, he spent every waking hour with her. He even took time off from work himself because he knew she would shortly return to Papua New Guinea for another month. He missed her so much when she was away. The house seemed so empty; he would wander from room to room, lost in his thoughts, his mind on Kara. It wasn't as if when she was at home they talked all the time; often, she would just be there studying, but the fact that she was at arm's length and he could plant a kiss just above her glasses or share a bath and even hold her tightly in bed was enough for him to feel contented.

However, this Papua New Guinea trip seemed to go on forever, and the week they had shared together, she wasn't quite herself; at the time, he'd put it down to jet lag and overwork. Yet, she had seemed oddly cold, even snappy, as if she was under a lot of pressure from work. He didn't push her, deciding it would be better if he left her alone.

The boredom, mixed with missing her, foolishly led him to soak up the attention from Lucy. He spent more time in the pub and in her company, and the incentive to do so was there. She was very flirtatious and the compliments she paid him boosted his ego, although he couldn't blame Kara for any loss of self-esteem he felt. Far from it, yet Lucy was making him feel very special indeed, and as a man, he lapped it up, until once more Justin found himself drunk and in Lucy's company.

Again, he couldn't remember anything until he woke up in her bed the next morning. When Kara was home for good, he pushed the incidents out of his head. Kara's mood swings and tetchiness continued and once again he assumed it was work. After a short while, Kara returned to her usual self and things were back to normal but then the unthinkable happened – fast. Lucy called him one night in floods of tears. Shocked that she even had his number, he managed to calm her down and agreed to meet up in the park across from where he worked. That was when she dropped the bombshell that hit him like a concrete post.

Justin was brought up never to shirk his responsibilities. It was bred into him, being raised by a mother and no father in sight. He could still hear his mother's words: 'You made your bed, now you must lie in it.' But it wasn't just his mother who had that opinion – he did too. All his life he had wished for a father and vowed if he had a child he would never abandon it.

Lucy removed his untouched plate and toddled off like a moving Barbie doll towards the kitchen. Justin followed her with his eyes and sighed deeply. It was all too fast and like a mad dream; sitting in the dining area with Lucy playing happy families was surreal. She was acting as if they had been together for years, and yet he was torn. On the one hand, he loved Kara, but on the other, he was faced with the cold reality that Lucy was having his baby.

He knew why he had liked Lucy initially: because although she was very different in personality, she was similar in appearance to Kara. It was not the overdone make-up or her hair, or the neat thin nose, but those amber eyes. He fell in love with Kara because of those hypnotic flecks and swirls like tiger stone. She was aloof at times with her head in a book and her oversized glasses perched on the end of her nose. But he loved the way she was so natural, with her blonde hair pulled up in a scruffy bun, and he was attracted by the way she could look highly desirable, even in just a loose tracksuit. Her beauty was innate, and if she did get dressed up in a tight sexy dress with a sprinkling of make-up, then she looked stunning and turned heads.

What he loved the most about her was that she never knew how beautiful she actually was. Despite her intelligence, she had a sweet naivety about her.

He watched as Lucy, in her high heels and skintight catsuit, came walking back with a confidence that emanated self-importance. She waved a bottle of wine and two glasses. 'Here you go, sweetie, I bought us a special pressie.'

'Lucy, firstly, I'm not in the mood. My house has just burned to the ground and Kara is in some prison somewhere. That's probably down to us. Secondly, since you are pregnant, you cannot drink.'

'Oh, don't be like that, darling. I thought it might take your mind off all the drama.'

Justin rolled his eyes and left the room. He was drained and needed to sleep and hoped things would be clearer in the morning. He stared for a while at the plain white sheets and the grey walls – there was nothing warm or inviting here – and then he looked at his bags. They were still packed, apart from the bare essentials. Maybe he was too hesitant to really put his feet under Lucy's table. He had no choice now, though. His home, their home, was totally destroyed. He just needed to be alone to think things over.

As he lay with his arms under his head, staring up at the

ceiling, he thought about Kara and wondered how she would ever cope in prison. She wasn't made for any such place. She was his delicate princess, his soul mate, and he'd let her down very badly. That said, she wasn't born with a silver spoon in her mouth – far from it. Not that Kara spoke much of her past.

Her mother, who wasn't rich by any means, brought her up in a cottage down in Kent; however, she managed to pay for Kara to go to a posh boarding school. Kara hadn't been exposed to the real world. He gritted his teeth, when he thought of how she would never survive if anyone hit her. She hadn't had a physical fight in her life, and he'd never seen her be rude to anyone. She didn't like confrontation. True, she'd certainly put up a fight to keep him when he'd delivered his bombshell, but the fact was he'd committed the act and he didn't blame her for defending her own corner, even though her intense anger was a shock and that expression on her face haunted him.

* * *

The first thing that hit Kara was the smell; it could be best described as sweat mixed with a school canteen odour. With the overpainted metal doors and polished concrete floor enhancing the harshness, Kara longed for her warm bed and to be wrapped in a blanket, safe and secure. She realised then that peace and tranquillity, words that had been so important to her, were now just words.

Every noise now had an almost frightening meaning to it. Every unexplained bang was making her jump, the rattling chains were setting her teeth on edge, and the periodic sound from the entry buzzer left her ears vibrating. The speed at which she was pushed from one section to another, expecting to take everything in, was alarming. She wasn't slow either, yet the list of dos and don'ts, times and places, all seemed to merge into one big blur.

The interview, the prison officers, and the stark coldness of it all was a world so far removed from her own that Kara could never imagine getting used to it. She was led through locked door after locked door, with her arms out holding prison issues, a plastic cup, and basic toiletries. The clothes they gave her to wear after the horrid strip search were too big, yet she wasn't in a position to complain. The fierce glare on the officers' faces was enough to imply she was fucked if she argued. Her head was spinning, feverish with fear.

Eventually, she was escorted down a long corridor with heavy doors on either side and was stopped at a door partially open. 'In ya go, Bannon!' ordered Anna Larson, the burly female officer. Kara shuddered at the small space and tiny cold-looking bed. 'Meet Colette Connor.'

The inmate, who was lying on the opposite bed propped up by pillows, deliberately sized Kara up. 'Aw, for fuck's sake, no one told me I was gonna 'ave a cellmate!'

Colette Connor was a heavyset woman with a fat face. Her menacing sneer was enough to shit the life out of Kara. Instantly, she stepped back, treading on the officer's toes and was roughly prodded on the shoulder. 'Move, Bannon! And you, Connor, can shut it. She's in with you, so be fucking nice and no nonsense.'

A faint smile lurked in the corners of the officer's broad mouth. Her narrowed eyes and her cropped hair emphasised the spiteful appearance. She chuckled, as she slammed the door shut.

Kara was still trembling when she placed the prison issues on the bed. The reality of her predicament was creeping into her bones, inch by inch. This was no university campus set-up where everyone could share a joke, relax, and have fun. This was a whole different ballgame. She gingerly sat down and tried to give the inmate a warm smile. It wasn't reciprocated. Instead, she received a stony glare that gave Kara the shits.

'Oh, my name's Kara Bannon. It's nice to meet you.' As soon as the words left her mouth, she realised how ridiculous they sounded. And to make matters worse, Colette repeated them in an over-the-top posh voice, trying to intimidate her.

'So, Posh, what ya in for, then?' asked Colette, with her cocky head tilted to the side.

'Well, I, er … arson, I think, and oh, yes, reckless bodily harm or something. I'm not quite sure.'

Colette, or Cole as Kara soon found she was commonly known, looked Kara up and down. 'Who did ya hurt?'

'My neighbour.'

'Why? Did she fuck ya ol' man?'

Colette was getting excited. She was bored, and this young woman might have something interesting to make the daily grind of prison life actually bearable for once. Colette loved aggro. It was in her DNA. Not only did she want to hear all the gory details, she needed to size up this Kara bitch. For all she knew, she could be a raving nutter, sharing her cell.

'I don't know. I, er … I mean, I can't remember exactly what happened.'

Colette frowned and thought it best to back off. If this posh bird couldn't remember what she'd done, then she didn't want to be the one who suffered from a red-mist moment at the hands of a fucking psycho.

'Right, Posh, lights are out in twenty minutes, so you'd better sort ya shit out and no fucking snoring. I 'ate noise, when I'm trying ta sleep. The last bird cried all night, and I swear to God, I gave her something to cry about, so no blubbering, right?'

Kara took a few deep breaths as if she was trying to stop herself from being sick. 'I don't snore, and I won't cry, but I might be sick. I have a virus I picked up from abroad.'

Colette noticed the girl's face looked almost grey. She pointed to the toilet tucked in the corner. 'Use that, and I swear, if ya fucking puke anywhere near me, I'll make sure you fucking eat my next shit.'

Kara's lower lip trembled. The tension was so hostile and

downright scary. Suddenly, the light went out and she had to feel her way around the cell. Running her hands along the bed and to the small partitioned wall, she finally found the place she wanted. Kneeling beside the chrome toilet, she hoped beyond hope that she wouldn't be sick anywhere near her cellmate.

For over an hour, Kara gripped the basin, with nothing but the tremendous feeling of guilt for company. She just couldn't get Mrs Langley off her mind; it was eating away at her. Silently, she prayed for the poor woman's full recovery. The nausea was relentless, so she sat on the hard floor with her chin resting on the stinking toilet bowl until she felt her head nod as she began to drift off to sleep.

The sickly feeling at last receded, so she crept onto her hard bed and entered the world of darkness. In no time at all, a loud sound pulled her from her nightmares. Doors were opening, and the small room lit up. Colette was rolling a cigarette, her fat tongue sliding along the sides of the rolling paper before she stuck it together. She didn't look at Kara but just jumped up and left, with the cigarette in her mouth.

Kara sat upright, trying to get her bearings; everything was still surreal. The night before when she was in reception, the officers were reeling off so much information, she couldn't take it all in. It was something about breakfast, showers, jobs, and times.

A few minutes later, in the doorway, a tall woman with wild black hair, grinning from ear-to-ear, was showing a neat row of gold teeth. Kara couldn't work out if she was black or white. Her features were African, but her skin was milky, and her eyes were green. Kara was uncomfortable because the woman's gaze was anything but welcoming.

'Cole tells me ya burned ya house down, fucked up the neighbour, 'cos she fucked ya ol' man.' She had her hands on the doorframe and was gently swinging in and out of the cell.

A bead of sweat trickled down Kara's back and her face flushed.

She recognised that feeling. The sickness was coming up, and this time she couldn't hold it. Ignoring the tall woman, she leaped from the bed and hurled her stomach contents down the toilet. As she pulled away, she noticed how disgusting the toilet actually was and then remembered she'd been leaning on it for some time during the night. With that thought in mind, she heaved again. There was nothing left to bring up.

With wobbly legs, she tried to stand up and had to grip the wall. As she turned, she saw the small sink and leaned heavily, bowing her head and catching her breath. She turned on the taps and ran her hot face under the flowing water, whilst slurping mouthfuls of the cold liquid. She spat twice and then wiped her mouth with the back of her hand. Falling back onto her bed, she glanced up at the woman in the doorway. The ordeal had no doubt made her own eyes bloodshot and evil-looking.

Kara took a deep breath. 'What did you say?' she tried to sound friendly, but her voice was hoarse and her expression demonic. The woman stopped swaying on the doorframe and stepped back, as if unsure what to make of Kara.

At that moment, the inmate was shoved away from the entrance to the cell and in her place stood a square-shouldered, tall, and heavily built screw, as they called them. Kara should have been relieved. Weren't they the good guys?

'Bannon, you're supposed to be back at reception!' the screw growled, her voice deep and husky. 'Get up and follow me.' Kara naively expected the officer to be less harsh and less manly. It was the big tits that gave her sex away. Dressed in the prison sweats, Kara dragged herself up, still shaking, and stepped forward. The screw huffed, 'Jesus, woman, what's the fucking matter with ya? Get a wriggle on. I ain't got all day!'

Kara gulped back a breath, hoping she could get enough oxygen to her brain to stay upright and walk on. Outside the cell, she noticed prisoners bustling from one place to another, all on some kind of mission. She tried to keep her head down, too afraid of making eye contact with anyone. This was so far detached from anything else she'd ever experienced, that it was hard to stomach. Even her first day at boarding school wasn't this intimidating. The banging and clanking of keys and doors was a stark call of reality to the situation.

As the officer marched ahead, Kara noticed the inmates looked away. The officer was the one who called the shots – that was a given. As they approached the end of the landing, an inmate, who was standing in the doorway of her cell, swiftly stepped out and unexpectedly pinched Kara's arse and whistled. A fear crushed her, and she could feel the tears welling up.

No, this wasn't happening. It couldn't be happening. How would she ever survive? She wasn't gay, she wasn't streetwise, and she certainly wasn't hard. She felt the tear trickle down her face and quickly she wiped it away. The screw unlocked the end door and pushed her through, locking it behind her. They marched down the stairs and along another hallway, until, finally, they were in the reception area. Kara was too afraid to look at anyone, until she heard a man's voice. 'Kara Bannon?'

Slowly, she glanced up and nodded.

There, a tall, dark-haired, and smartly dressed man in his mid-forties, who reminded her of a younger Hugh Bonneville, smiled compassionately, giving Kara a feeling of hope. *Please tell me I am going home?*

'You need to fill out this form. They forgot yesterday.' He spun a piece of paper around on the desk and handed her a pen. The female officer stood by her side like a concrete statue. Kara looked at the form. It had two questions: name and next of kin. She scribbled her name, and on the line below, she wrote 'no one'.

The male officer took the form from her, and then he raised his eyebrow. 'You have no next of kin?'

Kara shook her head.

'What, no parents, partner, brother, sister, or even aunts?'

Kara shook her head again. 'No one,' she whispered.

42

'Okay, now it was a mad rush yesterday. It always is on the weekends. Have you been told the process, like how it works?'

Before Kara could answer, the screw jumped in. 'Yep, Gov, she was given the full low-down—' She was cut short.

'Sandra, was I talking to you? Go back to the wing. I want to talk to Bannon alone.'

Sandra gave him a spiteful sneer and stomped away. Once the door was slammed shut, the man looked Kara up and down. She gathered he must be the governor or assistant governor. 'A lot to take in, isn't it?'

Kara raised her head and smiled nervously. 'Yes, I'm sorry, I don't know what I'm supposed to do, you see. It's all new to me.'

'Yes, I can see that ... Look, Kara, I won't pretend it's a bed of roses in here because it isn't. I suggest you keep your head down, don't listen to the other inmates, and sign up for a job right away. Of course, you don't have to because you're only on remand, but it might be better if you do. You have fifteen pounds a week for the canteen, which means money to buy stamps, treats, tobacco, and phonecards. Your breakfast will be left in the cell and the lunchtime and dinnertime meals will be in the canteen.' He chewed the inside of his mouth. 'You can order books from the library.' He probably guessed she liked reading, just by the way she spoke. 'What was your job on the outside?'

Kara swallowed hard. Her job was her life, except for Justin, and both were gone now. 'Epidemiologist,' she replied.

'Okay, Kara, well, mopping floors will be a drastic change.' He was clearly trying to make a joke, but Kara was still in shock and riven with uncertainty.

She stared at his deep blue eyes and noticed they had a kind sentiment about them. 'I don't know how I should address you or anyone for that matter.'

'My name is George, but you must call me Gov. You can't really go wrong with calling all the staff Gov. The other girls do,' he replied.

George had worked his way up through the system for twenty years and took no shit from anyone – the inmates or his fellow officers. He had only worked at Larkview Prison for a year, having been taken on by the number one governor. She wanted the prison cleaned up, and he was the man for the job.

In his time, he had seen hundreds of inmates come and go and some return time and time again, yet he had never come across an inmate like Kara Bannon. It was the sadness in her remarkable amber eyes that set her apart. She was sweet and naturally attractive. Her hair was fair and her skin flawless. He inwardly sighed. She wouldn't look so fresh after a stint in here. The bright lively waves of hair that shone would no doubt grow dull and lifeless, and her dewy glow would diminish, along with her soul.

'Right, I'll organise a job for you in a few days' time, but for now, you can get to know how things work on the wing. You can go to the canteen. That's where you buy your essentials, if you need anything.'

Kara shook her head. 'I don't usually smoke or eat sweets and I have nobody to write to or call.' She didn't seem to be saying it for the sympathy vote. George felt for the girl because deep down, he knew she would get eaten alive. Her posh voice, her naive manner, and her good looks would do her no favours. He smiled and nodded towards the door. 'Okay, I shall escort you back.'

* * *

On the surface, he seemed soft and kind, and yet Kara, with one exception, had never trusted anyone. She never had and for good reason. All except Justin; she had trusted him and look where that had ended up.

As they walked back to the wing, he went over the procedures again. This time, Kara took it all on board – she had to, if she

44

was to survive in this hellhole. She would have been put on the new inmates' course, a short introduction that gave them a run-down on how the prison operated, what to expect, and what they expected from her. However, the prison was very short-staffed and so the two-day course was wrapped up in two hours.

Back inside her cell, she noticed the box that was supposed to contain her breakfast. It was empty. That Cole woman had stolen it. Kara's stomach was now rumbling, and she thought back to the last time she had eaten anything. She couldn't remember, it was so long ago. She would have to keep up her strength. Colette was sitting smugly with her eyebrow raised as if to say, 'Yeah, go on, Kara, say something.'

Kara hesitated, but then she made a stupid mistake. It was her biggest blunder and a real learning curve for her, accusing Colette of stealing her food. 'That was my breakfast, I do believe.' Her tone was soft, but there was an undercurrent of sarcasm. She never meant it to come out that way, but it did, and it was too late to take it back. Colette was off her bed in an instant. She spun around, and with a clenched fist, she punched Kara clean in the mouth. The thud was hard and knocked Kara against the wall. She tasted the blood and winced, just as another punch hit her. This time, she felt her head smack against cold concrete. It was as if the wind was knocked out of her. Colette stepped back with a cruel, beady look in her eye and dared Kara to fight back.

Colette's fighting skills were gained from many a ruck inside. She had a reputation, and with her fast and furious blows, she would have an opponent on the deck in the blink of an eye. Some brave or stupid souls returned the violence, but the clued-up ones begged her to stop.

However, Kara was still in total shock. She had never been hit before and it wasn't as she had anticipated. Her cheek hurt like a dull cramp and she was left with a sore tingling. But it was the unknown that was the problem. It was the prospect of further aggression that was frightening her and also not knowing the possible damage that would be inflicted on her.

Her fear when she entered the prison was the brutality, isolation, and inhumanity, along with deprivation. After she wiped the blood away with the back of her hand, she stared at Colette with a dull expression that didn't match her thoughts. She was stunned and should have been terrified. Yet, for some odd reason, this initiation into prison life really wasn't as bad as she had imagined. Deep inside her mind, she'd gained an ability to detach herself. Besides, the pain of losing everything was worse and perhaps the smack in the mouth was a wake-up call to snap her out of the daze she'd been living in.

Colette was watching the younger woman's still countenance, gauging Kara's next move. But there was no move: Kara just continued to gape at Colette with no life in her eyes. It was a poignant moment, which Colette, for all her bravado, was at a loss to explain. Normally, if she gave a bird a good hard lump, they would either try to defend themselves, or, more likely, they would crumble on the floor in a ball, begging for her to stop. Either way, it was a win-win.

She was a bully in every sense of the word. Her accounts of GBH and ABH were as long as her arm and ended up with her serving four years. Prison didn't bother her in the least. In fact, she found it a doddle: three meals a day, a bed, and not having to think for herself – what was there not to like? She loved to be a plastic gangster, talking tough and exaggerating her crimes.

The truth was she lived with her elderly mother, fact; she was ugly and stupid, both incontrovertible facts; and she had nothing going for her. The only respect she got was from her ability to knock out grown men. Inside that hard-ass armoury, there was a sad, lonely woman longing to be loved by a man, to have a family, and to be cherished. Her father had run off when she was two and her mother was a shy, weak little woman who had no control over Colette at all. She was a victim of circumstances, and unfortunately, she knew it, which was why she was merciless inside the nick.

Kara's eyes were bloodshot again and it gave her an almost fiendish look. She continued to stare, as if not really knowing what to do. Colette slumped her shoulders and sat heavily on the bed. She slid her hand under the mattress and retrieved a Snickers bar, her favourite treat from the canteen. ''Ere, if ya are so fucking hungry, 'ave this.'

Kara still didn't move. She was intent on keeping her eye on Colette, in case she tried to bash her once again. She wiped her bloodied mouth for the third time and could feel the swelling of her bottom lip. It didn't hurt at all. It was strange because she knew it probably looked bad. She ran her hand over her cheek-bone to feel the lump protruding under her eye and again was astounded that the swelling was numb.

Colette watched her checking her wounds and waited for the backlash, but there was none. Kara sat herself down and shook her head. 'I don't eat chocolate. But, thank you, anyway.' Her response was typically articulated, her Oxford accent clearly pronouncing each and every word.

Colette wasn't sure if Kara was being sarcastic or that was just her normal way of speaking. 'You don't fucking accuse people of nicking ya gear 'cos you will get fucking hurt, right?'

Kara replied in a flat tone, 'But it isn't right. I was extremely hungry. I haven't eaten for days.'

Colette wasn't used to anyone speaking to her like that except for her schoolteachers, many years ago. Unbelievably, she felt like a child again.

Standing up and closing the cell door, she replied, 'Listen, Posh, I ain't got any beef with ya, and I s'pose it's easier if we gel, 'cos I'm gonna 'ave ta put up wiv ya. So 'ere are the rules. Change the way ya speak, or you are gonna get a fucking good hiding. The birds in 'ere don't take too kindly to you looking down ya

47

hooter at 'em, and ya best learn to be on high alert, watch ya back, keep outta people's business and …'

She paused and looked Kara over. 'And, if ya do get in any trouble, you be sure ya come and find me. 'Cos, I have a reputation, see. Not many will fuck wiv me. I'm one 'ard bitch.' She was showing off and wanted to be feared. For some reason, this waif of a woman was intimidating her. Perhaps it was her educated voice – Colette guessed she hadn't gone to her local state school – or the woman's weird expression when she was given a good thumping. Either way, she could be a force to be reckoned with, and Colette wasn't taking any chances.

Kara gave Colette a gentle smile. Her fat lip and the lump on her cheek made Colette unexpectedly feel a twinge of guilt. The girl was very pretty, and she'd just messed up her face, and for what? It had just been to prove a point, end of. It was wrong on every level, and she knew it.

'Thank you, Cole. I'll try to speak like you, if it helps.'

Now, Colette felt even more guilty. Kara wasn't like the others, that was for sure. She was sweet and innocent.

The door swung open, and in stepped the inmate who Kara had seen earlier, before the screw pushed her away. 'All right, Cole, so what's happening?'

The mystery woman looked Kara over, as if intrigued to know more about her. Earlier, Kara had felt a little uncomfortable to be alone with her.

Colette shuffled along the bed so her buddy could join them. 'Her name's Posh. She's all right, Dora.'

Dora's face changed and she gave a dirty grin. 'Oh, yeah, it's like that, is it?' She winked at Kara, who, of course, had no idea what she meant.

Colette gave Dora a hard nudge. 'Fuck off, Dora, it ain't like that – she ain't my type. You, of all people, should know that.'

Dora lowered her eyes and blushed.

Kara's mind was whirring. Was Colette a lesbian and Dora her

48

girlfriend? The image of an inmate coming on to her was worse than being violently attacked. Or perhaps it was much the same thing. She shuddered. She watched Dora run her hands down Colette's leg and wondered if long-term prisoners who weren't gay turned to each other for comfort. Assuming they wanted some privacy, Kara jumped to her feet and asked, 'Where's the library?'

Colette turned her head to the side. 'What's the matter wiv ya? Ain't our company good enough for ya?'

In normal circumstances, Kara would have chosen her words more carefully, but this situation was hardly normal. And she wasn't sure what saying the right thing would do for her credibility. There was no room here for decorum or polite niceties. No, she was going to have to play their game, and where she could, she would stay away from conflict. 'Cole, I'm going to leave you two to have some private time. I think if we are sharing a cell, it's only right that I let you have your space. It's obvious what you two intend to do.' She looked down at Dora's hand.

Colette really laughed at that, and then she winked. 'You can join in, if ya fancy a bit?' She stood up and ran a finger along Kara's uninjured cheek.

With her stomach now in knots, Kara instantly grabbed Colette's wrist. 'You can hit me, Cole, but don't touch me.' Surprised that those words had left her mouth, she swallowed hard and winced, awaiting the backlash. However, Colette didn't see the fear behind those words. All she saw was a flash of fury, which took her by surprise.

'So, I ain't ya type, then, Posh? Not good enough for ya, eh?' Her voice was climbing several levels, and Kara felt drained by being on edge all the time. She had to think quickly; backing Colette into a corner would not be clever. 'Look, Cole, it's apparent that Dora' – she pointed to the angry-looking woman still sitting on the bed – 'is your type, and you have a thing going. I wouldn't like someone to take what's mine, and my neighbour did just that, so do you understand where I'm coming from?'

Colette's eyes flicked from left to right, trying to take in the message. It took a couple of seconds for her to process the intent behind Kara's question before she dropped her guard and sat back down. Colette was not totally stupid, not by a long stretch. She realised that Kara had given her a way out, a face-saver. 'I get ya, Posh, I get ya. You are the faithful type. So, did ya do the neighbour 'cos she was muscling in on ya ol' man, then?'

Kara wondered if she could adopt an alter ego. She realised she would have to continue with the lie just to give herself some creds, if she was to survive. Telling lies wasn't her thing, and yet being in the slammer certainly wasn't either. 'Yes, Cole, I burned the house down and tried to kill the bitch.' She tried to sound cold and hard, but in her mind, she knew she probably sounded pathetic. Truthfully, even saying those words made her feel ill. Mrs Langley was a sweet woman who never deserved what happened, and worse, Kara was using the incident to save her own skin by coming across as hard and uncaring. Who the hell was she turning into? This wasn't who she was.

However, Colette was uneasy because Kara wasn't jumping about swearing and re-enacting the crime; there was a coldness to the woman's tone and manner. Through long experience of prison and life, she wondered if Kara was really a nutter behind that angelic façade.

'Was ya ol' man a bit of a dish, then, was he?' asked Dora, raising her eyebrows and licking her lips.

Gritting her teeth, Kara wanted to cry again. Of course, he was a dish; he was everything she ever wanted in a man, but he'd abandoned her, ripped her heart out, and left her in prison to rot.

'He was a class-one bastard!' she snapped.

'All fucking men are bastards; it's in their make-up. 'Orrible wankers, they are. Always after ya fanny or wanting their shitty pants washed. They're no good to us women, let me tell ya. Me ol' man ruined me muvver, then he fucked off, leaving her without a pot to piss in and me to bring up. I know how to treat men, though, just as they treat us. I use them for a free ride on their cock, get 'em to buy me a few bits and pieces, and then fuck 'em off.' She looked Kara up and down and sighed. 'I guess you ain't learned the rules yet, 'ave ya? I suppose he sucked you in, got what he wanted, and then he spat ya out, moving on to the next unsuspecting bitch?'

Kara wanted to say, 'No, it wasn't like that at all. He loved me and never used me,' but then, in this new environment, she would look a right idiot. 'Oh, I knew the rules. It's just a shame that my neighbour didn't,' she replied, with a smirk, even believing her own slander now. Nevertheless, it was easier than admitting the truth. It was her way of escaping the reality of the situation.

At once, the tension seemed to ease, and Dora, now looking more relaxed, giggled. 'No flies on you, gal.'

Colette joined in and smiled. 'I bet the bitch knows now, though, eh? With a face like Freddy Krueger, she won't be messing with no woman's man again. Who would want her now?' She slapped her thigh and laughed even louder.

Kara was feeling nauseous. That poor woman. What if she really was scarred … and worse, what if she was dead? Kara resignedly sat on the bed, her legs weak and wobbly, and yet Dora and Colette took it as if she was joining in with them and having a laugh at the neighbour's expense.

The inmates' levity was cut short by the appearance of a large woman, with jet-black hair half up and half down and a deep jagged scar across her forehead, standing in the doorway. Kara smiled but was sneered at. The woman was in her late thirties, good-looking and yet hard-faced. She had on the prison issues, a green tracksuit, but her sleeves were rolled up showing her tattoos. 'Cole, I want some gear!'

Kara watched the dynamics. Dora had her head down, and

Colette jumped to her feet, flustered. 'Er, Vic, I 'ave only got a bit of puff.'

Victoria Meadows, commonly known as Big Vic, was obviously someone with clout. She exuded confidence and her demeanour said, 'Don't fuck with me'. She was scratching her neck, and as Kara's eyes followed her hand, she could see the raised swirls of red inflamed skin.

'I need something now, Cole. You'd better call on everyone on the wing, or I'll be smashing a few heads in.' Her beady dark eyes glared at Colette, who was clearly shitting herself.

'What do ya need, then, Vic?'

'I need anything that's gonna stop this fucking itching, something to knock me out, and I don't care what it is, meth, brown stuff, or puff!'

Kara bravely stood up and stepped towards the woman.

Vic stepped back with her forehead creased. 'What are you fucking looking at?'

'The rash on your neck,' replied Kara, totally unfazed by the woman's harshness.

'Go fuck yaself.' She turned to face Colette. 'Who's this fucking numpty?'

Colette was still uneasy. 'Er … that's Posh. She's in with me. Tried to kill the neighbour who was sniffing around her ol' man. She burned the fucking house down.'

'You got any gear, Posh, or are you just another waste of space?'

'I don't have any gear, but I can tell you what's wrong with you.'

In a flash, Vic snatched Kara by the hair, bending her back. 'You can tell me about meself, yeah? Ya cheeky fucking whore. I run this wing, so you'd better know ya fucking place, or I'll show ya!'

Kara then realised what she'd said had been taken the wrong way. 'No, I mean your neck. I know why it's inflamed.'

Vic dropped her like a hot brick and glared at Colette and

Dora. 'Get out!' she hollered. Instantly, the two women darted out of the cell. Vic then closed the door behind them and glared at Kara. 'Oh yeah, some kinda doc, are ya?'

Kara looked at Vic unblinkingly and nodded. 'Yes, sort of.'

As Vic sat down on the bed, Kara noticed the woman's demeanour soften. 'So ya know what this is?' She lifted her baggy green tracksuit top revealing swirls of raised red circles covering her chest.

Leaning forward, Kara ran her finger over the inflammation. 'Does that irritate you?'

Vic was like a patient in a surgery. 'Yeah.' Slowly, she rolled her top back down.

'What did the doctor give you for it?'

'That ol' cunt said it was a heat rash. Four weeks I've had this, and it's getting worse. The blind ol' fucker, I could smash him round the 'ead. So, what is it?'

'It's a fungal skin infection.'

'What!' screeched Vic. 'You better be joking! You mean, I have a fucking fungus growing on me skin?'

Kara knew it would make anyone feel ill, imagining a fungus growing over their body. 'Yes, but don't worry, it's easily cured. I promise you, all you need is an antifungal cream. You know, like athlete's foot or thrush?'

With wide eyes, Vic slowly nodded. 'Yeah? So, that's all I need, just that cream?'

With a compassionate smile, Kara replied, 'Yes, that's all you need, and within a couple of days, it will be gone. Try not to scratch it and keep it cool for now.'

'Right, I'm going back to tell that idiot fucking doctor. I swear if he don't give me that cream, I'll smash the living shit out of him.' She jumped up and went to walk away, but then she turned back. 'Er, listen, this is between me and you, yeah?'

Kara nodded. 'Of course. Oh, by the way, my name is Kara. Cole just calls me Posh.'

'Yeah, well, you are posh. Everyone calls me Vic or Big Vic ... Er ... if ya need anything, give me a nod, yeah? But you'd better be right. I don't take too kindly to being mugged off.'

With a warm smile, Kara nodded again. She had got the picture loud and clear. It was going to be a testing time. She had to prove her worth and use everything she had, if she was going to survive. She lowered her eyes and sighed. If she believed in God, she would pray that she hadn't got the diagnosis wrong. Then the muscles in her jaw relaxed. If she had got it right, then perhaps she would have a friend on her side.

At that moment, Colette and Dora hurried back in. 'So, what did she say?' asked Colette, looking flushed.

'Nothing much. It was personal, really.'

With a deep laugh, Colette went on, 'Personal, there's no such thing in 'ere. Anyway, no matter, whatever you said, ya got her off my back.'

Perhaps she was making headway at last for a peaceful life.

Chapter 4

The sun was just starting to rise. While Lucy was in the shower, full of the joys of spring, Justin sat on the end of the bed, with his hands cupping his tired face. It had been a long night, a stressful one, and he felt like shit. He'd rolled on his side just to avoid any affectionate contact and had found himself almost hanging off the bed most of the night. He took a deep breath. *What the hell am I doing? I don't even know her. It's all madness.*

Lucy obviously hadn't taken the hint, as she casually walked into the bedroom from the bathroom completely naked. He'd looked up and thought about Kara. She was never so provocative, more sweet and shy. He was always the one doing the running, making the first move, but he liked it that way, not having it handed to him on a plate. Something about Lucy's body made him blink. He thought perhaps his longing for Kara had messed with his mind because Lucy's figure with her neatly shaped breasts and slim thighs was almost identical. He looked away.

'Justin, please don't tell me you don't find me attractive, not after you were all over me before.'

Even her higher-pitched voice was irritating him; so much so, that he stood up from the bed and reached down to pick up his bag. 'Lucy, I know that I slept with you and we're having a baby, but it doesn't feel right that I should live here as if we've been dating for years. We don't know each other all that well, and so to play the happy family game right away doesn't sit comfortably with me. Surely, you understand?' He looked at her with his face half turned away, but it was definitely not easy, with her standing there naked. 'I think for now I'll stay elsewhere until I can figure this out. I don't intend to shirk my responsibilities, but I need time. You do realise that, don't you?'

Lucy felt like a schoolgirl. The way he pronounced his words – with no trace of an accent or slang – he bordered on being posh. She wasn't used to it, and she felt a little intimidated. She wouldn't be put off, though; his looks and money more than compensated for his more genteel and less manly ways.

'Don't be like that. Look, Justin, if you want to sleep in the spare room, then do that. Christ, all those things you said to me, I guess you never meant them, eh?'

'What things?' he snapped.

'That you really liked me a lot, how you wished you were with me, and how things would be so different. Well, Justin, you have me now and a baby on the way. For fuck's sake, she burned our … sorry, I mean *your* bloody house down and nearly killed the neighbour. Seriously, you aren't telling me you're having second thoughts, are you?' She began to snivel and left the room.

It was bizarre. One minute, he was in his perfect world with Kara, where they shared his lovely home and enjoyed a comfortable lifestyle, with a deep sense of closeness between them, and now he was facing a life with Kara in jail and Lucy swanning around like she'd been with him for years. What the hell was he doing? Was being a father so important that he was blinded by the notion? He thought back to his childhood, and yes, he longed to have his father in his life, but could he really sacrifice Kara for this unborn child and Lucy? Who the hell was she, anyway? He knew absolutely nothing about her.

Still gripping his bag, he sighed. Perhaps he'd gone too

far. 'Lucy!' he called out. She didn't answer, so he wandered to the bathroom to find her sitting on the edge of the bath sobbing. She looked vulnerable and very different from a few minutes ago. With a towel wrapped around her, she whispered, 'I'm so sorry, Justin, I guess you're right. This is all too soon. I never knew I could get pregnant. The doctors said I couldn't. I would never have put you in this situation, but you did say how much you liked me, and when you came back here for the second time, I assumed I wasn't just a one-night stand. But it's okay. I understand. You never really did like me.'

She wiped the tears away and pulled the towel tighter around herself. 'You're a good man, Justin, and I will admit I fell in love with you the first time I met you, and so having your baby is not a heartache for me. I just hope he or she grows up to be just like you. But, I promise you, I'll be a good mum, so never worry about that. I'm just sorry you don't feel the same way about me. I'm not Kara, and well, I couldn't possibly be. I grew up in a foster home, a few actually, so I'm a bit wilder, I suppose. I can't take her place, and so it's best that you go and forget you ever met me.'

With a heavy sigh, Justin placed the bag on the floor. 'It's not you, Lucy – you're probably a lovely person. It's just so soon. We don't even know each other, and I wish you wouldn't act like we have done so for years. I feel suffocated.'

'I only wanted it to be nice for you. I didn't want you to feel awkward. Perhaps I wanted too much.' Her voice was softer and gentle, and it tugged on his heartstrings. It wasn't Lucy's fault. After all, the only person who had caused all this mess was him. He needed to man up. Only he could put it right. He had played away from home and got this woman pregnant. He couldn't bring himself to mess up two women's lives.

'Why she had to burn the house down, I don't know. She could have stayed there. I suppose, she really hated me for what I did.'

Lucy looked away. 'Babe, she did something terrible. The neighbour is in hospital, fighting for her life. That could have been you. Kara isn't the person you think she is.'

Justin chewed the inside of his mouth, going over Lucy's words in his mind. Perhaps she was right. Maybe Kara did have a vindictive side to her. 'Okay, I'll stay in the spare room, and we'll see if we can work this out. I'm not ready for a full-blown relationship, so give me some time, eh?'

With an obliged, compassionate smile, Lucy nodded. 'I understand, love, and I'll back off, although it will be hard, because I do love you, Justin.' She paused, as if wondering if she sounded convincing.

Those words kept repeating themselves in his mind. Still numb and racked with guilt and grief, he made his way into the spare room. It was little more than a box room, with just a single bed, one pine wardrobe, and a bedside table. The window looked out over the row of houses opposite, and as he stared, he shuddered.

This was worlds apart. His house was in a close and the property opposite was so far away, that he never felt hemmed in. Lucy's flat was in what was once a large house with three floors. The property was now split into two flats. The basement flat that was accessible from the side door to the building was on one level, whereas Lucy's flat had an upstairs as well as a downstairs floor. There were two separate entrances, but the back garden was only available to the basement flat. At least it was kept very neat and tidy by the old lady who lived there.

* * *

Lucy smiled to herself. She had to keep him there, close to her, and work on him. Acting as if they had been together for years wasn't working, so she would have to change tactics. But she noted how he responded to her when she appeared needy. She would have to put on a first-class act, although she shouldn't denigrate her acting skills. They'd made her what she was today. They had been honed to a fine art, and she knew she was good at disguising her true inner self.

She believed she'd been dealt the shitty hand, being left with her father, while her mother upped sticks and got on with her life, leaving her behind to live with a bastard of a man. She didn't care what anyone said. Even the shrink, Julien Spinks, with his stupid ideas that she had an unhealthy vivid imagination. What did he know, anyway? As far as she was concerned, her father was a short-tempered, evil bastard.

The tears she'd put on for Justin, though, were fake. As she recalled it, all her life, no matter how much she cried, she was told to stop snivelling, don't be a baby, and grow the fuck up. Her recollection from the age of six was that she'd had to cook, clean, and pander to her father's needs or suffer a violent backhander. The freezing cold bath or the metal cabinet were two of his favourite forms of retribution, although no one believed her. She vaguely recalled being locked away overnight, unable to sit down because the space was too small, and standing in the dark, desperately hoping that he would let her out soon, feeling the cold walls and hearing the rustling of rats outside and the scurrying of spiders.

Then, there was her father's face when he opened the cabinet, and her blinking furiously with the bright light and the silhouette of his big frame and thick neck. 'Have ya learned ya lesson, then? Now, will you stop telling lies?' he would bellow.

Lucy remembered a woman from the social services, called Rhonda, a big black woman, smiling sweetly at her father and then tutting at her, shaking her head, and with those condescending words, saying, 'Now, now, Lucy, this has to stop. You have to attend your weekly appointments with Dr Spinks and take your tablets every morning.' But they had her all wrong – even Dr Philippa Shelby, her GP, the condescending bitch, with her curt words and sharp tongue, telling her that without the medication, she would be sent to a home.

She hated Rhonda and Dr Shelby nearly as much as Spinks, and she also detested her teacher, Mrs Lyons, who always insisted she sat at the back of the class and refused to believe a word she said. Still, what did they know? They never had to take the vile gag-inducing pills. They were probably all being bribed by her father, Les, anyway, to pretend she needed psychological help. She put up with the shit until she was old enough to change it all.

Naturally, as a teenager, she found men were extremely attracted to her. Not only could she turn a head or two, but she had the guile and the confidence to wrap any man around her little finger. She'd already had practice when it came to sex, as she believed her father had sold her to his friend. For most young teenagers, it would have been a terrifying, traumatising experience, but for her, it wasn't. Now, at thirty-one years of age, she looked back and concluded at that time it was rape. Of course, it was. And yet her rapist didn't pin her down or hurt her.

Carl was his name. A man in his twenties, he was smart and handsome. From the weekly gatherings, which Les called their poker night, she soon realised that Carl was a villain. Carl would eye her up and pay her the most flattering compliments, which she wasn't used to, but which gave her butterflies from all the attention. He was much younger than her father, and he had a sleekness about him and soft eyes that could make him everyone's friend when he needed to put on the charm.

After she poured their drinks, she hid in the shadows, but all the time she did so, she listened to their conversations of money scams and prostitution and her eyes lit up. She was well on her way to becoming a minor player in the life before most boys her age actually knew where to find the hidden jewel of the female anatomy.

So as the years went by, her knowledge of the criminal underworld gave her the self-assuredness to think about getting into it herself. After all, it was easy money. And besides, who would stop her? Her own father could hardly look down on her for it, and he didn't care about her anyway.

Then, one evening, when she was fifteen, she endured a particularly bad weekend, although her memory of the events was not clear in her mind. After she'd been out with her friends to a party, she put the key in the door only to be dragged the rest of the way into the house by her hair. Her father's thick sausage-like fingers gripped her arms and shook her so hard she bumped her head on the back wall. He was screaming. As foam and spittle left his mouth, his eyes were red and violently angry, and his voice held an ear-piercing screech to it. In his rage, he threw her to the stairs and demanded she stay in her room, or she would be locked in that metal cabinet.

The recollection was vague, but the next morning, he gave her some pathetic lecture about her being drunk and rolling in at all hours, not knowing where she'd been or who she'd been with. How he was sick of her going so late and he was going to get someone to give her a good talking-to, who may knock some sense into her. Never mind what he said, she was convinced that the marks on her face were caused by him manhandling her. Okay, she'd had a little to drink, but she couldn't have given herself the bruises.

Shortly after her perceived assault, the men had another meeting at her home. She had been getting ready for another night out, secretly downing a few shots of neat vodka before she applied more make-up to hide the bruises. The sound of the men downstairs seemed more appealing than the invitation to a house party put on by a few of her mates.

Carl noticed the marks on her face, and he immediately curled his finger for her to come closer to inspect the bruises. As she approached him, she noticed the compassionate smile that spread across his face.

'You need to be careful, Lucy. Don't you go ruining that beautiful face of yours,' he uttered, quietly. Amazed at that time by his concern for her, she'd put it down to the fact that he'd been drinking, and yet, she felt goose bumps all over her arms and her face went bright red with embarrassment. He must have noticed how coy she was, and he played on it, running the back of his hand down her cheek. She didn't move.

His eyes then darted to Les and then down at the cards in his hand. With a low sarcastic tone, he said menacingly, 'You owe me now, Les. I don't think you can trump three aces, can you?' His eyes darted to the pot of money on the table.

Lucy looked at her father who appeared to be nervously chewing his bottom lip as he focused on the cards in his hand. He suddenly shot her a look and shook his head in disgust. She hated that expression.

'Right, I think I will call it in. Come on then, pay up, Les – ya can't beat my hand.' Not looking at Les, he ran his hand down her face again.

Once again, Lucy looked at her father who lowered his eyes, studied his own cards, and then nodded with a heavy sigh. She never really knew if it was shame, guilt, or humiliation. Did he look down because he had sold his daughter, or was it because he'd reached the depths of fear of the repercussions if he had said no? Either way, as far as Lucy was concerned, it didn't matter. She didn't care. In her head, she guessed what he meant when he said, 'pay up'.

The meeting over, the men left, one by one. Les took Carl into the kitchen and then re-emerged, giving her another one of his critical looks. 'Carl wants to talk to you.'

With that, Carl nodded for Les to leave the room.

'Come and sit by me, beautiful.' He winked. Those words were like wandering into a Disney world, a magical place. She did as he said, and as he stroked her hair, she felt alive, with his warm breath on her neck and his gentle words of affection. Her ears buzzed, and her heart rate quickened. Whether or not it was the alcohol in her system or the closeness of a real man, she didn't care: it felt good either way. That longing look of his sucked her in, and as he leaned in to her, she detected the subtle sweet-and-sour aroma of his aftershave.

She closed her eyes, as his words reverberated somewhere in the distance. Her hands covered his, easing them inside her school blouse. Immediately, he pulled away, but not before his eyes narrowed, sending a cold shiver up her spine. She hated that look of disappointment; it was the same one her father constantly wore. She wanted, longed even, for the attention, and could have cursed, just when things were getting interesting.

Get a grip, Lucy, she told herself. This is big school not play school and those soothing fingers and wanting eyes were sending furious signals to her brain. Leaning in to him, she arched her back, encouraging him to caress her. He held back as she urged him to touch her. All she could hear were words of adoration; those kind, sweet words were like music to her ears, words that flooded her mind with candy and lifted her spirits to a new height. It didn't matter what he was saying; his voice was somehow hypnotic and addictive, like a drug.

If this was Les's way of "paying up", then she was going to ensure it was well and truly paid, and her father could live with the guilt for the rest of his miserable existence. It was then that she realised she could have this effect on men. She would become a player by using her looks and sexual powers to control them. But not just any men. They would need to be charismatic, wealthy, and stunningly good-looking, just like Carl. She wouldn't settle for less.

He left that evening with a warm smile and an incredibly seductive wink. She remembered giggling and him saying, 'Goodnight, my little darling, sleep well.' And she did – for the first time ever, she slept like a baby.

By the morning, she felt alive, although, for a moment, she wondered if it had all been a dream. Les staggered into the kitchen, still reeking of booze. She had her back to him and snatched the toast as it popped from the toaster. In her head, she was singing a tune, but not aloud; he would hate any noise in the morning, usually suffering from a hangover. She placed the buttered toast on a plate and slid it under her father's nose. This time, she didn't feel so petrified of him. That morning was probably the first time ever he'd said, 'thank you'. She then placed the coffee by his plate.

She didn't have to look at his chunky, puffy face to know he was tormented with guilt; she could hear it in his breathing, by the way he quietly sat down, and by the tone in his voice when he asked if the talking-to from Carl had helped her in any way. She rolled her eyes and smirked. 'Some pep talk, eh? My fucking arse. You know what he did to me? Call yaself a father. You should be ashamed of yaself!'

She glared at her father's expression of resignation, rolling her eyes once more when he asked if she had taken her tablets again. Finally, she stomped off, after he accused her of such mad and disgusting lies. They weren't mad, and she wasn't going to stand there and allow him to fill her head with bullshit.

A week later, the firm gathered again for their poker night, but Les ushered her to her bedroom. 'Stay up there and don't make a fucking sound,' he demanded, before he opened the front door to let the men in. Lucy listened at the top of the stairs and then she heard Carl. She could visualise his smouldering eyes, his command for attention, and then the soft glance he would give her, but she was upstairs, hidden away. She wanted him and pondered how she could let him know she was there.

She added another layer of mascara and lined her lips with red lipstick, swigged another mouthful of neat vodka, and waited for her chance. The problem was, if she made a sound, her father would beat her or send her to the metal cabinet. Then, she heard her Prince Charming. 'You fucked up again, Les,' came the sarcastic laugh from below. There was a long pause, as she strained to hear.

'No matter, Les, I suspect you are holding an ace up your sleeve or calling my bluff. How's Lucy, and where is she this evening?'

Her heart skipped a beat. She wanted to yell down the stairs, 'I'm here! Come and get me, take me away. I will do anything, but just get me out of this fucking house away from my monster of a father.' But she said nothing and waited whilst imagining her father sitting there counting the ten-pound notes that Carl was carefully slapping in front of him, all to have a piece of her. She took another swig from her bottle of Smirnoff.

'She's upstairs,' her father uttered, defeated.

Lucy remembered the grin on Carl's face, as he stood there in the doorway to her bedroom. The butterflies were back, along with the fast beating of her heart, and she was ready for him. Looking back at that time, she shivered. *Her father had sold her again.*

Before Lucy's mind returned to the present, a chilling thought entered her head. Where was her diary? She couldn't leave that lying about for Justin or anyone else to find. It contained her innermost personal thoughts and feelings. Years ago, Dr Spinks had suggested that she made a diary to help her control her somewhat aggressive tendencies and fanciful recollections. It had been the only good advice she felt he'd ever given her. She knew her head was still in a mess. But she truly believed that until her present plans came to fruition, she would not become the person she had always wanted to be … she needed to be … for her own sanity.

Lucy's thoughts returned to the present. Leaving the bathroom, she hurried to the bedroom, where she quickly got herself dressed in a soft woollen dress. She liked to feel wrapped in cotton wool, but the long black dress would have to suffice. She would allow Justin his space and work on him slowly but surely. She had come this far now; she wasn't going to give up on such a good catch so easily – not without a damn good fight, anyway.

Chapter 5

The exercise yard was a bleak place with the high barbed wire walls and the officers keeping a keen eye. Groups of women stood smoking and talking. Kara was alone and had no idea where she would fit in. A few necks craned her way, and she could feel the tension as the other women whispered and laughed. Her blood was rampaging through her veins like spears of ice, and she could feel her heart beating wildly.

Then, she saw Vic and didn't know whether to go over or keep away. She was surrounded by a crowd of hard-looking women, with tattoos, meaty arms and scars, cold smirks, and toothless smiles. There was no one like herself. The black inmates huddled together, a few Chinese formed their own group, and then there was Big Vic. She was like a showpiece, with a following all looking up to her.

Kara was completely out of her depth. She looked who she was: a well-off person who would have been at home perhaps in one of the enclosures at Epsom Racecourse, but here, standing on Larkview Prison's exercise yard, she was ill at ease. What was even worse was the rest of the inmates knew it. But try as she might to find someone like herself, she couldn't.

But, then, who was she? All she'd ever been was Justin's girl-

66

friend. She didn't have friends, too busy with her head stuck in a book. Now, she was still a nobody, but she was a nobody who was caught in a car's headlights, ready to become roadkill. Vic looked her way, and for a second, Kara was gripped with fear. *Had the cream worked? God help her, if it hadn't.* Vic flicked her head for Kara to join her. Reluctantly, she ambled over and smiled nervously, searching her face for any small indication that she was about to get her head kicked in.

'This is Posh. She's a doctor, a friend of mine.'

As if all her fears collapsed at once, Kara could breathe. She acknowledged the others, with a shy nod.

The short heavyset skinhead, with massive jowls, laughed. 'Ya mate? Yeah, Vic, she don't look like your kinda pal.'

A deliberate glare from Vic to the skinhead changed the atmosphere immediately and everyone stood around feeling tense. 'Listen, if I say she's me mate, then she's me fucking mate. Now, if ya wanna argue the point, Teri, me and you are gonna fall out big-time.'

Teri, the skinhead, stepped back, realising she'd engaged her mouth instead of her brain. 'Ahh, nah, nah, Vic, I was just saying she looks, well, ya know, soppy, like.'

With a deep, raspy laugh, Vic heavily patted Teri's shoulder. 'Posh, 'ere, is far from soppy. She will burn ya in ya fucking bed, if ya even look at her the wrong way, and if she don't, Teri, I fucking will. Got it?'

Teri's eyes widened, as she peered over at Kara. But Kara knew what Vic was doing. She was protecting her, by giving her a reputation that she didn't really deserve. She'd never had a fight in her life.

'Er, sorry, Posh, I mean, not that you look soppy, ya just look kinda cute, if ya know what I mean.'

Another wrong move. Vic's hand gripped Teri's shoulder, pushing her down. 'And she ain't into women either, so touch her, or even wink her way, and I will seriously fuck you up.' She eyed the others in the group: it was a warning to everyone.

Vic walked away with her arm around Kara. 'It worked, kiddo. That silly ol' cunt of a doctor put his glasses on and had a closer look, and then he gave me the cream, just like you said.' The older woman looked at the downtrodden expression on Kara's face and sighed. 'I know, love, it's hard, trust me. I've spent most of me life inside. Ya don't belong 'ere, and that's a fact.'

She stopped talking and turned to face Kara. 'I must be going soft in me old age, but ya did me a favour. I owe you one, not that I ever owe any fucker anything, like, but you, I do. Any nonsense from the bitches in 'ere, you tell me, all right?'

Kara was nodding like her head would fall off. 'Thank you, Vic, you're right. I'm so out of my comfort zone, I'm scared to death, to be honest. Those women look as though they could eat me for breakfast.' She looked back at the coven of inmates whispering in their little circle.

Vic laughed out loud. 'That lot are a bunch of fucking pussies, but ganged together – 'cos they can't fight one-on-one – they are nasty. You stick with me and you'll be all right … Aw, before I forget, ol' Deni is sick. She ain't left her cell. In agony, she is, the poor cow. The doc reckons she's got a migraine, but I've never seen her cry in pain before, so take a look for us, will ya?'

'Deni?'

'Yeah, everyone calls her Deni. Her real name is Denise Rose Denton – famous, her crime, ya know.'

Kara swallowed hard. She wasn't a GP and had only received three years' training in medicine before she became an epidemiologist, but how could she say no? 'Yes, of course, I'll take a look.' Her upbeat tone, she thought, should instil confidence, if not in herself, at least in Vic. She closely followed her new best friend, hoping that she wouldn't get stopped by one of the officers because she had absolutely no idea of the rules. She was still in shock and struggling to take it all in, although she needed to learn fast.

However, Vic seemed to know the ropes. She wondered what

she was inside for. It must have been pretty bad, if she'd spent most of her life locked up. Her thoughts returned to her own predicament and what her life had mapped out for her. She wouldn't hold her breath, that was for sure.

Just as they were about to enter B Wing, an officer, Vic's personal officer, came up behind her. She was a tall long-legged woman, with a red short-back-and-sides style, thin features, and eyes that turned down at the corners. 'Meadows! A woman called Julie Meadows has arrived from court this morning on remand. She says she's your sister. I'll put her in with you, yeah?'

Kara stepped back. This was none of her business. The officer looked her up and down. 'What are you doing here? This ain't your wing, is it?'

Kara put her head down, not knowing what to say or do. The tall woman looked spiteful and ready to lay down the law.

'Look, Gov, she's on B Wing to see Deni, her aunt. All right with it, are ya?' dared Vic, giving the officer a hard stare.

'Her aunt? Oh, yes, and me mother's a monkey's uncle,' snorted the officer.

With a quick laugh, Vic replied, 'Well, with a face like yours, it don't surprise me, and no, Julie ain't sharing with me. For Christ's sake, what has she gone and done now?'

The officer shrugged her shoulders. 'Not sure, GBH, ABH, maybe. Well, anyway, I'll tell her she's on her own, on C Wing. Right, you take this inmate over to see Denton. Her aunt, my arse. Don't like your sister, I take it?'

Vic slowly looked the officer up and down. 'Barbara, listen to me. I like to be on me own in me own cell. It *don't* mean, I don't like me sister, so don't go spreading dirt, all right?'

Barbara gave Vic a sneering look and stomped away.

'Fucking no-good shit-stirring screw – I hate her. She's the only screw we have to call by her first name. She hates her last name, it's Pratt, but she is a prat an' all. Ya wanna stay away from her. She loves a good ruck and stirs the shit spoon just to get the girls wound up. I swear to God, if I came across her in the street, I would cut her fucking pointed hooter clean off.'

For the first time, Kara found herself laughing, which spurred Vic on to make her laugh even more. 'She walks around like she's got a carrot shoved up her arse and talks like she's chewing a fucking lemon.'

The interaction between Barbara and Vic intrigued Kara. She assumed that she would get into serious trouble if she so much as answered any of the officers back. 'I can't believe you got away with saying that stuff to an officer.'

'Ahh, see, this is where you have a lot to learn. Firstly, I keep some kind of order on this wing, and they know it. Barb is one 'orrible screw, and even her own kind don't like her. I won't take any shit because they fucking know that throwing me in solitary does fuck-all other than leave the girls on the wing restless. The truth is, kiddo, I came from a big family, piss-poor, had me baby took from me, got beat near to death by me ol' man, learned to fight to stay alive, and then I ended up in 'ere on an attempted murder charge. So, what do I have to lose? There ain't much the prison can throw at me that I can't handle.'

She sucked her back teeth and then winked. 'But I ain't no bully, and see, the likes of you, I know, don't belong 'ere, so I'll watch out for ya.'

The change in Vic when she was away from the others was remarkable. She had a softer side and a sense of humour, and she was obviously a good judge of character too.

Kara felt at ease. 'Vic, I'm grateful you know, well, just to have some support. It must be nice having a sister. I was an only child, you see.'

'A sister? More like bleedin' three sisters and two brothers. Me mum was Catholic. Either that or she liked a good bunk-up. Yeah, Julie is a feisty bitch. She's a few years younger than me. Got a baby. But she's a bit handy with her fists and has a mouth on her. She reminds me a bit of meself, a few years back. I just wish she would keep a lid on her temper. I don't want her in here on the same charges as well.'

They continued past the heavy painted doors and up the metal staircase to another row of cells. It was much like her own wing – dull, grey, and depressing. They stopped outside a cell six along from the staircase. Kara expected Vic to knock or something, but instead, she barged straight in. The room was the same size as hers, and yet there were pictures on the walls, a few books neatly lined up along the shelf, and a few knick-knacks – family photos, a pottery cat, and some lipsticks. The clothes were neatly folded on the opposite bed, and the sink and toilet looked immaculate, very different from Colette's cell. It even smelled better.

Kara's eyes settled on the older lady who was lying flat on her back with her hands over her face. She was roughly sixty years old, plump around the middle, and her ankles were swollen. Her toenails were yellow and in need of a serious pedicure.

Vic sat on the edge of the bed and slowly the older woman removed her hands. 'Gawd, girl, how long you been sitting there? I was just dozing off. This bleeding headache, and my eyes, they're killing me, Vic.'

As Vic looked up at Kara, her hard features softened, as if she was tending to a sick mother. 'Can ya have a look, Posh?'

Deni tried to sit herself up but wobbled and needed aid from Vic. 'Oh, my living. Is this what it's like to get fucking old? Ain't nuffin graceful about that, eh?' She blinked, and her eyes streamed. That was when Kara noticed the tiny blisters. As she peered down to get a closer look, Vic got out of the way.

'Posh wants to have a look.'

Finally, sitting up straight, Deni looked worn out. Her wiry grey hair was flat at the back from lying down. 'I ain't mutton, Vic, I can 'ear ya.'

As Kara sat down gently on the bed, she moved Deni's hair away from her left eye and then she searched her head, like a monkey defleaing her baby.

''Ere, what ya doing?'

'Is it your left eye that hurts and is the pain stabbing, shooting, or burning, by any chance?'

'It's like red-hot needles digging in me. I swear to God, I think I'm dying. I can't sleep, I can't open me eyes. It's something bad, I just know it is. I ain't never felt anything like it.'

Vic was wide-eyed and looking at Kara for an answer. 'Is it serious, Posh?'

'Well, it is in as much that if she doesn't get treatment soon, she could damage the eye. I think I know what it is, though. It's unusual to get it on the face, but it does happen. It's shingles.' She moved Deni's hair away from her temple. 'Look, see those blisters? That's the herpes blisters and the pain is herpetic neuralgia. It's extremely painful and is certainly not a migraine.'

'That fucking quack needs shooting. Right, I'll call the senior officer and get Deni back over to the hospital wing. A fucking migraine, my arse,' spat Vic.

A gentle smile crossed Deni's lips. 'I knew it weren't no bleeding headache. Thanks, my gal. Now, what shall I tell the doc?'

'Tell him that you have shingles of the face and you want suitable treatment, including the cream to put on right away. You may need to see an eye specialist to ensure you don't lose the sight in that eye.'

Gripping Deni by the arm, Vic helped her off the bed. 'Come on, Deni, let's get you to the senior officer and get ya sorted, eh?'

As hard as Vic was underneath, Kara knew her new friend had a heart of gold.

Deni held on to Vic, whispering, 'What would I do without ya, Vic, aye?'

'Get yaself in fucking trouble, Deni.'

There and then, the damp depressing mood lifted. Kara knew there was hope. In among the hard, the tough, and the frightened, there was a sense of morals. There was a pecking order for those who wanted to fight for the top spot; some were natural leaders and others just liked to be the followers, the hangers-on. She was now gaining friends or allies, but, either way, she wasn't alone or so terrified.

Kara returned to the exercise yard, and instead of lingering stares, she received a few nods, and surprisingly, some inmates even smiled her way. Teri, however, sneered but didn't do much else. Kara, with her new-found confidence, glared back, which was enough to force Teri into lowering her gaze. Perhaps she had believed Vic when she said she would burn her in her bed.

Inside, Kara was laughing to herself. Exercise was over, and they returned to their wings, some to their allotted jobs. Kara, of course, was on remand and didn't have a job right away. Just as she followed the last of the inmates back inside, Barbara, the tall officer, pulled her back. 'Bannon, I have moved you to another cell.'

'Oh, why is that?' Her voice aired confidence.

Barbara looked her over. 'We have turned over yours and found illegal substances, and I'm assuming they ain't yours. Connor is down the block and you are in with Julie Meadows.'

'The block?' asked Kara with her head tilted to the side.

'Solitary confinement, for now. We don't like drugs in this prison. Oh, just so you know, she said they were yours. She tried to rat you out, she did.'

Taking a deep breath, Kara responded, 'So how do you know they aren't mine?'

'Because you've only been here two days and you haven't had a visit. You were also searched on arrival. We ain't stupid, love!'

'And Cole would have known that, so why would she even attempt to blame me? It makes no sense.' Kara had sussed her out. Colette may be mouthy and hard-faced, but she wasn't a grass. Vic was right: her personal officer was a real shit-stirrer.

Barbara shuffled uneasily. She wasn't used to listening to a smarty-pants or being spoken to in such a manner. Normally, the prisoners were bolshie, brash, and foul-mouthed, but they didn't have the intelligence to tie someone like her up in knots and make her look thick.

'I dunno, but get a move on. Your transit box is in ya new cell and so is Julie Meadows,' she jeered.

Her tone was ugly, like her face, and Kara sensed that the officer was trying to have the last laugh. Kara wondered who Julie Meadows was, apart from being Vic's sister. Her heart sank, and she just hoped that Julie wasn't about to throw her weight around as well. Begrudgingly, she followed Barbara along the corridor and past her previous cell, which was now completely bare, and on to the last cell on the left.

'This is it, Bannon, your new home.' She chuckled.

Gritting her teeth, Kara entered. She was mortified when she saw the woman sitting on the bed with a face like thunder. There was Julie. If it wasn't for the fact that the young woman's jaw was clenched so tightly and those eyes, which were narrowed to a furrowed frown, the girl would be very pretty. She was slim enough and had an attractive figure. But Kara could tell that despite being in her thirties, Julie had already lived a harder life than most women her age.

She still had that same ugly tone as she had the day Kara met her on the estate when she'd screamed, 'What are you fucking gawping at? Ya fucking snob!' Kara had been scared of the woman then, and now, the mouthy madam was going to be sharing a cell with her.

'Oi, I said I want to bunk in wiv me sister!' she hollered at the officer, totally dismissing Kara.

'Tough, Meadows. Ya sister don't want ya, don't like ya, so you're on ya own. Get on with it.'

Before Julie had a chance to say another word, Barbara shot off.

'What are you fucking looking at?' spat Julie, in a temper.

Kara stared for a few more seconds. It was obvious that Julie didn't recognise her, but then she was in prison issues, wearing a bruised nose and a fat lip.

It was a case of putting on a very brave front, so Kara replied, 'Don't take it out on me. And for the record, your sister, Vic, never said she didn't like you at all. I was there. That screw is a shit-stirrer.' She was even getting used to the lingo.

'Know her, do ya?'

Kara nodded. 'Yes, she's a decent woman, your sister.'

'Yeah, well, not decent enough to have me bunk in wiv her.' Her pitch softened.

'Look, I'm not so bad, honestly. I'll keep myself to myself.'

'So what ya in for?'

This was it. As soon as Kara told her, she would know who she was. But there was no point in lying. The word would go around soon enough. 'I burned my house down and almost killed the neighbour.' She was plagued with guilt every time those words left her mouth.

Julie put her hand to her mouth and cocked her head to the side. 'Fuck me, I know you. You live up the road from me. I've seen ya walking about, on the bus, and ...'

Kara overfilled her lungs with air. 'Yes, you did.'

A sudden laugh almost made Kara jump. 'Well, ya fell flat on ya fucking arse ending up in 'ere. That'll teach ya for being such a snobby bitch.'

Kara sat tentatively on the bed opposite with her head down in shame. 'Is that what I looked like to you, a snob?'

Julie nibbled her lip. 'You are stuck-up, walking around with ya nose in the air, in all ya fucking designer clothes, not even saying hello to anyone. And me sister Angie cleans for ya. She said you and ya ol' man think ya shit don't stink.'

There was a long pause before Kara looked up and sighed. 'I suppose to you and Angie, I did look like that, but you've formed the wrong impression of me, you know. I wasn't stuck-up, I was scared.'

'Of what?' Julie sounded narky.

'Of you and the people on the estate. You all seemed to shout at each other, and I saw a few nasty rows where people threw bricks at each other. I wasn't looking down my nose at all, and as for Angie, I was never horrible to her, I just kept out of her way, usually with my head in a book. I was always busy studying. So, she thought I was stuck-up as well, then?'

Julie was taken aback; she thought perhaps she'd got the woman all wrong. 'Yeah, well, I dunno about that. I remember the way you were looking at me on the bus, like I was dog turd.'

Kara waved her hands. 'No, no, you're mistaken. I wasn't looking at you like that. It's hard to explain ... You are worlds apart from me. I was being nosy. Yes, I admit it, but I was thinking how hard you had it, jumping on the bus with no money. I wasn't being a snob, I felt for you, that's all. Oh, and I was looking at your beautiful baby, thinking how sweet she was.'

'Um, well, we ain't all got a good job and a posh house, ya know.'

'I know, and by the way, neither have I now. I fucking burned it down. My boyfriend has gone off with another woman, I got fired from my job, and now I'm in prison for how long, I don't even know.' She laughed. 'So, Julie Meadows, I'm in your shoes now, and I'm still bloody scared.'

Julie sat back, raised her eyebrows, and smiled. 'Guess you are, then. So, what's ya name? Karen or something, ain't it?'

'No, it's Kara, but I seem to have been given the nickname Posh.'

Julie's face turned from a harsh, tight-lipped expression to a young fresher-looking appearance. 'Stands to reason. Posh, eh?'

'May I ask what you're in for?'

'I stabbed me sister, the lying, cheating cunt. I knew she was 'aving it away with me ol' man, the lazy fat bastard, he is.' Kara gathered this was the fourth sister she hadn't met, rather than Angie.

Kara noticed Julie's eyes fill up, but she instantly sniffed back the tears.

'But he was my lazy fat bastard, not hers. Me own frigging sister, what a fucking skank. I should have stabbed her in the face instead of her leg. Then, she might think twice about going after my ol' man again. S'pose it don't matter now. I'm in 'ere and they are out there, probably fucking as we speak.'

'I doubt that, if you stabbed her in the leg.' Kara smiled, trying to lighten the mood.

With an unexpected childish giggle, Julie went on, 'Yeah, I should have knifed her in the fanny. That would have well and truly fucked her up, eh?'

After an hour or so, Kara found her tongue and they spoke for England. Julie's foul language had muted, and in some ways, Kara's words had rubbed off on her. She had nothing to prove – no axes to grind, just relaxed conversation. And Kara found she was using some of Julie's terminology and had ventured into throwing in the odd swear word. Their discussion around cheating husbands was halted when Vic arrived. 'Fucking cosy, this, eh?' she commented.

'All right, Sis?' responded Julie.

Kara had half expected them to hug, but they just eyed each other over and gave approving nods.

'So, ya silly bitch, what ya gone an' done now?'

Lowering her gaze, Julie said, 'I stabbed our Sharon in the leg.'

'You what?' Vic's voice was bold and gruff. Kara then knew why people feared her; just her tone alone was frightening enough.

'All right, all right, keep ya fucking hair on. I ain't killed her, the no-good muggy cunt!'

'What the fuck did you do that for? She's ya sister. We stick together, remember, or 'ave ya gone mental in ya old age?'

'She's 'aving it away with Billy, my Billy.'

Vic shifted Kara over and sat down on the bed. She was a good foot taller than Julie, but there was an obvious family resemblance; their almost olive skin, high cheekbones, and black hair, were similar, but it was their eyes that narrowed and cast doom; that was their striking trait.

'Aw, don't tell me you are still with that fat fucker? Ain't you learned ya lesson by now? He's shagging half the estate … Gawd knows what they see in him, 'cos it ain't his good looks and sophisticated ways. Jue, he is a nasty no-good pain in the arse, and you need to woman up and kick his lard-arse to the kerb. As for rucking with our Sharon, I'm ashamed of ya.'

Julie took a deep breath. 'You wouldn't understand, but it's not that she was shagging Billy. It's not like a jealous thing. I'm just sick of her taking the piss outta me.'

A chuckle left Vic's lips. 'You sure about that? Only, didn't you punch that kid at the end of your road, all 'cos Billy whistled at her?'

'Oh, whatever, anyway, it ain't the point. Sharon pushed me too far, laughing in me face like that, telling me she was better in the sack and said she would do it again. She laughed at me baby an' all, saying she looked like a French bulldog.'

Kara watched and listened; somewhere in there was a moral code.

'She called the baby names, did she? Well, then, she deserved it. Poor little Harper. She's a dear sweet thing. Fancy her own aunt calling her a French bulldog. What a cunt.'

Kara's hunch was spot-on and she was learning fast. There was the moral code. Calling the baby names was a no-no in their way of life, and although Julie's actions seemed over the top, almost laughable in a gruesome way, in fact, Kara could see why Julie and Vic were on the same page. The Meadows were a big family and probably tighter than a fat guy in spandex. Fighting among themselves might be tolerated under exceptional circumstances but calling the baby a bulldog had crossed a line.

Sensing she was in the way, Kara got to her feet and was quickly pulled back down. 'It's all right, mate, you can stay. It's your cell, so don't mind me.'

Very pointedly, Julie studied Kara and then her sister. 'Mates then, eh?'

'Yep, Jue, so you treat her nice. She knows how ta fix ya up, so she will know how to bring ya down. Lotions, potions, and poisons.'

With a curled lip and a raised eyebrow, Julie looked the epitome of confused.

'Gawd, Jue, Posh is a doctor, right? She knows how to make ya better, so she will know how ta kill ya.'

Kara's eyes widened at Vic's conclusion.

'Anyway, she sorted me out, so she is fine in my book. And ol' Deni, the poor cow, I've just left her in the hospital wing. Mind you, I gave the nurse a fucking warning. I said she has shingles and not a bleedin' headache. You should have seen the look on her face, as if I had just told her she had the plague.' She pulled a roll-up from her scruffy bun and lit the end, puffing furiously. 'So, where's the baby? Muvver surely ain't fit enough, the bleedin' piss 'ead.'

'Our Angie's got Harper. Mind you,' she said, with a penetrating stare at Kara, 'she ain't got her job no more.'

'Oh yeah? She didn't tea leaf anything, did she? She was on a right good earner. She reckons the woman gave her a monthly bonus to spoil herself an' all,' Vic said, with a quizzical frown.

Julie was still looking at Kara, a grin forming across her face. 'No, her employer burned the flaming house down. Didn't ya, Posh?'

Vic spun around with her hands to her mouth. 'Oh, fuck me, it was *you*! Jesus, ya really did go to town. My Angie said ya didn't leave a brick standing, not a blade of grass in the front garden. She reckons you used a bomb … I need to change your name to Bomber Bannon.' She laughed at her own joke and pushed Kara almost off the bed. 'Cor, small world, eh? So, Bomber, you're a sly horse. I thought it was an accident. I didn't know you were serious. Fucking bombed the house! Well, you have respect from me … But why, though?'

79

For a moment, Kara felt comfort. Two women, a world apart from hers, were treating her now as one of their own. 'My boyfriend went off with someone else and then asked me to get out of the house, our home that we had shared for years, so I thought, if he wants to move the bitch in, then he can sleep with her on a pile of ashes.' Just as she spoke her innermost thoughts, she realised she was just like them. The only difference was that she portrayed more finesse, but it all boiled down to the same thing at the end of the day.

'This neighbour, then. Was she shagging this fella of yours?' asked Julie.

With an inward groan, Kara replied, 'No, that's just a story that grew legs and ran. I didn't know my neighbour was in the driveway, and the truth is, I didn't know the boiler was going to explode. It all happened so fast. I doused the house and lit the match and headed for the back garden. That's all I remember, really, apart from ending up in here.'

There was silence. You could have heard a pin drop. Julie and Vic looked at this attractive and slim woman in front of them and just stared, totally dumbfounded by the precise and unemotional words leaving Posh's mouth. It was left to Vic to speak up. 'So, you're a bit of a reckless fucker on the quiet, then?'

A soft chortle left Kara's mouth. 'Well, I guess I must be.'

'Right, I'm off to the canteen. I need to get a few bits. Jue, show Posh the ropes, will ya? She's walking around like a tit in a trance.' With that, Vic jumped from the bed and was gone.

'You already know the ropes, I take it?'

With a big huff, Julie replied, 'Yeah, well, me ol' man, the wanker, don't work, ya see, and I needed a few bits for the babe, and I got caught choring 'em. They gave me three months. I already had a suspended, for nicking out of Waitrose. Some snooty cashier caught me, but it was the thump on her nose that got me inside. Anyway, I ain't never done anything too serious like burning down a big posh house.'

For the first time, Kara realised that inmates like Julie saw her crime as more serious than stealing and violence, and yet she hadn't given it a second thought, assuming that hitting someone was far worse. Perhaps Julie was right, and the judge would come down hard on her. She'd been racked with guilt since the incident and would take whatever the judge decided to throw at her if the neighbour was seriously injured. She would deserve to suffer and yet she was also terrified of being locked away for years.

'What's up, Posh? You don't 'alf look white.'

'Just the thought of that innocent woman dying and it's all my fault. I will never get out of here. I don't deserve to either.'

'So, what's ya brief say? I mean, is she outta hospital yet?'

She guessed Julie meant her lawyer. 'Er, no, I don't have a brief, or family, or a boyfriend anymore, so I haven't a clue.'

'You best speak to your personal officer and get a brief, sharpish. You will need all the bleedin' help you can get. I'll give ya the name of mine, if ya like. I'm seeing him on a legal visit tomorrow. Shall I put a word in? He does legal aid.'

Kara nodded, feeling totally deflated. 'If you wouldn't mind, that's so kind of you.'

'No worries. I'm going down to the canteen. I need some sany towels. I came on early. All the bloody stress, I guess.'

A sudden thought almost knocked Kara sideways. She hadn't even considered her period. She was late, the sickness over the last few days having put everything else to the back of her mind. And what with worrying about herself and Justin and now being incarcerated in this absolute shit-hole, it was no wonder that her once logical and formidable brain was out of kilter.

She did a mental recap of when she'd last had a period and an uneasy feeling gripped her stomach. It had been her last trip to Papua New Guinea where she'd thought she had contracted the lingering gastro bug that had been infecting the villagers. She could quite easily have thrown up the pill then. She calculated back the dates and sat there numb; she was possibly two or three months pregnant. How the hell could she have not known? She was medically trained. She'd put it down to sickness and stress, and she hadn't thought a baby was on the menu yet – not this side of thirty anyway.

Chapter 6

Two weeks had passed. Lucy was keeping up her end of the bargain, as she saw it. Justin worked late most evenings and slept in the spare room. She cooked his evening meals and they joined in small talk – how he had got on at work and what she had been up to during the day. Then, believing they were getting somewhere, she decided to up her game. 'So, Justin, I was thinking perhaps I should meet your family. We can break the news together.'

He was just about to place a fork full of mashed potatoes in his mouth when he stopped and placed his cutlery down. Taking a deep breath, he declared, 'I haven't even told my mother about my break-up with Kara, let alone the house burning down. I think she needs to deal with one thing at a time, don't you?' His curt tone pricked her nerves.

'Christ, Justin, she must already know. It was in the papers, and she will think it odd that you haven't called.'

'Look! My mother doesn't read the news, except her local rag, and she knows if I'm busy, then I won't call, but if she got wind of it, she would be knocking down my office door. Let me deal with one thing at a time, eh?'

Lucy noticed the fine lines that had appeared around his eyes.

Maybe it was the overhead light that highlighted his face, but he looked older, not so fresh. She couldn't even say they were laughter lines because his expression of late was so sullen. Being patient was wearing thin and she had to batten down the urge to shake him. She wasn't used to men denying her affection.

'But surely your mother will be excited when you tell her she will be a grandmother?'

His face tightened to an angry glare. 'You what? Are you delusional?'

Lucy forced her eyes to water. 'But, it's not fair, Justin. I feel like I'm being hidden away, like your dirty secret, when I should be embracing this pregnancy, showing off like other mothers-to-be, buying baby clothes, and enjoying the experience. It's not my fault that Kara burned your house down and ended up in prison.' She allowed a fat tear to fall. 'I didn't think you two were such a big deal because you wouldn't have been in bed with me … twice. She wasn't your wife, you never married her, she was just a girlfriend. If you really loved her that much, you wouldn't have been seeking solace in another woman's arms, my arms, would you?' She didn't raise her voice but kept her tone neutral.

He shook his head. 'Hello? I was drunk,' he replied, coldly.

'Maybe you were a little tipsy the first time, but you weren't drunk the second time, when you came over to chat me up in the bar. If I remember rightly, Justin, you were stone-cold sober and moaning about Kara always being away and how you were getting bored with her. I would never have got involved with you, if I had thought for one moment you still had feelings for her. How do you think I feel? I thought we had something special. I know it was all very quick, but now we're having a baby and looking forward to the future, it's just not fair on me. Your suffering from guilt is affecting our baby. It's not even born yet, and they say unborn babies pick up on things.' She allowed another tear to fall, hoping that it would stir a reaction.

For a moment, as Justin stared into her speckled amber eyes

with that innocent expression, he saw Kara. It was so strange, he took a deep breath and blinked. He did miss Kara and would do anything to turn the clock back, but he couldn't, and the sooner he accepted it, the quicker he could move on, and perhaps telling his mother would be the best thing.

'All right, this weekend, I'll drive to my mother's and let her know what's happening, and then, once she gets over the shock, I'll take you over there to meet her.'

Clasping her hands together, she tried to control her excitement. 'Aw, thank you, Justin, I so want to meet her. I don't have a mother. Well, I do, I just don't know her, so it will be lovely to have your mum in my life and plan for the arrival of our precious child.'

At that point, Justin realised that he knew very little about Lucy, and a sadness crept over him. Lucy didn't have a mother. 'You said a while ago you grew up in foster care, didn't you? Didn't you have a mother figure, then? Wasn't there someone you cared about and who cared for you?'

For a second, Lucy forgot she'd told him that she was brought up in foster care. 'Oh, no, I went from home to home. No one really wanted me. They all wanted babies, and when you're older, they want the money. I was worth a hundred pounds a week to the last foster carers.' She stared at nothing, giving the impression she was somewhere in a dark place, recalling a distant horrible memory. In reality, though, she was plotting the next lie.

'You never really had any family, then? That's pretty sad, Lucy. I'm so sorry, love.' He genuinely felt bad for her because he did know what it was like to have a loving mother, although not a father because his had run off. But, still, his mother more than made up for it, in love and kindness. He stretched his neck, trying to ease the strangling feeling. How was he going to tell his mum that Kara was in prison and his house was just a pile of ashes? And to top it all, he'd done the one thing his mother detested and that was to be unfaithful.

He could hear her words ringing in his ears. 'Son, I'm so proud of you. You have grown up to be a fine young man with morals and values and you never went off the rails. I feel I have done my job.' He remembered it well because it was the day she'd given him her grandmother's engagement ring for Kara. That was twelve weeks ago, but Kara was overseas for the second time, and so he'd hidden the ring in his sock drawer. He'd wanted the time to be perfect and had planned a trip to Italy in order to propose.

He snapped out of his thoughts, when Lucy said, 'So, yes, having your mother will be like having my own.'

He so desperately wanted to go along with the notion that Lucy and his mum would be friends and the idea that a baby would make everything okay, but how could it? His mother loved Kara; she doted on her, in fact. She took over very quickly from Joan, who was eager to move to Australia, a long-term dream of hers. So, as soon as Kara mentioned that she would be moving in with him, Joan sold up and emigrated. Crippled with arthritis and suffering from extreme pain, she hoped the warmer climate would do her good. The truth was, Joan was very poorly and showing signs of dementia. Consequently, she would forget to call or even answer the phone, and so Kara resorted a lot to texting her.

Christ, how would his mother, Mollie, take it all? They were already a family: Mollie, Kara, and him. He looked across the table at Lucy, who was still teary-eyed. Knowing he had to get the past out of his head, he said, 'Hey, why don't we go out tomorrow tonight for a meal and properly get to know each other?'

Her face lit up. 'Really, do you mean it?'

'Yes, I think I need to move on. I can't help Kara. She should never have done what she did. It was unnecessary, and you and I have a baby that needs looking after.' He reached across and held her hand.

Lucy knew she had him: hook, line, and sinker. Now, she would sleep easy; she had finally cracked the nut.

Justin left the next morning for work. He had slept in her bed, and although they didn't have sex, he did hold her. Lucy didn't tell him that she had a scan that very morning; she couldn't reveal the birth date or he would have smelled a rat, so, instead, she went alone. The baby was five months not four. She paid for the photo of the scan and put it in a card ready for when he arrived home from work.

* * *

That evening, Justin arrived with a bunch of flowers, much to Lucy's surprise.

'There you go. I've booked a table at Desperados, a new Mexican restaurant.' He didn't want to go to any place that he'd been with Kara. It just didn't seem right, and also, he wanted to remove any thoughts that could possibly darken his future, although he was well aware that it was an uphill struggle. Every time his mind wandered to Kara, he thought about the baby and how he would be a good father. Lucy was sweet; he hadn't really noticed at first, but as the weeks passed, he was beginning to find her loving nature a real asset and could easily plant a kiss on her cheek or rub her now protruding belly.

The restaurant was bright and full of exotic pictures, sombreros, and Latino music. Dressed like one of the bandits in the film *Three Amigos*, the waiter guided them to their table after which he reeled off the chef's special menu.

'This is wonderful, Justin, such a fun place. Have you been here before with …?'

He smiled and shook his head. 'No, never, I wouldn't take you to the same places I took her. We need to have a fresh start, and with our baby on the way, I'm going to make some changes. The insurance company will be assigning a building company to rebuild the house. Everything has been approved, and so fingers crossed, we can move in, hopefully in six months. There is a big team of contractors who should have the place up and ready in record time.'

The waiter returned with Lucy's virgin cocktail in a huge glass topped with fancy decorations and sparklers. Lucy giggled. 'Oh, I feel so spoilt.'

Inside, though, she was irritated; this was not the expensive restaurant she was expecting, but still, she had to look impressed.

'Here, Justin, take a look at your baby,' she said, as she handed him the photo scan.

His eyes widened. 'Oh my God, is this really our baby?'

The question was not taken in the way he meant it, and Lucy, for a second, forgot herself. 'What do you mean?'

Justin was staring at the alien-looking picture from the scan at the hospital, and his face changed from a look of surprise to one of wonderment. Gazing at her with a huge smile, he replied, 'No, I mean, I never expected to see a photo so soon. When did you go to the hospital?' He was still grinning like a Cheshire cat.

Quickly, she had to regain her footing. 'Oh, I went today. I thought I would surprise you.'

Puzzled, he looked at her. 'Why didn't you ask me to come along? I would have gone with you.'

The sparklers fizzled out. 'I know you are busy at work, and I didn't want to be a burden, Justin, and demand your attention. Anyway, our baby is perfect, so they said.'

As Justin glanced from the menu he was studying to look up at Lucy, he noticed a look of pure horror on her face. Slowly, he turned around, following her gaze. A group of men had walked into the restaurant. They scanned the seating area, presumably looking for a table. Wearing dark grey suits, cutaway collar white shirts, and classy ties, they could have been pin-up models in a

Hugo Boss catalogue. They clearly thought they looked the business too, with their cocky expressions. Justin looked back at Lucy who was getting up from her chair. He grabbed her hand. 'Where are you going and who are they?'

She shook herself free from him. 'I need the ladies,' she whispered. But it was a bit late for that.

'Well, hello, Lucy,' came the distinctive East End voice from behind Justin, a voice that was deep and harsh. He didn't need to turn around because the man in his forties with a sleekness about him was there by the side of the table. 'And how are you, little Lucy Lou?'

Justin was about to smile politely at the tall suited man, but pulled back from doing so, as he saw the sneer on the man's face. There was a daunting air of menace that gave Justin a bitter taste in his mouth. The two other men, who looked like bouncers from a nightclub, gave Justin an ice-cold stare. Lucy was frozen to the spot.

'What's up, Lucy? Not got a hug for ya Uncle Carl, then?'

Her eyes flicked from Justin to the two sidekicks and then back to Carl, who was still wearing his half-cocked smirk. Swallowing hard, she looked at him, as she tried to regain her composure, but her mind was in a spin. 'Oh, come on, you're not really my uncle, but anyway, I'm good, thank you.'

'So, ain't ya gonna introduce me to this nice young man 'ere?'

Her hands shook so much, she had to grip the table. 'Justin, this is Carl.'

Getting to his feet, Justin held out his hand and received an almost bone-crushing handshake for his trouble. 'Nice to meet ya, son, so ...' Carl looked down at Lucy's bump, which was clearly on show in her tight tube dress. 'A baby's on its way, then, eh, Lucy Lou?'

She nodded coolly and sat back down. She needed to regain the upper hand, before this evening went pear-shaped, but trying to dismiss Carl and his bruisers out of hand wouldn't go down well at all. 'Look, Carl, it's nice to see you but maybe another time, yeah?'

'Aw, don't be like that, Lucy, we have a lot to discuss. As ya know, it's been a while. How's ya dad?'

Justin sensed the tone of sarcasm and the atmosphere around them was becoming tenser by the second. Even the waiters and bar staff were looking over at their table and standing to attention. He watched as Carl pulled up a chair and sat facing Lucy. Nervously, Justin took a deep breath and took his seat. Then Carl clicked his fingers, and immediately the waiter, dressed like a Mexican, with a sombrero and black moustache, was by his side.

'Tony, bring over the best champagne, will ya?'

Lucy raised a hand. 'Look, Carl, I'm having a private meal with my boyfriend, so, like I said, let's do this another time, eh?'

Glancing up at the two meatheads standing in the gangway, he laughed. 'Looks like we're not wanted, boys. Our little Lucy Lou is too good for us now.'

Justin intervened. 'I'm sure Lucy didn't mean it that way, only we are celebrating tonight. Maybe another night, we could all enjoy a meal together. It would be nice wouldn't it, Lucy, getting to know your friends?' said Justin, casting a questioning look at her.

Carl tapped Justin's face. 'You, my son, haven't a fucking clue.' For a moment, Justin was expecting all hell to break loose, but the moment passed. Carl sucked in a lungful of air and stood up. 'All right, you two lovebirds, the meal and drinks are on the house. My treat.'

Lucy glared at him with utter contempt. She hated him just then with every bone in her body and wanted nothing more than to pick up her knife and stab him in the neck, but instead, she smiled sweetly and nodded.

The waiter hurried over with the champagne. 'It's on the house.' Tony's eyes watched, as Carl got up to leave.

'No, thank you, it's fine,' stated Justin, as he waved his hand, dismissing the waiter.

Tony looked at the men slipping away though the front door and then back at Justin. 'But the boss just said …'

'I don't give a flying fuck what the boss said. In fact, sod the meal, I'm leaving.' He shot Lucy a fierce glare and jumped up from his seat. 'Are you coming, or what?'

She hurriedly followed him, desperately trying to think of a way out of this bloody cock-up. He didn't look behind him; she knew then he was pissed off with her. Not bothering to open the door to his BMW for her, he just got in the driver's seat and stared directly ahead, whilst she hastily climbed inside. 'I'm so sorry, Justin. That man is just a pervert friend of my foster father. God, I thought he would never leave. I'm so glad you stuck up for me.'

She paused, holding her breath, awaiting the argument that was clearly brewing. As they headed back to the flat, he was silent, driving faster than normal, but his tight lips and tense brow told her he was fuming. She'd never seen him act so manly, standing his ground with Carl; perhaps he really wasn't the pushover she'd imagined him to be.

He stopped abruptly outside her flat and marched on ahead, shoving his key in the door and leaving it open for her to follow. But he didn't wait. He carried on, jumping up the stairs two at a time and then charged into the bedroom. Lucy was panicking and scurried behind him. 'What's wrong, Justin, what are you doing?' She looked at him filling his sports bag with his clothes, throwing them in as if he were on a bank heist.

Grabbing his arm, she asked, 'Justin, what the hell's going on?'

He shrugged her off. 'I'm not living in this flat with a fucking liar!'

'What?'

'You heard! That man clearly knows you well, saying he's your uncle, and who the fuck is Lucy Lou? I said I would take it slowly, get to know you, but it seems you are a liar. You told me you were fostered. Those men aren't doting uncles, more like hard-faced villains, and I'll tell you this, Lucy, I'm no idiot. They know you and for reasons that are beyond my comprehension. The way he looked at you and spoke to you was too familiar. It was as if you were used to his company. I'm beginning to wonder if that baby is even mine. Are you sure it's not Carl's?'

Jumping back in shock, Lucy put her hands to her mouth, and her eyes brimmed with tears. Justin stopped what he was doing and sighed. 'Look, sorry, that was a bit over the top. I didn't mean that, but back there, it was like you were a different person, not some sweet young woman, who, from what you told me, had a very sad life.'

The tears tumbled down her cheeks. 'All right, if you must know, Carl …' She paused, snorting back the tears. Then, she sat on the bed, with her head in her hands, and began to sob.

She felt the bed sink, as Justin sat beside her. 'What is it, Lucy? Who is this Carl bloke?' His voice softened.

'He was a friend of my foster dad, but Carl … Oh my God, I can't bring myself to say it … he raped me when I was fifteen.'

Justin gasped. 'He what? Jesus!' His hands slid around her shoulders. 'Why is he still wandering the streets? Why isn't he locked up?'

Shaking her head and wiping her eyes, Lucy looked up at Justin's face. 'You will never understand what it's like to be caught up in the system – foster care homes and children's homes. No one believes a word you say. It's easier not to rock the boat. If you do, you end up with a name for yourself, and if you're not careful, they section you off.'

Her words were so utterly believable that Justin had a rush of guilt again for the umpteenth time. 'If you had said, I would have bashed him myself.'

She ran her hand down his cheek. 'You are so sweet, Justin, so innocently sweet. That's why I never told you too much because how can I compare myself with Kara? She had it all, and she wasn't damaged goods, like me. It's taken a long time to get over what happened to me, and now I have you, I don't want to lose you. I have a family now, at long last a family – me, you, and our baby. I never want to ruin it. I'm so sorry, Justin, I should have told you about my past, and then, perhaps, you would have understood.'

Her words were so credible that even she began to believe them herself, but that wasn't unusual. She had an ability of exploiting her warped imagination to conjure up a life that she believed she'd been living – well, so the psychiatrist had told her.

Justin stroked her hair and wiped away the tears. 'Hush, it's fine. I'm sorry, I should have believed you right away. I promise you, I'll make things better. You will never have to live in the past. We have our own future to look forward to – as you say, me, you, and the baby.' He pulled her close and hugged her like an injured child. As she looked over his shoulder, she sadistically grinned; she knew how to lure him in.

Christ, I'm a clever girl, she thought. *I should have auditioned for EastEnders.* It was now just a matter of time for her master plan to unfold.

Chapter 7

Alone in her cell, Kara looked up at the ceiling. It had been two months since the day she'd arrived at the prison. Not a day went by when she didn't think about Mrs Langley and the guilt roiled around in her stomach like a rotting egg. She often wondered if Justin missed her as much as she missed him. Even though he'd done the dirty on her, she still loved him, and it was still hurting so much. She could feel the tiny being inside her move, and that made her smile because she knew that at least she would have someone to love who would love her back without breaking her heart.

Her court case was looming, and if they sentenced her to more than two years, she would have to hand over her baby to the social services. Vic and Julie were becoming more like her own family, which was quite a shocker. Especially Vic – she made sure that Kara was at the front of the queue when they handed out the food. 'Get in there, gal, and grab yourself a good piece of chicken. Ya need ya protein for the little one,' she would say.

Deni had also become a real friend, although she'd had to stay away from Kara for a few weeks, in case the young mother-to-be contracted the virus that caused shingles. Her priority must be her unborn child's safety. Once the cream and tablets ensured a speedy recovery and the rash was diagnosed as shingles, Kara was held in high esteem. It took a while before she worked out the dynamics, but it finally fell into place.

Deni was the matriarchal character who everyone respected, and she was useful to have in your corner. At one time, in the late Sixties, she ran a brothel, and her reputation for treating her girls with respect and keeping them off the streets was nothing short of legendary. She was apparently a big woman, in stature that is, who no one messed with, if they wanted to keep their pretty smiles. A no-nonsense woman, with a punch as hard as any man's. So her girls didn't need any pimp because they had her.

Her sentence started twenty years ago when she murdered two punters, both judges, who had fucked up one of her girls so badly, she could never work again, and when they came back for more, Deni set about them with a meat cleaver. The incident had captured the interest of the nation for weeks, helped by an article in *The Sun* that coincidentally had drawn its readers' attention to the way some of the so-called privileged members of society treated prostitutes as pariahs. And so by the time she was sentenced and had arrived at the nick, she was given a standing ovation and a pat on the back from the inmates.

The screws smiled because although what she did was legally wrong, it wasn't morally wrong in their eyes. Inside the prison, she was seen as fair, ensuring no one got bullied and the real nasty bitches got their just desserts. Just a nod and a flick of her eyebrow, and they would get a handmade knife in their ribs. So, when Deni came to visit Kara to thank her, everyone knew that Kara was protected. She had Vic and Julie, but more importantly, she had Deni watching her back and fighting her corner.

She remembered well the day Deni came into her room with a huge smile on her face and a strong smell of lavender. 'You must be me own private little doctor, then? I can honestly say, I didn't get ta see ya face properly, I was in that much bleedin' pain.' She stepped closer and eyed Kara over, while Vic and Julie watched. 'Cor, pretty little thing, ain't ya? Well, Posh, I just wanted to say, I think ya saved me life, 'cos if that pain had got any worse, I was gonna hang meself.'

She sat on the bed and nodded for Kara to take a seat.

'It was nothing, honestly. I have seen that condition before.'

Deni looked different from the last time Kara saw her. With her cheeks round and rosy and her eyes wide open, she would probably have been a very good-looking woman in her younger days. And the stories Kara had heard about this hardened woman somehow didn't seem to match her soft face and voice.

'No, no, I'm not 'aving that. Ya didn't 'ave ta come and see me, but ya did, and you put me right, so if you ever need me, you just call. Someone will find me.'

'That's very kind of you, Deni,' said Kara, still marvelling at the woman's presence in the room. Deni's inoffensive cherubic face, grizzled hair, cut to shoulder-length, and motherly presence belied her true self. Her reputation and standing among the inmates and officers was such that when she wanted something done it was. No one mugged her off and got away with it.

'I can see why they call ya Posh. I like it. It suits ya, gal. It's nice to hear a well-spoken voice, instead of all the bleedin' slang. So, Vic tells me ya just found out ya got a bun in the oven? Ahh, that's a real shame, darling. This ain't the place to be 'aving babies, but you 'ave us 'ere, babe, if ya need us.' She looked up at Vic. 'Ain't that right, Vic?'

Vic gave a sobering smile and nodded. Kara then realised that whilst life in Larkview wouldn't be a bed of roses, at least the women in the room were rooting for her.

Much of her time now was spent either contemplating the future, meeting with Alan Cumberbatch, her solicitor, or playing doctor to the inmates' minor ailments. Luckily, the court case was only a few months away and her verdict would be confirmed. Alan said she was lucky that it wasn't murder by recklessness that

96

she was facing since the neighbour had recovered with no after-effects, apart from post-traumatic stress disorder. However, Kara could still be looking at a few years. He had assigned a barrister who would be meeting with her soon.

As she lay pondering in her cell, a commotion on the landing caught her attention. She eased herself off the bed. When she looked below at the landing to the recreational area, she could see a few of the inmates gathered, and a deranged-looking woman with a screw on either side. Then, Kara clocked Vic step towards the newcomer with her arms folded and a daring nod. Kara had never seen the inmate before, but she was obviously new, judging by the way all the onlookers stood staring at her. Vic was giving her plenty of front from the expression on the newcomer's face. Clearly, this person was not going to be made welcome in this nick. But she didn't seem the least bit bothered. In fact, she looked a real cocky bitch. 'Thought you was up in Durham, Meadows?'

Vic laughed. 'Ahh, yeah, you would like that, eh, Esme?' The tone in her voice alone was provocation.

'Get back to your cells, recreation is over!' screamed Barbara. Really, she was nervous because the two hardest women in the prison system were now face-to-face, and there would be a riot, if she didn't clear the area before getting Esme Lonergan, an Irish tinker, into her cell.

Kara was glued to the situation below and felt her stomach turn over. It was a sobering face-off, and the assembling crowd were enthralled by the two protagonists who were giving it large, every bit as much as watching two professional fighters at the prefight weigh-in.

The crowd reluctantly dispersed, when it became clear the prison officers had the situation under control. As Esme was pulled away, Vic ran a finger along her throat. Kara shuddered. It was frightening to watch; there was so much hate here and now rumblings of real violence. So far, she'd been lucky, apart from the smack in the mouth from Colette, who was now licking her feet in adulation. Kara knew she was one of the lucky ones: so far, she'd never faced any serious brutality.

A few moments later, in walked Julie and Vic, their faces flushed with excitement. But Kara could see that they appeared agitated and Vic was breathing fast.

'Who was that?'

'That, my friend, is what's known as a right royal cunt. Esme Lonergan is serving a life sentence for killing her own mother and slashing her daughter's face. She is a psycho but not according to the shrinks. I have had my run-in with her.' Vic lifted her top and turned around to reveal a nasty scar just below her rib cage. 'She caught me a good 'un. Nearly killed me, the sly fucker.'

Kara had her hands over her mouth in shock. 'She knifed you?'

Vic laughed. 'Yep, make that twice now.' She pulled down her tracksuit bottoms to show a long scar the length of her thigh.

Kara's face went totally white and she had difficulty swallowing. Just as she thought she was coming to terms with life in prison, she experienced a glimpse of the real potential violence and it knocked her for six.

Vic gave Kara an encouraging smile. 'Oh, don't worry, she will get it from me, if she tries another stunt like she did before. I run this prison, not her, not here.'

Vic meant it too because three days later it all kicked off. Kara had taken herself to the showers; she had suffered all night with heartburn and night sweats and wanted nothing more than a warm shower to bring herself back to normal. With just a towel around her middle, she now felt confident enough to make her way to the bathrooms. A few nods and smiles along the way gave her a lift in her step and also in her mood. Unlike the first time she took a shower, when she was petrified knowing all eyes were on her and from hearing about the horrendous injuries inflicted on inmates in the cubicles, she was now able to take a more sanguine view of life in prison.

It stemmed from an inbuilt ability to assess the risks. Her

safety was bolstered by influential inmates higher up the food chain than herself, and she had life-saving skills that the others could only dream of. So, on balance, things looked pretty good.

But on the negative side, she had been inside now for two months and it felt like years. Understanding the psyche of prisoners was helped by Vic and Julie, who, for some reason, enjoyed teaching Kara about their world whilst learning about Kara's. Drug abuse was rife in Larkview, as elsewhere in the world of prisons. She learned that having a steady supply of any illegal substance gave a prisoner credence and power. Obviously, she didn't have access to that source. However, what she did have – and what the others didn't – was medical knowledge. In the currency of prison life, that was priceless.

Identifying the drug addicts was easy: their gaunt faces, sunken eyes, and nervous twitches, along with the scars from self-harming, gave them away. Sadly, many were victims of their upbringing due to their weak personalities or child abuse. The only correlation to her own experience of incarceration was at boarding school, where she had to stay there, even though she didn't want to. However, circumstances at the time deemed boarding school to be the best option – well, so her mother professed.

Most of the women had already gone to their jobs, so it was the ideal time for Kara to take her shower. However, when she arrived, one of the showers was already occupied. As she turned her shower on to feel the warm massaging sprinkles of water, she felt an uneasy prickling sensation. She rotated to find another occupant almost on her toes, and as she looked up, her eyes focused on the grim shape of Esme Lonergan. Esme had one of those faces that was the stuff of nightmares – and that was if you caught her on one of her good days. Her deep-set eyes were cold, almost lifeless, and yet her cruel smirk and threatening stance scared the shit out of Kara.

Quickly glancing to her left, she prayed that someone else would be there. There was no one – just Esme and herself. Nervously, she let the bar of soap slip through her fingers. It made her jump as it hit the floor. Esme's smirk turned to a lip-curling grin. 'Well, pick it up, or someone will slip and break their neck, and you sure wouldn't want it to be you, would you now? Not in your condition.' She looked at Kara's neat bump.

Kara ran her hands over her belly, feeling a new unfound fear and an inner sense of protection. She couldn't bend down and pick up the soap because she would have to take her eyes off Esme. She had to protect her unborn baby, whatever the cost. The images of Vic and Esme's alarming standoff whirled around in her head. Esme was ruthless with a stance and look that held no conscience or remorse.

'Pick it up, I said!' yelled Esme, twisting her head to the side like some nutter. She stepped forward and yelled again, this time in Kara's ear. 'I said, pick … it … up!' Her words were spat through gritted teeth.

So close was Esme's face that Kara could smell the stale odour of cigarettes and what seemed like the evil taste on her breath. In a panic, Kara tried to flee, but Esme's hand slammed her face against the cold white tiles. She felt her cheek smash and she yelped. 'Please, let me go,' she snivelled, terrified the woman would really hurt her in some malicious manner.

'You go back to that fecking whore, Vic, with a message from me!' Without warning, she snatched a clump of Kara's hair, pulled her away from the wall, and rammed her face into it again, but this time, it was so hard that Kara's legs buckled, and her attacker, with a swift, violent, and unforgiving kick, landed her foot into Kara's stomach.

'Nooo!' screamed Kara, clutching her abdomen. Slumped on the floor, she curled into a ball to protect herself, but then came the next kick, harder than the last. Kara could only think of one thing and that was to scream. And she did. She filled her lungs and opened her mouth, letting out a guttural, blood-curdling holler. Again, she screamed, as loudly as she could, and when she finally opened her eyes, Esme was gone.

Racked with fear and pain, she sobbed, rocking on the cold shower floor, as the water continued to pour. Too afraid to get up, she watched as the blood from her wounded face diluted to a pink colour and swirled around the drain. 'Please be okay, baby, please don't die, you're all I have,' she whispered in despair.

The screams were so loud now that everyone in the vicinity came running, including Colette. Instantly, she was by Kara's side. 'Fucking 'ell, Posh, what happened? Are you all right?' She stood back up and turned the shower off but seriously struggled to help Kara to her feet. Two officers arrived. As they moved Colette aside, a crowd of onlookers were all trying to see what had happened. Officer Brent, a seasoned screw, who mothered everyone, was the first to offer support. 'It's okay, Kara, don't move. Pass me a towel someone.' Colette found the towel on the floor and handed it to the officer. 'Is she gonna be okay, Gov?'

Barbara was standing there like a wet weekend. 'Get back to your cells! Bannon is fine, nothing to bloody see!' she yelled.

Colette, however, didn't move; instead, she bent down beside Brent and tried to help Kara stand, but as soon as Kara turned her head to look up, Colette gasped.

'For God's sake, Connor, get out of my way,' screamed Barbara, before she radioed through for help.

'Listen, Kara, you are going to be okay. Just take a few deep breaths and we'll see if we can get you to your feet,' whispered Brent.

The shock had hit Kara hard and she began to shake violently. Sharp pains gripped her stomach, and as she attempted to get up, she doubled over. 'Oh, no, no, my baby, please help me!'

Colette had run into Dora's cell, grabbed her blanket, and hurried back, trying to put it around Kara. As their eyes met,

Kara saw the fear and compassion staring back. She stopped moving and grabbed Colette's arm. 'Thank you,' she whispered, before she doubled over again, the pain ripping through her.

'Shall I get Vic?' Colette asked, as she looked up at Brent.

But Barbara was quick to intervene. 'Certainly not. Get back to your cell, or I'll have you on report.'

Colette stepped back, looking hurt. She'd only wanted to help. She felt for Kara because the same thing had happened to her, only back then, the officers had done bugger-all to help and had just left her all night locked up for her to miscarry down the toilet alone and frightened. She was damn sure it wouldn't happen to Kara.

Ignoring the warning, she hurried down the flight of stairs and then along the recreation room before entering the laundry room where she was almost blinded by the steam from the industrial steamers. 'Vic!' she screamed. 'Vic, where are ya? Kara's been beaten up! She might lose the baby!' Fortunately, the steam cleared and there in front of her were Deni, Vic, and a druggie called Vivienne.

'You what? Where is she?'

Colette was out of breath. 'Upstairs … in the showers … her face … it's a hell of a mess. She … is holding her stomach … I think … she's gonna have a miscarriage,' she gasped, as her breathing returned to normal.

Vic lifted the lid on the steamer and hurried past Colette and took the stairs two at a time. But, by the time she reached the showers, the area had been cleared. She spun on her heels to face Colette behind her. 'Who did it, Cole? I want a name!'

With a shrug of her shoulders, Colette replied, 'I dunno. I was in Dora's cell, when I heard this horrible scream, and when I got here, she was on the floor.'

Barbara had cleared the wing, but as soon as Kara was led away, the inmates all came back out.

'I wanna know who the fuck did that to Kara?'

Deni was way behind the rest of them. Like Colette, she too was puffed out. 'Where's Posh?'

'Gone to medical. They may have taken her to hospital,' replied Colette.

'Well, ya know who did it, don't ya?' said Deni, with her hands on her hips and a scowl on her face. 'It was that scumbag Esme, 'cos unless one of the junkies lost the plot, that kid has no enemies …' She glared at the gathered crowd. 'Unless one of youse can tell me any different?'

Vic took a deep breath. 'Let's hope Posh ain't told the screws who did her in, 'cos they will have her on watch. They know full well this won't get brushed under the carpet, not all the while I have a head on me fucking shoulders and fire in me belly.'

Dawn Leonard, a woman in her late forties, convicted of setting up one of the biggest skunk farms in the country, screwed her face up. 'Tell me, Vic, 'cos it's puzzled me for ages now. Why do you look out for this Posh bird?'

Deni, Vic, and Colette gave Dawn a dirty glare. But it was Deni who answered her. 'Because, like me, you, and most of us, we deserve all the crap we have to put up with in this shit-hole, but that kid doesn't. She wasn't cut out for this life. She's never done no one any harm. She helps us when that cranky quack is fucking useless, and she has no one. You, though, Dawn, you 'ave it all. Ya have your fancy clothes, ya own bedding brought in, visitors' letters, and enough fucking gear so you can sleep at night. That kid has fuck-all. No family, no friends, and she never asks for nothing. I have always been a fair woman, as well you fucking know, and she didn't deserve any beatin', so either you are wiv us, Dawn, or you can sign ya own death warrant, along with the bitch that beat Kara.'

The warning was harsh and heartfelt. Dawn never wanted to upset Deni; the repercussions were just not worth it. She nodded. 'I never said … what I mean is, I just wondered, nothing more, and I'm wiv ya. You're right, she didn't deserve that.' Dawn slunk away with her head down. Deni had a point. She did have family and money. Her cell was like a luxury fitted bedroom, with her own bedding from Harrods and curtains to match, and her stash of designer clothes was a sight to behold. And a big plus, she had regular contact with her family.

With that thought in mind, she decided to help in any way she could. Under her bed was another set of bedding and a few new sweatshirts not even out of their cellophane packets. She pulled out a big bag and filled it with whatever she could and headed over to Kara's cell. Vic was sitting on Julie's bed, smoking a roll-up, when Dawn appeared, looking a tad sheepish. She raised her eyebrow. 'Got any news, Dawn, like, who did it?'

Solemn-faced, Dawn shook her head. 'Nah, but Deni was right, and I thought Kara might like a few bits. The kid's got fuck-all, and well, I've got enough.'

With an approving nod, Vic took a deep drag on her roll-up. 'A guilt trip, I'm guessing?'

Dawn shot Vic a reproachful sideways glance. 'Er, no, I just thought about what Deni said, that's all. I had nothing to do with it. Ya know that, surely?'

In a flash, Vic was off the bed, with Dawn's chin gripped between her fingers. 'That's exactly what I meant, you long streak of piss. But it looks to me that you just put yaself in the frame. So, before I ring your neck like a fucking rooster, you'd better start talking.' She removed her grip on Dawn, but glared, waiting for an answer.

Flicking her eyes to the door, Dawn contemplated bolting, but it would be no use. Esme didn't have enough backup and Vic had a small army of wannabe soldiers. 'Look, Vic, it weren't like that, I swear, right? Esme collared me in me cell, wanting to know stuff. I didn't say anything except—'

She didn't have a chance to finish. Vic grabbed Dawn's hair, pulling her to the ground. 'What the fuck did you tell her?' she snarled. Her tone was enough to put the fear of God in the woman.

It was no use. Dawn was caught between a rock and a hard place. 'I just said that Posh was like your little sister, that's all.'

'And why would you say that?' Vic asked, as she went for the woman again, clenching her face in a vicelike grip.

'Ahh, let go, please, you're hurting me! She just asked who she was, nothing more, I swear, Vic. Please, let go. I don't want no trouble. I ain't getting involved.'

Releasing her grip, Vic spat in Dawn's face. 'You slimy bitch. Ain't you learned to keep ya mouth shut, eh?'

Dawn slid herself up the wall. She was seriously petrified now. Esme was hard, but the combined threat of these nutters was scaring her more. 'She had a blade at me throat, but I promise, Vic, that's all I said.'

Sitting back on the bed, Vic glared. 'A blade, yeah?'

Dawn was nodding so fast, it was a wonder her head didn't fall off. 'Yeah, about four inches. Watch yaself, Vic. She's after your blood.'

As she flared her nostrils and narrowed her eyes, Vic wondered if it was worth grassing or taking on Esme herself. Grassing went against the grain, on every level, but then, she had her little sister to think of as well. Either way, she would have to have it out with Esme once and for all – it was a case of calling a truce or beating the mad bitch to death.

* * *

The ambulance arrived at the prison to take Kara to hospital. The senior officer had insisted because she knew that there would be serious consequences, if Kara was given less than the best treatment. She was too much in the know, when it came down to medical dos and don'ts. Brent was well informed that the regular doctor they had in the prison was as useless as an ejector seat in a helicopter, so she called it in and would make her case to the number one governor tomorrow, if arranging the ambulance was an issue.

She decided personally to escort Kara. She wouldn't leave it to Barbara; she never liked that woman anyway. The paramedics took charge whilst Melanie Brent stayed back. She stared at the look of complete despair on Kara's face. Her polite ways and soft nature had been noted by all the officers, especially George, who made sure he popped in to see her on a regular basis. They had thought at first that he had the hots for her, but as time went by, Melanie realised Kara just wasn't like the other inmates, and so his careful watch over her was warranted.

'I can't lose this baby, I can't …' Her voice was trailing off, as she sucked on the gas and air.

One of the paramedics, a young thickset woman, patted her arm. 'You may not be miscarrying; it may be a shock. Just try to relax, and we will get you seen to as soon as possible.'

Kara pulled the mask away from her face, revealing the black bruise and wounds to her bloodshot eyes. She looked at Officer Brent. 'Thank you, Gov, I'm so grateful.'

Melanie felt the urge to cry. Even though she'd become so hardened to prison life, she was taken aback by the state of the poor young woman. 'Hey, it's okay. Tell me, Kara, who did this to you?'

Kara gently shook her head. 'I slipped.'

Melanie knew damn well this was not the case but decided not to push it. 'Look, is there anyone you would like me to call? I have my mobile on me.' Brent was breaking all the rules, but she didn't care. Kara didn't deserve this treatment.

Again, Kara shook her head and a sudden tear pricked her eye. Justin should be here with her. She had tried so hard to hate him, but deep down, no matter how much she was sickened by what he'd done, she couldn't stop loving him. 'It's ironic. Justin, my partner, left me because he was having a baby with another woman, and there I was, already expecting, and he didn't even know it.' She sucked hard again on the gas and air.

Melanie reached across and held Kara's hand. 'Does he know now?'

'No, there's no point. He'll be setting up home with her and their child. He doesn't want me because he's never even sent a letter, nothing at all, so I suppose he's moved on without giving me a second thought. I loved him, you know. I mean, I really loved him so much, and all I have now, God willing, is his baby. I can't lose this as well.'

'You won't, you'll be fine. Look, you're not in pain now, are you?' Melanie smiled.

Kara blinked and took a deep breath. 'Er, no, actually, the pain has stopped.'

'Aw, let's pray, it was just a bruise, shall we,' said Melanie, kindly.

Childless herself, Melanie was over the age of childbearing and had wished she hadn't been so into her work that the potential fruitful time had just flown by. She'd yearned for a child for many years, and now she longed for the well-being of Kara's baby. 'What will you name your baby?'

'Well, if it's a boy, I don't have a family name because I never knew my father, and I'm not sure I would want to name my baby after him anyway. I couldn't bear to call him Justin. It would hurt too much, and, well, I don't have a name either for a girl. Perhaps, nearer the time, I'll think of something sweet.'

The ambulance came to a stop and the paramedics eagerly helped Kara from the back of the ambulance, careful to be gentle, lowering her down in the lift. Luckily, the ultrasound suite wasn't busy, so she was wheeled in and seen to right away. Melanie held her hand. To the radiologist, this looked strange, seeing an officer and an inmate acting as though they were best friends. She poured the gel over Kara's small bump, and after a few minutes, she sighed, but the look on her face said it all. 'Kara, you have nothing to worry about. Your little girl is doing just fine.'

'A girl, oh, my goodness, a little girl!' Instantaneously, the floodgates opened, and the tears flowed down Kara's face; it was relief and heartache all at once. This should be Justin holding her hand, watching their tiny baby girl on the screen. She was real: she was hers, wriggling around.

After allowing Kara to cry and get it all out of her system, Melanie helped her off the bed. 'You know what, Kara? I think God was watching over you.'

After her eyebrow was glued back together and her face cleaned up, Melanie escorted Kara to the awaiting prison van that had followed them behind the ambulance. George was in the driver's seat. 'All good?' he anxiously asked.

Melanie winked. 'Yes, the baby is okay. Kara is shaken up, stitched up, and is now ready for her bed.'

Chapter 8

As the sun streamed through the kitchen window, Justin swallowed his bitter coffee and remained silent, ignoring Lucy's comment. He had run out of excuses for not taking Lucy along to meet his mother.

'Justin, look at me, I'm not getting any smaller. This bump is your mother's grandchild. How long will this go on for? Are you going to wait until he starts school before you spring it on her?'

Spinning around, he faced her and rolled his eyes. She *was* getting big, and she did have a point, but he was being ground down by all the whining. There were still days when he found he was thinking about Kara and comparing both women. Kara never moaned. She would even take herself off to the spare room, if she was unwell, so as not to make him miserable. Lucy's negative attitude, particularly her rudeness to other people, was wearing thin. His mother's words were popping into his mind. 'Son, judge people on how they treat others.'

Lucy was impatient and downright bitchy at times. The waiter, the gas man, and even the poor woman who lived in the basement flat below received a smart remark when she accidentally dropped her black sack of rubbish and it spilled onto the pavement, just as they were about to get into the car a few days ago.

Lillian was in her late seventies, and not so nimble on her feet, and he could see she was riddled with arthritis, yet Lucy had to have a go.

'Watch what you're doing, you silly woman!' she snapped. Justin was mortified and raised his hands to mouth the word 'sorry' whilst he hurried over and helped the old dear retrieve the rubbish and place it in the big bin. Lucy was already moaning in the car. 'You shouldn't have to help her. I'm sure she has sons to do all that. Now, we're going to be late.' At that point, Justin knew he had to get back out of the car and go inside before he said something he would regret. Once again, Lucy was hanging on to his shirt-tails, crying and blaming her hormones.

Now, a few weeks later, they were drinking coffee in the kitchen. Justin had had a bellyful of Lucy's pleading and whining. 'Okay, okay, Lucy, I'll call her today and make arrangements for you to meet her, if, of course, she wants to meet you—'

Unable to even let him finish the sentence, Lucy jumped in, 'What do you mean, "if"? Why on earth would she not? I'm having her grandson. I'm a person, you know, not just a bloody oven. Besides, she can't honestly have any feeling for your bloody ex. Christ, Justin, that woman burned your house down, and nearly—'

'Yes, I know,' Justin interjected, 'and nearly killed the neighbour. How many more times are you going to say it?'

Pulling her fluffy pink dressing gown tighter around her big bump, she sneered, 'Well, I just think no one seems to get the seriousness of what she did. You act as if it was nothing, but, Justin, until that house is bloody built, we will have to live in this cramped flat that you can barely swing a cat in. If she'd not been such a firebug, then we would be in there now decorating our son's bedroom.'

'That's enough, Lucy. Will you stop going on? You act as though you hate the woman. You don't even know her. In fact, let's be brutally honest here, she should be the one hating you, but she hasn't even said a word, not a phone call, a letter, nothing.'

Jumping from her kitchen chair, Lucy flew into a rage. 'How dare you! That fucking bitch burned the house down, to spite you. She never loved you, but she couldn't bear to see you with me. Strutting around like she owned the pla—' She stopped dead, her eyes wide as saucers. 'Well, that's what I imagine, anyway ...' Her voice trailed off into a pathetic whisper.

Smashing the coffee cup into the sink, Justin stormed past Lucy and headed for the door. 'I'm off to see my lawyer. I'll be back after work, when, hopefully, you have calmed down.'

When Justin used his reasonable voice it made Lucy want to punch him in the mouth. The door slammed shut, and she waited until she heard his car pull away before she searched at the back of the cereal cupboard for her bottle of brandy. Pouring a large measure into her coffee, she sat back and allowed her daily fix to soothe her mind. Unexpectedly, her secret phone rang. Normally, she would have it turned off, if Justin was around. The number was withheld. She knew exactly who it was and sadistically grinned.

* * *

Justin had calmed down by the time he reached Lucas Lane's law firm. Taking a deep breath, he opened the car door and took long strides towards the offices. Lucas had been a long-term friend of Justin's; they had been to school together and stayed in contact over the years.

Sitting on a high-backed executive chair behind a long mahogany desk, Lucas grinned. He still had a round baby face with smooth shiny skin and waves of fair hair, but married life coupled with good food had piled the pounds on him. 'Come in, come in, Justin, good to see you, buddy. How are things?'

'Well, I would love to say things are grand, but I think I'm living with one hormonal pain in the arse.'

Leaning back in his chair and clasping his hands together,

111

Lucas protruded his lower lip. 'Justin, you don't have to be with her. Look, I get that you want to be a good father and not let your baby down, but you can still be that. My dad, as you know, left when I was young, but I saw him every other weekend, and he is still in my life. We go deep-sea fishing every month. You should come along, on one of our trips.'

With a full smile, Justin chuckled. 'I get seasick. Now, if you said a footy match, then I'm there, but fishing, nah, it's not my cup of tea.' He stared up at the pictures adorning the wall, all of which were family photos enlarged and put on canvas, many with Lucas and his father.

'Justin, I have to tell you something as a friend. I had a call from Alan Cumberbatch.' Justin tilted his head. The name meant nothing to him.

'He's a solicitor … on Kara's case.' He waited for Justin to absorb the information and gauge whether or not he was interested.

'What did he say? Will she get released or will she have to serve a sentence? Christ, I feel so sorry for her.' He ran his hands through his hair that was now in need of a trim. Justin had let himself go recently.

'He wants a copy of the letter I was supposed to have sent her.'

'What letter?' asked Justin, now bemused.

'Apparently, Kara claimed that when she received a letter from me stating that she had to get out of the house by the end of the week, she lost her mind. The news tipped her over the edge, and so that was the reason she burned the house down.'

Shaking his head, as if he'd just woken from a nightmare, Justin said, 'But I never said she had to get out.'

'No, exactly, and I never wrote that either. I sent you a copy of the letter, and I have one here.' He leaned forward and picked up the letter that lay on the desk in front of him. 'It clearly says that all you would like for now is a valuation done for future reference.'

Justin took the letter and read it. 'Yes, it says nothing about her having to leave. I guess she misread it or something, I don't know. Besides that, I had already changed my mind. I thought after you sent me that copy, it would be a bit too soon, and so I was going to tell her to leave it for a few months, and then, well, there was no house to value.'

'Yes, exactly, Justin, and by the way, I never sent the letter.' Lucas huffed and rolled his eyes. 'I'm sorry, but I have to say this. Why? I mean, Kara is such a lovely woman, a stunner, sweet, a girl-next-door type, if you know what I mean.'

Justin clenched his fists and gritted his teeth. 'I hate myself, I really do. I don't condone what Kara did, obviously; but I wish I could turn the clock back.' He breathed out through his nose, annoyed with himself.

Lucas knew Justin was being honest, and he felt for the man. Kara had certainly been a catch, and for years, they were like two newlyweds. He'd envied Justin because although he loved his own wife, she did nag and moan and had let herself go. In comparison to Kara, who was the same age, his wife looked ten years older. But it was a joke among the lads, the friends who had shared a regular drink or a round of golf, that Justin and Kara were like Posh and Becks.

'Are you going to court, because you may be subpoenaed? Cumberbatch gave me the court date.' He scribbled it down on a piece of notepaper, turned it to face Justin, and then neatly rearranged his pens. 'Here, take it. I think you may be wise to go, or you may never forgive yourself.' He looked down at the desk and sighed heavily. 'She doesn't belong in there, Justin. I know you are with this Lucy bird now, but Kara has no one. Her mum is in Australia, so who does she have?' He paused and looked at the despair on Justin's face and quickly said, 'Sorry. Really, it's none of my business.'

'No, no, Lucas, you're right. I've been a first-class shit. I feel so bad. I haven't even sent her a letter. I just can't imagine what she's going through. She wouldn't even raise her voice. They'll eat her alive ...' His voice cracked, and he coughed, but Lucas saw his eyes fill up and his face redden.

'There's no time like the present. Write to her, go to court, let her know you still care, and this Lucy, what does she think about it all? I mean, she must feel terrible, mustn't she?'

Justin rubbed the palms of his hands over his eyes and gave a sarcastic laugh. 'No, she doesn't, and for some reason, hormones or pregnancy, she's hateful towards Kara. She doesn't even know her. I stormed out this morning, after listening to her moaning.'

He got up to leave, folding the note in his jacket pocket. 'It's good to see you, Lucas. I'll be in touch.'

With a generous smile, which turned his eyes down at the corners, Lucas stood up. 'Call in, any time. We'll go for a drink, and remember, you don't have to stay with Lucy, unless of course you've fallen for her.'

With a screwed-up face, Justin replied, 'No! Er ... I mean, not like, well ... like I loved Kara.'

Lucas corrected him. 'You mean "love". I know you still love Kara.'

The drive back was filled with mixed emotions. Of course, he still loved Kara, but in constantly pushing her to the back of his mind, it was eating away at him. At the same time, he also felt sorry for Lucy because he was well aware that he was comparing both of them on a daily basis; not that he would ever admit it, but that was the case, even down to the way Lucy walked, talked, and ate her food. She was not serene and sweet like Kara; she was harder and cold at times. The main thing that bothered him was she was reluctant to talk about her past. He had to accept her reason for not doing this was because she'd had such a hard time.

* * *

Looking at the clock with less than clear eyes, Lucy wondered if Justin would be home soon or had gone off to work straight from the lawyer's office. She knew she would have to be in bed before he smelled the drink on her breath. It was a regular thing; if he was at home and she was in the main bedroom sleeping, then he would leave her there and sleep in the spare room.

A sudden rapping at the door shook her out of her contemplation. She guessed it wasn't Justin because he had a key. She pulled her dressing gown tighter around her waist, ensuring her burgeoning breasts were covered, before she swung open the door. To her horror, it wasn't the postman or any delivery driver but Carl, standing cocksure and leaning against the doorframe. He gave her his trademark smirk and casually walked past her into the living room.

'What the fuck are you doing 'ere? Justin will be back any minute. You need to leave.'

He was silent, looking her up and down, but still wearing that confident grin. 'Nice, Lou Lou.' He moved towards her, and in a flash, he pulled her dressing gown open. 'Well, well, look at you, all fat and pregnant.' With a quick squeeze of her breast, he laughed. 'I think I like a bit of baby bump.' He slid the dressing gown off her shoulders, leaving her shocked and naked and wondering why she hadn't fought him off.

'You owe me,' he said, as he grabbed the back of her neck, pulling her close. He slid his other hand between her legs.

She tried to push him away. 'Fuck off, Carl. This body ain't yours to cop a feel whenever you please, so get out!' She bent down to pick up her dressing gown but was beaten to it.

With one swift move, he retrieved it and held it up for her to slide her arms into. 'I said, Lou Lou, you fucking owe me, and until your debt is paid, I think I'll take whatever I want.'

She relaxed her shoulders and looked up at the ceiling. 'Hurry up, then, and then do one.'

With that, he looked down at her body. 'Nah, you know how I like it clean, fresh, and smelling of fucking roses.'

Lucy laughed. 'Well, in case you haven't noticed, I have a dirty great bump in front and Justin likes my fanny just the way it is, thank you, so, fuck off, Carl.'

She watched as he paced the floor, scratching his head. He was still bloody handsome, but everything was different now. The days of turning tricks and giving out freebies were long gone.

'You know what I do to people when they mug me off, don't ya, Lou Lou?' His voice became cold and hostile.

'Listen, Carl, that money, yeah, I took it, and I didn't mug you off because if I'd wanted to really take the piss, I would have taken every fucking last fifty-pound note from your safe. But I never did. I only took twenty grand, as payment.'

'Ha, payment, you say? Well, as I see it, I didn't owe you fuck-all, and you, Lou Lou, went snooping around, helping yaself. The funny thing is, I would have given you money had you done the right and proper thing and actually asked!'

She slumped down on the sofa. 'Yeah, 'course ya would, Carl. Don't give me that. I worked hard for you. You made a bleedin' mint, and what did I get, eh? A poxy flat and a fucking dose of clap.'

In a fit of rage, he snatched her arm, dragging her off the sofa. 'You, my little Lou Lou, left me in the fucking lurch. You were supposed to be sucking off a cunting toff in Farnborough Park by the name of Judge Herman, a real shyster, while me men were doing over his mansion, but not you. No, you packed ya bags, stole me money, and fucked off to Australia.'

Lucy's eyes widened.

'Didn't think I knew that bit, did ya? I know a lot more than you think, including what poxy lies you feed people.' He narrowed his eyes and nodded his head. 'But here's the thing, see. I have enough on you to have you put away for a very long time, so I think you need to listen, my little sugar plum.' With a sarcastic grin and a quick jerk of his head, he let her go.

Her heart was pounding, and her mouth felt like she was sucking on talcum powder. But she liked to think she was a good bullshitter. 'You know fuck-all, Carl.'

'Try me, darlin'. So, unless you want to see the inside of a prison or my fucking basement, you will do as I say.'

She swallowed hard. 'Like what?' Her confidence was gone, and she was now shitting hot bricks.

'For starters, let me remind you, I know everything you do. The scam with the lawyer. Yeah, I taught you well, but you, in your stubborn and know-it-all way, went behind my back. You played the mistress, which, we both know, you do very well. While the stupid fucker was tied up and blindfolded, you went and helped yaself to his wife's jewellery. What a complete idiot! That man was my next customer, and you may think you were clever in grabbing a few pieces of tomfoolery, but he had half a fucking million pounds in that house. Between me and you, we could have had it right off, but we didn't, did we? You made a huge mistake and his wife went to the Ol' Bill. I have photos of you leaving that house. That lawyer's wife is the daughter of the local MP, so you could easily have found yourself in very hot water. That, my little toffee-apple, is just one example. And the list goes on.'

She stared with her mouth open. Once again, she had under-estimated Carl.

'Well, now I have your attention, I'll go and leave you to think about things, but I'll be in touch, so be a good girl. Your little college boy is probably very green behind the ears, and my guess is, he has no idea who you really are, does he?'

'In case you haven't noticed, I'm not that person anymore.'

With a look that said 'dream on', he replied, 'Lucy Lou Lou, you, my darling, are delusional, but I have to give it to ya, you really are a good act, and I've never met a woman that can change her colours like a chameleon better than you. I bet you could even pass a lie detector test because you obviously believe the shit that spews from your gob. You, my sweetness, are the best pathological liar this side of the fucking Thames!'

With her body now trembling, Lucy bit her tongue, to stop the hurl of abuse that was itching to escape from her mouth. However, she had to be calm and play it cool. Carl could be so reckless and unpredictable that she really didn't want to wind him up now. As the door slammed shut, she took a deep breath, relaxed her shoulders, and bowed her head. What did he want from her? Surely not just the money she owed? Whatever it was, it wouldn't be above board or simple.

She shuddered and thought back to her old way of life, the life she wanted to escape from. Carl, her father, the firm – they were all out for what they could get. But, to be fair, she had been too: she'd been a very successful money-maker.

* * *

It began not long after Carl had dropped her like a hot brick, well, so she'd believed at the time. Really, he'd left her wanting more, after pushing her as far as he could. She went back to finding fun in her own way, enjoying a good drink, the odd drug she could get her hands on, and comfort in the arms of anyone who wanted her.

She'd just turned seventeen when the first package arrived; it was a small parcel with her name on it. She hadn't expected anything for her birthday because all she ever got from her father was a pat on the back and a grubby card. The last one had even had "congratulations on passing your test" instead of "happy birthday"; that showed her how little interest he had in his only daughter. The parcel though was exciting; it was wrapped in pink foiled paper with a fluffy shiny oversized bow as big as the box itself. It was there on the dining-room table. 'Is that for me?' she'd asked her father.

Standing in his black trousers and white shirt, undone at the waist, her father, nodded. 'Yep.'

'Oh, wow, thanks, Dad,' she said, excitedly.

He undid the cufflinks and turned to face her. 'It ain't from me.' His face was sallow, tired from being on the door all night at the club owned by Carl. 'It's from the club.'

He pulled his shirt off and headed up the stairs to bed. The house was silent, cold, and far from the atmosphere she should have expected on her seventeenth birthday. She made herself a cup of tea while glancing over at the pink box. Slowly, to savour the moment, she sat down and fingered the parcel, looking at all the neat folds and how the foil changed colour in the morning light. After carefully removing the bow, she set it aside to keep it as a memento.

She gasped as she unwrapped the gift. Clearly labelled on the black leather box inside was the Rolex logo. Her heart skipped a beat, as she opened the lid, to find inside a beautiful ladies' watch with a diamond-edged front. She stared in disbelief at the alluring gift, and then she chuckled, thinking how it would look against her cheap off-the-peg clothes, which were faded from the wash. On second thoughts, with that on her wrist, she could wear anything and look dead classy. Quickly, she fastened it and paraded up and down, admiring in the mirror how exquisite it looked.

The second present came the next day. She'd been given gift vouchers to use at a high-end fashion store in Knightsbridge. She wasted no time in hurrying off to scan the racks of clothes. Never before had she tortured herself by going in and wandering around. That day, however, she spent three hours trying everything on and struggled to carry the bags home. She really didn't give much thought to the gift giver; her father had thrown the envelope enclosing the vouchers at her, and with a miserable face, he'd said that the present was from the club. She didn't question it, in case he snatched it back.

The third gift arrived, but this time by delivery; it was a black full-length leather coat and it fitted like a glove. But that was not all. She also received a large bottle of very expensive perfume, and once again, there were vouchers, but this time, they were redeemable at a luxury beautician store.

She remembered looking in the mirror at herself – the new woman – dressed in a fitted woollen dress, black high-heeled shoes, and her face made up to look like a celebrity. Up to that point, she'd never really known how attractive she was. Now, she knew: there stood a stunning beauty, a young lady of class and sexy as hell.

Yet at seventeen, how could she have guessed it was a ploy? It was a masterstroke by Carl, the deceitful bastard. That evening, her father didn't go to work. She had cooked his dinner, as she normally did, and once they'd finished, he wiped his mouth, leaned back on the chair, and said, 'You'd better get yourself dolled up, girl. Carl's on his way. He wants to take you out.' Then, he sighed, shook his head, and walked away.

'But, Dad,' she called after him, 'what if I don't want to go?'

He stopped in his tracks and she could see his head bow. 'Lucy, what other choices in life do you have, eh? He wants to take you out. If ya don't go, then God knows where you'll end up!'

Well, at least that's what she thought she heard.

She watched him walk away, not even turning to face her. At that moment, she despised him. Why couldn't he have been like other fathers, fighting off any potential suitors, instead of making her sell her body and soul to the highest bidder? The truth of it was, she didn't really mind going out with Carl; it was just the fact she didn't have a choice that hurt her the most.

She did as she was told and got herself ready. Little did she know that this was no ordinary date, a nice drink or two in a wine bar or a nightclub perhaps. This ended up being one crazy affair. But, looking back, it had been an incredible evening all the same – a steep learning curve, definitely, which showed beyond any doubt that she possessed skills in the art of sex that very few women could emulate.

In her expensive clothes and shoes too high to walk properly in, Lucy was waiting nervously in the living room when Carl arrived. She followed him outside and he held the door open to his top-of-the-range Mercedes, allowing her to awkwardly clamber inside and make herself comfortable in the front seat. Excited to the point she could hardly breathe, goose bumps covered her skin. *Is this what it's like to be a grown-up?* she thought.

Carl was, as ever, smartly dressed and the sweet-and-sour aroma of his aftershave filled the car's interior. She remembered the evening air being warm for October and felt slightly sticky in her woollen dress and long black leather coat; but still, she didn't mind because she knew she looked damned good. The initial part of the drive was spent in silence, Lucy being too afraid to say the wrong thing and put him off taking her out to this special place that she assumed he'd planned. However, when they parked in a lay-by, in a leafy road outside of town, opposite the entrance to a park, she looked at him, her eyes filled with disappointment. Was he just like the teenagers, wanting a quick grope or shag in the bushes? 'Where are we? I thought you were taking me out?'

He chuckled like a kid, wiping the stern expression away. 'Right, my little sugarplum, how do you like your new rig-outs and watch? Makes ya feel classy, eh?' He raised his eyebrow. 'And it's my guess, you would love to live your life enjoying the finer things, not running around getting into pointless trouble, with fuck-all money and being pecked at by kids with acne, right?'

Lucy nervously nodded, fearing what he had in mind and thinking: *What the hell have I let myself in for?*

'This is what's gonna happen.' He pointed to a private drive. 'That, there, is the home of a very well-respected banker, and you, my girl, are going to knock at the door, where he will be expecting you.'

'What! No way! I know what you want me to do, but I'm not

a prostitute.' She tried to get out, but the car's child safety locks were on.

Shaking his head, he chuckled again. 'No, of course not. You, my gal, are gonna make a shedload of money without even sucking his dick. How about that?'

Lucy chewed over the idea. There had to be a catch somewhere, but the excitement on his face was infectious, and so her initial fear receded. Money talked, in her world.

Slowly, she nodded. 'How much, then?'

Carl had her eating out of the palm of his hand. 'Two hundred smackeroonies.'

The excitement level shot up, but as calmly as she could muster, she held it in. 'Two fifty and you have a deal.' She was pushing her luck, but so what. Unbeknown to her, though, Carl would easily have gone to five hundred, if she'd played hardball.

After gently planting his lips on hers, he pulled away. 'You are my best girl, you know that? Me and you will go a long way. I like you, Lucy. You are more like me than you could possibly imagine, so here's what you have to do.'

She nodded, listening carefully.

'You knock at the door. A banker, Frederick Palmer, will answer. I want you to go in. You'll tell him your name is Sapphire and he will offer you a drink. Take it.' He watched her eyes, ensuring she was taking in every last detail. 'Now, he thinks you are a prostitute, right, but here's the important bit. He likes bondage. His speciality is to be tied up and gently whipped. You must flirt until the man is gagging for it. You have to take control because that's what he wants, so make him sit on a chair naked, parade up and down in front of him, and then tell him he's been a bad, bad boy. Got it?'

Lucy gasped and frowned. *This couldn't be happening, surely?* Paradoxically, she felt her face flush despite a chill down her spine, as she tried to assimilate the implications of what Carl was telling her. 'You what!' She screamed at him so loudly that an old geezer, walking past with his dog, turned back to the Mercedes in surprise. 'This is bleedin' mental, Carl.'

Carl laughed. 'Keep your voice down. Now, listen, darling, there are many men, of all shapes and sizes, who take great pleasure from being treated like a slave. It's the world of the dominatrix.' He dangled a pair of handcuffs in front of her face. 'Put these in your pocket.' Then, he pulled a short horsewhip from the side of his seat. 'This is what he loves, but don't beat the shit out of him. Make him take his clothes off, tell him not to move whilst he does so, then handcuff him. You blindfold him, 'cos he likes that too, and then you open the front door.'

'What if he doesn't like me?'

Carl rolled his eyes. 'Firstly, darlin', this ain't no first date with a man you met on eHarmony, and secondly, when he sees you, babe, he's goin' to have an erection of a lifetime, trust me on that. He just wants to be treated like a slave. Anyway, don't worry about that – you just make sure the cuffs are on and the doors are open. I'll sort out the rest.' He looked at her black dress. 'Have you got decent underwear on?'

She bit her lip and nodded. This evening was turning out to be a right scary affair, and she hadn't even got to the perv's front door yet. 'Yeah, but you said—'

'Lucy, you don't have to even let him touch you, but he will be more comfortable, if he sees you strutting about in ya sexy briefs before you put the blindfold on, yeah? Stands to reason. Who wouldn't be totally besotted with a beautiful body like yours. The man will be so turned on, he will do anything you say.' Her confidence went up a notch and continued to climb when he said, 'I wouldn't let a man touch you, my darling. You're my bit of gold dust, and I will look after you.'

She nodded, feeling a little uneasy, but she was up for it, and besides two hundred and fifty pounds was a fortune to her at seventeen. Along with the promise that she was his, and he would protect her, she was on cloud nine.

Frederick and Genevieve Palmer lived in a relatively secluded house on the outskirts of Brockwell Park. Married at forty, with no children, it had been a marriage of convenience, if the truth be known, at least as far as Frederick was concerned. Genevieve held all the cards in this relationship. It was she who had massaged her daddy's ego as chairman of a merchant bank in the city, enabling her husband to take up a senior role there. Her ambitions steered more towards ensuring that the scallywags in society were given short shrift when it came to sentencing. As a justice of the peace, she had carte blanche, and she wasn't afraid to wield the big stick, which she did – mercilessly.

Whilst she might see herself as an extraordinary woman, she was boring, loud, and manly – in looks that is. Even her closest bridge-playing acquaintances would struggle to come up with anything nice to say about her, although to her face they pretended to like her because she had connections that were useful to their husbands.

Poor Frederick. He had married into money, but his pecker – of which he was justly proud because he was well hung – received very little attention from his wife. Sex to Genevieve was a dirty word. She couldn't fathom why couples needed children at all, never mind the scum who chose to have lots of them because in her eyes they were simply breeding to steal money from the state in benefits.

It was, therefore, little wonder that her bedroom door was locked at night to her long-suffering husband. It had been that way almost from the get-go. But she could be flexible. Frederick was allowed into her bedroom, and ergo her bed, on just one day in the year: on his birthday.

So, in Frederick's eyes it was entirely understandable why he had his sexual foibles. Not only was he starved of sex generally in his home life, but he craved sexual adventure, and in his opinion, nothing could be more exciting than being the object of domination from the opposite sex.

Cautiously and somewhat curiously, Lucy wandered up the long drive to the large detached house, her high heels killing her. Bushes and trees lined the perimeter and then the sensor lights came on, making her jump. She stopped for a second, and in her peripheral vision, she saw a man. Her eyes tried to focus, and she was at the point of turning around to beat it back to the Mercedes, when the man, hidden in the bushes, whispered harshly, 'Lucy, it's me. Go on, girl, go and knock at the door.'

She squinted, trying to get a clearer view of the man, and then she recognised him as Paul Shelter, one of Carl's men. She wondered what they were up to, but her mind was on this crazy job she'd been told to do and the money deal; the sooner she got this over with, the quicker her pockets would be lined. She lifted the heavy brass knocker and stood back, waiting. Her heart was thumping and yet she felt confident she could pull this off.

The door swung open, and there, wearing casual black trousers and an immaculate white shirt, stood a middle-aged man. He was roughly five feet eight and well toned. However, his eyes looked tired against his smooth, clean-shaven skin. She raised her eyebrow and curled her lip.

With her shoulders set back, she gave him a confident smile. 'Well, are you going to ask me in?' she said, in her most sophisticated voice.

Frederick looked her up and down and responded with a huge beaming smile of his own. He hesitantly stepped back, allowing her to enter, and took her into the drawing room, still eyeing her over. Lucy knew she had him in the palm of her hand: firstly, he was nervously licking his lips; secondly, he was ogling her from the top down; and finally, Carl was spot-on, the front of the guy's trousers was positively bulging. He didn't have a confident stride and she noticed the traces of a shuffle. He poured a drink. 'Would you like one?'

'Of course!' She had to get into the role of being the boss. As he turned his back to pour her drink, Lucy marvelled at the room, with all its expensive furniture, grand gilt-edged paintings, and hi-tech entertainment equipment. The fireplace was enormous, and the Persian rugs were far larger than the entire ground floor of her dad's house.

With her heart beating wildly, she kept her eyes on him, and a slow smile formed as she began unbuttoning her long leather coat and placing the whip slowly and provocatively on the grand settee. That's when he approached her.

'Here you are, madam,' he said, as he nervously handed her a glass of Chardonnay.

She had to get into this new character. *To hell with it*, she thought. *It's now or never. Let's give this creep something to jerk off on until the next time.* She was going for an Oscar-winning performance. She snatched the whip and tapped the glass that he held in his hand. 'Put it on the table,' she ordered, loudly.

Frederick's eyes were alive with excitement at the young woman's body language. He couldn't wait to get the proceedings started. His wife was out for at least a couple of hours at the local bridge club, so the evening was his, and he was going to make the most of it.

'Don't look at me until I tell you to!' The words were spat out like an AK-47 on automatic fire.

Instantly, Frederick looked away.

Lucy couldn't believe it. Here she was, a seventeen-year-old girl, controlling a grown man. With all his wealth and obvious standing, he was eagerly doing everything she said. It beggared belief. But, she was well up for this. She hurriedly stripped down to her black bra and knickers, leaving only her stilettos on. 'Now, Frederick, look at me!' she demanded.

When he looked up, she could see his nostrils flare, as he tried to control his excitable breathing. 'I like my men naked, and I think you've been a *very* bad boy. You have, haven't you?' she said, with the trace of a mocking smile.

Again, Frederick licked his lips nervously, but there was a schoolboy eagerness to please her.

'Take off your clothes this instant!' she commanded, in a dry voice. She realised that she sounded a bit silly, and even wondered if he would do as she told him. He was a grown man, for fuck's sake, and she was barely out of nappies, relatively speaking, of course. It was crunch time.

The banker appraised her, and he did as she ordered. As he turned away from her briefly to remove his socks, Lucy eyed the high-backed wooden chair and mentally worked out whether she could handcuff him with his arms behind his back. She needed to ensure he would still be able to release himself once the fun had finished. Slowly, she stepped back and snatched the chair, dragging it to the centre of the room. Then, holding the whip in her right hand, she cracked it twice in his direction, thinking, *Let's get this show on the road.*

Lucy pointed with the whip at the chair. 'Sit. I think you need to be taught a lesson, don't you, Frederick?'

Frederick gave her a nervous glance and held his breath, as if anxiously wondering how far she would go with him. His cock was straining at the leash.

Lucy noticed a slight grin forming on his face, as he fought back the urge to smile. He did as she instructed, and then she pulled the blindfold from the pocket of her coat. But to maintain his interest, she straddled him, as she tied the black material over his eyes and round the back of his head. She thought he might come, there and then.

She stepped back and lightly whipped his leg. 'You naughty boy! You moved. Now, I will have to restrain you!'

Gently, she pulled his hands behind his back and clicked on the handcuffs. She considered whether he might panic because he was totally helpless, sitting naked on a chair and so vulnerable. She was shocked, and then, for a split second, she felt a pang of guilt. The banker had never done her any harm and he completely trusted her. Her job was done, so she thought; all she had to do, once she'd got dressed, was to open the front door and scarper. *How bloody simple was that?*

'Now for the entrée,' she said, silently. Remembering Carl's instructions, she opened the front door. She was on her way back into the drawing room when Paul appeared behind her, putting his finger to his lips. He then pulled a balaclava over his head. Behind him was another man she didn't recognise; he looked really menacing with wide pupils and a demeanour like a coiled spring.

'Sit on his lap and look fucking sexy,' Paul whispered, holding a camera. Lucy bit her lip. Carl had never said anything about this, but she couldn't run outside partially clothed. Paul nodded and winked. Frederick was still in the same position as Lucy straddled him again. She looked at Paul who was nodding with encouragement. Running her hands down the banker's neck, she began moving up and down provocatively, as the other menacing man began to take pictures. Without the flash on, the camera made no noise.

Once again, Frederick's penis began to come alive and he was groaning with pleasure. Out of the corner of her eye, she saw Carl with a pair of black gloves on; he put his thumb up and disappeared into what she assumed was another room. On she continued, rubbing herself up against the man's appendage. When, finally, Carl appeared with a bag and he held it up and nodded, she knew that her work for the evening was reaching a conclusion. She was almost in the process of climbing off her client, when Paul wagged his finger for her to continue.

The other man moved to within two feet of the banker and took a close-up of Frederick's ten-dollar-bill tattoo, which was etched along his rib, and he couldn't resist getting another shot of Frederick's prize possession. Then, in a flash, the men left. Lucy climbed off the banker leaving him to finish himself off, assuming that's what would happen in mistress and slave scenario.

She got herself dressed, unlocked the handcuffs, pulled the blindfold off, and said, 'Right, now you be a good boy, or next time, I will leave you tied up for longer.' She felt awkward because, really, she had no idea what she was supposed to do. Surprisingly, he smiled and nodded. 'Yes, mistress,' he replied demurely.

As Lucy left the house, ideas were almost popping out of her head with excitement. This little caper could easily turn her into an overnight sensation. The rewards were there, and she'd not even needed to engage in sex. Carl had shown her a whole new world, and she guessed he was going to try to be her puppetmaster. But as young as she was, she now had ideas of her own.

What a life she could have. She couldn't wait.

Chapter 9

Eventually, Kara made her way to the front of the phone queue, hoping for answers to troubled thoughts in her head. Constantly idling in the back of her mind was that eerie phone call from the almost demonic voice she'd received that day back in the tearoom. She wondered if she'd imagined it, due to the sickness and the stress at the time. Had that phone call actually been a dream?

Unfortunately for her, it seemed that it hadn't. The same voice asked, 'How's prison, dearest Kara? The green sweats fit you okay, do they?'

For a second, Kara was stunned. Her brain was in overload mode, such were the thoughts that were ripping through it like a force twelve hurricane. Her mother's carer sounded almost deranged. She had a flashback to watching Chucky the doll in the movie *Child's Play*. 'How do you know I'm in prison? What's going on?' She tried to sound firm, but her nerves made her voice falter.

'Oh, dearest, sweet Kara, I know everything about you, absolutely everything, even what you have for breakfast. How fucking perfect your life was …' There was a cackle that made Kara grip the phone tightly and hold her breath for so long, that she thought she was about to faint. An unearthly feeling, a cold shiver, swept up her spine and sent a tingling feeling from her neck to her head.

'But it's not so perfect now, dearest Kara, is it? And what about Justin? Where's he, when you need him? ... Oh, yes' – she sniggered hideously – 'in my bed, waiting for me to join him. You see, Kara, I can satisfy that man in more ways than one, but you, sweet Kara, couldn't, could you, or he wouldn't be fathering my baby.'

Like a thunderbolt, Kara's whole body jolted. 'What? Who is this? What do you want? Why do you have my mother's phone?'

There was silence on the other end of the phone, with just heavy breathing. Then she heard a faint chuckle before the phone went dead.

Lucky for Kara, Deni was in the queue for the phone when she saw Kara slump to the floor in a pitiful pool of sobs. Pushing the others out of the way, she helped Kara to her feet. 'There, there, my babe, what's happened?'

Kara couldn't speak, the sobs taking her breath away. Her world had just crashed down around her, and for the first time in her life, she wanted to die, to get out of her miserable existence. Keeping up the pretence that she could cope after being dumped by Justin, incarcerated for arson, and then, nearly losing her baby, had all taken its toll. Now the call as well, it was too much to handle.

Holding the trembling body, Deni tried to calm the poor, wretched woman. 'Let's get you back to your cell and make you a nice cup of sweet tea and you can tell me all about it.' Looking back at the queue of women eager to get to the phone, she smarted. They were all ignorant of the fact that Kara was on her knees. It meant nothing to them; all they wanted was to make their calls. Kara had no one, except, as she saw it, herself, Vic, and Julie.

All the way back to the cell, Kara was inconsolable and unable even to string a sentence together.

131

Holding her up under her arm, Deni could feel just how slight Kara's body was. Her own daughter, should she have lived, would have been the same age as Kara; she had been a petite girl and weighed next to nothing the day she died. Deni remembered holding her limp body and feeling so helpless.

'Aunty Deni will look after ya. Nothing will ever be that bad. God only gives us shit we can handle.'

She helped Kara into her own cell, pulled off the blanket that was neatly folded at the end of the bed, and wrapped it around Kara's shoulders. 'Now, my babe, you've been through a hell of an ordeal, nearly losing the baby. Thank Gawd, she's all right, so, what's upset you so much? Who was on the phone?' asked Deni, with her back to Kara, making a cup of tea.

Sniffing back the sob, she replied, 'I tried to call my mum. She's sick, you see, but this strange woman, I think she's my mother's carer, answered and said she knew I was in prison. Oh my God, she was cruel and wicked … It was like … she was taunting me. I don't know, perhaps it's just the stress. Or, maybe, I'm hearing things.' How could she say that she may have just had a conversation with the person who had taken her Justin away? Deni would think she was going barmy. Nothing made sense; she needed to work it out, before opening her mouth and sounding ridiculous.

Deni felt a lump in her throat and wondered if the saying about God giving a person only what they could handle was true. She gritted her teeth; life was so hard sometimes. Possibly, the recent events were pushing Kara over the edge. Sadly, she knew full well, once Kara's mum departed this world, Kara would have no family left, and an unexpected tear trickled down her face. She quickly wiped it away and shuffled along the bed, handing Kara a mug with a slogan that said, "KEEP CALM, IT'S ONLY PRISON". Kara held it up for a second, and then she smiled.

Deni grimaced. 'Oops, sorry, I didn't read it. Well, it's either that one or mine.' She held it up and smiled. The logo on her mug said, "KEEP CALM, LOVE A CONVICT". She put her arm around Kara's shoulders and pulled her close. 'You let it all out, my babe, 'cos the truth is, there ain't nuffin I can say that will make ya feel any better, well, except, I'm 'ere for ya, me and Vic, if ya just wanna shoulder.' She could smell the clean scent of Kara's hair and felt the wet cheek on her neck, and for a moment, she was holding her own daughter. Kara was a sweet untainted child, an innocent kid with her whole life in front of her.

The one good thing she had done in her sordid existence was giving birth to her little Phoebe. At no time did it matter that she never knew the father, but it was a fact that her little girl was pure and not subjected to a life like her own. Deni had run the brothel from a big seven-bedroom house. The girls of all ages and types paid rent; it wasn't a fortune, but it was enough for her to keep the roof over their heads.

She had the two rooms at the back of the house for her and Phoebe. All the prostitutes knew the score, so there was no foul language or talk of punters to be had when the little girl was around. Lucky for them, they knew Deni's wrath and wouldn't dare go against her rules, not that there were many. No one had ever looked out for them as much as Deni, and so she was held in high esteem. She nursed their wounds, she lent them money, and she made sure they had food in their bellies.

Any punter who pushed their luck would be turfed out on their ear, with a swift kick and a severe word of warning. If Deni kicked off, the whole house would hear, and the girls would appear from their rooms like a pack of wolves; no cocky little piece of shit would dare take on a load of women wielding deadly hot curling tongs or pointed hairdressing scissors.

Yet little Phoebe was kept away in the back room, reading her library books. Deni loved the girls, but her Phoebe was the apple of her eye, and the reason she got up in the morning. She didn't care what the neighbours or the other mums at the school said behind her back; she held her head high and walked her daughter to school, dressed in the smartest uniform, with her polished black Clarks shoes and her long fair hair tied back in a big red ribbon to match her red coat.

As a child, she was a cute little thing, with her large brown eyes that would melt your heart. By the time Phoebe left school, she had grown into a beautiful teenager, polite and kind – looking just like Kelly Clarkson when she won *American Idol* – but all the niceness in the world couldn't save her from the drunk driver on his phone who was rowing with his girlfriend. He didn't see her, and as he went to throw his phone out of the window, he mounted the kerb and crushed Phoebe against a brick wall. She died instantly.

'Thank you, Deni, for being there for me. I feel a bit of a fool, really, on my knees, crying like a baby.'

Deni was still thinking about her own daughter; she wished she'd been there that day and taken the hit herself instead of her little Phoebe. 'You had a shock, is all, Kara, and you, lovey, have been through enough lately.' She looked at Kara's bruised face and felt a tightening in the pit of her stomach; life was so cruel at times, and this was one of those times.

'Why don't you write her a letter?'

'To whom?' questioned Kara, looking dazed.

Deni frowned. 'Your mother.'

'Oh yeah, of course, sorry, yes, maybe I should.' Kara chewed her fingernail. 'Let's hope she gets it before she hears about what happened.'

'Where's your mum?' asked Deni, thinking that Kara was being naive, as the arson attack was all over the papers. Surely her mother would have known?

'Australia. She went over a few years ago. She always wanted to live there, and when I moved in with Justin, she sold her house and moved shortly after. My mum suffers with arthritis, you see, and thought living in a warmer climate would help her. I guess, as she has a carer now, she must have got worse. She doesn't even answer the phone anymore. Christ, I had no idea when she said she was poorly that she was so sick, and with all that's been going on, I have been so wrapped up in my own problems. It hadn't crossed my mind that she was … well, maybe dying.'

She stared off into space. 'I should never have struck that match. I can't believe that was even me, back then. I've never even swatted a fly, and in that minute of madness, I burned down his house … and that poor neighbour … I just hope she doesn't suffer any long-term damage.'

'I have phonecards, babe. You take mine. There ain't anyone out there that I need to call regularly.'

Kara gave her a thankful smile. 'That's so kind, Deni. Thank you for everything. I mean it.'

Deni got up to make them both another cup of tea and hide her glossy eyes, when Barbara appeared in the doorway, looking stony-faced and spiteful. 'Get back to your own wing, Denton.' She looked at Kara's tear-stained, battered face and smirked. 'A Dear Jane letter, was it?'

'Go fuck yaself, Babs!' spat Deni.

'Carry on, Denton, and you will be on report or down the block.'

'What's up with you? Batteries run out on ya Rampant Rabbit, did they?'

'I'm warning you, Denton!' Barbara's face was screwed up like a dried-up prune.

'Yeah! And I'm warning you, ya fucking ugly bitch. You put me down the block, and you'll have another riot on ya hands … Remember the last time?'

Barbara did remember, only too well. Denton was marched down the block for mouthing off, and within five minutes, the women went nuts, pressing all the buzzers in their cells, screaming and shouting, causing the officers on duty that night no end of grief. They had to check every cell, in case they had any code blues. They couldn't afford to have any more suicides, and if they missed just one, then their necks would be on the line, so every call had to be addressed. The inmates all played merry hell, demanding to see the doctor, pretending they were sick. And all because she had locked their leader, the old tom, in solitary confinement.

'You didn't get permission to come over to this wing.'

'Shove your permission up ya jacksie and do one. Can't ya see the girl's been through enough, or do you get off on seeing young women on the fucking floor, eh? You know what, Barbara, I thought you would have softened in ya old age, but you just get worse … The poor girl's mum's sick. Have some bleedin' compassion, will ya!'

Barbara looked Kara up and down, huffed, and then stormed off.

'Sorry about that, Kara. I hate that woman with a passion. One day, she will have a knife in the ribs, because the trouble is, wearing that uniform, she thinks she's invincible, but it's only because she ain't been hurt yet. But, mark my words, someone will do it, if I don't do it first!'

'She's probably just doing her job. It must be miserable for her too, I guess.'

Deni shook her head and sighed. 'The thing about you, my babe, is you really don't see bad in anyone. I wish I was like you, but people are bad, especially her.'

Kara knew only too well that there was a bad side to people; her childhood wasn't exactly a Disney script. In fact, her housemistress had given her a useful maxim before she left to face the outside world. Kara could remember what she said as if it were yesterday. 'Kara, it's a wicked old world: if you expect the worst in people, you will never be disappointed.' The trouble was, she didn't believe those words at all. She only wanted to see the good in people.

Just as Deni was about to pour more boiling water into the cup, she heard a rumbling of voices downstairs in the recreation area. At first, she thought it was all the women coming back from their jobs, but then the noise was louder and in among the sound was a scream. Deni and Kara both hurried out of the cell and looked over the landing to the floor below.

Vic was lying there with four other women surrounding her. Kara could see she was laid out clutching the inside of her leg, and then she saw the blood. 'Oh my God, she's bleeding!' she yelled, as she rushed past Deni and jumped down the stairs three at a time.

The four bystanders were standing there looking helpless, as Vic rolled around trying to hold the top of her thigh. Kara pushed two of them aside and fell to her knees, to see what was going on. Vic's tracksuit bottoms had turned from olive green to almost black from the blood flow. Kara grabbed the waist of the trousers and pulled them down, as Vic tried to catch her breath. 'Fuck! Fuck! Posh, she's stabbed me!' Her face was white, and for the first time, Kara witnessed terror in Vic's eyes.

Kara looked down at the neat but very deep wound and the blood pumping out in spurts. The force at which the claret shot out told her that the femoral artery was sliced, and if they didn't stop the bleeding, she would be dead in minutes. She put her hands over the wound and pressed as hard as she could, screaming at everyone to get the screws. Deni had already pressed the emergency buzzer and was now on her knees supporting Vic's head.

'Kara's here, babe, you're gonna be all right. Will someone get the fucking screws!' she screeched at the four inmates who were standing there looking gormless.

Barbara heard the commotion and came tearing along the bottom landing, pushing the women aside. She then tried to push Kara. 'Move away, let me see!'

But Kara knew that if she took the pressure off the wound, she would reduce Vic's chances of surviving. 'No! Quick, give me your belt,' she yelled.

Once more, Barbara tried to shove Kara aside. 'Get away, Bannon!'

That was enough for Kara. She turned and glared with total venom in her eyes. 'Give me your fucking belt. I need to slow the bleeding or she will die. You need to call for help. Do you understand me?'

Barbara didn't even have a chance to answer back. Deni grabbed her around the waist and tried to unbuckle the belt herself.

'Get off me, I'll do it myself.' She looked at the surrounding crowd and knew she had no choice. She slid the leather belt from her waist and called on the radio for help. Kara snatched her makeshift tourniquet and handed it to Deni. 'Tie it around her leg just above the wound and tie it as tight as you can.'

Deni wasted no time, and with sweaty, shaking hands, she followed the order. Within two minutes, the medical team arrived and took over. Deni turned to Kara. 'Will she make it?'

White-faced and sickly, Kara slowly shrugged her shoulders. 'If she doesn't get to the hospital in time, then no, she could bleed out.'

Seconds later, Julie came hurtling along the corridor, having heard the news. 'Where's me sister?' she screamed.

Deni grabbed her arms. 'She's gone to the hospital.' Julie was looking past Deni, over her shoulder. 'Is she all right? What the fuck's happened?'

There was silence, as they waited for Julie to calm down. Deni stared into her eyes. 'Listen, Julie, Vic's gone to the hospital with a knife wound.' Julie pulled away and looked at the blood on the floor and on Kara's hands, her hair, and her face.

'Jesus fucking wept. Please, don't tell me that's her blood?'

Slowly, Kara nodded but jumped when the siren went off. It was lock-up, and the landing was now awash with officers, all escorting the prisoners back to their cells. Deni, Julie, and Kara headed upstairs, only to be stopped by Barbara, who had returned from the hospital wing. 'Oi, Denton, back to your cell!'

Kara was still angry with Barbara for not freely handing over her belt. She stopped dead on the stairs, covered in Vic's blood, and turned to face her. 'You have a nerve. I can't believe you are even here dishing out orders. You really don't have any regard for anyone's life, do you?' She took a step down, closer to the prison officer. 'I have a good mind to report you,' she said, poking a finger in Barbara's face, 'to the number one governor; so think very carefully about what you say in front of me, lady, because I'm far more intelligent than you, and I'll have every damn news-paper knowing the truth about you … yes, you, Barbara. I'll endeavour to ensure you never work in a prison again. You will be lucky if you're not scrubbing floors in Tesco, by the time I'm done with you!'

With eyes like saucers and breathing fast, Barbara retorted, 'Watch ya mouth, Bannon, or I'll have you down the block!'

Kara gave an almost hysterical laugh. 'Now, how good will that look? A young inmate attacked in the showers, face brutally smashed, nearly losing her baby, trying to save a woman's life, and then being marched down the block, all because some vindic-tive officer would rather see an inmate bleed to death than take her belt off to save her life!' Puffing her chest out and pushing her shoulders back, she stood defiantly.

Other inmates were now outside their cells, all glued to the confrontation between Kara and Barbara. Deni looked at Julie; both were thunderstruck. Then came the silence, as Kara stared, and Barbara, sizing up the situation, was clearly unsure what to do. But all eyes were on them: the big standoff.

Barbara looked at the sea of gaping eyes, all awaiting her next move. This was going to go one of two ways, and she had to think quickly. Dragging Bannon down the block would cause a riot, and she was well aware of Kara's following. She was under Deni's and Vic's protection and the women respected her for her medical knowledge.

What Barbara didn't know was that Kara had reached her

tipping point; with no one on the outside, and the pain of deep loss, Kara was ready to take on the world and stand up for what was right, even if it meant she would suffer in the long run. Vic could be dead, and Barbara was acting like a malevolent bitch.

'Go on, Barbara Pratt, take me down the fucking block. I would love you to because you will have to write a report as to why, and I'll have my say, and not just to the governor, but to every reporter who will listen! I'm not a convicted prisoner, remember. I'm on remand, and in a few weeks, I'm in court. I'll make sure my lawyer has the press there ready and waiting, and your name will be the first to roll off my fucking tongue!'

The blood began to rise, and Barbara's face was glowing red to match her hair. Humiliated and stupefied, Barbara funnelled herself away, ordering the other inmates to get back to their cells. A number of officers started rounding up the prisoners on the corridor above and below and hadn't witnessed the impasse.

Julie stared at Kara in disbelief, never imagining that the girl would even swear let alone be so brazen and hard-faced against the nastiest screw of all. They hurried inside their cell, and as soon as all three were in, they closed the door. Julie slumped on the bed with her hands over her face. 'Is Vic gonna die, Posh?'

Before Kara could answer, Deni piped up, 'Listen to me, Julie, your sister is one hard bitch. She will fight for her life. If anyone can, she can, and I'll tell ya this for nothing. If it weren't for Kara, she would never have stood a chance. I swear to God, the girl's an angel.'

Julie removed her hands from her tear-stained face and snivelled. 'Oh my God, if she dies ... well, I can't even imagine it. She's like a mum to us. Me own mum's a fucking waste of space. It was our Vic that brought us up. She can't die, it won't be fair.'

Kara noticed for the first time how Julie, who she thought was a really tough cookie, had become so vulnerable, hunched up with her lips drooping and her eyes full of sadness. 'She will be okay. The paramedics got here fast enough. She was still conscious. I think she'll be fine.'

That evening, the three women shared the cell. Deni lay on Julie's bed whilst Kara and Julie shared the other one. As Kara lay there with Julie's arm over her belly, she felt a comfort and warm feeling. And she also felt something else – being part of a family.

Chapter 10

The excitable noises, as the cells were unlocked, woke up the three inmates. Deni stretched, farted, and then giggled. 'Aw, excuse me.'

Julie yawned and cupped her hands over her mouth to smell her own foul breath. 'Jesus, I stink.'

Kara was now sitting at the end of the bed, trying to open her heavy eyelids, still tired from talking until three in the morning. When she did finally fall asleep, that creepy Chucky voice, taunting her about Justin, weaved its way into her dreams. She shook the aftermath of the nightmare away from her thoughts. 'I wonder if there's any news about Vic? Surely, one of the officers would let us know?'

'You'll be bleedin' lucky. We'll be the last to know, especially if it's left down to ol' ginger minge, Barbara, to inform us. Now, see, there's one sick, evil bitch, if ever there was one.'

Kara noticed the discriminating veil that cloaked Deni's face. 'You hate her, don't you, Deni?'

'Yeah, babe, I do, and talking of that streak of piss, you be careful, Kara, because she will be after you. Maybe not now, but she'll find a way of harming you. I don't mean physically, either.'

What could hurt her any more now? She had nothing, no one,

and her future was looking pretty bleak. So what else could Barbara take from her?

Just as they were about to get up and get showered, the door opened, and there in the doorway, almost touching the frame, stood George. Like three schoolgirls, they stood to attention. He very rarely came on to the wings, usually pen-pushing. He nodded at them to relax and entered, closing the door behind him.

'Are you ladies okay this morning?'

Julie burst into tears, fearing the worst. 'Oh my God, she's dead, ain't she?'

Quickly, he shook his head. 'No, no, Julie, she's fine. Well, she's not fine, but she had a blood transfusion, so they are keeping her in until tonight, but she's going to live.'

The relief was palpable. Her shoulders slumped, as if all the worry had been lifting her up, tightening her muscles. She let out a sigh, mixed with a giggle. 'Oh, thank God!'

George unexpectedly sat on a bed; it was unknown for an officer to do such a thing. 'No, not God, you need to thank Kara. Apparently, the doctor at the hospital said if she hadn't acted so quickly, then Victoria would most certainly have died.'

Kara bowed her head, not used to being praised or held on any pedestal.

'So, the reason I'm here is because Victoria's incident was attempted murder and I want the culprit named.' He held up his hands, before they said anything. 'And, Denise, if you are about to tell me you have no idea, then I'm assuming you will want to seek retribution in your own fashion. Let me tell you categorically, you will be arrested, any of you, if you do.'

Deni stood with her hands on her hips and a smirk on her face. 'Seriously, we don't know who did it. We just heard a commotion, and Kara, here, ran down the stairs and helped Vic, stopping all that blood. I followed her and pressed the alarm button, but we never saw who did it.'

George gave her a gentle smile. 'That, Denise, may well be

the case, but you will do by the end of the day. I will bet my last tenner on it.' He looked at Kara. 'And I will also bet it was the same person who did that to your face. So, just to warn you, we are keeping a close eye. If you want to talk, it will naturally be confidential, and action will be taken to arrest the inmate.'

They all looked at each other and then back at George, but he knew they wouldn't grass. They were after Esme's blood. He knew full well it was her, and yet without a witness, his hands were tied.

He closed the door behind him, and Deni checked to see he was out of earshot. 'That bitch Esme starts a war at every prison she ends up in. Still, when she met Big Vic a few years ago, she met her match.' She sniggered. 'I wouldn't want to have gone a few rounds with Vic when I was her age, I'll tell ya that for nuffin. Esme did, though. She wanted to run the nick. What a slag. She stabbed Vic on the sly, but she came a cropper. Vic don't go down too easily. I'm gonna kill that Esme, I am. She's a no-good wrong 'un. Besides, what have I got to lose?'

There was silence, as the three of them pondered over the idea. Kara then spoke up. 'You can kill her without stabbing her, or even getting caught, you know.'

With eyes round like saucers, Deni stared, trying to fathom what Kara was proposing. 'Tell us, Kara.'

'Well, it can't be done right away. I have to grow some bugs first.'

Julie laughed. 'In case you haven't noticed, Posh, this is a prison not a lab. How are ya gonna grow bugs?'

'I don't need a lab, I need a kitchen, and we have all the bugs we want right under our noses. Deni, you work in the prep area. Are the chickens frozen?'

With a huge grin, Deni replied, 'Yep, proper shit pieces too, with fucking feathers and claws still on 'em.'

'Have you got an area that's hidden but warm?'

Nodding, Deni laughed. 'Are you thinking of that Sam and ella bug?'

Kara laughed out loud. 'Salmonella, you mean. No, I'm not. I'm talking about another bug that can kill. Campylobacter found on chicken skin is deadlier.'

Both Julie and Deni stared in astonishment, but Deni assumed Kara was getting carried away with the idea of revenge. She flicked her eyes across at Kara's face, nibbling her bottom lip. 'Right, listen, let's not talk about this anymore, babe.'

With her nose screwed up, Kara asked, 'Why not?'

'Well, because, my darlin', you ain't like me. You're good, kinda wholesome, whereas me, well, I'm used to this. I have lived my life by the skin of me teeth, done many a thing I ain't proud of, and I do still 'ave nightmares. I still get this sickly feeling when I have flashbacks, and I will do 'til the day I'm pushing up daisies, but you won't, not if I can help it. So, let's leave this idea of poisoning alone. If the nasty bitch gets mullered, then it won't ever be on your conscience.'

''Ere, hold on a minute, Deni, Kara don't 'ave ta poison anyone. She can tell us how to do it. I might poison ol' Billy Big Bollocks when I get out.' Julie's eyes were alive and eager. Sitting on the edge of the bed, she urged Kara to go on, but Deni stood up. 'No!' She gave Julie a glare that said, 'Don't push it'.

Julie lowered her head. 'Sorry, yeah, you're right. If Esme died of poisoning, and you told us how to do it, I guess it's like giving us a loaded gun, eh?'

'I guess you're right. But she did try to kill my baby. It was her, you know ...' She paused, as she thought carefully what she wanted to say next. 'I appreciate what you are trying to do, Deni, but I have changed a lot. Trust me, when I say, life is not all it's cracked up to be. It's a bag of shit, really, and I only have this baby to look out for. Esme nearly killed her. She tried to murder her, so listen to me, and what you do after I give you the information is up to you.'

Deni was taken aback and sighed. 'Go on, then.'

'Right, campylobacter can be deadly. As I said, it grows on the skin of chickens. If you don't cook chicken properly, you suffer from the bacteria poisoning. It will initially cause gastroenteritis, and then, if it's not diagnosed properly, it will get into the bloodstream and can be fatal.'

'But all the chicken is cooked almost dry, so there's not much chance of poisoning.'

A crafty smirk crossed Kara's face. 'You're right, but who said it has to be undercooked chicken? No, it has to *come* from chicken, well, that's the easiest contaminant, but it doesn't have to be *served* as chicken. So, all you need is a piece of chicken with the skin on, frozen if possible. Keep it in a sealed bag, so the fluids don't leak out, and in a warm place for a couple of days, and then remove the liquid. As long as you don't heat the liquid, it should contain enough campylobacter and salmonella to kill her off. If she doesn't get to the quack in time, and if he is as useless as you all say, then he won't recognise the symptoms and will just assume it's a common bug. By the time it's in her system, she should be dead. There are a few ifs. I mean, if the bug has grown enough to contaminate and if it attacks her body. You see, some of us can naturally fight it off.'

She suddenly regretted what she'd said. Of course, she couldn't kill Esme; her baby was unharmed and she herself was only bruised.

'Yin and yang!' said Deni, to everyone's puzzlement. She smiled. 'Yeah, like good and bad. See, Dr Posh, here, can heal and can kill. If you can save someone, you can take them out. Power of knowledge, see. Our Kara is more dangerous than any of these silly tarts in 'ere.' She stood up, walked to the small cabinet, and held up her cup. 'Reminds me, I think I best make me own tea. Never know if I've upset ya. Don't wanna get poisoned.' She was joking, but now the thoughts of millions of tiny bugs eating away at her insides caused her to shiver. 'Let's not do anything until

Vic gets back. I know we are all assuming it's Esme, but what if it isn't?'

Deni looked at Kara surreptitiously and felt an odd sensation. It was all very well jesting but in that joke was the truth. It concerned her, though, how Kara had changed. A few months ago, the girl would never have talked about murder and certainly wouldn't have given them a hypothetical loaded gun.

Julie was still thinking about poisoning Billy, her sister Sharon, and anyone else who had pissed her off. 'It must have been Esme. What other retarded bitch would attempt a stunt like that?' spat Julie, still thinking about her Vic and how awful it would have been if she'd died.

Vic was the eldest sister and had been put in the care system for five years until their mother began breeding again. Then she was taken out and put back into the growing family. She was basically her mother's skivvy: fetching and carrying, babysitting, cooking, and cleaning. Marsha, their mother, was partial to a bottle of vodka and a man. It could be any man, as long as he could bung her a few quid, give her a quick shag, and hand her a litre of the hard stuff.

Vic learned from a young age to look after herself; she could fight because needs must. The school had said to her mother that she was particularly good at sports and could run faster than the school record held by a boy. Having won all the inter-school races locally and having competed at county level, Vic had been further encouraged by the school to take part in the English Schools' Athletics Championships, something that every young athlete aspired to.

But Marsha told the school to forget that idea. She wasn't having her girl taking two days off to travel up to Gateshead International Stadium to take part in some snobs' event, when she was needed at home. It was a travesty, but Vic was powerless where her mother was concerned. The reason for Vic being able to run so fast was because the security guard at Tesco was a sprinter himself, and she had no choice but to be able to have it on her toes in record time.

As young as thirteen, she'd learned to fight men to save herself, including the dirty perverted men her mother brought home. It wasn't surprising because Vic turned heads – tall, olive-skinned, and with long black hair, she was a looker, but her eyes were cold. It was through no fault of her own; it was just her lifestyle that made her appear so hard-faced. Julie, like the other sisters, looked up to Vic because she fought all their fights; she made sure they didn't go hungry and ensured they were warm in their beds at night.

Bringing up six children with not a pot to piss in should have run Marsha ragged, and if it was all down to her, it would have been like herding cats, but it wasn't. Vic took control because she had no choice: turning her back on her siblings wasn't an option. The younger ones, Sharon, Angie, Julie, and Teddy were all just a year apart. But Vic was seven years their senior, and Rocky, as they nicknamed him, because he looked like a very young Sylvester Stallone, was the eldest brother, a year younger than her. He was her sidekick, but he got off the estate as soon as he turned sixteen, with his own pad, a few quid in his back pocket, and a name for himself.

Vic and Rocky were close; they'd always had each other's backs. He respected her because she in effect became the *de facto* matriarch of the family and saw his kid brother and sisters were all right. Every Friday afternoon, he called in and handed her money, a new bit of clobber, or any other knock-offs. The freezer was always full of stolen Waitrose steaks, so although he left the nest, he still cared for them in his own way.

When the kids grew up and left home, Rocky was the man who looked out for them. Even Billy was shit-scared to look the wrong way, if he was around. Julie would use her brother's name to threaten him, if he got too handy; it was a sure move to make Billy reel his neck in.

'I think I'd better tell me brother Rocky what's been going on,' said Julie, out of the blue. She had been thinking about him for a while and was worried how he would take the fact that she'd stabbed Sharon. She never wanted to upset him, not because she was afraid of him, but because he'd earned her respect.

'Oh, don't do that, love. Wait until Vic gets back. He will want to know that she's all right,' replied Deni, shaking her head.

'No, I was thinking that ol' shit-legs Sharon will turn him against me, playing the fucking victim. 'Cos, I bet she ain't told him that I called her and said I was sorry. I mean, I was angry, but maybe I shouldn't have stabbed her in the leg. Christ, I could have killed her, like Vic could have been. I never knew it could be that dangerous.' She bit her nails, as if she were starving, but it was just the nerves.

The morning brought with it gossip, accusations, and a hive of excitable inmates acting like a brood of clucking chickens. All three women went about their daily business, with a lot on their minds. Kara mulled over everything. Her main focus was on leaving another message for her mother.

* * *

Gripping the toilet basin amid gasping mouthfuls of air, Lucy tried hard to stop the next wave of puke spewing through her nose and burning the back of her throat. She gasped again and cursed aloud. 'Fucking bollocks!' It was apparent that she'd gone too far with the whole pregnancy thing. She never wanted a screaming brat and certainly never remembered pregnancy being so bloody awful. The sickness, the tiredness, and the early signs of stretch marks that slithered across her hips didn't help either. She should have terminated this one too, along with the other five.

In fact, it should never have happened, according to her doctor. How she had ended up pregnant was a mystery; the doctor told her after her fifth abortion and the umpteenth morning-after pill that she wouldn't be able to have children. At the time, it was a relief because she really was sick of going through the motions of terminations. The last one made her ill and the pain was unbearable, but she assumed it was because she was so far gone. The contraceptive pill was not an option as it made her fat, condoms slipped off, and the coil gave her cramps.

She had Justin, her man now, and with the new home – once it was rebuilt – a baby, and a new, respectable, and clean life, where her husband brought home the bacon, she could live like any decent, upstanding member of society – like fucking Kara, in fact.

A smirk adorned her pale sickly face. Kara was no upstanding citizen; she was a jailbird, a homeless, loveless convict. Justin would never want Kara again, not after a few years in prison. Prison would rip the niceness right out of her; she knew that only too well herself. Not that she'd spent years inside, but a short three-month sentence gave her an inside seat as to what it would hold for someone like Kara.

Lucy could deal with prison; it was nothing to her. Carl sent her money and a few grams of Charlie to stuff up her crotch. Her little supply had some of the hardest inmates eating out of her hand. Not that she couldn't handle herself; she was as tough as old boots and brutal as the other prisoners. She'd learned to stick up for herself from the age of seventeen – against men, not women.

Easing herself away from the cold bathroom floor, she hauled herself up and washed her face with the cold running water from the new modern single tap. Slowly, she stood upright and glared at the face in the mirror; the brown rings under her eyes and an unsightly puffiness had spread across her nose and cheeks. Pregnancy was not good for her looks. She appeared older, much older; the seventeen-year-old with round fresh eyes and an innocence about them had gone.

She shouldn't be surprised though; life had dealt her that wicked hand, what with a father who didn't give a shit and Carl who she thought back then cared but clearly didn't. Of course, he never cared; he was a selfish, evil, arrogant bastard, yet for some reason, maybe familiarity, she still went running back to him. It was a strange relationship … but needs must when the devil drives. Perhaps she still clung on to the past, when he'd made her feel alive, special, and loved. Then again, was it really love, and was he even capable of loving anyone but himself?

She wandered to the bedroom and lay on the soft quilt covered in a brushed cotton, feeling the gentleness against her skin. Carl's words swirled around her head. 'Lucy Lou, you are dangerous when you don't need anyone and weak when you do.' She often thought about those words because he knew there were many times in her life when she needed him. And he was right: it made her weak. He fascinated her, drew her in with his mysterious ways, his philosophical statements, and with the crazy reckless look in his eyes. Perhaps in some ways he was her mirror image – only older, male, and even more insane than herself.

She carried out his clever scams, and at the time, she thought she was being rewarded fairly with a few hundred quid shoved down her knickers. But he was right about being stronger alone, and so she began finding work for herself. She hooked up with an agency as a call girl, and within a week, she was in the world of the streetwalkers, except she didn't walk the streets – she had clients who wanted her. The dominatrix earner was great, and she could pull it off easily, but there was more money to be had in other areas, and without a conscience, she was learning the game fast, leaving Carl behind to go it alone.

By the age of seventeen, she was tall, leggy, and could ooze sex just by the way she walked; it was that sultry eyebrow lift and then a flutter of her heavily mascara-laden lashes that would have her drinks paid for by any unsuspecting punter. Her ability to have men eating out of her hand and begging for it gave her a status – a high-class prostitute, who could demand an outrageous price for a night in an expensive hotel. It meant nothing to her. Whether they were tied up and whipped just for the turn-on, or whether they liked full-on sex, it didn't matter, it was just that – sex. She never had high expectations of saving herself for the right man or worrying that her past would come back to haunt her because she didn't care.

She was rewarded financially but she also had a certain status. Yet, always there in the background was Carl, turning up at her father's home, when Les had retired, so he put it. But the truth was Les was washed up, too fat to fight, and too pissed to think straight. He never questioned her line of work, but he knew she was on the game; the tell-tale signs were there: the flash clothes, the heavy make-up, and the sensual manner, too suggestive for a girl her age.

Carl had a strange obsession to keep one hand in her life; he took her out for the odd meal for two, and it was always followed by sex. He referred to her as his number one woman, his pleasure, and of course his money-maker. She too liked to have him on speed dial, if ever a rough punter needed bashing up, or she was too drunk to get home.

Their relationship was symbiotic; she wasn't his partner, girl-friend, or best friend, but his go-to girl. He didn't flirt with her either; he just said in matter-of-fact terms that she was sexy, reliable, and perfect to have at hand, if need be. What it amounted to varied from week to week. She could never guarantee his intentions when he pulled up in that flash car of his to take her out. Perhaps that was her guilty pleasure – the unknown.

Then things changed.

One evening, she was propped up at a bar, sipping a glass of Grey Goose and tonic, awaiting her favourite punter, Gerry Johns, when Carl strode in. He nodded her way but didn't come over; instead, he walked with his cocky swagger over to the tall and very beautiful brunette who was seated by the open fireplace.

Lucy followed him with her eyes and watched closely how he greeted the mystery woman.

Lucy's heart beat faster when she saw him gently rub the woman's arm and sensually kiss her cheek. The brunette smiled coyly and fluttered her eyelashes. This was no business meeting; it was a date. Lucy stared harder, clocking the attractive woman's response to him. She was clearly besotted and made no bones about oozing her sensuality. He ran his hands through his long loose waves and almost blushed – that was a first.

It was at that point, Lucy realised she was jealous and would have loved to have swapped places. The one thing she had always noticed was that no matter what scam he was pulling off, he wore an Armani suit or designer jeans, an expensive leather jacket, and a gold watch. As she continued staring, whilst he was whispering in the woman's ear, he glanced Lucy's way and winked. She spun back to face the bar to digest the meaning of that sexy wink. She couldn't be sure if he was teasing her or mocking her.

As soon as Gerry arrived, she sighed with relief; she could play Carl's game and flirt. Gerry was a looker himself, being tall, fit, and almost pretty with round glassy eyes framed by extra thick dark lashes and a contrasting pale skin. His hint of an Irish accent gave him an edge. She had asked him why he needed to pay for it when he could have any girl flocking at his feet. He smiled and replied, 'Yes, I can have girlfriends, but I can't stand the ag, the neediness, and the bloody whining. I've enough money to pay for what I want, so why have some tart hanging on to my shirt-tails?'

That was good enough for her, although if he hadn't been paying for it, she would have given him a piece of her anyway. She liked sex with him and actually enjoyed his company, but once he'd given her his reasons for not having a girlfriend, she decided to keep it as it was and not upset the apple cart. That evening, though, she wanted to flirt, and so she laughed louder than she would have and whispered more than she needed to.

She tickled his back and ran her hands up the back of his neck, pretending she was gooey-eyed and in love, and yet, all the while, she hoped Carl was watching. *Two can play at that game,* she thought.

As soon as Gerry got up to use the gents', Carl was at the bar to buy another round. He slid his way over to her and whispered, 'I hope he's paying you well for all the effort you're putting in?' He winked and ordered two Bacardi Mojitos, leaving her biting her lip with rage. She felt foolish and wanted to slap him for mocking her.

A week later, he called at her father's, holding a bunch of keys and laughing. 'Fancy ya own pad, treacle?'

She naturally grabbed the offer with both hands, packed her bags, and left within an hour, without even asking what the flat was like, how much the rent was, or what she had to do to return the favour. She'd misunderstood him and assumed they were going to live together.

The flat itself was a two-bedroom pad, along with three other small flats, which had been converted from a shop in Webb's Road just off Clapham Common. He pulled up directly outside and grinned in her face. 'So, what do you think? Better than Lewisham, eh?'

She looked at the modern frontage and smiled. 'This will do us both nicely. Have you moved all your belongings in already?'

He jerked his head back in surprise. 'You what? Lucy Lou, you didn't think I was moving in with you, did you?' His tone was contemptuous.

Her eyes flicked across his face, searching for an explanation, but his deadpan countenance told her all she needed to know, and with a downtrodden expression, she replied, 'No, of course not, a silly assumption on my part.' Yet, deep down, she was gutted, and then the realisation hit her; he wanted something in return. 'So, Carl, do enlighten me. What's the reason for the flat?'

He shook his head and laughed. 'Oh, come on, Lucy, me and

you, we have a thing. I look out for you, and, well, you work for me.'

She couldn't disagree, but the flat would cost an arm and a leg, so he would want payment, in one way or another. 'Carl, me and you are just two lost souls, really. Yeah, we fuck, and I work for you sometimes, but I'm not ya sister or ya bird, so, come on, spit it out, what's the catch?' She fingered the set of keys and waited for an answer. His side profile was just as handsome as his front, and she gazed while he stared ahead.

'All right, there's no messing you over, is there? I'll be straight with you. I know you have your regular punters and I turn a blind eye—'

'Blind eye?' she interrupted. 'What the fuck does it have to do with you?'

With a half-cocked grin, he ran his index finger down her cheek. 'Because, Lucy Lou, you are supposed to work for me. No sidelines, no nonsense, just be ready when I need you.'

She shuddered, feeling a little intimidated by his words. There was no hint of a joke; he was serious. 'Carl, since when do I solely work for you? I mean, I have scratched your back, and you, in some ways, scratch mine, but that's as far as it goes.'

'That, my little treacle dumpling, is where you're fucking wrong. I have toms set up in twenty flats all over London, and each one does as she's told. You have got away with too much, and anyway, why ask?'

Her face was scrunched up in confusion and disgust. 'I ain't one of your fucking dirty whores. I've my own clients, rich decent men, who wine and dine me and don't take fucking liberties. They see me all right for cash, so why on earth would I be in one of your whorehouses? You ain't my pimp.'

He chuckled sarcastically. 'You have a funny idea of a pimp. Well, let me educate you, Lucy Lou. You don't have to sleep with a man for money to prostitute yourself. You've been doing it for a few years now. But, although we make a good team, with our little scams, it still comes down to the same sordid act. Whether you are dancing around half-naked cracking a fucking whip or jumping up and down on some geezer's cock, it's still prostitution. And another thing, Miss High and Fucking Mighty, your so-called selected clients can just as easily put a knife across your throat and would probably have the brains to get away with it. So, in my eyes, princess, you need a pimp.'

He paused and wiped his mouth. 'Whether you like it or not, I'm your pimp. I always have been and probably always will be.'

With flared nostrils and a livid expression on her face, she grappled with the lock to get out of the car. She wasn't going to listen to his bullshit. She didn't need him, she was independent, or so she thought. He could shove his fancy flat up his arse. But the door was locked, and Carl laughed again.

'Hey, slow down, you're gonna wreck me motor. All right, listen. I said I would turn a blind eye to your private clients … the truth is, it was me that sent you them, not that poxy two-bit escort agency. Christ, Lucy, I thought you would have guessed by now that everything you do has your good old Uncle Carl's name behind it.' He waited for her to digest all of this, enjoying the frustration on her face. In fact, he revelled in getting one over her – he almost got off on it.

She stopped trying to escape from the car and froze, feeling as though she'd just experienced an electric shock. Slowly, she understood his satisfied expression and lunged forward, clawing at his face. 'You bastard, you fucking dirty sly bastard!' She began to scream and, enraged, she continued trying to claw him, but he gripped her wrists, allowing her to scream and shout obscenities, until, unexpectedly, she began to cry – deep heartfelt sobs that made Carl think perhaps he'd gone too far this time. Lucy never cried.

She genuinely thought she'd escaped her father's miserable council house and was going it alone, to make a life for herself. Selling her arse was just the start, until she would have enough savings to set up her own business. Whatever that would be, it didn't matter, but one day, she would make a life for herself.

He waited until her sobs subsided before he spoke. 'I knew you went to that agency, so I told them to only give you the best punters, and I checked them out myself. Ya see, babe, I still have your back, so directly or indirectly, I'm your pimp.' He softened his voice and spoke slowly. 'But, you're right. You ain't like my whores I have in the flats. No, Lucy, you, my babe, are different.'

She sniffed and wiped the snot with the back of her hand, pulled down the sun visor mirror and looked at her blotchy red face as she tried to wipe away the black mascara that stained her cheeks. 'Why, though, Carl? Why me? Why couldn't you just leave me be? You always seem to have your hand in my life. What is it, Carl, eh? In love with me, are you?' In a way, she hoped he would say yes.

He didn't, though. He laughed in her face and those words hit her like a brick. 'Don't be silly, I'm not capable of loving anyone. I don't want to, either.'

She rolled her eyes and stared at the flat. 'So, I guess I'm in there, then, and you will send clients to me, eh? And I s'pose I will pay you a percentage to cover the cost of the flat. Am I right?'

For just a second, she thought he looked sad or guilty as his head dipped down, but maybe it was just wishful thinking.

'Aw, Lucy, no. Look, treacle, I don't want to play happy families. I can't. I'm not into that, and no, I don't love you, well, not enough for anything serious. Look, I owe your ol' man a big debt, and I made a promise that I would look out for ya, and yeah, you have chosen your own path in life, and I can't change that, but I *will* look out for ya. I have to admit there's something about you that has me coming back for more, but I don't want you all the time – it's that simple, really. Anyway, enough about us, 'cos there is no us, but listen, the flat's yours. I have a few little jobs coming up, and I want you ready. It's a good earner for me and you, so there's the flat. Keep ya silly punters but be ready when I call.'

He tapped her nose and gave her a look of narcissistic satisfaction. 'Now we have that straightened out, how about we try out your bed? It's all fresh and ready for your naked body. You know how I like it, Lucy Lou.'

For a second, she contemplated the idea. His eyes were beckoning her; that sexy twinkle, it always turned her on, yet she was still furious, and so she laughed back in his face. 'No way. You want my arse, then you fucking pay like the rest – five hundred pounds, take it or leave it.' She noticed his arrogant jubilation diminish, and she smiled inwardly. *That will teach you, you cocksure prick.*

But she wasn't prepared for what happened next. All at once, his hands were around her throat and his eyes burned into hers. 'Listen to me, baby doll. You ever think about talking to me like that again and I'll rip you a new fucking arsehole. No punter, no matter how desperate, will want a piece of you.'

As she spluttered, and stared at him in horror, he released his grip. The situation had turned tense, but he realised he needed to be the bigger person. Accordingly, he lowered his tone. 'I didn't have to take care of you. In fact, as a kid you were a fucking nightmare, but I made a promise to ya ol' man. You have a short memory, Lucy, and you need to remind yourself where you really would have ended up, if it weren't for me. I can take you to King's Cross, right fucking now, and you will see for yourself!'

She tried to remain cool and not let on it terrified her. Instead of making exaggerated gasping noises, she took a slow but large intake of air through her nose and fixed her eyes on his, trying hard not to show any emotion. She didn't want to give him any clues that she was afraid of him; he was a dangerous man, a secretive and powerful man. But whilst she had to be mindful he would hurt her if she took the piss out of him, she was no soft touch herself. She had her pride and an inner steel about her. No way was he going to get the upper hand, not whilst she still had breath in her body.

That was the beginning of their adult relationship. She was almost eighteen and he was in his late twenties. He'd achieved a lot in his young years. It was hard to imagine her own father being powerless to Carl; even at his age and size, her dad was still bloody scared of him. Perhaps that fear had rubbed off on her. Maybe that was part of the thrill, imagining her father being scared of the man and her shagging him.

Whatever it was, it never changed over the years. Carl made demands that increased as the months rolled into years. She went along with it – she had to – even with the men he sent for services, and to add insult to injury, they weren't the nicest either, being old, fat, hairy, and some smelly, but in the back of her mind, she was afraid that if she pushed Carl too far, he would harm her.

Now, as she lay there on the bed, feeling the brushed cotton between her fingers, she experienced a sudden rush of emotion: it was hate. Being away from Carl had made her see things for what they really were and getting her life in order and taking what she *wanted*, and not what she was only *allowed* to have, gave her a sense of freedom. Biting her nails, she just wished that he would leave her alone, and let her get on with her life. And as for the twenty grand she stole from him, that was peanuts to a man like Carl; he probably carried that much around as pocket money.

But she had stolen it to go to Australia, to start a new life on the other side of the world. Carl, however, saw the money she owed as his reason for pulling her back into his clutches. If he was insistent, then she would have to get the money, and the only way that was likely to happen was if she could somehow wangle it from Justin. Perhaps a trust fund for their son would be the answer.

She'd spent all of her own money and also what she'd cajoled out of Joan Bannon before she died. Joan, the poor unsuspecting woman, had no reason to ever imagine that the young person who had moved to within a few yards down the street and who offered to clean her house and care for her would be a leech for information. Lucy had spent enough time with Joan to learn everything about Kara because the woman was so proud of her precious daughter; it was like taking candy from a baby. And she had all the tools she needed to step into Kara's shoes and take her man, her house, and her money.

Without any warning, Lucy felt the baby move, only slightly, but it made it all the more real that in a few months she would be giving birth, and then she would have her hands tied. Of course, she would play the sick wife and insist they had a nanny.

Her thoughts returned to Kara, and once again, she bit her lip, as there was always that nagging doubt that Justin could leave her at the drop of a hat, as he'd done to Kara. For, deep down, she knew in her heart that Justin was still very much in love with Kara.

She looked at the small bedroom and sighed. She wanted to have what Kara had – that idyllic home and the man who Joan had bragged about. Once Joan was on the subject of her daughter, she wouldn't shut up; she would go on and on about how proud she was, how beautiful and brilliantly clever and happy Kara and Justin were – even to the point of describing the size of their perfect home and what wonderful parents they would make.

It gripped her every time and raised her anger. She hated Kara, a woman she didn't even know, but with every compliment that Joan paid her daughter, Lucy's contempt for Kara increased. It reminded herself of how little she had, with no mother figure, no one proud of her, and the lack of a decent man to adore and cherish her and give her everything she wanted. She imagined that conceited look on Kara's face, the confidence and smug attitude because she'd had it all. The jealous anger building up inside her was like a giant tidal wave that had the force to wreak havoc in its path, and she would too, if necessary.

All the tablets that were there in packets and bottles, a whole cupboard full – it was a massive temptation. She could easily open a hundred capsules and pour them into a drink, and Joan would have been out of her miserable existence of constant pain; besides, she would be doing her a favour, wouldn't she? For days, she contemplated ending the woman's life. Many times, while Joan cried in pain, Lucy stood staring at that cabinet, eyeing up the pills and picturing Joan swallowing a long cold drink of iced tea with a concoction of medication, and her drifting off into a deep sleep, never to wake up.

It was such a shame that she wasn't there at her bedside when she'd died. She remembered her last words. 'Sweetheart, you go and enjoy your party. I will be fine.' She'd looked sprightly that day, not bent double in agony; even her face seemed to be glowing. Lucy had made her one last drink of her favourite iced tea and placed a mound of tablets on the bedside table and left. If Joan wanted to end it all, she had the means right there, an arm's reach away.

The beach party was a new experience for her. The fire, the barbecues, and the endless flow of drinks had Lucy in her element. She got drunk, took some ecstasy tablets, and was reluctant to leave because she was having the time of her life. She couldn't remember the guy's name, except that he was a real chunky handsome man in his late twenties, with broad shoulders and hair tied back in a ponytail. He was the central attraction, and some of the other girls there were fighting for his attention. But he'd been drawn to her English accent and wasn't shy in coming forward.

The beach party went on through the night, and then, as the crowd slowly drifted to their own homes, she was left alone with him. The drugs had kept them awake until the sun came up. He grabbed her arm and led her to an open-top jeep parked on the beach. He insisted she went back to his apartment, which she was only too delighted to do, hoping that he lived in some sophisticated pad where she could perhaps start a new life for herself. The sun, sea, and a handsome surfer – what could be more perfect? – except for the fact his apartment was essentially a wooden shack, and she soon realised he was a beach bum; nevertheless, the shag they'd had had been fulfilling.

The following day, they slept for a few hours, and when they awoke, she realised that he wasn't as handsome as she'd first thought. The drugs had blurred her vision and all she really remembered was his handsome face from the golden glow of the fire. But, in the cold light of day, he was pretty ordinary.

She returned to Joan's only to find her in bed in a very poor state, with incoherent mumblings and burning up a shocking fever. On the cabinet beside her bed was the empty glass and next to it was another glass half-full of what looked like a red berry drink. Joan pointed to it; Lucy took a few sips herself, trying to rid herself of a dry mouth from all the weekend drinking. She then helped Joan into a sitting position so that she could sip the rest.

Joan's thirst was still unquenched, so Lucy went to the kitchen and made an iced tea and placed it on the cabinet. The room was stifling hot, and she assumed that in her dazed state Joan had turned off the air conditioning. She was a little daft at times, due to the pain she was in, and she did things like put the sugar in the teapot. Lucy noticed the iced tea tumbler was empty and the tablets she'd left there seemed to have been disturbed. Some were on the floor and scattered under the bed, and some remained on the cabinet. Lucy wasn't sure if Joan had knocked them over, trying to take them all, or had accidently moved them in her sleep.

The next morning, Lucy got herself dressed and dawdled into Joan's bedroom. She stopped dead in her tracks and stared. Joan was lying flat on her back with her mouth open and her skin unnaturally grey and yellow. Her eyes were wide open, cloudy, and lifeless. Lucy held her breath and observed Joan for any movement, but she was still; there was not even a gentle rhythmic motion of her chest. As she continued to gaze at the body, she wondered if she'd died in pain or just drifted off to sleep with the help of the tablets.

Naturally, the coroner carried out a post-mortem examination, and on inspecting the enlarged liver and looking at her medical records, he determined that all the medication she was on had finally led to liver failure. He took samples but concluded there were no suspicious circumstances, and in so many cases where the patient is in severe chronic pain, a few extra tablets could easily lead to an overdose or possibly suicide.

She was cremated within a week, and as much as Lucy wanted to stay in Australia and enjoy a new life, her visa had almost expired. She'd sold all of Joan's belongings, packed up the gifts Joan had given her, and returned home. Now she'd tasted a small part of good, clean, and contented living, she wanted more of it. She wasn't going to give up her ideal future that easily. She had now reached the point where she was convinced she deserved the life that Kara had, and nothing would stop her now.

She would have told Kara that her mother had died. However, she realised that in not telling Kara, it would work to her advantage. She'd taken Joan's pay as you go phone with her. The calls were costing her a fortune, but it was worth it to hear how frightened Kara was.

A thought hit her. To achieve the life Kara had and one that Joan continually boasted about, she would have to get her head into gear. There would be no more pussyfooting around. Therefore, she had to entice Justin into her web of deceit – and then marry him fast – to secure everything she was working towards.

163

Chapter 11

Two days passed before Vic was allowed out of the hospital and back to prison. Julie, Kara, and Deni had collected goodies from the canteen: a few chocolate bars, Mr Kipling cakes, and crisps. They wanted to give her a small party, just the four of them. Colette tried to ingratiate herself into their company, by offering a small pouch of skunk and a bottle of homemade booze, otherwise known as prison hooch. Deni looked her up and down, as she stood in the doorway. 'Brown-nosing are ya, Cole?' She smirked.

Colette tilted her head down and shuffled uncomfortably. 'Nah, it ain't like that. I thought I might be included.' She looked at Kara. 'Well, since I kinda helped you with the blanket and …'

With a genuine smile, Kara nodded. 'Yes, Cole, you did help me, didn't you, and I'm grateful.' She chuckled. 'Deni, Cole nearly got put on report, trying to help me.'

Deni relaxed her shoulders and stepped back for Colette to squeeze into the cell. 'Okay, Cole, come in, love.'

Kara noticed that Colette looked different. Her square shoulders and thick trunk were slimmer, and her close-cropped hair had grown; she even wore a dusting of mascara, which definitely improved her appearance. Kara didn't say anything because she didn't want to humiliate Colette.

'Now, Cole, don't you eat all the bleedin' Snickers bars. I know they're your favourite,' said Deni, with an exaggerated rise of her eyebrow.

Colette laughed coyly and pulled from her pockets three chocolate bars and slapped them on the bed. 'I brought me own.'

It was Julie who had to make a comment regarding Colette's transformation not only in looks but personality; after all, Julie wasn't the shyest of people and was as blunt as you like. 'What are you after, Cole, a new fanny muncher?'

Colette blushed crimson. 'No, I ain't into that anymore – I'm not gay.'

'Who are you trying to impress, then?' asked Julie, redoing her messy bun.

'You'll think me a fucking weirdo, if I tell ya, so leave it at that, eh?' she replied nervously, fiddling with her small plastic pouch of weed.

'Nah, Cole, we won't laugh, so, what's going on?' Julie was like a newspaper reporter, once she sensed a good story. Deni was also intrigued, but Kara felt it was none of her business.

Slowly, Colette lifted her head and looked at Kara. 'All right, I've been thinking. I ain't done anything with my life, and to be fair, I never wanted to either, but I've watched Posh help out, even save Vic's life, and then I got to thinking about myself. What do I ever do but talk about fighting and shit?' They were all glued to her, waiting to hear the big reveal.

'Well, I've been to the library—'

'Cor, fuck me! Can you even read?' squawked Julie.

'See, I knew I should 'ave kept me mouth shut,' retorted Colette, looking thoroughly fed up.

Kara waved her hands and leaned forward. 'No, carry on, Cole, Julie's just jesting.'

'Okay, so I thought I would try and better meself. If I ever get released, I got to thinking about me future, and, well, I've been reading about midwifery.'

165

'What!' screeched Deni, followed by a chuckle. 'A bit fucking random,' she scoffed.

'You might think so, but, well, I've always wanted to be a midwife, ya see, before I got locked up in here, and I wish to God I'd studied it back then, ya know, when I lost me own baby.'

Kara moved closer and placed a hand on Colette's knee. 'I never knew.'

Colette shook her head. 'Nah, well, there weren't much to know. Ya see, I was about six months pregnant when I told the fucking screws I was in pain, but they locked me up anyway, and I miscarried on the fucking toilet. I couldn't even reach the panic button, I was in that much pain.'

Instantly, Kara placed her arms around Colette. 'Oh my God, it must have been awful.' She choked back the tears, feeling the woman's grief.

'Ahh, no worries, Kara, it was a long time ago now. Anyway, I just thought I should sort meself out. I need to give this shit up for starters.' She held up the small packet. 'And, well, do some studying and educate meself. I've lost a bit of weight, 'cos I was reading those health books, too.'

Deni nodded, with an empathetic expression. 'Aw, babe, I'm proud of ya.'

'Another thing. I dunno if you're up for it, Kara, but you know you can have a baby buddy, like a friend that helps with your baby? Well, if I study enough about that too, I thought you might wanna let me help. I mean, you'll probably have Deni or Vic, but well, if they don't fancy it, would you consider me?'

A tear made its way down Kara's face, and she looked at Deni, who nodded. 'Sounds like a good idea to me, babe.'

'Yeah, why not, Cole. I would love you to help me. I see how caring you can be when you aren't putting on that hard act of yours. I remember when you tried to place that blanket around my shoulders and the look on your face. You were genuinely worried for me.'

The serious conversation was stopped in its tracks. In the doorway, being held up by George, was Vic, whose complexion was pale and sickly.

'Hey, 'ere she is,' clapped Deni. 'Move up, Julie. Let ya sister get comfy.'

George would not normally assist a prisoner back to a cell, but he wanted to make sure she got back safely and wasn't going to entrust Barbara because word had got around how she'd behaved when Vic was nearly on her deathbed.

'Thanks, Gov,' she said, as she gave him a sorrowful look. The wind had well and truly been taken out of her sails, and she appeared pathetically vulnerable. She was assigned a crutch because she was not allowed any pressure on that leg, not until the wound had healed properly.

Carefully, she eased herself down and placed the crutch on the floor. A huge sigh left her mouth followed by a smile that looked as though it had taken a great deal of effort. 'Posh, they said without you doing what you did, I would be dead now. I don't remember much, and I ain't spiritual or religious or shit like that, but I do remember feeling as though an angel had my back.'

You could have heard a pin drop, as they all listened to the words leaving Vic's mouth. This was serious. No one mocked or made light of it because it was big, hard Vic and she never said anything more than what needed to be said. To their surprise, her eyes shimmered, and the tears were about to tumble, but she quickly brushed them away.

''Ere, girl, get ya laughing gear around that,' said Deni, handing Vic a cup of hot chocolate. She knew Vic would never want to be seen in public teary-eyed; she had a reputation to uphold.

Vic swallowed hard and took the cup. Kara was flabbergasted because it was as if Vic was a completely different woman.

'I owe you big-time, Kara. Ya do know that, don't ya?'

Kara shook her head. Her eyes were already moist. 'No, Vic,

that's what friends are for. Besides, you are one tough cookie. You probably didn't need my help.'

Vic's eyes remained fixed on Kara. A warm feeling engulfed Kara, as though she really was some kind of angel, and in her heart, she knew the older woman would always look out for her.

* * *

Two weeks later, much changed. Esme was shipped back to Durham Prison. George had no proof she'd attacked Vic, but while she was in sick bay, he turned over her cell and found enough gear and a knife to have her nicked. He didn't like the idea of her in his prison. In his eyes, she was a psychopath, and she shouldn't have been put into a mainstream prison in the first place.

Luckily for them, Esme didn't die from food poisoning. Their usual doctor was off sick and his replacement took over. Dr Miles had concluded fairly quickly that Esme had something more serious than an upset stomach. Esme was going downhill rapidly, and without the antibiotics and saline drip, she would have died.

The news had spread like crabs at an orgy, and by the time it reached Deni, she was folding sheets with Julie in the steam room. Vivienne, the junkie, came with the gossip and left seconds later to spread the word, leaving both Deni and Julie with deep smiles on their faces.

'Well, I'll be buggered. Kara did give us a loaded gun.' She laughed.

Julie was gobsmacked. 'I can't wait to tell Posh.'

Suddenly, Deni looked concerned. 'No, don't do that. You know what she's like. It'll worry the life outta her.'

'But …'

'No, Jue, she spent months worrying over that neighbour of hers. I don't want her bothered, and trust me, she will be. I thought about it a while back, ya know. And I came to the conclusion that when she told us what to do with those bits of scabby chicken, she probably didn't think we would.'

'Well, that's fucking mental and I thought she was brainy.'

'She is, Jue, she's just not used to thinking like us.'

* * *

Kara had a legal visit called at the last minute, all in preparation for her court case. As she anxiously waited in the cold, ugly square room, she ran her hands over her now protruding bump. She could feel her little girl moving and a wave of warmth covered her. She knew that all the time her baby was inside her, she was safe from the cruel world she would be exposed to.

George appeared with his rosy-cheeked face and a gentle comforting expression. 'Kara, your barrister is here.' He stood aside and allowed the man to enter. Kara watched as he took confident strides towards the table. Stuart Venables was in his early forties, his short hair professionally styled. His unusually large round eyes were crystal blue and his cheeks had folds stretching down to his wide mouth that offered a generous smile. Kara noticed his exceptionally white teeth and wondered if they were veneers. His clean-shaven face had a soft glow from the perfumed shaving balm. She assumed he was a confident man; his upright and perfect appearance showed no signs of exhaustion from overworking. He could have been a salesman, judging by the ambition in his eyes and his enthusiastic, eager smile.

Holding out his hand, his smile grew bigger and his eyes lit up. 'Hi, Miss Bannon. I'm Stuart Venables, your barrister, instructed by your solicitor, Mr Cumberbatch. How are you today?'

Kara shook his hand and smiled, and yet, she felt her face redden. Maybe it was the way he looked at her so fondly that made her feel suddenly shy and self-conscious. 'Hello, it's lovely to meet you.'

Stuart was surprised to hear her speak so softly with a pronounced accent. Yet, dressed in prison issues and with her hair in a ponytail, she could pass for one of the rougher inmates.

'Okay, you don't mind if I call you Kara, do you?'

She shook her head. 'No, please do, Stuart.'

'Good, I like to get to know my clients before I represent them in court, and I think surnames are so formal.'

She coyly smiled and looked at her lap, knowing she appeared scruffy.

'Well, I would love to bring good news, Kara, but there seems to be an issue. This letter that you said you received, stating that Justin Fox asked you to vacate the property only a few days after he left, was quite frankly denied by his solicitor.'

She looked up in amazement. 'What! No, I did receive a letter. I know I did. I read it twice because I couldn't believe he would do that to me, not Justin. I mean, he wouldn't do that to anyone. He is a … I mean, he is a very kind-hearted man.' She glanced across at Stuart's face and then down at the table where his long, manicured fingers pushed a letter under her nose.

'Apparently, this letter, here, is the only one he sent to Justin. In fact, it was for Justin to agree to before his solicitor posted it to you, which, by the way, he never did. Of course, slip-ups do happen, and his secretary may have posted it by mistake, but I very much doubt it. Please read it.'

Kara scanned the letter. It was short and contained nothing like the harsh words she'd read just before she burned the house down. In fact, it was almost the opposite. She wondered if she was going mad, so she read it again.

Dear Kara,

Under the present circumstances, Justin has instructed me to oversee the legalities regarding the separation for both parties. In order that the house is either sold or solely owned

by either yourself or Justin, he has asked for a valuation to
be carried out.

Of course, there is no hurry, and you are welcome to remain
there as long as necessary. Please could you let me know when
you will be available to show an estate agent around?

Yours sincerely

Lucas

Shaking her head and fingering the letter, she replied, 'No, I didn't receive this letter. I've never seen it.' She looked at the date and frowned. 'Hang on, this is not right. The fire ...' She paused, feeling a deep sadness and regret, not being able to bring herself to say, 'when I burned the house down ...'

He urged her to go on.

'That letter is dated the day of the fire, so if it was sent, the earliest I would have received it would be the next day, surely? And the letter I received was sent in the post ... I think.'

He nodded. 'Yes, Kara, this is the strange part about it because those were my thoughts exactly. So, I called Justin's lawyer and asked him if the date was correct. He informed me that he'd drawn up the letter and sent one to Justin for his approval four days before the fire. However, he then drew up the official letter on the day of the fire, and it lay on his desk awaiting confirmation from Justin to send it, which he never gave. Therefore, if the secretary posted the letter by mistake, you would have received it at least two days after the fire and possibly even later.'

Kara was going over in her head the ramifications of how the letter could have been delivered two days after the fire. There would have been very little of the former house left to deliver it to.

'I checked with the post office. There are letters they have kept back for obvious reasons, but not one from the solicitor. So, I'm as confused on this matter as you appear to be. However, this is where the problem begins. Without that letter, we will have difficulty proving you acted with temporary insanity. That letter you say you received could have pushed you over the edge and possibly helped to provide a reason to commit the crime, so, without it, we are hard-pressed to get you off, and more problematic, newspaper headlines such as "Mrs Langley fighting for her life" will resonate in the jury's minds.'

Covering her face with her hands, Kara felt almost strangled by the lump in her throat. She could accept her punishment, but her baby shouldn't have to suffer, growing up inside a cell or being taken from her. She fought back the tears and removed her hands to reveal the grief-stricken expression.

Stuart was struck by the sadness and desolation in her eyes. Normally, if he gave a client bad news, especially in prison, he would receive a barrage of abuse and demands of 'well, do something', but Kara just nodded, accepting her fate. It saddened him because she clearly was one person who didn't belong there, and he hoped the judge would see what he saw.

'Stuart, I know I have to face what is coming my way, but do you think I could ask a huge favour? You see, I think I can handle being in here, but it's my mother …'

He leaned forward on his chair. 'What about her?' He asked so gently that it caused a fat tear to trickle down her face.

'She lives in Australia, and well, every time I call to see how she is, there's no answer. I spoke with her carer the other day, but since then, I've heard nothing, and I have no way of knowing what's going on. Can you help me? She's sick, you see.' She kept the request simple, not wanting to discuss the very strange conversation she'd had with the person she presumed was the carer.

His heart went out to her, and he knew only too well what that felt like. He had lost his mother only a year ago, and he was so distraught, he worked every hour to avoid thinking about it. Obviously, this was outside his normal professional remit, yet a call wouldn't hurt, if it put his client's mind at rest. At this stage in her case, he was her only link to the outside world.

'What's her number and her address? I will make enquiries and let you know.' He could tell she was distrusting and of course she would be. He'd read the case notes, and for a young woman with so much going for her to end up in prison, he would be surprised if she didn't hate the world right now. He stood up to leave. 'I came today to introduce myself and to ask about the letter. Now, it's Monday, today. I will be back on Thursday to go over the details of your case in full. Sorry this is such a short visit, but we will have more time on Thursday.'

She smiled generously, wiped away the tears, and stood up to shake his hand. His eyes were drawn to her protruding stomach, which had been hidden behind the table. She wasn't overweight, but how could he be sure? Then, he saw her hand stroke the bump.

'Are you expecting?' he asked, and then he wished he hadn't. It was unprofessional, and yet, he felt the strange urge to befriend her.

'Yes, a little girl. Oh, you won't say anything? I mean, Justin doesn't know, and to be honest, I don't want him to. You see, he left me because he got a woman pregnant, and they're now living together.'

'Yes, I know, I read his statement.' He sat back down, not ready to leave. This news was a surprise. It would no doubt help her case enormously; hormones could play a major role in a case.

'So, you were pregnant when the fire happened, then?' He didn't like to say, 'when you burned the house down'.

She nodded. 'Yes, that's why I also lost my job. I suppose I was feeling so sick all the time, and I assumed I was ill. I remember, I seemed to cry constantly, and then, when Justin left and that letter arrived, I just saw red. I'd never felt like that before. It's hard to explain. It was like it wasn't me.'

Stuart nodded. 'Well, you know, Kara, it will all come out in court, and I'm afraid you cannot hide the signs.' He looked at her midriff.

She eased herself back on the chair. 'I don't want him to know because he obviously loves this other woman. I know what he did was wrong, by going off with her, but he is a good man, and I don't want to get in his way. The baby and I will be fine.'

Stuart felt his stomach turn over because he knew exactly what would happen. 'Kara, do you have any other family … in the UK?'

She shook her head. 'No, no one. It was only Justin and me, and, of course, his mother.'

Chewing the inside of his lip, he worried over how to approach the issue of the baby. 'Look, Kara, your situation before the fire may influence the judge, and he or she may reduce your sentence by a few years, say from five to two years. We won't be looking at a life sentence luckily because Mrs Langley didn't die. But, I cannot guarantee you will be out within eighteen months, and at that point, the baby will be taken in by social services … You do know that, don't you? Have they told you this?' He cocked his head to the side, concerned that she would face an unthinkable situation.

The blood drained from her face, and he could see she was visibly shaking.

'Oh, Jesus, has no one told you?'

Slowly, with her eyes full of tears, she shook her head. 'Yes, Stuart, they told me, but what can I do? I can't let them take her. She is all I have in this world.'

'As I intimated, you will be able to keep the baby for a year and a half or so, but then they will find her a home, a foster home, until you are out. But, I have to be honest, it's not that easy to get the baby back. Kara, try to think who could take the child on until you are released and settled.'

* * *

174

His departure was a blur. She was too numb from the harrowing experience to think straight, but that was exactly what she needed to do. Vic and Deni were awaiting her return, anxious to hear what her barrister had to say. But, by the time she reached her cell, her face was white, and the little make-up she'd worn for Stuart's visit had been ruined by her tears. Deni jumped up from the bed and placed an arm around Kara's shoulders and guided her inside. 'Sit yaself down. Let me make a brew.' She'd sensed that the brief had burdened her with bad news.

'What's he say, babe?' asked Vic, in her kindest tone.

'Social services will take my baby after about eighteen months and foster her out.' Her bottom lip quivered, and more tears tumbled down her cheeks.

Vic felt her throat tighten; she was looking at a face that would have melted anyone's heart. That look of deep sadness was heart-breaking.

Deni spun around. 'Aw, fuck me, haven't they told you anything about how it works in 'ere?'

Kara shook her head. 'I knew it might happen, but I hoped it wouldn't. I didn't even think that if I get more than two years, they will take …' She couldn't bear to say the words.

Vic reached across and grabbed her hand. 'Listen, Kara. Don't you go worrying about all that now. We will sort you out.'

'How, though, Vic? I have no one, I mean no one, to look after my baby.'

'What about your mum? I know she's poorly, but she may help ya, you know, between her and a carer.'

Kara glanced up. 'No way, she's not capable.' She realised she sounded abrupt and instantly transformed her expression. Upsetting her friends wasn't called for.

Vic shot Deni a look. 'Deni?'

'Listen, my babe, I know you don't want this Justin fella to know, but … well, maybe he should know. Perhaps he could take over until you do get released. Let's not get carried away. We're talking as if you will get a long bird. Let's just wait until after the trial. The judge might only give you six months.'

Kara realised that going on about it and passing her worries on to her friends wouldn't change anything, so she smiled, trying to hide the torment, and graciously took the cup of tea from Deni's shaking hands. She was just grateful she had friends. And they were right: she had to get the court case over and done with first.

Chapter 12

Justin sat in his office, staring at the pile of invoices. As much as he had to get stuck into the accounts, his mind just kept wandering off. It was no use; he had to call his mother. She'd left umpteen messages to return her calls, and he could only assume that somehow the news had reached her ears. She wasn't one for listening to the news or even buying a newspaper. Fortunately for him, he usually got away with texting every so often, or otherwise she would have discerned something was seriously wrong. However, had Justin thought about it, he would have realised that ignoring her calls would make her anxious.

He pulled out his mobile phone from the inside of his jacket pocket and stared for a while at his mother's number, before he called her. Instantly, she answered, as if she already had the phone in her hands. 'Justin!' she almost screamed.

'Mum, how are you?'

Her morning voice was gravelly. 'Where are you, Justin?'

He paused. Did she mean where was he living or where was he now?

'At work,' he decided to answer.

'Right, drop what you are doing and get here this instant!'

He'd never heard her so cross, and in all his years, she'd never put a demand on him.

'Mum, I can't just leave work.'

'Justin, you are the bloody boss. I will not take no for an answer.'

'Okay, I'll see you in an hour.'

'Good,' was all she said, before replacing the receiver.

Nervously, he tidied his desk, thinking about how he would explain the situation to his mother. It had been months now and delaying the inevitable had only made matters so much worse. His dear mother would be hurt that she was the last to know. Yet it was guilt and embarrassment that had driven him to hide it from her.

The drive was quicker than expected; he'd missed the rush hour and was able to get a clear run. Reluctantly, he pulled up outside his mum's three-bedroom semi in Lenham – a pretty house with an abundance of carefully pruned bushes that framed the meandering footpath. Normally, he would get a warm feeling as he walked towards the red-painted front door, because it was the home in which he'd grown up. Not today, though. Today, he was going to have to break the news of his complete cock-up, his life-changing mistake.

His mother had the door open before he even put the key in the lock.

Mollie stepped aside, but right away, she noticed the expression on her son's face. Her anger subsided when she saw how sad he appeared, and so her initial intention of tearing him off a strip was put on hold.

'I'll put the kettle on.'

Justin watched her waddle off in her carpet slippers and pink tabard that she rarely took off unless she was out shopping. The living room hadn't changed in ten years: the walls were still coated in magnolia paint and the beige carpet was immaculately clean. The brown Dralon three-piece suite, with throws draped neatly on the arms, was placed facing the flame-effect electric fire.

He looked up at the wooden framed photo of him and Kara on holiday. His mother had hung it above the fireplace, for all to see. He stared at it all the while she was making the tea and tried to think of the right words he would use to explain his predicament.

'Here, Son, did you want something to eat?'

He waved his hand, dismissing the idea, and then his eyes met hers, as she sat on her usual chair opposite him. At sixty-two years old, Mollie was a real mumsy woman. Her hair was kept short for ease and she wore no make-up, apart from on special occasions. Her thick frame and soft grey eyes were open and shone against her rosy cheeks. She was always wringing her hands on her apron after any chore in the house, and she eagerly fussed over her visitors, with offers of homemade food and endless cups of tea.

And then there were all the other offers before he'd had a chance to sit down. They weren't long in coming this morning. 'Shall I turn the heating up? Are you warm enough? Do you want a cushion?'

'No, Mum, no to all those. Look, I'm sorry, Mum—'

'Stop, Justin, I know what's happened because I had a visit from your old school friend, Joshua's mother, Iris. Gawd, she couldn't wait to bring the gossip to my door. She even slapped the bleedin' newspaper cutting under my nose. What was worse was, I couldn't even answer her because, Son, I am obviously the last one to know.' She stopped, to gasp for breath. 'So where is Kara now?'

Justin bowed his head. 'In prison.'

'I know that, Justin – Iris told me everything – but which prison? I can't have that poor girl inside without letting her know I'm here if she needs me. She's like a daughter to me and …' She paused, choking back the tears. 'And to think of her inside a prison. Oh my goodness, she must be …' She stopped and swallowed hard, before saying, 'And how is Joan? Have you spoken to her?'

Justin frowned. So much had happened that Joan had gone out of his head; besides, he would be the last person Kara's mum wanted to speak to right now. 'Well, Mum, no I haven't.'

'Well, she's obviously very angry because she hasn't called me or answered my calls, and we always speak once a month. She likes to hear how you two are doing. She sent me a text, months back. It's strange because she rarely sends text messages. She knows and so do you that I'm bloody useless when it comes to these new-fangled gadgets. Mind you, that's all we ever do these days, so I feel like I'm becoming a dab hand. Anyway, I managed to return the text, but I haven't heard anything since.'

Justin would usually have laughed at his mum and teased her, but not today. Mollie shuffled in her chair and looked her son over. 'So,' she sighed heavily.

Justin looked into his cup of tea and shook his head. 'I messed up, Mum, and the truth of it is, I don't even know how or why. I loved Kara—'

'Loved?' questioned Mollie.

'Um, well, I still do, but …'

She could see his bottom lip quivering.

'When Kara was away on one of her work trips, I met this woman … Lucy. I got so drunk, I didn't realise I'd had so much. I don't remember anything, and then I woke up in her bed. Stupidly, it's happened twice and …' he hesitated '… she ended up pregnant.' There, he'd said it.

'So? That doesn't mean you have to stay with her. Aw, for Christ's sake, Son, I *have* moved with the times you know. This happens all too often. I don't know if kids today know what it's like to have a mum and dad. It's all stepmum this and stepdad that.'

'Well, that may be so, but I don't want my son growing up without his father.'

Mollie's eyes widened. 'A son? How do you know?'

He waved his hand again. 'The scan picture showed it's a boy. Mum, she wants to meet you. It might be an idea to get to know her before the baby arrives. It's not that far off now.' He didn't have the exact date but he'd worked it out for himself. It was five months ago when he'd woken up in her bed.

Mollie was caught between a rock and a hard place. She loved her son more than life itself and was relieved he hadn't been hurt, but she also adored Kara, who'd always been the perfect daughter-in-law, and there was no way that this Lucy could fill Kara's shoes, not in a million years. 'Have you been to see Kara? How is she?'

'No! Of course not, so I haven't a clue!' he replied, with a sharp tongue.

'You heartless sod. If that's how you are now, then no wonder she burned the bloody house down. I would have done the same.'

Placing his cup on the coaster, Justin looked up. 'You would? What, you don't think she's a bit cuckoo?'

Mollie frowned and jolted her head as if to say, 'You what?'

'Cuckoo, no, Son. Upset, heartbroken, distraught, or devastated, yes, but cuckoo, no.' She felt her anger rise. 'And as much as I love you, Justin, I think what you've done is terrible. I'm surprised that Kara didn't run a knife through your chest, as I might have done.' She thought back to when Justin's father ran off with her former best friend, leaving her alone with a baby and debts that led to her becoming temporarily homeless. 'Jesus Christ, what is the matter with you? Oh, let me flaming well guess. This Lucy is filling your head with shit about Kara, isn't she? I know, Son, because I'm a woman and you are a sucker. I don't blame Kara for burning the place down, and as for meeting Lucy, well, no, not until I've seen my daughter-in-law.'

'Mum, she isn't your daughter-in-law.' He clammed up, knowing he'd said the wrong thing.

'Don't you dare, Justin! Kara *is* my daughter-in-law. Goodness, you lived together long enough. You had your whole lives mapped out beautifully, what with a lovely home, holidays, a wedding to plan, and children …' She stopped and swallowed down a lump in her throat. 'So, as far as I'm concerned, Kara is my daughter-in-law until the day she marries someone else.'

Those words cut Justin. There was no doubt that his despicable behaviour had led to unforeseen consequences. Kara's incarceration was testament to that. And how would he feel once she'd left prison? Would he still feel guilt, even be jealous if she had a new partner?

'Mum, I have to go. Look, Kara is in Larkview Prison. The lawyer told me, and if you want to visit, you can contact the prison. You won't need a visiting order.'

'A visiting order? What's that?'

Justin shook his head. 'It doesn't matter. Just call the prison and request a visit. They should explain how it all works, but be warned, Mum, she might not want a visit. And I'll tell Lucy that you need more time.'

Mollie shot Justin a spiteful glare. 'Well, then, I'll write to Kara, and I don't care what you tell Lucy. It's not all about her, you know. There are far more important things to worry about right now, like Kara and her mother, who, in case you have forgotten, is very poorly. She must be in a right state, worrying about her daughter rotting away in prison, and I wouldn't be surprised if all this has made the poor woman even more ill.'

Justin could feel his mother getting bitter and decided to make a swift exit. Leaving the house, angry with himself, he wondered if this day would get any worse. 'Fuck!' he said quietly, as he reached his car. Putting his seat belt on as he drove away, he felt more confused and guilty than ever. He'd heard his mum saying only recently what goes around comes around. He wondered anxiously if this was actually a prescient warning sent from on High. But he wasn't particularly religious, and he wasn't into all that psychic bullshit. 'Fuck!' he shouted. *Life could be such a bitch.*

* * *

Stuart was still pondering the issue regarding Kara's mother. He'd tried several times to make contact, but the calls were being diverted to an answerphone. He tapped on the huge oak desk and sighed. This wasn't his job, but, somehow, the look on the poor girl's face had weighed heavily on his shoulders. It was the least he could do.

Opening his notebook, he looked at the address and decided to investigate. First he should call the Australian police. He looked at the details on his computer screen. There was a records and reports department. He looked at the time on his Raymond Weil watch, a twenty-first present from his mother. Although it would be well into the evening over in Melbourne, he decided to call them anyway. A quietly spoken woman answered. After explaining the predicament to her, the officer on the other end offered to contact the patrol officer in that vicinity and have them knock at the address on their night shift.

Reading through Kara's notes in preparation for the case, it hit him she must have received a letter from Justin's lawyer because she was so specific; and yet, how puzzling that it was a different letter. How he could spin that in court was more of a concern. There simply was no evidence.

His thoughts were interrupted by the phone ringing; it was the same woman with the quiet voice. 'Hi, it's Rachael Woodstock from Victoria Police. I've just had a call in from the officers out at the lady's address and apparently her neighbour said Mrs Bannon died a month ago. I can get you more details, if you like, but I will need to go into the records.'

Stuart felt his body go cold.

'Sir ...? Are you still there?'

'Oh, yes, sorry, I'm surprised because my client said she spoke with her mother's carer a few days ago.'

'Sir, she must have that wrong because the house has been empty for some time, but I will call back with more detailed information, if you would prefer?'

Stuart's head was in a spin. 'Oh, er … yes, please. Could you e-mail me with all the details? It may be more serious.'

'No worries, sir. I am only too pleased to help.'

He gave her his e-mail address and his mobile number, and then sat back on his bespoke cream-coloured leather chair and stared up at the ceiling. *Poor Kara doesn't even know her mother is dead.*

Looking over at the photo of his own mother with her confident smile, he made up his mind to help Kara. Regardless of the fact that he had a tower of paperwork from more boring cases, he felt this situation was worthier of his time.

* * *

Jayne Williams, Stuart's secretary, rapped twice before entering. She was always full of the joys of spring and Stuart admired her. Dressed in an emerald green dress, and with her thick raven hair piled high, she placed a steaming cup of coffee onto a coaster by his telephone. 'Stuart, I have lined up three clients this morning. You have a lunch break at one o'clock and your dry cleaning is in reception. Shall I order up lunch or will you be working?'

With another heavy sigh, Stuart replied, 'No, that's fine. Um … Jayne, I know your father is a local detective. I was just wondering. Do you think he would meet me for a coffee, just to run something by him?'

Jayne frowned. 'That sounds ominous.'

He shook his head. 'No, it may be something and nothing.'

'Well, actually, my dad has retired and he's driving my mum

184

up the wall with his OCD antics. He's like that when he's bored. I'll call him and let you know.'

With a full smile, Stuart thanked her.

Literally two minutes later, she returned. 'Stuart, my dad says he can meet you today for lunch. I told you he was bored.'

'Perfect, so order in something special for two, please, Jayne.'

She smiled, winked, and then coyly giggled. He often wondered if she was flirting, but he wouldn't like to assume so, not since he'd misread the last secretary's toying and almost got himself disbarred for sexual harassment. That incident had been a right wake-up call; now, he kept his mind firmly on his work. Boring it may be, but better safe than sorry. The next woman he made advances to would have to be stripped naked and begging for it before he even brushed her lips.

The trouble was he was unhappy with his solitary life; he'd been married for all of five years when his wife decided that being a lawyer's wife was no life for her, and so she ran off with a guitar player from Manchester and that was that. Fortunately, he and his wife had no children, so the settlement was a fair fifty-fifty split, at least in her eyes, anyway. His mind wandered back to Kara and her predicament. In the cold light of day, his problems seemed like a walk in the park. He read over the statements of her upcoming case and racked his brains to find a way to get a reduced sentence, but there was nothing there except for the fact she was hormonal.

Along the deep mahogany shelves was a vast array of books all neatly lined up in order of specialism: law, company, civil, and criminal. Pushing himself away from his chair, he headed to the bookshelf. Tilting his head to the side, he read the spines, before finding what he was looking for – a book referencing trials that set a precedent with pregnant women who had committed murder.

The weighty volume had to be carefully removed from the

shelf before being placed on his desk. It was a long shot, but the fact that she was fired from her job because of her sickness and then feeling beside herself, vulnerable, and devastated, might well help the case. He hoped a female judge would be presiding, if he decided to go down the crime of passion route due to temporary insanity.

He kept the appointments with his three clients to a bare minimum, to spend more time on Kara's case.

One o'clock arrived, and he was still reading through past verdicts and trying desperately to match a similar case, when Bruce Williams knocked on his door.

Stuart looked up at the clock and realised who it was. 'Come in,' he called.

'Hi, Stuart, Bruce Williams.' Bruce's hand was firm and cool as both men greeted each other. Ten seconds. That's all it takes to appraise people and each man had made their initial assessment of the other by the time they had sat down. 'Jayne told me to just knock. I think she's going to fetch a sandwich.' Right away, Stuart could see the resemblance to Jayne. Apart from the thick mop of grey hair and rotund middle, the two of them were uncannily alike.

Stuart realised that the former detective was unusually nervous, which was uncommon in his experience when meeting professionals of his ilk.

'Thank you, Bruce. Like I said to Jayne, it's probably something and nothing, but I thought you might be able to help me.'

Sitting comfortably on the chair that was offered, Bruce leaned forward. 'A tricky case, then?'

Stuart scratched the back of his head. 'Well, no, not exactly. This young lady I'm representing has a mother in Australia, and she asked if I would contact her because she has tried on various occasions and can't get through. Now, this is where it's very strange. My client says she spoke with her mother's carer only days ago, and yet when I called the Australian police, they said

186

the mother, Joan Bannon, died a month ago, the exact date not yet confirmed.'

It was obvious from the way Bruce's hands shook that the probable reason for his nervousness was alcoholism; the rose-coloured cheeks confirmed it.

'Was she a wealthy woman?' His eyes told Stuart that Bruce was straining at the leash with interest.

'To be totally frank, I have no idea about the situation other than what I've just told you. Like I said, it's probably nothing.'

'Yes, but your gut instinct tells you otherwise, and there's a lot to be said for gut instinct. Look, Stuart, let me tell you where I'm coming from. As you know, I'm a retired detective. I left the force a year ago, and I'm thinking of becoming a private detective. I left because …'

He stopped and looked down at his hands. 'I messed up a few cases, you know. I took my eye off the ball, shall we say, and, well, the choices were early retirement or get the boot. So, I retired with a good pension and all that, but I'm bored shitless, so this will be a good little project for me to see if being a private detective suits me. I'm happy to do it for free, and if I come up trumps, then perhaps you could be my first referee, and to be frank, I'll need a professional one. Plus, it gives me the chance to test myself, you know, to see if I'm up to it.'

'That's brilliant, because to be honest, I hadn't thought through the payment side of things. I guess I was acting on impulse. It's a bad habit of mine. If it means a trip to Australia …'

Bruce waved his hands. 'No worries, and if I do find something sinister, we can hand it straight over to the police, and they can take up the expense. Anyway, I've always wanted to visit Australia.' He winked and chuckled. 'Without the wife.'

Stuart warmed to Bruce. He appreciated his honesty; it was refreshing in his line of work. With a generous smile, Stuart held out his hand, a gesture that the deal was done, and over a sandwich, the two men went through Kara's file.

Bruce felt alive and keen to get stuck in. Pottering around the garden pruning and weeding and collecting antique jewellery were not cutting the mustard.

They wrapped the discussion up, and Bruce was on his way out of the office when Stuart called him back. He had another thought.

'There's something else that's not adding up. Kara received a letter asking her to vacate the property, and apparently, it was sent from Justin Fox's solicitor. I contacted him, and he said he hadn't sent any letter.' Holding a copy, he went on, 'He did have this letter drafted up, but he is adamant he never sent it. Perhaps you could do some digging around? Again, it may be nothing.'

Bruce walked back to the desk and took the letter. Reading it there and then, he frowned. 'Maybe she has misunderstood, but again, your gut feeling can be very helpful in cases like this one.' He laughed. 'Women use it all the time, and I've never known one to be wrong.'

Stuart nodded and looked at the photo of his mother. Bruce was right. Women did usually get it right; his own mother was meticulous and very much spot-on with her instincts.

As the door closed behind the detective, Stuart sat back and sighed. Kara's court case was fast approaching, and he would stay up all night, if necessary, trawling through the books to find anything he could use to help her. It was nine o'clock, as Stuart was about to leave the office, when the phone rang. Jayne had already left for the day, and so he answered it himself and was surprised to hear Rachael's voice from Victoria Police.

'It seems I made a mistake. I've been talking with your detective, Bruce Williams, and whilst I didn't regard the situation as serious at the time, his line of questioning made me concerned. So, I looked into the death of Joan Bannon and requested her death certificate. I have it. The coroner's office has staff on call throughout the night. It appears I was wrong. Mrs Bannon didn't die a month ago, she's been dead for five months. The neighbour is in her eighties, so that's the reason for the mistake. I will e-mail over all the details we have, if it helps.'

Bruce clearly hadn't wasted any time and Stuart was impressed. The Melbourne police officer's findings were troubling. He would have to break the news to his client, something he certainly didn't relish the thought of. Kara had been in prison for more than two months now, but the mother had been dead for five months, so whoever this carer was, they'd obviously been stringing the daughter along. The thought sickened him and yet intrigued him. Who would do such a malicious thing, and more to the point, why?

He looked at his mother's photo again. If he'd been in the same situation, he would have called out the whole army to track her down. He looked at the notes and realised that Kara had been in Papua New Guinea, and then, not long after she was home, she'd ended up in prison – with no one to help her.

* * *

Justin drove home from work, with the radio on low, listening to Will Young's 'All Time Love'. Was that fate again, telling him something? His head felt like it had been through a washing machine, with so many negative thoughts running through his mind. And he was now especially concerned about the atmosphere between his mother and himself. It was never that way, yet today, it was as if they were strangers.

He had a lot to think about and his mother's words continued to whirl around inside his head. Then the image of Kara with another man churned his stomach. He felt overwhelmed by guilt that he didn't have to worry because she was locked up inside. What a pitiless thought. However, there was Lucy and their baby, his son, and their new life, which wasn't off to a good start.

So, racked with mixed emotions, he stopped the car at the end of the road and contemplated going to the pub. He debated whether to turn left or drive on and face the fact that Lucy would be upset that his mother didn't want to meet her yet. He felt for Lucy, but on the other hand, he could see his mother's point of view. She'd made it perfectly clear that she didn't think Kara was a nutjob, and, shockingly, his mother had said she would have burned the house down, had she been in Kara's shoes. He took a deep breath and sighed loudly. 'Oh, God, what do I do?' he said, looking up at the darkened skies.

There was only one thing to do and that was to face the music. He'd fucked up and now he was living with the consequences. Gingerly, he inserted the key in the door and crept inside. It was quiet and dark. He flicked on the switch and called for Lucy, but there was no answer. Thinking this was strange as she was always in, he hurriedly climbed the stairs and went into their bedroom. Lucy was sprawled across the bed, with a dressing gown hardly covering her bare back. He switched on the light, but she didn't move. Straightaway, he panicked and kneeled beside her, shaking her arm.

'Lucy!'

She murmured and tried to tug her arm away.

'Lucy, are you okay?'

She shrugged him off and mumbled incoherently. Then he smelled the alcohol. At first, he thought it was nail varnish remover. As he leaned closer to her face, he could smell the stench of stale alcohol and jumped back as if he'd discovered a rats' nest. His eyes scanned the room for the bottle, but there wasn't one, and then his gaze fell on her protruding stomach, and his anger raised its head. She was pissed and inflicting harm on their unborn son.

He spun on his heels, left the room, and headed for the kitchen. He would sober her up this minute, whether she liked it or not. In such a rage, he almost threw the nearest cup at the wall. He took a deep breath for a moment, before filling the kettle and pouring heaps of coffee into the cup, ignoring the fact that she shouldn't be drinking strong coffee whilst pregnant. Then, with a sudden movement, the anger resurged, and he punched the cabinet door. *How fucking dare she?* Instantly regretting it, he now had a throbbing hand to match a throbbing head.

* * *

Lucy tried to focus her eyes, unsure whether or not Justin had woken her up. She heard someone in the kitchen and a wave of panic gripped her. Had he realised she'd been drinking? Still wobbly and pissed, she hurried to the bathroom to clean her teeth and slap cold water on her face. He mustn't know she'd been drinking. She stared in the mirror and there was no denying it – she looked a wreck and was obviously drunk. Closing the bathroom door, she turned on the shower.

She had to straighten herself up or he would be livid; good old high morals mister perfection would be turning himself inside out. Buying all the vitamins and ensuring she was eating her vegetables seemed nice and sweet, but it was getting to be a right pain in the arse. Christ, if he knew she liked her daily drink, he would have her up at the hospital having her stomach pumped. She heard him climbing the staircase, and quickly she stepped into the shower, hoping he hadn't sussed her.

He had. 'Lucy!' he almost screamed.

As he banged hard on the bathroom door, she pretended she couldn't hear him.

In her sweetest and most upbeat voice, she called back, 'Hold on, Justin, I'm having a quick shower.' She held her breath, hoping she could hear him walking back downstairs, yet he was still outside.

'When you're done, we need to talk. There's a very strong coffee on the windowsill. I'm damn sure you fucking need it.'

Lucy felt sick. The alcohol and the shock of Justin knowing made her stomach flip over. She decided not to reply but ensure she was stone-cold sober by the time she was finished. The shock was enough to clear her head, and so by the time she climbed out of the shower and cleaned her teeth for the umpteenth time, she was ready to face him.

Wearing a fresh nightdress and her long robe, she slowly descended the stairs only to find Justin was not in. She looked out of the window and searched for his car, but he was gone. In a panic, she ran upstairs and opened the wardrobe. A sigh of relief left her lips: his clothes were there, hanging in a line.

* * *

Justin had to get out of the house and away from her. The Sydney Arms, the nearest pub, was brimming, and Justin, still in his suit, made his way to the bar. The occupants were obviously having a few drinks after work. Some workmen, still dressed in their paint-covered overalls, were at the bar chatting up the young trendy barmaid, whilst in a corner, a group of young men and women were huddled around an iPhone, looking at some video and laughing their heads off. The petite barmaid bustled her way past the landlord to serve him, her face beaming with a smile that showed her gleaming white teeth.

'What can I get ya, handsome?' she said, in such a matter-of-fact voice that Justin assumed she called everyone handsome.

'Double Jack Daniel's, please.'

'On the rocks, babe?'

He smiled back and nodded. She was refreshing really, with a cute smile that for a second took his mind off his troubles.

'There ya go. Don't drink it all once.' She chuckled, and Justin found himself laughing along. Perhaps that was what he needed, just to get away from work, his mother, and Lucy.

After a few more drinks and a bit of chit-chat with the barmaid, he felt his tense muscles relax, enabling him to switch his mind from his troubles. By now, the early evening punters had all left and it was too soon for the Friday night party-goers. He distinctly sensed someone behind him. Turning around, he saw a man dressed in a smart tan leather jacket giving him a faint smile along with a confident wink. He was standing with his legs apart and his shoulders back.

For a second, Justin thought he'd seen him before but couldn't think where until the penny dropped. The restaurant. His relaxed mood changed instantly. This was the man who had raped Lucy as a child; this was the man who was still out walking the streets and not locked behind bars.

With a few drinks inside him, Justin had the guts to confront the bastard. 'You've got some front!'

The barmaid, who was leaning on the bar and having a banter with Justin, swiftly hurried away. She knew who Carl was and didn't want any trouble.

Carl smirked. 'Dear me, I guess Lucy Lou has been filling your head with bullshit again.'

Justin didn't expect that reaction at all. It took him completely by surprise, and for a moment, he stared, appraising Carl's cold eyes.

'You no-good scumbag, they should lock you up for what you did to her.' Justin's voice remained on an even keel; he didn't want to draw attention, but he certainly wasn't going to leave the issue alone.

The tension was building, and Justin waited for Carl to either defend himself or start a fight because he didn't look the type to run away – that was for sure – and he wasn't alone. His men were now at the bar, standing just a couple of feet behind him.

Unexpectedly, Carl put his hand on Justin's shoulder and gave him a compassionate smile. 'Well, I have been called many things in my time but not scumbag, and I can see why you would have the gall to front me like that. Most men don't get away with it, but you, my friend, are different. I guess that Lucy Lou has filled your naive brain with all sorts of wonderful fantasy stories, but that's okay, 'cos as much as she's full of shit, I have a soft spot for her. So, do yourself a massive favour and take whatever she says with a pinch of salt.'

Justin was shocked and tried to digest those words, but after a few Jack Daniel's, he was struggling. He was, however, sober enough to know that if he laid into Carl, he would get a good kicking from any one of his mates or minders, whoever they were, so instead, he shot him a dirty look and said, 'Just keep away. You've damaged her enough already.'

Carl wiped his tongue over his teeth and sucked in a sharp intake of air. 'You'd better watch ya mouth because you really don't know anything about me and her. Cut the wisecracks and do some research before you start slandering my name, or, sunshine, I will ensure you eat your words.' He winked and nodded to the barmaid for a drink.

Justin felt the hot breath from Carl's followers down the back of his neck and made the astute decision to leave, to the apparent disappointment of the young barmaid. He could hear what sounded like Carl laughing and was tempted to turn back and have it out with him, but the surge of adrenaline had completely sobered his thoughts, and he left, but with the bit between his teeth and a bitter taste in his mouth.

Life had been so much simpler with Kara. It seemed to him that Lucy might be having his baby, but she came with a whole heap of trouble; although he was partly to blame. For a while, he drove around trying to digest Carl's words and the fact that he'd found Lucy zonked out, stinking of booze. The rain began to pour, and the streetlamps, mixed with the raindrops on his windscreen, were making his vision blurred and his eyes tired. There was nothing much more he could do except return home.

* * *

Lucy was sitting in her night robe, her face soft with moisturiser. She hoped she looked somewhat gentle and motherly from the glow emanating from the table lamp. She was pretending to read a mother and toddler magazine. Really, she'd bought them for show and had no intention of looking after the baby; she wanted a nanny for that.

Justin stood in the doorway to the living room, his hair wet from the rain and his eyes glassy from drink. 'We should talk.'

'Is everything okay, love? I mean, I got out of the shower and you were gone. I couldn't hear what you were saying through the bathroom door.'

He stepped inside and took a seat in the small armchair. Running his hands through his hair, he leaned forward and stared at the floor. 'Why were you drinking, Lucy? I came home, and you were out cold.' He looked up. 'Oh, yes, and fucking drunk.'

She gave her best frown. 'What? Of course I wasn't drunk. I had what's called Braxton Hicks contractions, and my stomach muscles just wouldn't loosen up. I was in agony. I mean, it was really painful. The midwife said a small glass of wine might help relax me. She said I could have a small drop at this stage of the pregnancy, as it wouldn't hurt. The truth is, Justin, I didn't like to worry you, but I haven't been sleeping well at all, and I guess it all caught up with me.'

With her tone so convincing, she could have had the Pope believing he wasn't Catholic.

'You what? The midwife actually said you can drink?' He didn't want to push it too far because what did he really know about pregnancy – zilch.

'Yeah, well, this midwife I called was old-school, really down-to-earth, and it helped no end, I can tell you. Within five minutes, the pain went away, and I was able to sleep. Oh, Justin, I must have given you an awful fright, then?'

He sighed heavily. 'Yeah, well, I guess you did.'

'Shall I cook us a nice dinner, babe? You look worn out.'

He shook his head. 'No, thank you, I, er … I went to the pub and that Carl was there. I said to stay away, and the cocky piece of shit laughed at me. I told him he'd damaged you enough, and he then said, you are, and I quote, "full of shit"'. He paused and tried to read the reaction on her face. She looked surprised, but then he noticed a dark look in her eyes and wondered if she was hurt or angry.

'He would say that, wouldn't he? No way would he ever admit what he did to me. How could he?'

Justin was torn; he wanted to believe Lucy, but Carl's words were not said in jest; it was as if there really was some meaning behind them. 'Lucy, did he really rape you when you were a kid?' He'd no sooner asked than regretted it. After all, he wasn't just questioning the incident, he was also questioning their relationship and his trust in her.

He realised he'd asked the wrong question. Putting her hands over her face, she instantly gave a deep gut-wrenching sob, rocking herself, as if he'd hurt her more deeply than he could ever have imagined. A rush of guilt enveloped him, and he hurried to her side to hug her. 'I'm so sorry, really sorry, it's just so much has messed with my mind today. Please, Lucy, forgive me. Of course, he did. I know that. I should never have asked.'

She slowly stopped the fake tears and wiped her eyes, before clearing her throat. 'It's okay, Justin, I don't expect you to believe me. No one ever does. I've had it all my life, in foster home after foster home. I was the one always taking the blame for anything that went wrong. I just want a normal life now, with us as a family. Me, you, and our little boy. Carl is a nasty person, a dangerous person, and he will try to find a way to ruin it for me. Please, Justin, don't be taken in by him. Don't let him mess things up for us.'

He pulled her close and stroked her hair. 'No, love, I won't let him ruin things for us. I won't let anyone.'

She lay with her head against his chest and smiled. 'I think the baby is playing football in there.' She pulled his hand over her stomach, so that he could feel the baby move.

An unexpected feeling gripped him. This was his baby; his son was real. Before, it had just been a bump, but now it was a person moving. With overwhelming excitement, he made a decision. Usually, Justin was cautious, and yet, he was about to make the most impulsive gesture of his life. Out it came.

'Let's get married.'

Lucy sat up straight, gobsmacked. 'Oh my God! Do you mean it, really?' With her face glowing with excitement, she searched his face for any hint of this being a joke. To Justin, her eyes held an innocence that was so attractive.

'Yes, I mean it – nothing lavish, just me and you, and a nice meal afterwards, or did you want the whole kit and caboodle?'

'No, no, just me, you, and our little one, that's all we need … When were you thinking?'

He hadn't thought that far. 'Um … well, why don't you get on that laptop of yours and see what you can find? We could even go abroad and get married on the beach, if you like?'

Her eyes widened. 'No, I think here is just fine. I'll get on to it now.' She tried to pull away to get the wedding booked before he could change his mind, but he stopped her. 'No, not now, do it tomorrow, while I'm at work. Surprise me, when I get home.'

She gave him a coy smile, which enhanced her ingenuous look. 'Oh, it will be wonderful, and our little lad won't be born out of wedlock. It's perfect, Justin, just perfect.'

She laid her head back against his chest and smiled.

What a clever girl I am, she thought.

Chapter 13

Kara went over in her head everything she'd told Stuart and wondered if she'd left anything out. Her body shuddered when she thought about her mother, and to make her sleep more restless, the baby had been kicking all night. Her stress levels were going through the roof, and the thought of getting a long sentence and then having to hand over her baby just didn't bear thinking about. For the next three days, she walked around in a trance, with the world on her shoulders. Vic and Deni tried to cheer her up, but their efforts were in vain.

By Thursday morning, she was exhausted, but she had to get her thoughts in order because she was expecting a visit from Stuart, and she hoped that he'd managed to make contact with the carer and would arrive armed with some news.

Julie yawned and stretched. 'Cor, blimey, I slept like a bleedin' baby. How are ya doing, mate?'

Kara was sitting upright, her mind an unassembled jigsaw of questions and worries. 'I'm all right. I'm seeing Stuart in an hour, so I'd best get sorted out.'

Feeling helpless, Julie watched as her cellmate slowly sauntered away. There was nothing any of them could do except be there if Kara needed a shoulder to cry on.

* * *

As George entered the laundry room, he waved his hands to clear the steam and turned to the first inmate. 'Where's Denise?'

'I'll get her – she's loading the sheets around the back, Gov.' The woman hurried away, clearly realising George looked flustered.

George nodded and waited outside. He was hot under the collar anyway and all this steam was working him up into a state. In a few seconds, Deni appeared, wiping her hands down her tracksuit. She eyed him warily. 'Everything all right, Gov?'

He shook his head. 'Come with me, Denise.' She was one of the few he called by her first name; it was all about respect with someone of Deni's stature at Larkview.

'Aw, fuck me, what 'ave I gone and done now?'

He tapped her shoulder. 'Nothing, Denise. I need your help.' He continued to walk on with Deni hurrying to keep up. 'What's going on, Gov?'

He stopped and looked up and down the corridor. 'Kara's lawyer has just told me some disturbing news, and, in a few minutes, he is going to have to break it to the poor woman. I want you on hand to help her. She could do with a real friend right now, and you are probably best to deal with this kind of thing since you are used to …' He stopped and tried to backtrack.

'It's all right, Gov, I know what you mean. I ran a brothel, so I had many a girl crying on me lap.'

He inhaled a fast gasp of air. 'Exactly. Sorry, Denise, I wasn't judging you. I just thought, well, yes, I guess that's exactly what I thought.'

She gave him a big smile and nodded. 'Ya know, of all the staff here, Gov, you're the only one who doesn't judge us. Besides, I can't get away from what I was, and that's that, so, of course, I will be there for the kid. She don't belong in 'ere, ya know.'

He nodded and sighed. 'I know, Denise, I know.'

'So, what's the bad news? Is it her mum?'

'Sadly, yes, but that's confidential, okay?'

'Oh, no, the poor little cow. As if she ain't been through enough. Right, no worries, Gov. You leave her to me, love her heart.' Deni swallowed the lump in her throat and blinked back the tears.

* * *

Just outside the legal visiting room was a waiting area. George nodded for Deni to take a seat. 'Would you like a cup of tea, Denise? I'm going to fetch one for her and her lawyer.'

Deni sat on the plastic chair screwed to the wall and nodded shyly; it was all a bit strange. The assistant governor putting himself out in such a way, fussing over tea, this wasn't the norm. She took a deep breath and then frowned to herself; there was more to all of this. She had known many an inmate to get bad news, but they just got on with it; never did someone like George make tea – well, not like this. She waited with bated breath, her mind an assortment of fears.

* * *

Inside the visiting room, Kara sat anxiously, eager to hear the news, but Stuart was quiet whilst he pulled a pile of papers from his briefcase. She searched his face for some answers. On his arrival, she'd straightaway sensed something was wrong. He looked downcast and struggled to make eye contact. He'd asked how she was feeling, and if the staff and the inmates were treating her well, but it felt a bit like the calm before the storm.

She couldn't bear it any longer. 'Did you contact my mother?' she blurted out, now irritated that he was silently fiddling with paperwork.

With that, he looked up and placed his hands on the table, away from the folder. 'Kara, I have some dreadful news, and I'm not sure how to tell you, but I guess I should be frank.' He paused and looked at her frightened eyes. 'Your mother passed away. I am so sorry.' He paused again, waiting for her to absorb the information before he revealed any more of his findings.

Her face was like a stone statue. He remembered watching the implosion of the Hackney Downs tower blocks where his grandmother once lived. That complete destruction took seconds to happen from the moment the detonation took place. Here, in this room, Stuart had regrettably provided the detonation himself, so he was dreading the effect it would have on his client after the news registered. And then it happened.

At first there was stunned disbelief across her face, but seconds later, there was a barrage of questions all tripping over themselves. 'How did she die? Was she alone? What did the coroner say?' Her expression showed she was desperate for facts.

Stuart looked at the papers, conscious that in among them was a copy of the death certificate dated five months ago. *How was he going to tell her?* But he couldn't save her from the pain because she had every right to know the truth.

A knock at the door came as a temporary relief. George entered, holding two mugs by the handles whilst manoeuvring the door with his foot. Stuart got up from his seat to help. 'Here you go, two teas.' He glanced at Kara's face, now flooded with silent tears. He gave her a sympathetic smile. 'I'm sorry, love. When you've finished in here, Denise is outside. Would you like her to join you?'

She looked up at George and frowned. 'Denise?'

'Deni.' He corrected himself.

She nodded, but really, she wasn't listening; she wanted answers.

George left and Stuart coughed delicately, bringing Kara out of her vacant and confused state.

'Kara, I need to tell you something more, and I'm afraid it's further bad news.' He placed his hands together on the table and waited for her to acknowledge what he'd just said. Slowly, she lifted her head, waiting to hear what he had to say. What could be worse than what she'd just heard? He'd just said her mother was dead. Her heart pounded so fast, she could feel her whole body rhythmically pulsating and her neck burning up.

'It appears, from talking to the Australian police, that your mother died five months ago.'

'No! That's not possible! You must have the wrong person because I spoke with her recently.'

'Did you actually speak with her, though? I mean, verbally?'

Kara stared into space. 'I, um … I mean, we texted each other a lot, and I spoke with her carer only a few days ago. She said my mother was very sick, but I didn't speak with her in, let me think … Oh, Jesus, it must have been months ago. I was in Papua New Guinea, working, and she texted me to say she was unwell, but she had this carer, and so I was not to worry. The lady, I think her name is Lucille, was taking good care of her. I never thought my mother was so ill. My God, I would have flown over to see her. I would have called more often, I would have … I don't know, but hang on, it has to be wrong because her carer said—'

Stuart intervened. He could see she was struggling to hold it together. 'Kara, I'm so sorry, love, but I have a copy of her death certificate, which confirms she died five months ago. It concerned me enough to employ a private detective. I hope that's what you would have wanted, under the circumstances?'

An unexpected vibration filled her limbs and she found herself shaking uncontrollably. She grabbed her mug of tea, but her hands trembled so much the contents spilled over the side.

'A detective?'

Stuart was concerned. Kara's face was drained, and a deathly grey shadowed her; her body was quivering so much, she almost looked as if she was having a fit. He said no more but jumped up and opened the door. Unsure what to do, he looked over at

Deni, sitting outside. He didn't have to say a word; she was up off her seat and in the room, just in time to catch Kara before she fainted. Holding her in her arms, Deni lowered Kara onto the floor.

Stuart watched in horror as she lay unconscious. Deni pulled Kara's hair away from her face and stroked her cheek. 'There, there, my girl, come on, wake up.' Kara's eyes were blinking, and she slowly opened them.

'It's all right, lovey, Aunty Deni is here. I will look after you.'

Stuart looked at the middle-aged woman and at the hardness on her face, the rough skin, and the messy hair, with scars a testament to a life most people in his world couldn't comprehend. He listened to the East End accent, which was somewhat soothing in the circumstances, rather like his own late mother's. Deni was like an angel herself right now. He'd been concerned when he'd first met Kara because she was so well spoken and almost fragile. What her life would be like in a prison with the hardest of women worried him.

However, for sure, she would get sympathy and she had a good mate in Deni. He was aware from talking to colleagues that the truth behind the walls, when serious shit hits the fan, was that female inmates still had their natural instinct to care and nurture, so inevitably they would pull together. He kneeled down next to Deni and had the urge to stroke her shoulder and thank her. They both helped to get Kara back onto the chair. Then Stuart dragged his own next to Kara's for Deni to take a seat. 'I think it's better if you stay here with us. Do you mind?' he asked her.

Deni gratefully smiled and sat next to Kara with her arm around her shoulders. As soon as Stuart was out of the room to find another chair, Deni pulled Kara closer. 'Listen, babe, try and hold it together while your brief is here because you need to listen. I'm here for you, and you can cry on my shoulder when we get back to the cell. But, trust me, darling, we need to concentrate on what he says.'

Kara took a deep breath and tried to pull herself together. She ran her hands over her bump and nodded. 'Yes, Deni, I will. I'm determined to fight now to get out of here. I just cannot believe that my mother is dead. He said she died months ago. Nothing makes sense.'

Deni wiggled herself around in her chair to face Kara directly. 'Let's just see when he comes back. Do you want me to stay with you?'

Kara grabbed her hand. 'Yes, please.'

Stuart returned with George who was looking somewhat flustered. 'Are you okay, Kara?'

Kara smiled at George with a gentle crease of her lips. 'Yes, I just had a fright. It was the shock, I suppose, but thank you, and, er … can Deni stay with me?'

'Of course.' With that, he slipped away and left them to it.

Stuart retrieved the copy of the death certificate and placed it in front of Kara, so she could see it for herself. There was no denying it; her mother had died months ago.

'But, I just don't understand. The carer said – well, actually, I can't exactly remember what she said. The conversation was kind of eerie, as if she was laughing at me. I may have misheard or been stressed out at the time, but she certainly did not tell me that my mother had passed away.'

'Yes, well, that's why I have this chap Bruce Williams, an ex-detective, on the case because although she hasn't broken the law, there may be more to all of this, unless, and I hate to say it, this carer was just a vile woman.'

Kara's eyes widened. 'Oh my God, a vile woman has been caring for my mother? Well, are the police tracking her down? I mean, if she keeps calling me or answering my mother's phone, could she not have had something to do with her death? What if she killed her?'

'Well, I can't truthfully answer that, but the death certificate says hepatitis and enlargement of the liver due to several possible factors, one being the fact that a large quantity of her own pain-killers may have been ingested. However, considering your mother was very poorly and on various medications the coroner didn't rule out suicide in his notes.'

'Was a note left for me? What did the coroner say was in her system?'

He shook his head. 'In answer to your first question, apparently not. All the Australian police could discover was that she was found dead in her bed. But regarding what was in her system, the post-mortem showed that she had taken a possible overdose of the medicine prescribed by her own doctor. She was on high doses of drugs, although the report was not one hundred per cent conclusive. However, the probability of having taken an overdose outweighed the other potential causes. I know this is very harsh for you to hear, but they had no information regarding any family, so she was cremated a week later. Apparently, the little funds she did have were used for her funeral.'

'None of this makes any sense whatsoever. I know my mother used the proceeds from the sale of her house to go to Australia, but she could never have spent it all in the time she lived there. She wasn't an extravagant woman. This carer, do you know any more about her? Maybe you should have her investigated because although she seemed genuine to me, it could all be an act. Does anyone actually know this woman?'

Stuart was relieved that Kara was now on the ball. Her eyes were alert, and he could sense she was not going to wallow in self-pity but was determined to find out the truth. 'Kara, all I can offer you right now is my word that I will do everything in my power to get to the bottom of this, because like you, I feel that something stinks. However, for now, we need to go over the details of the court case and try to get you a reduced sentence. I need your company's details, including your manager's name.'

Kara frowned. 'Why?'

With a deep grin, he replied, 'Because I think we should go

down the route of diminished responsibility. You were pregnant and hormonal, and this, Kara, may well be your get-out clause. Of course, I cannot promise you anything, but I will do everything I can to get the maximum penalty reduced.' He then looked across at the older woman and smiled. 'It seems to me, Kara, you have a good support network, so I suggest you try to remember everything you can about how you felt leading up to the fire, every little detail. I want you on that stand with the jury in tears.'

Deni chuckled. 'Well, best we get you some acting lessons, kiddo, eh?' She rubbed Kara's back. Most of that conversation had gone right over Deni's head because she'd no idea about medical stuff. Still, she did know about courtroom antics – she'd taken part in many herself – and so she could at least help Kara with that side of things.

'I know this is a particularly tough time for you, but please, Kara, try to remain focused and leave the business regarding your mother to me. I will do all I can to help.'

Kara stood up to shake his hand. He nodded to Deni and was gone.

After a moment, Deni tried to make light of the dreadful situation. She nudged Kara's arm. 'Cor, he's a right nice bit of stuff, and he has a soft eye for you, babe.'

'He is very nice, Deni, and I just pray that he can get me off. I cannot bear the thought of anyone else bringing up my baby, and I really don't want Justin having her, not when he's with some woman I've never even met.' She broke off, near to tears again. Her mind cast back to the eerie conversation where the carer implied she was Justin's girlfriend. Perhaps she should have mentioned it. Nevertheless, she hoped that Stuart would take this carer's odd behaviour seriously.

'Come on, let's get back on the wing and have a nice hot chocolate, eh?' Deni realised that Kara was focusing her mind on the baby, as if the news about her mother had never happened. It was perhaps not such a bad thing. Kara needed to stay strong, and if blocking her mother's death from her mind helped, then so be it.

* * *

Lucy clapped her hands together. The registry office was booked, and they didn't have to wait long. The big day was set for a weekday – *who gets married on a weekday?* She then looked at the brochure of the cottage in the Cotswolds – an ideal retreat away from it all. She had to make this work because all she wanted was that heavenly life that Joan had banged on about – her daughter and future son-in-law had had this blissful life, in a perfect world, so far removed from her own miserable existence. She'd been sick to death of the conversations with Joan, and her tolerance of what she'd discovered had turned to hate, and then the hate had turned to jealousy, and she'd wanted what Kara had so much that she would do everything in her power to have it.

So far, her plan was in place, and as long as Justin didn't change his mind, they would be saying 'I do' in less than a week. She searched the internet for an exquisite wedding dress and shoes to go with it. There would be no bridesmaid; after all, she didn't collect friends, she used them and ditched them. There was no time for niceties in her world. How could she be that woman with friends who do lunch or coffee mornings, sharing gossip or cake recipes? Her life had been too real and hard for all that silly girlie stuff. Her baby kicked, and she flared her nostrils; that was another issue she wasn't prepared for – motherhood – but she would find a way around that little annoyance.

With a click of a button, the long white princess-cut dress was ordered along with the crystal-embellished shoes to match. Lucy was in seventh heaven. She hurriedly pulled her mobile from her pocket and called Justin's number – he answered within a second. 'Well, my darling, I have managed to book the registry office.

There was a cancellation – how lucky was that?' Her voice was upbeat and full of enthusiasm.

Justin was staring at the paperwork that had piled up and the ten cars all ready to be collected by their owners. It was a huge deal for him. Most car dealerships did a big push to sell their stock at the end of March to boost their sales at the close of the tax year. But the last few months had steered him off course and he was now having to play catch-up. He'd realised that all the excitement of feeling his baby move had led him to act impulsively. 'Um, that was quick, Lucy. When is it?'

'Next week on Thursday at Bromley Registry Office and then a week in the Cotswolds, just you, me, and the bump. It looks beautiful and so relaxing and peaceful. I thought you would love it.' She was rambling on and on and all Justin could do was listen with his silent sighs.

'I've ordered the dress, but I haven't done anything about your suit because I don't know your exact measurements. Mind you, babe, you have a beautiful grey suit hanging in the wardrobe. I can buy a red tie to go with my red rose bouquet. It's going to be so special. I can book a fancy restaurant for afterwards. I was thinking of a short ride, maybe in a vintage car, to a romantic country restaurant. Oh, and—'

He cut her short. 'Lucy, can you talk to me about it when I get home? Only, I have customers I need to see to.'

'Oh, um, okay. We can talk then. I can show you all the pictures of the cottage but obviously not my dress because that's bad luck before the wedding.'

He hung up, without saying goodbye. The impetuous act of yesterday was now coming back to haunt him, and it was dragging him down. He had to face facts; he'd said they should get married, and she'd taken him at his word, so he only had himself to blame.

* * *

Vic was well on the way to a full recovery. She joined Kara and Deni for a natter. Julie was being much sweeter and had ditched her often sarcastic comments, partly through empathy and partly because she was told to be good to Kara or Deni would scalp her.

'Only a few days now and it will be ya big day. Me brother's sent you in a nice bit of clobber. I gave him your size, and bless him, he has an eye for a smart outfit. Let's hope it all fits.' Vic smiled, itching to brighten Kara's day.

'Really? Oh my goodness, how kind of you and of him. He doesn't even know me ...' She paused and looked at the eyes staring back. 'You know, I never in my wildest dreams believed I would experience kindness from women who I was once so very afraid of.' She looked at Julie and smiled and then she turned back to face Vic. 'I used to look at the estate and shudder. I imagined all sorts – violence, aggression, and a cold existence – but now, when I think back, it was my world living in that big house that was probably the coldest. I mean, I never even knew my neighbour very well, and to think the women I really feared are the ones who have helped me the most. I think I get it now. You are tough and hard with each other, but when it really counts, you all stick together.'

Deni gave her something to think about. 'When you have fuck-all, my babe, you tend to share what you do have, 'cos ya know how hard it is to go without. You're all in the same boat, and it's the state that becomes the enemy, not each other.'

Vic laughed and nudged Julie. 'Yeah, remember when old man Jake nicked that Sainsbury's lorry and drove it straight into the estate? Fuck me, once those back doors were open, the boxes were unloaded and shared out before the police even got a call. That was hilarious. Everyone on the estate had fucking sirloin steaks and bottles of champagne and no one went hungry for months. Poor old Jake got three months, but when he got outta prison, we all put on a big party for him in the square with steaks and burgers on the barbecue. That was a night to remember, eh, Jue!' She was laughing so much her face went red.

Julie was joining in. 'Yeah, my Billy even siphoned all the diesel out of the truck. We had enough juice to take us down to the coast for the day. He weren't happy that I had six kids join us, but that was a lovely day. Remember, Vic, we had a convoy down to Margate. There must have been thirty of us. Those poor holidaymakers must have wondered what hit them, with Billy's ghetto blaster on the beach and ol' Sharon getting everyone up dancing. Little Tommy Sutton fucking insisted we brought the crabs back with us. He wanted to keep them in the bath. Cor, yeah, that was a laugh and a half. We all came back with our hair sticky from candy floss, sunburned shoulders, and fucking sand in our knickers.'

Kara listened and understood. They tried to make the most out of life with the little they had. Whereas she could have gone anywhere in the world and enjoyed a five-star hotel with cocktails on the beach if she wanted, they seemed perfectly happy with a trip to Margate. What struck her the most was they shared everything: the diesel, the food, the fun, and, most importantly, each other's company.

Julie was still laughing. ''Ere, ya know what? When we all get outta this shit-hole, we should save up, hire a minibus, and have ourselves a day on the beach. You with your new baby, my little 'un, and whoever else wants to join us … Seriously, Posh, you will love Margate. It's got a sandy beach and everything.'

Kara chuckled. 'I think I will, Jue, so it's a deal. When we all get out, we'll meet up and arrange it.'

There was a long silence as reality hit them all; it would be years before they were out of stir all together again, and Kara could be the last one out, if she got a five-stretch. Deni was due out in two years, Vic in a year, and Julie in probably six months or less.

'I should send your brother a thank-you card. I'm very

grateful. I guess, standing in the dock dressed in this won't look too good.'

'Me brother's beholden to you. He knows ya saved me life. He's got a heart of gold considering ...' said Vic.

Deni nodded. 'Yep, he has, but you wouldn't want to mug him off, that's for sure.'

Kara turned her head. 'Oh, do you know him, too, Deni?'

'Who don't? Yeah, he's, shall we say, in the same line of work as I was.'

Kara frowned. 'What, he runs a ...?' She didn't like to say what Deni had done for a living.

'No, well not exactly, but he sees the girls are all right. He took over, when I got locked up. The girls love him, don't they, Vic?'

She nodded, with a proud expression on her face. 'Me brother's a looker, and no mistake, but he's also a naughty boy. Done well for himself, though. He already owns a little club. I'd like to say it's all above board but that would be stretching it.'

Kara tried to stop the gasp, but it escaped anyway. 'Sorry, I didn't mean to sound so shocked, but it's all a different world to me.'

'Why don't you meet him? He's coming to visit me, and he can ask for a double visit, as you're on remand. It will get you outta this place for a couple of hours. What do you say? And yes, he is a bit of eye candy.'

Before Kara even had time to think, she agreed. Her world was becoming weirder by the minute, but what did she have to lose? A visit from a handsome stranger might lift her desolate spirits. The girls had so far been a godsend. They'd made sure she was never alone and they were always ready with a shoulder to cry on. Kara wished she could be more open with the girls as they were with her, but the details of her childhood were too sickening to divulge. And as much as she trusted them, she could never fully put her faith in anyone again. Justin had made sure of that – when he slept with another woman.

Chapter 14

Kara looked at her face and blinked furiously; the puffiness from endless crying was still there. She splashed cold water on her cheeks and took a deep breath. Her hair was in a bun and so she pulled the band away and let it fall messily around her face. It had grown extensively in the last two months.

'Are you ready, kiddo?' called Vic, leaning on the doorframe.

'Yeah, all ready. I feel a bit silly, really. I don't even know your brother,' she said, skipping alongside Vic.

'Well, it gets you outta here, a change of scenery, and plus, he can buy all the chocolate and cakes you fancy from the tuck shop.'

Kara's face lit up. She'd been craving anything sweet; her mouth watered, just thinking about it.

The girls gathered in the search room, each ready to have their name called, and all very excited, as it was the highlight of their week or month, depending on whether they had used up all their entitled visiting orders.

Barbara was calling the names with her nose in the air. She glared menacingly at Kara. 'I'm not sure you're on the list, Bannon.'

Vic pushed past Kara and unexpectedly ripped the clipboard from Barbara's hand, pointing to Kara's name before Barbara could snatch it back. 'There, ya blind bitch.'

Barbara gave a snort and a huff and nodded for them both to go in. Kara followed, not having been inside the visiting room before. It was bright and quite cheery compared to the wing. Visitors were sitting on the edge of their chairs, giving oversized smiles, and children were hugging their imprisoned mothers. It was a lot for Kara to take in all at once, but she did so, following Vic, until she stopped by a table where a very handsome man jumped up and greeted them. 'How ya doing, Sis?' He let her go and put his arms out to hug Kara, who was now frozen to the spot. With his arms around her, he whispered, 'Vic's angel.'

She felt her body stiffen but she gently hugged him back. The smell of his classy aftershave impressed her, and then she looked into his eyes, his big grey eyes, lined with black lashes. She felt herself redden and shied away.

'So, this big hunk of a man is me brother Rocky.'

'Right, girls, while that queue is low, I'll grab us some bits.' Kara nodded but hung on to his deep gravelly voice and those intense eyes.

Vic turned to face Kara. 'It's all right, Posh, he don't bite. He's all right, ya know.'

He returned, trying to balance a tray overflowing with all sorts of treats, including the huge iced buns. 'I bought two, one for you, sweetness, and one for the baby.'

As Vic went on about her parole hearing, Kara helped herself to the bun. She couldn't take her eyes off it, heavily topped with thick icing, and juicy raisins in the middle. She savoured every bite, allowing the sugary topping to melt in her mouth.

Rocky looked at Kara out of the corner of his eye. He smiled, and Vic turned to see what he was grinning at, only to find Kara in a world of her own, thoroughly enjoying the cake. 'Aw, bless her, she's craving sugar, eating all our chocolate rations, she is.'

Kara stopped and chuckled. 'Oh, yes, sorry.'

'Me skin and blister tells me you saved her life, and, well, I'm glad I've got to meet ya, because, my sweetness, Vic 'ere means a lot to me.'

Kara waved her hand. 'I only helped.'

He stared for a moment, and a full smile crossed his mouth, before he winked slowly, causing Kara to blush once more. Her heart rate climbed a notch, and she felt an attraction, but then again, she was locked away with women. It was probably just the fact that he was a handsome man, there was no denying it, and that he'd given her a smouldering wink.

'So, Kara, now that's a pretty name. Vic told me you burned your home down.'

Kara nodded, and the smile left her face. 'Yes, I did, and it looks as though I will have to face my fate next week. I can only hope they don't throw away the key.'

He unexpectedly reached for her hand. 'I can't do much for you whilst you're in here, but ...' he looked at his sister and smiled '... I've just got meself well and truly on the straight and narrow, and I have a flat you can have. It ain't much, but it'll help you to get back on ya feet with ya baby.'

Kara's eyes were wide; she never imagined in her wildest dreams that anyone would offer her a flat. She assumed she would end up in a hostel on some endless council waiting list. Then she had an uneasy feeling. What would he want from her? 'Um, that's very kind of you, but I'll be fine, honestly. Besides, I think your other sister Julie might be needing that.'

Vic threw her head back and laughed. She guessed right away what Kara was thinking, just by the sheer panic written on her face. Rocky, though, was bemused. 'What's so funny?'

'Oh dear.' She chuckled, trying to get her breath. 'Kara knows you looked after Deni's girls and we told her you are a bit of a naughty boy.'

Rocky gave Kara another wink. 'Treacle, that's a world I live in, not you. The flat was just to help ya out. Ya see, me big sis, 'ere, never asks nuffin from me, so when she does, I'm all ears and will help if I can. 'Cos, sweetness, my Vic brought me up and made sure I was looked after, and so I'm returning the favour, that's all.' His voice oozed conviction, and once again, Kara blushed.

'I'm sorry. As you say, this is a world very different from the one I'm used to. Please forgive me.'

Rocky soaked in her innocence. She was unwittingly playing with his emotions, and he had to remove his gaze and look back at Vic. 'As for Julie, well, the day she decides to ditch that fat bastard Billy is the day she can have her own place, but I won't help her. I've done it too many times. All she does is go running back to him. Talking of which, our Sharon is playing the incident down. She don't want Jue inside.'

Kara picked up the other bun and devoured it in minutes, unaware that Rocky was casually watching her. Vic noticed, though, and raised her eyebrow; he responded, with one of his infamous winks.

Kara listened to their conversation and soon realised that Rocky was as Vic said, a bit of a bad boy. He'd all sorts of scams running, and although Kara was whiter than white except for the fire, she felt somewhat excited. It was also very apparent that he looked to Vic for advice; they shared a very close bond that Kara admired, and she wished that she'd had a brother. She lowered her eyes and swallowed hard. She had no one, except for her unborn baby and these new villainous friends.

Rocky noticed her downturned expression, and as if she were his girlfriend, he reached across and grabbed her hand. ''Ere, sweetness, what's the matter?' His face was so full of concern.

His eyes drew her in, and she allowed him to hold her hand. 'Nothing, I just wished in some ways I had a family like you have.'

She realised she sounded pathetic and tried to laugh it off, but Rocky grabbed her other hand. 'Well, Vic tells me you *are* like family. Besides, having a doctor in the family can only be a bleedin' good thing.'

Vic placed her arm around Kara's shoulders. 'Course you're our family. I thought you'd have guessed that, by now.'

'Oh no, sorry, I don't mean to sound ungrateful. It's just, when we all get out of here, you will go your way, and me, well, I'll go somewhere and …'

Vic hugged her closely. 'Nah, Kara, you're special to me, mate, and as for Deni, the silly ol' gal, she thinks she's ya adoptive muvver.'

'See, treacle, we don't drop people like hot bricks. Anyway, you just remember, you have a place as soon as you get out, and Rocky will look out for ya. Any good at bookkeeping?'

Kara knitted her brows. 'Er, I can use spreadsheets.'

'Good, 'cos I will have a job for you too. I'm getting a right bashing from the taxman, so I need to keep me books up to date, now I'm sort of going straight.'

Vic laughed and slapped his arm. 'Get on with ya, you straight – and bears don't shit in the woods.'

'No, seriously, Sis, I've got the club all above board. It has to be, 'cos the poxy taxman drinks in there, the cheeky fucker. So, are ya up for it, then, Kara?'

She nodded enthusiastically. 'Gosh, how can I thank you?'

He winked again and replied in a very seductive tone, 'By letting me visit you again and giving you a little peck on the lips, should do it.'

Kara's heart was beating faster again. Kissing this gorgeous man was not such a bad idea; in fact, she quite liked the thought of it.

'If I'm not mistaken, Rocky, I would say you have a little crush on our Kara.' Vic laughed.

He leaned back on his chair and ran his hand through his thick mop of black hair. 'Who wouldn't? She is beautiful.' He grinned in Kara's direction. He meant it. To him Kara was a breath of fresh air, a natural beauty, with such innocence and sweetness about her. He was pleased that his sister saw fit to look out for the girl or she would never survive inside.

As the visit came to an end, Rocky hugged his sister and then put out his arms to hold Kara. She didn't resist or stiffen up; instead, she gently hugged him back, the embrace being a little longer than she expected, but she wasn't going to complain. The sweet aftershave and the warm breath on her neck gave her butterflies, and as he gently pulled away, he stared into her eyes, and for a second, she really did want to kiss him.

Vic nodded to him and waltzed away, but Rocky was still holding both of Kara's arms; he wasn't ready for her to follow. Barbara, the officer by the door, called out to tell everyone visiting was over, but it was as if there was a magnet clamping Kara and Rocky together. She didn't want to read too much into it; even so, his eyes bored into hers, as if the two of them were meant for each other. He rubbed her nose with his, and then, as her heart beat faster, he brushed his lips against hers. She didn't move but her breathing quickened.

He could clearly feel her getting nervous and wasted no time in pulling her closer and giving her a long passionate kiss. The officer screamed, and as Kara reluctantly pulled away, she realised they were the only ones left.

He looked over at the prison officer and grinned, mumbling under his breath, 'She's got a face like a smacked arse, ol' fucking vinegar tits, the jealous bitch.' Kara nervously giggled.

'I'll see you soon, sweetness, if you want me to?'

Her cheeks were pink, and her eyes lit up. Shyly, she nodded.

As she was escorted away, Kara waved back at him. He responded by giving her a last sexy wink and left, feeling upbeat and yet blown away. Vic had said that Kara was a lovely person, although she didn't add that she possessed such natural beauty and was so fresh and untainted. Once outside, he headed to his latest top-of-the-range car. He sat inside, staring out of the window, his thoughts all over the place. Kara had really knocked him sideways; he'd had a fair few women in his time, but he just couldn't get Kara off his mind.

A deep sigh left his mouth. What was he thinking? She could be inside for several years and was expecting a baby. He had no time for kids and never even contemplated having any. He laughed out loud. It was ludicrous; he'd only met the girl once, and she was a doctor, all posh and clean, not forgetting the fact that she was up the duff. As he pulled away, he tried to clear the image of her out of his mind, but that was proving to be quite difficult.

* * *

Kara walked back to her cell with a fixed grin on her face. Vic was already there with Deni; they both smiled with raised eyebrows when she arrived.

'Well, fuck me, he didn't eat you, then?'

Kara looked at Vic with a puzzled expression. 'What?'

'I saw you two. I thought he was fucking eating ya face.' She turned to Deni. 'I've never known an attraction like it. Me brother was salivating over her.' She laughed again. 'And you, kiddo, you can't tell me ya didn't fancy the fucking pants off him. I felt like a bleedin' gooseberry.'

'Well, no matter, it's put some colour in her cheeks and a smile back on her face,' said Deni.

Plonking herself on the bed, Kara blushed. 'He is gorgeous, and it was a lovely kiss.' She raised a cocky eyebrow. 'And, you are right, it has put a smile on my face. Gosh, I feel all giddy and silly, but, yes, Deni, he was very flattering, and after being stuck in here all day, every day, he has lifted my spirits. I can't deny it.'

Vic's face took on a serious expression. 'I've known me brother all his life, and I've never seen him like that. He's usually cold with people he doesn't know. I mean, he's never really shown a lot of public affection.'

Kara could feel her butterflies back again; at least she had something to take her mind off the awful situation of the court case and the possibility of having to give up her baby. Then her smile turned to a solemn pout. What was she thinking? Her mother's death should have been at the forefront of her mind, and here she was, acting like a kid and snatching a minute of excitement with a stranger.

* * *

The morning arrived. It was bleak for April, and a chill in the air made Lucy curse. Her dress was beautiful, but with her arms bare as well as her neckline, she was freezing.

Justin was fiddling with his red tie and not in the best of moods. He looked in the mirror and noticed the few grey strands of hair and the bags under his eyes. He stepped back and looked himself up and down. The weight had fallen off him and his trousers were loose. He took a deep breath and looked again at his own sorrowful expression. He knew he was a wimp, but whether it was because he was going along with the wedding arrangements to make his relationship with Lucy more manageable, or he just wanted an easy life was debatable.

He shuddered. It didn't matter either way now. Kara would never have him back, and there was his and Lucy's little baby to think of. That's really what was keeping him going.

'The car's here, love,' Lucy called up the stairs.

He was halfway down the stairs when he stopped abruptly at the sight of her: he had to admit to himself she did look beautiful. Her hair was piled up like a Grecian goddess and she only wore a small amount of make-up. As the light poured in through the hallway window, it struck her face and she looked angelic. She smiled sweetly and lowered her gaze, as if she really was a virgin bride.

He held her hand, as they walked down the steps to the awaiting chauffeur. The Bentley was white with a red ribbon tied in a V across the bonnet. She tottered along, careful not to crease her dress, and placed her neat small posy of red roses in the footwell.

'Oh, Justin, I cannot wait, and to think our baby will not be born out of wedlock.' She knew throwing that nugget in again would lighten his mood. For him, it was all about that fucking moral code. In matters of honesty and sincerity, they were worlds apart.

'You look beautiful.'

She tried her best to look the shy, apprehensive bride.

He turned away and looked out of the window. A sick feeling gripped him. But his thoughts were interrupted by the postman, a friendly chap who always had time for pleasantries, and who was now tapping on the window, just before they drove away. Justin smiled and before Lucy could stop him, he jumped out. The postman handed him a letter, waved, smiled at Lucy, and went on his way. Justin climbed back into the car and laughed. 'Ahh, the postie just offered his congratulations.'

Lucy was clearly annoyed and glared at the franked envelope, seeing it was from Justin's solicitor, and in a quick effort to stop him reading it before the wedding, she snatched it and tried to shove it into her small vintage bag. But he grabbed it back. 'Don't be silly, I can leave it in the car.' But as he looked at the letter, his eyes widened.

'Justin, please don't bog yourself down with things now. We have a wedding to get to. Don't let this spoil our day.'

He contemplated the notion for a few seconds and agreed, placing the letter on the back shelf.

The registry office building looked grand enough, but it wasn't Justin's idea of a perfect wedding. Still, he didn't want to dampen Lucy's enthusiasm, and so he forced his mouth to smile every time she looked his way.

They walked together through the main doors and were escorted to the ceremony room where two of his mechanics were waiting, having agreed to get dressed up and be the witnesses. The small room was already laid out with a few rows of chairs, each one tied with cream bows. He guessed they were having another ceremony soon after. Griff and Lee, both in their early twenties, nodded in his direction and made their way towards him, whilst the lady who would be conducting the service escorted Lucy into a side room.

As soon as she was out of sight, Griff grabbed Justin's shoulder. 'Boss, you look like you're going to a fucking funeral not your own wedding. Are you sure about this? I mean, I don't want to cause offence but …' He looked around the room. 'No one's turned up, Boss. Is anyone else coming or what?'

Justin fidgeted, now a complete bag of nerves. He needed to get a grip. Glancing down at his shiny black patent shoes, he replied, 'No, Griff, it's just a formality really, you know, to get married before the baby arrives.'

Lee, the taller, slimmer of the two young men, coughed discreetly as the registrar walked in. She hurried over to the men. 'Right, if you will take your places, we'll play the music.' She was assertive and seemed to be in a hurry. Justin shadowed her to the table whilst Griff and Lee followed with their heads down, as if they were standing before the headmaster.

As soon as the music began to play Adele's 'Make You Feel My Love', Griff nudged Justin. 'You don't have to go through with it, you know,' he mumbled under his breath but received a nasty sneer from the registrar for his boldness.

Lucy entered the room and gracefully glided up the short aisle as if there were a hundred people watching her. Justin felt his legs wobble slightly and his mouth dry up with so many emotions ripping through him. His mother not being there, not even knowing he was getting married, the guilt – he knew this was madness. That was until he glanced across at his bride and her small protruding bump, and then, he took a deep breath and smiled.

Within ten minutes, the ceremony was over, and he was married. It had all happened so fast, that he was surprised when the registrar said, 'You are now husband and wife.' His two friends signed the register and it was done. They didn't even go for a celebratory drink with the newlyweds; instead, they headed off together to a local pub to have a good gossip like two old women.

In the back of the Bentley, Lucy pulled out her phone and took a few pictures of them both. 'Aw, Justin, come on, smile, love. What's the matter?' she said, as she tried to take a selfie.

He felt his cheeks tighten, and his smile was more of a thin grin, but she didn't seem to mind; she had her photo.

The plan was to drive back to the flat, get changed, and head off to the Cotswolds, where she'd booked the cottage for the week. However, as soon as they were in the flat, he felt a cold, unearthly sensation, as if reality had slapped him again. 'Listen, Lucy, I know you're looking forward to our honeymoon, but I'm so worried—'

'About bloody Kara, I bet!' she spat angrily.

'No! I just have so much work that I'm struggling with. I'm so behind, and I don't want the business to suffer. Can we postpone the honeymoon for maybe a couple of weeks?'

Like a spoiled child, Lucy threw the bouquet onto the chair. 'It's just not fair; none of this is fair. I couldn't have the big white wedding with family and …' she paused and snivelled '… I can't even meet your mother. And I tried, Justin, I really tried to make this wedding as sweet as possible. All I wanted was for us to be married and spend a week together. That's all, just a measly week, away from everything, to start our lives anew.' She placed her hands over her eyes and cried.

With a heavy sigh, Justin caved in. 'Okay, I'll call the boys and tell them what needs to be done, and we can be on our way.'

Lucy squealed with delight and threw her hands around his neck. 'Thank you, my husband.'

With that, she ran up the stairs to get changed out of the dress that had looked a little tight. Justin stared out of the living-room window and noticed the Bentley was still outside. The driver was in the final stages of removing the red ribbon. All at once, Justin remembered the postal delivery and hurried out of the building before the chauffeur left. Opening the back door, Justin snatched the letter. 'Sorry, mate, I forgot something.'

'No worries. And congratulations, you look a very lovely couple.'

Justin hadn't even thought about what they looked like together; in fact, he hadn't thought about a lot when it came to him and Lucy. He gave a wry smile and slowly sauntered back up the steps to the front door, where he paused to open the letter.

Dear Justin,

After not hearing from you after the previous letter and the messages I left for you, I am writing in regard to the court case on 14th April. I appreciate this is short notice. However, as I mentioned earlier, I was only informed a week ago. I think it would be prudent to come to my office as soon as you can. I need to discuss some other matters that have come to my attention.

Also, as I indicated previously, you may be required to take the stand as a witness. However, if you would rather not, then you can mention that you would be a hostile witness, due to the nature of your relationship with the defendant, Kara. I would be obliged if you would call me at your earliest convenience.

Yours sincerely
Lucas

Justin stood shivering, at a loss to know what to think. Loosening his tie that was almost strangling him, he reread the letter and folded it away before he entered the house. Lucy was so busy getting herself ready that she hadn't even noticed him go to the car.

How was he going to tell her that he would have to cut their honeymoon short, and, more to the point, go to court? He was contemplating lying but he would only trip himself up. The best solution would be to explain the situation calmly and decisively. He took a deep breath and called up the stairs. 'Lucy, sorry, love, but we can only go for four days. I have to attend the court case, which is next Monday.'

He listened but there was silence. He called again but there was still no response. Taking the stairs with large strides, he reached the top and peered into the bedroom. Lucy was staring out of the window.

'What's the matter?' He knew the answer to that already. She whirled around with a face devoid of any happiness. For the first time, he understood the expression 'Hell hath no fury like a woman scorned' and he shuddered. There would be ructions.

'You don't need to go, do you? But I guess you want to see Kara!' she said with a spiteful undertone.

'I have no choice. They'll call me as a witness.'

Without thinking, Lucy met him head-on. 'Not if you're a hostile witness. How can you be on the opposite side, if you—?'

'What did you just say?' Justin placed his hands firmly on his hips and inclined his head, waiting for an answer.

'What I'm trying to say is, the prosecution wouldn't risk putting you on the stand, if they suspected all along that you had strong feelings for her.' She lowered her aggressive tone, as if realising she'd put her big foot right in it.

'No, no, Lucy, you said, and I quote, "not if you're a hostile witness". Now, where would you have heard that phrase?'

With an exaggerated raised eyebrow, Lucy sniggered, 'I do know a bit about the law you know. I'm not a complete dunce.'

Justin decided perhaps he was reading too much into it. The first letter could have got lost in the post, messages get so easily deleted, and as for Lucy's knowledge of legal procedure, who was to say Lucy didn't know more about this than him?

'Well, anyway, my solicitor has asked me to meet with him

before the case, so I think it's best under the circumstances. After all, Lucy, we don't want any issues to stand in the way of the insurance company continuing with the rebuilding of the house, do we?' he replied sarcastically.

Lucy flared her nostrils and threw the last cashmere jumper into her suitcase. 'Oh well, a long weekend it is, then,' she said, with a deflated tone.

'I'm sorry, Lucy, I know how much this means to you. Look, I'll make a quick call and we'll be on our way.'

With no expression, she nodded and continued packing.

Justin headed back downstairs out of earshot and phoned Lucas Lane.

'Well, about time, me old son. Three messages I left for you on your new landline number. Anyway, never mind that, how are you doing, Justin?'

'Sorry, Lucas, I must have missed them, but yeah, I'm good. I don't have much time, so just to let you know, I'll be there for the court proceedings.'

There was a pause. 'Justin, it's not my place, but as a mate, to you *and* Kara, she needs a character witness. Her lawyer, Stuart Venables, a good barrister, has informed me that she's going into court with no one backing her because her poor mother is dead.'

'What!' cried Justin.

'Oh, didn't you know? Has Kara not been in touch at all?'

Justin felt his nerves on fire. 'Oh my God, no, she hasn't. Joan died? When?'

Lucas coughed quietly. 'Listen, Justin, I'm breaking all confidences by telling you this, but Stuart told me something pretty awful. I want you to know because I want you to do the right thing. Joan died five months ago, but Kara insists she made contact with her carer only quite recently, so something very dodgy is going on. Nevertheless, whilst it has nothing to do with Kara's case, I know you wouldn't want her rotting away inside.'

At once, his tone became cold and firm. 'After all, Justin, let's be honest, Kara may have acted totally irrationally, but she stayed faithful to you, didn't she? I think you have two options: either stay in the gallery and watch the proceedings or offer to be a character witness. She needs you, Justin, that's all I can say, and trust me, without divulging anything else, as I'm bound by a professional code, I really do recommend you attend.'

'What is it, Lucas? Tell me!'

'I can't. I've already breached a confidence by telling you about her mother, but please go to court, and you'll see for yourself.'

'I'll be there. Have you heard how Kara is? I mean, how did she take the news and how the hell did her mother die five months ago? And how did Kara not know? Surely, she would have told me or my mother? No way it could have been that long ago, could it?'

'Justin, I can't say any more, mate. Just be there.'

He ended the call and turned to find Lucy, standing in the doorway. 'Oh, I didn't know you were there.'

'Clearly,' she replied. 'So, are you definitely going to court, then?'

Justin was still reeling from the shocking news about Joan. He'd loved her too and was gutted, and even more so now that Kara was inside a prison cell, alone, and having to deal with her mother's death. His heart felt like a lead brick and his stomach was in knots.

'Yes, Lucy, I'm definitely going. We're not together anymore, and I did wrong by her, but I'm not a complete bastard, you know.' He looked her up and down. 'You and I are married now with a baby on the way. But that doesn't change things.'

Lucy asked sorrowfully, 'What do you mean?'

'It's obvious what it means, Lucy. We can move on with our lives, as we're bloody well doing, but that doesn't mean I should leave Kara to it, to rot inside. I can help, and I will help, whether you like it or not. Kara isn't a bad person, and really, as I see things, she shouldn't be in prison. I'm partly to blame. I drove her to burn the house down. My mother said she might have done the same, if she'd been treated the way I treated Kara. I'm going to court and I'm going to be a character witness. It's the flaming least I can do.'

He tried to judge her expression, expecting her to be sarcastic, but the smile that greeted him seemed genuine enough.

Lucy wanted to launch another attack but thought better of it. She had to change tactics, or her marriage could easily be for nothing.

'Okay, darling, you do whatever you think is best, and of course you should go. If the poor woman gets a lighter sentence for it, then at least you will have done your bit.'

Playing it cool was in her long-term interests, so she needed to rein in her legendary temper and focus on pampering Justin and enjoy the long weekend. The last thing she needed was for him to fall back into Kara's arms.

* * *

The long drive started with Lucy trying to make conversation. Justin, though, was miles away and seemed irritated by her babbling. After a few one-word responses, she gave up and sat in silence, seething at the thought that her Justin was going to help get his ex out of prison. He should be concentrating on them and their new baby. She looked at his profile, as he drove, and she had to admit to herself that he was a very good-looking man.

But, there again, he was such a pathetically faint-hearted person. She was used to men with so much more gumption than him. He was an intelligent kind of guy, and often she found herself agreeing with him simply because she'd no idea what he was talking about. Politics, religion, anything with an academic core to it, he had her baffled. She'd never been a keen student; in fact, she'd absolutely hated school and saw the endless hours in the classroom as missed opportunities when she could have been out there earning a crust.

Meeting Justin was a godsend – after she'd done her homework on him. A successful businessman with garages and a fat bank balance, his own classy home, and to top it all, the good looks, he ticked all the essential boxes. In theory. Now she had him, she would fight tooth and nail to keep him, even if he was a bit weak and full of garbage with his conversation that bored the pants off her. But his moody side somehow stirred a fire in her belly, and in a sadistic way, she quite liked it. The icing on the cake was she had claimed part of Kara's life for herself.

The silence allowed her to think of a plan. One thing was for sure: the attendance at court was a complete no-no. Deep down, she knew that if he saw Kara looking all vulnerable – maybe battered and bruised – he would ditch what they had and return to her. She had the measure of the man now, and he would find that out soon enough.

Just as the skies darkened, they arrived outside the small stone cottage with its rambling rose gardens. It was as picturesque as the photos.

The red and black skies were the perfect backdrop, lifting Justin's mood. He hurriedly jumped from the car, stretched his long, weary legs, and popped open the boot. A big smile adorned his face when he saw the basket of food, like a Christmas hamper, all carefully selected and secretly hidden under a blanket to one side next to their cases. He looked over at Lucy. 'This is a nice touch. When did you do this?'

She chuckled. 'Yesterday, when you were working. I bought all your favourite things, so our honeymoon would be perfect.'

For a short while, his mind drifted away from Kara and back to his wife. Perhaps he had been a bit short with her, had neglected her, and really all she was doing was trying to please him. The wedding, the cottage, she must have put so much effort in, and here he was, being a real grouch.

'Come on, then, I know this is not our home, but let me carry you over the threshold.'

They laughed together and began their honeymoon on a positive note.

* * *

Two days before Kara was to appear in court, Stuart was there in the legal visiting room armed with a stack of papers.

Both were more relaxed, compared to the last traumatic visit, and each of them was looking forward to a positive outcome at the trial. He was pleased to see she had a glow to her face and not that distinctive prison pallor. And likewise, he felt fresher compared to the last distressing visit.

As he moved the chair towards the table, he smiled. 'Right, then, down to business. I have ...' he held up the large files '... as you can see, been doing some serious research regarding hormones, and I think I have nailed a loophole in regard to your case, so we should be looking at a reduced sentence. These are some of the cases that have set a precedent regarding acquittals and reduced sentences for those women who found themselves in not entirely dissimilar circumstances to yourself. So, there is nothing for you to prepare for except to answer my questions honestly. The prosecution will try to prove that the whole incident was premeditated by you, but as I have got to know you a little bit, I am confident that although this is a way to help your case, it is also the truth. I will do my darnedest to prove it. So how do you feel?'

Kara was listening intently, but other issues weighed on her mind. 'I feel nervous, naturally. Have you heard any more regarding my mother? You mentioned a private investigator.' She fiddled with the tissue under the table, anxious to know more.

'Bruce has taken a trip over to Australia, and as soon as he has recovered from his jet lag, he'll be visiting the police station in the suburb of Melbourne where your mother lived.' He leaned forward. 'I know it's at the forefront of your mind, but please concentrate on your own case, and leave the other business to us.'

She nodded. 'I know you're doing everything you can to help, and I really do appreciate it, as I'm sure you're going well beyond your remit, but why?' She wondered if he had a crush on her.

He bit his lip. 'Well, yes, that's true, but I had a relationship with my deceased mother like you obviously had with yours. I like to sleep well in my bed at night and not be plagued by niggling worries. This situation deserves an explanation. I just feel, somehow, justice needs to be served.'

Kara felt awkward and Stuart seemed to read her expression.

He rapidly changed the subject. 'Oh, there is one other thing that will help your case. Lucas Lane has informed me that Justin will be at the trial, and he has offered to be a character witness.'

Kara gasped. 'No! He mustn't see me like this.' She looked down at her bump.

'Kara, I don't mean to interfere because your personal life is simply that – personal. However, I strongly recommend this, as you do need someone on your side, and the fact that it was his house that was burned to the ground and he is still willing to give a character statement goes a very long way.'

She looked down in shame. 'Yes, I can see that. I just don't want him to know about my baby.'

Stuart sighed. 'Kara, similar cases to yours have very rarely resulted in more than five years. I can do my best to get you out sooner, but I cannot guarantee anything. You may need him to look after the baby for a few months.'

With her eyes firmly fixed on his, she nodded. 'Maybe you're right. I don't have anyone else, do I?'

'Honestly, Kara, it's for the best. You don't want your child in the social service system and then have a big fight on your hands to get the baby back, do you?'

'I know you're right. It's just that I feel sick about the idea of handing my baby over to anyone.'

'I understand, but for now, just prepare for the court case, and we'll sort out all the other details as they arise. When the trial is over and done with, we'll know what your options are.'

She agreed. Stuart wasn't a flashy man or a dismissive one: he really showed he cared. He was right of course, and so she trusted him completely. Strange that: she hadn't been at all trusting of anyone until she arrived in prison.

Chapter 15

The evening before the trial, the girls gathered at teatime in the large dining room, all eager to make sure Kara was okay. It was a tense occasion for any inmate awaiting their fate. Holding her tray, Deni eased herself onto a chair and put her small Angel Delight on Kara's plate.

'There ya go, girl. For the baby.'

Kara giggled. 'Gosh, this baby is spoiled already.'

Julie was hyper with excitement. 'Well, it seems that they're fast-tracking me case. Sharon has withdrawn her statement and hopefully they're gonna let me go.'

Vic kicked her under the table.

'Aw, what was that for?'

'You insensitive bitch, Jue.'

Julie cast an eye in Kara's direction. 'Sorry, mate. Anyway, who knows, you could be out even sooner than me.'

Deni was fiddling with a necklace. Her arms were stiff, so she cursed. 'I'm fucking useless. Vic, unclip this for me, will ya?'

Vic got up from her seat, still walking with a slight limp. She moved Deni's hair aside and unclasped the gold chain.

Deni then pulled the chain from her neck and held it in her

hand. 'Kara, I want you to have this, for good luck, babe.' She held out her hand, showing a gold cross and chain.

Kara looked at the beautiful gift and was overcome with emotion. 'I couldn't, Deni, it's yours. You always wear it.'

'It was me grandmuvver's. Loved that ol' girl. It's always been me lucky charm.'

Julie almost choked on her sausage. 'Well, a fat lot of good it did you. It didn't keep ya outta 'ere, did it? Ouch!' she squealed at Vic, who had just sat back down again and kicked her once more under the table.

'Actually, Jue, it did, 'cos, by rights, I should 'ave been looking at another ten years, so shut ya mouth.'

Kara took the chain and smiled humbly. 'I will wear it for the trial, and I promise, I will return it right away. It's very kind of you, Deni.'

It was Deni who now blushed. 'No, Kara, I want you to keep it. I was gonna give it to me own little girl, but, well, she's not 'ere, so I want you to 'ave it, babe. I can't replace ya mum, but, nevertheless, I can be there for ya, can't I.'

Goose bumps covered Kara's skin, and a warm feeling enveloped her as though Deni was her own mother. If only. She held back the tears, knowing that if she started again, she wouldn't stop.

Colette came over to join them. Her appearance had been changing weekly; her hair had grown, and her weight loss had given her chunky boyish frame a more feminine look. She even wore a softer expression.

'I wanted to wish you good luck for tomorrow, Kara. I er … I made something for you, a handkerchief with ya name embroidered on it. It's in ya cell.'

Deni put her arm around Colette's shoulders. 'Good girl. So, I take it, you ain't stabbed anyone with the scissors in your sewing class, then?' She chuckled.

'Nope, and the teacher reckons I'm a dab hand with the sewing

233

machine. When I get out of here, I'm gonna start designing dresses, a baby range. I did want to be a midwife, but the truth is, I'll never get employed, not with my record, and besides, I like making stuff.'

No one teased or joked because they knew that Colette was making headway with her new look and attitude; maybe it was Kara's character rubbing off on them. She was always the first to encourage anyone to make something of their life, all except herself. She was just waiting to find out what the future had in store for her. They all knew it too and tried desperately hard to make what she had as bearable as possible.

In between mouthfuls of food, Julie said, 'Oh, yeah, the parcel from Rocky is on ya bed.' She looked at Vic. 'The fucker never sent me anything, though.'

Vic was clearly a little irritated by Julie's behaviour. 'Jue, that parcel was a surprise. You and ya big mouth. And as for Rocky buying you anything, shouldn't it be ya ol' man, Billy Big Bollocks?'

Placing her fork beside her plate, Julie huffed. 'Well, he ain't got no money, 'as he?'

Vic shook her head in annoyance. 'That's why Rocky won't put his hand in his pocket for you. But he don't see ya baby go without. He makes sure she has nice clobber and baby milk, but, Jue, like I keep telling you, all the time you are with that fat slob, Rocky won't help ya.'

'Yeah, all right, message received and understood and all that bollocks. Maybe I need to kick the fat slob to the kerb.'

Kara turned her head to face Julie. 'Not that I'm worldly-wise, like you, Julie, but I know you're afraid that being without Billy will hurt you, and it's heartbreaking; but you will get over it, and with all your family's support, you will heal. I know I have, and I can tell you this. I loved Justin with all my heart, and his betrayal hurt so much that I burned the house down, but I'm over him, thanks to all the love from you girls.'

There was stunned silence. They knew they'd helped her to

survive this far in prison; what they didn't know was they had also nursed her heartache.

* * *

Justin had to admit to himself that during their honeymoon Lucy had been every bit the copybook wife. They had enjoyed the romantic strolls in the beautiful countryside and the intimate moments sitting in front of the open fire toasting marshmallows. It was picture-perfect: the rugs on the floor, the smell of the wood-burning stove, and the exquisite meals she cooked. They played games – cards and Scrabble – and they really laughed together.

She was somehow very different, more graceful and serene, and more like Kara. She had ditched her Barbie doll look and taken to not wearing loads of make-up and allowing her hair to fall messily around her face. She was learning very quickly what Justin liked and didn't like and was doing her best to morph into the ideal woman for him. They had relaxed the first evening; she drank orange juice whilst he managed two bottles of wine. At every opportunity, she topped up his glass, so that when he fell asleep on the floor, she gulped back the rest, gagging for a drink. That set a pattern for the remaining days of their honeymoon.

On the final morning, they were to leave at five o'clock to get back in time for the trial, but the previous evening, he didn't want to drink; he needed to be fresh for the long drive back and decided to have an early night. It must have been the invigorating country air that had knocked him out. She paced the floor, with the bottle of wine in her hand; a few swigs were all she needed, just to take the edge off her craving. Come what may, she was adamant he wouldn't be at court tomorrow. Without him, Kara could rot inside. She'd burned his house down, their home for their baby, so she deserved to be in there, and she would have a taste of how her own life had been.

235

As the clock gently chimed midnight, Lucy hurried to the bathroom. She splashed water around her hairline, cleaned her teeth, and then she yelled as if she was in extreme pain. She waited. There was no response from Justin. So, she yelled again, even louder. She could hear the floorboards creak, a sign he'd woken up and was on the move. It was time to use her formidable acting skills once more.

* * *

As Justin wandered into the bathroom, all bleary-eyed, his heart nearly stopped. There was Lucy, all curled up in a ball, clutching her stomach.

'Jesus!' he yelled, as he kneeled down by her side. 'What's happened – is it the baby?'

She groaned and nodded. 'Oh my God, Justin, something is wrong; it hurts. Oh, please don't say I'm losing him, not our boy.'

He moved the wet hair away from her face. 'It's okay, babe. Listen, I'm going to call an ambulance. I've no idea where the nearest hospital is. Can you get up?' He tried to help Lucy to her feet while she was bent in half.

'Oh, Justin, I can't lose our baby. He can't come yet; it's too soon. He'll never survive.'

Justin shook all over. She was right. He would never survive. He had to get her to the hospital and fast. Easing her onto the bed, he hurriedly looked for his mobile and was dismayed when he realised there was no signal. He ran around the small cottage, hoping to find a landline phone. But there wasn't one. 'Damn! What fucking house doesn't have a bloody phone?' he mumbled under his breath.

Little did he know the cottage was a peace retreat: there were no phones, no TV, and no internet. He should have guessed by the shelves of books and games.

He ran back up the stairs, panicking. 'Right, let me help you get dressed. I'll have to drive to the hospital. It will be all right, love. The satnav will guide us there.'

Her face was full of sorrow and sadness, which made him feel so guilty for how he'd treated her over the last few months. He would make it up to her; he would put everything right.

She gave him a pitiful smile and slowly edged herself from the bed and allowed him to wrap her long coat around her shoulders. He walked very carefully with her down the rickety oak staircase, and on the way to the door, he grabbed a knitted blanket. She slid her feet into her long fur-lined boots, and wailed again. 'Oh, no, it hurts so much!'

Justin told her to wait while he started up the car and drove it a foot away from the front entrance to the house.

He opened the door for her and helped her inside. 'Right, I need to set up this satnav.' He turned the heating to full blast to warm the car up and hopefully to stop himself from shaking; he had to remain in control. In a panic, his fingers fumbled with the directions on the screen in trying to activate the device and find the nearest hospital. 'Damn thing. I'm sorry, babe. I'll get you there soon.'

Lucy smiled inwardly; the longer he took the better. The satnav sprang into action, but Justin was panic-stricken: the hospital was so far away. 'Oh my God!' He looked at Lucy in horror. 'It's going to take ages. I don't know what to do.'

What if the situation was different and she really was having a miscarriage? It was a sobering thought.

At that moment, Lucy felt as though she'd been released from a coma. Justin wasn't acting like a man taking control; he was a bumbling idiot, putting the panic back onto her. Her shoulders slumped, and her heart felt heavy. What the hell was she really doing, taking another woman's man, wanting everything that the perfect Kara had? The house, the lifestyle, the money, a handsome man. She now wondered if she'd actually thought it all through.

It had been a game that had gathered momentum. It was a

sick, twisted scheme that toyed with her sanity and urged her on to win, to take everything she could. At every step of the way, she'd been able to tick the boxes: reeling Justin in, making sure he woke up in her bed, making him believe the baby was his, the wedding, and now this. He was no hardman: he was weak and easily led, and she hated him for it.

She really should have known that months ago. The signs were there, staring her in the face. He left Kara without delay, he assumed the baby was his, and he agreed to the hash of a wedding. What man in his right mind would ever do all that? Carl wouldn't have. He would have laughed at her; in fact, he did laugh at her, often. She dipped her head and sighed. A glance at Justin told her all she needed to know at the moment. He was hell-bent on saving his baby and hadn't even noticed that she was no longer groaning.

He drove as fast as he could, along the black rolling hill lanes, gripping the steering wheel tightly. He never even looked her way, but just kept saying repeatedly, 'Don't worry, I'll get you there. It's going to be all right.'

Even his pathetic voice now grated on her. Perhaps this was all normal. Maybe life with a hard-working successful man was different. She imagined his friends over for dinner with polite conversation and reliving pranks from their schooldays. She saw herself hosting the dinner parties with the wives of his business associates, their small talk of fluff and fairies. And then there would be the shopping sprees with his toffee-nosed acquaintances, stopping for coffee, whilst admiring each other's children, and talking about schools and the brats' achievements.

Then her mind turned to picturing Kara, with her nose in the air and the intelligent conversation about politics or economics and discussing the latest horror of the day's news. She imagined her serving quails' eggs and beef Wellington followed by lemon sorbet, their guests clapping at her culinary delights. That had never been her. Yet it should have been. She should have learned about the finer things in life: the good job, the skiing holidays, trekking around the world discovering the rainforest, and enjoying the fine wines and exclusive dishes. She should have had it all: that beautiful house with the well-kept garden, and the vast kitchen as big as her entire poxy flat. She stared silently into the darkness of the rambling hills and black skies.

She hated Kara for everything she stood for, and now she was in so deep that the game she played was not a game anymore, and her need to win seemed pointless. She wondered if she really could spend a life with a man she had no respect for. He wasn't like Carl; she respected him, even though she hated him. But that was it. There was such a fine line between love and hate. She hated Carl for not loving her. Why couldn't he love her?

But he didn't: he'd made it so clear that she was his go-to girl, nothing more and nothing less. All his bullshit about saving her from her bleak, miserable life and getting on track away from drugs and streetwalking was just that: bullshit. She could have done that herself. Why he had to come into her life and why she had fallen in love with him was incomprehensible. He knew it, though – he must have done. She'd played it cool and had acted like she didn't give a shit, but she did; she cared very much.

Fuck him. Then, as if she'd experienced a revelation, her devious mind went into another direction. Justin was weak and that only meant one thing: she could wrap him around her finger, and just like he'd left Kara in the blink of an eye, she could kick him into touch too. Once the house was built and she had her feet well and truly under the table, half of what he owned was legally hers. Her lips slithered into a smirk and she let out another groan. 'Oh, no, it's hurting again.'

Justin grabbed her hand. 'It's okay, Lucy, we're nearly there.'

The local district general was unexpectedly busy, and so he wasted no time in parking in the ambulance bay and helping his wife from the car. The panic on his face caused the nurse to take control and Lucy was wheeled right away to the scanning department.

'Shall I come or—'

Lucy stopped him in his tracks. 'No, Justin, I'll be fine. You wait here.'

He frowned. 'But …'

The nurse gave him a compassionate smile. 'I'll take care of your wife, and as soon as she's settled, I'll call for you. Don't worry, sir, she's in safe hands.'

Justin nodded and kissed Lucy on the forehead.

* * *

The morning alarm rang through Kara's ears, but it hadn't woken her up, as she was already awake, nervously contemplating her immediate future. It wasn't long before Deni and Vic made their way over to her wing, the governor having given them permission to help Kara prepare for court.

Dressed in her new outfit, sent in by Rocky, she gave a twirl. The navy-blue swing dress hung perfectly, without completely drowning her, yet modestly covering her bump. 'How do I look?'

'Cor, Kara, like you should be swanning around some posh office somewhere.' Deni laughed.

'It's okay though, yes?'

Deni was admiring the girl's gentle nature and elegant outfit, set off by her grandmother's gold pendant, when Julie piped up, 'Wanna wear a bit of me lipstick?' She was showing off a bright red stick.

Deni shrieked at her, 'No! Julie, she wants to look innocent and sweet, not like a fucking tart.'

Julie pouted.

'Me brother's got good taste, I'll give him that,' Vic said.

'Oh, I don't know.' Kara chuckled.

240

'All she needs to do is get that judge on her side and fingers crossed. Yeah, and if you get on the stand and the judge looks foreign, hide that cross – get what I mean?' insisted Vic.

'Yes, I will do, and I just want to thank you, all of you. If they send me to another prison from there, I'll write and let you know how I'm doing. I really hope they don't do that because I don't think I could cope alone again.'

Deni waved her hand and turned her face, too choked up to talk.

Vic patted Kara's shoulder. 'You just stay strong and remember we're family now,' whispered Vic.

Julie gave Kara an awkward smile. 'Yeah, they'll probably send ya back, just to annoy me,' she teased.

Barbara was now in the doorway, wearing a smug grin. 'Right, Bannon, your sweatbox awaits.'

'Cunt,' mumbled Julie, under her breath.

'What did you say?'

'I didn't say anything, I coughed.' Julie laughed, as she winked at Kara.

* * *

The journey to the court was spent wondering about Justin. She hoped that seeing his face wouldn't put her off and cause her to screw things up. She had to be on the ball and not let herself or her baby down. She wondered if he would look different now. Had he grown his hair? Did he have a beard? Would his girlfriend be there? She shuddered at the thought.

What was it that he'd seen in this woman? Perhaps she was prettier or sexier. She peered down at her protruding belly. He had thought her sexy, once upon a time. He wouldn't now, though, not with a bump, swollen ankles, and a couple of stretch marks. Her mind switched to her mother and her throat tightened; she had to stop drifting back there, as it would do her no good. She would have time to concern herself about her mother and the carer, once the trial was over and done with.

The holding cell was a blank canvas: there were no pictures or soft furnishings, pretty much like the one she'd been in when she'd been waiting to go to court months ago. She sat nervously on the edge of her seat and tapped her fingers, her heart beating wildly. The door opened and in bounded Stuart. He had a black gown on but no wig. 'Good morning.' He beamed, as if pleasantly surprised by her appearance. 'You are looking well, Kara, but more to the point, how do you feel?'

She stood up to shake his hand. 'Yes, okay, I guess. I'm just anxious.'

'Right, good news. We have Helen Blackthorn, a lady judge, who I am sure will be more understanding.'

Kara smiled, and his face lit up.

'She has four children herself.' He winked. 'So, it's time, Kara. Are you ready to take the stand?'

A look of horror shot across her face. 'What, now? I mean, has it already begun? What do I say?'

He took her hand. 'It's just the plea. All you have to do is plead guilty to the charges and then you will come back until we call you again. Don't be nervous. She is a good judge, actually, a very fair one.' He squeezed her hand tighter, as she trembled.

As soon as Kara was led up the stairs by two officers to stand in the dock, she felt her stomach turn over. The men and women of the jury, along with some of the other lawyers, were eyeing her over. She, however, was surveying the room and then searching the gallery. She had a sudden urge to see a familiar face, but there was no one she recognised, not one friendly spectator. There was only her legal team comprising Stuart, her barrister, and Alan Cumberbatch, her solicitor.

An instant wave of sadness swept through like an ice-cold wind. Was she really so alone in this world? Just as she went to lower her gaze, the side door to the gallery opened, and squeezing in, past some random reporters, was a real sight for sore eyes. Rocky. He was brazen enough to wave and wink. She held his gaze and watched him with admiration as he sat there confidently surveying the court. He could have been a lawyer himself, dressed impeccably and with his mid-length hair tied back in a tiny ponytail. He was more handsome than when she'd first met him.

Before she even had time to take it all in, she was sworn in, gave her plea, and was led away, back to the holding room. She slumped on the bench seat, with mixed emotions. Justin hadn't even bothered to turn up, unless he'd been and gone. But, surely, if he had any feelings for her, he would have been here, in the courtroom? Rocky jumped into her thoughts; his big suck-me-in eyes and that very sexy wink had given her butterflies, and she admitted to herself that she was drawn to him. Whatever it was they had between them, be it nothing at all, she would take pleasure from it. Even if it was just a wink.

An hour or so passed, leaving Kara racked with worry. If she were to get ten years in prison, how the hell would she cope? This wasn't what life was supposed to be about. And what about her baby? Not being able to hold her hand on her first day at school, the nativity plays she wouldn't see, the birthday parties she would miss – it was unimaginable. A ten-year-old wouldn't know her from Adam, by the time she was released.

She stroked her bump and shivered. Years inside, with just constant stress as company, was a hard thought to deal with. Just as her anxiety levels were almost at breaking point, her solicitor appeared. Unlike Stuart, Alan was his usual more aloof self. 'It's your turn to take the stand.'

He nodded for her to follow him, and she did, escorted again by two court officers. As she reached the top of the wooden stairs to the witness box, she took a deep breath and looked around. Rocky was still there. He smiled again and gave her another wink. She wanted to smile back but Stuart had told her not to wave or smile to anyone.

As Stuart had said, the judge was very nice and had a genial countenance about her. At the same time, she didn't look as though she would suffer fools gladly. Initially, Kara had no idea what was going on. Various papers were passed back and forth between the judge and the lawyers, and then the former instructed Stuart to examine the accused.

'Please tell the Court about the weeks leading up to the fire, in your own words,' instructed Stuart.

Kara had been told to expect this question, so she had her story prepared and reeled it off, beginning with the lack of concentration at work, the formal warning, and how Justin had conducted himself towards her. She was told to include how she felt and that part she found easy because she would never forget the day Justin walked out. She admitted to the court she'd taken huge doses of sleeping tablets but then came the description of how and why she started the fire.

She looked at the judge and then at the jury. 'I only remember how I was feeling. I don't remember exactly what I did – it's all a blur. After reading the letter, demanding that I was to move out, I could see Justin and his girlfriend in my home, changing the décor and living happily …' She paused and wiped her eyes. 'I hadn't thought for one moment about the consequences, and I would never hurt anyone. I feel so terrible that I have harmed my innocent neighbour … I, er … I was angry, I was upset, I wanted to die.' The words tumbled out and ended with Kara sobbing into her hands.

The jury was with her, feeling her torture, and watching the refined young woman, with the neat bump and gentle eyes, beside herself with pain.

'Do you need a moment, Miss Bannon?' asked the judge, kindly, as she glanced first at Kara and then at the defence team.

Kara shook her head. 'I am sorry. It's just so awful what I did and so unforgivable, that I can't remember the details.'

Stuart cleared his throat. 'Miss Bannon, you discovered you

were almost three months pregnant when you were in prison. Had you no idea at all?'

She shook her head. 'No, well, so much had happened. I was sick whilst in Papua New Guinea, and when I came back, I was sick again. But after a while, I assumed I had a bug and never thought anything of it. When Justin left me, I was so overwhelmed with grief that I naturally assumed the sickness was due to that or a prolonged tropical stomach infection. I had absolutely no idea I was pregnant. Nothing was further from my mind.'

Stuart couldn't have been happier with his client. 'That's all for now, Your Honour.'

Jasper Bellingham, the barrister for the prosecution, was a younger man, mid-thirties, with a nervous disposition and a troublesome stutter. He would have been the laughing stock of the judiciary, if his somewhat lightweight adversarial skills weren't trounced by his phenomenal record in achieving guilty verdicts. His red wavy hair and almost translucent skin were softened by his deep brown eyes.

Looking Kara's way, he genuinely smiled. Then his smile turned to a smirk. 'Three months pregnant!' It wasn't a question but a mocking statement. Holding up a sheet of paper, he repeated, 'Three months pregnant. Well, it seems unbelievable to me.' He looked at the sheet of paper. 'Here is a list of body changes at three months' gestation. A gain in weight, sickness, sore breasts, cravings … quite astounding, wouldn't you say? And an intelligent woman such as yourself would surely recognise the significance of these symptoms right away, would you not?'

Unexpectedly, the judge called to dismiss that evidence. 'That is not relevant. Every woman's pregnancy is different. Members of the jury please take note that evidence of that nature is not permissible.' She shot Bellingham a frosty don't-mess-with-me-in-my-courtroom look. It was at that point, Stuart knew the judge had read all the evidence and had already made up her mind.

Yet, it was down to the jury to decide whether or not Kara was guilty by diminished responsibility or just recklessness.

Duly admonished, Bellingham cleared his throat. 'Miss Bannon, it's clear from your records that you are a well-educated woman, in science no less, and yet you expect us to believe firstly you didn't know you were pregnant and secondly don't remember burning down the house.'

Instantly, the judge intervened again. 'Is there a question there, or are you making a statement?'

Stuart wanted to laugh, as he didn't even need to say anything. But, notwithstanding the fact that the proceedings were finely balanced at best, Kara's sad expression was speaking volumes. The judge's interventions were putting pressure on the prosecution's case, and the jury appeared to be showing some sympathy for the young woman on the stand.

Stuart presented various cases that had set a precedent and crossed his fingers that these would be enough.

As soon as it was time for the summing-up, Stuart knew exactly how Bellingham was going to play it. Even so, he felt he was one step ahead, pre-empting the prosecution's final closing statements. The prosecution in this case was to go first.

Bellingham strode with confidence over to the jury. 'Ladies and gentlemen of the jury, the case before us today is by no means uncommon. Arson is a very serious offence and can result in death, but luckily for Mrs Langley, she didn't die but did spend a substantial amount of time in a hospital bed fighting for her life, and so we must assume that the emotional scars will live with her forever.'

The jury was not engaged because Kara was in floods of tears. The judge asked for tissues to be passed to her. Bellingham coughed, now thoroughly irritated by the interruption. 'I want you to imagine this was your mother, aunt, or daughter, blown six feet into the air, almost at death's door, all because a young woman was so angry with her boyfriend, that she set fire to the house, just so that he could not live in it. She acted recklessly, selfishly, and didn't care about the consequences. This letter that she was supposed to have received ... Where is it?' He flung his arms in the air. 'I put it to you that there was no letter asking her to leave the house. She wanted to ruin her boyfriend's life, and to that end, she dragged the petrol cans into the house and maliciously poured fuel over every piece of furnishing.

'Members of the jury, she then struck a match, running for her own safety in the process, which is not the action of a woman with diminished responsibility. No, no, no, she would have burned to death herself, if that had been the case. Are we to believe she didn't know she was pregnant, or is it not the case that these are the actions of a woman scorned? If we allow pregnant women or menstruating women to go around breaking the law because of their hormones, then, members of the jury, we will be giving free licence for most women at some point in their lives to carry any act of violence with impunity.

'I put it to you that Kara Bannon was fully cognizant of her actions and is now using the diminished responsibility plea to have a lengthy sentence reduced.' He'd said enough on a point of law. Stuart wondered if he'd done enough, though, to win any emotional battle with the female members of the jury.

Stuart stood up and some members of the jury immediately sat a little straighter and became more engaged with the proceedings. The barrister for the defence was certainly more appealing, with his wide smile and confident walk. 'So, we have heard the prosecution remind you that, yes, Miss Bannon's case will set a precedent, but that, ladies and gentlemen, is how our justice system works in making laws current for society's needs. It is ever-changing and quite rightly needs to be, or we will find ourselves hung, drawn, and quartered for stealing a loaf of bread.

'We have to make a decision based on whether we believe Miss Bannon did this act deliberately, knowing the eventual consequences of her actions, with an intelligent clarity of mind. Imagine in a matter of days, her long-time partner walks out, leaving Miss Bannon for another woman, who is expecting his child. Then, through no fault of her own, she loses her job due to the effects of her own pregnancy. And, finally, she receives a letter stating she has to leave the property, her home, almost immediately – a letter, may I add, which was obviously burned in the fire and therefore could not be produced as evidence.

'Just try to imagine all of that happening in literally the space of a few days. Yes, she admitted that she took too many sleeping tablets, and as an intelligent woman and a medically trained person, she would never have taken any medication unsuitable for someone who is pregnant. Of course, her hormones would play a huge part. Tormented with grief, pain, and fear, these would have exacerbated her emotionally fragile state, and so what you have is a young woman who lacked the ability to act rationally and who admits that she doesn't remember actually setting the house alight.

'So, members of the jury, if there is any doubt that she was of sane mind at that time, you cannot find her guilty of reckless arson. Reckless arson can carry a prison sentence of up to life imprisonment. I want you to bear that in mind when reaching your verdict.' He smiled and looked over at Kara whose face was red and puffy from crying. The jury's eyes followed his. That would be the last image they had in their minds before they fought it out among themselves as to her state of mind at the time she committed the arson attack.

Before Kara was led away, she looked up at the gallery and noticed Rocky was still there. He was on the edge of his seat, but as soon as he clapped eyes on her, his face beamed, and he nodded as if to say, 'you did well'.

* * *

Awaiting the final verdict was like sitting on a bed of nails. She couldn't get comfortable. She knew that she could be painfully anticipating the verdict for some time, and as the hours passed, food and drinks were brought to her. Stuart popped his head in to say she would be escorted back into the courtroom when the jury returned. She took solace in the fact that his face looked upbeat.

Finally, at three o'clock, she was called to the dock, escorted by the same two officers. Stuart was already in place, ready for the verdict. Again, Kara took a very deep shaky breath and walked the final steps up into the dock. Feeling sick with nerves, she glanced at the back of the courtroom where the public were seated. There were a few reporters, a couple of nosy people, and still there in the gallery was Rocky.

Then, her eyes landed on a smartly dressed middle-aged lady. At first, Kara didn't recognise her only because she never expected her to be there. Mollie was wiping her eyes and very subtly waving. Kara gave her an empathetic smile but was jolted out of her gaze by the court clerk asking the people present to rise as the court was back in session. Kara's eyes moved to watch each member of the jury return to their seat. She studied their faces as they sat down, but she reached no conclusion as to the likely pronounce-ment due any minute now.

She peered over again at Justin's mother. Kara could see the grief written over Mollie's face. She wanted to leave the stand and run over to her and to feel the warm embrace of the woman who would have been her mother-in-law. Kara noticed her quietly sob into a tissue and felt her own eyes filling up. Rocky slid across and placed an arm around the lady's shoulder, handing her another tissue. She couldn't make out what they were saying, but what did it matter now? In a few minutes, she would know if she was going back inside for a long time or a couple of years.

Within a few moments, it was over. It took Kara a second or two to register the outcome, but Stuart was smiling wide, and she saw his shoulders relax.

The judge, as Stuart had said, was fair.

'The jury have found you guilty of diminished responsibility, and as this still remains a custodial sentence, I am sentencing you to four years and six months in prison.'

Kara had no time to say anything. She was swiftly taken away.

Chapter 16

Lucy felt proud of herself. She'd managed to secure a bed on the ward until the consultant could discharge her. She looked up at the clock. It was five minutes past three. There was no way Justin could have reached the court in time to support Kara. She could imagine the look on Kara's face, with no one there by her side, like she herself had been whilst growing up. The school plays, the sports days – she'd been all alone.

The nurse had gone to fetch Justin, but Lucy was so determined to delay the drive back home, she hadn't even noticed that there was concern on the faces of the medical staff as they carried out the scan. In fact, she didn't even bother to look at her baby on the screen. Her eyes were firmly on the clock and her mind was on devising a story she would tell Justin if the nurse mentioned the due date that gave away the date of conception. She already had the lie figured, once the baby arrived – simply a premature birth.

As soon as Justin arrived, she noticed he looked agitated. He held her hand, as he took a seat next to the bed. 'The doctor will be along shortly. He wishes to talk to both of us.'

Lucy didn't like his sympathetic tone. Her eyes shot over to the nurse who also wore a face that said, 'I feel so sorry for you.'

'What is it, what's going on?'

Justin looked at the nurse for answers.

The unease was cut short by the arrival of a very tall doctor, to the extent he had to stoop below the top of the doorframe as he stepped inside the room. He was reading through some notes, and then he peered over the top of his glasses and smiled. Both Lucy and Justin stared, waiting for the results of the scan. They watched, as he carried a chair across the room and sat just a foot away from the bed.

'Has the pain stopped now?'

Lucy nodded. 'Yes, so what's the matter? Everything is normal, isn't it?' She assumed it would be, because she'd only faked the pains.

Dr Conway placed the notes on his lap and clasped his hands together. 'Well, no, there is a concern with the baby's growth and development. At this stage, there is nothing we can do, only wait and see. I suggest, however, that you maintain a good healthy diet and go back to your doctor in two weeks' time. I will fax over the notes and your GP will refer you for another scan to ascertain if the baby is developing as he should or if there is an underlying issue.'

He paused and waited for the floods of tears and endless questions, but to his surprise, Lucy didn't seem at all bothered. Perhaps she didn't quite understand what he was saying.

'Doctor, what does this mean? Is our son at risk, or disabled, or what?' asked Justin, with the fear of Christ in his eyes.

'Well, at the moment, it appears that his organs are not the size we would expect at this stage.'

Lucy was now cringing, concerned that the doctor would expose how far gone she really was.

'But that is not to say they won't develop to a satisfactory size. We need to keep an eye on things over the next few weeks. Please don't be alarmed. The problem may well correct itself.'

Justin looked at Lucy's expression, but, unbelievably, he couldn't read it.

'There must be something we can do,' Justin said. 'Can you do some more tests to find out exactly what's wrong?'

The doctor nodded. 'Well, we have blood samples, but at this stage, we don't have the results, so I suggest you talk it over with your GP. He can organise further tests, after the second scan.'

'Thank you, doctor,' replied Justin.

Dr Conway looked over at Lucy and found her disinterest strange. He made a mental note to write up his concerns, along with his findings.

Justin turned his head to face Lucy, only to find she still had a vacant look on her face. But she quickly seemed to snap out of it and asked, 'Can you take me home now?'

He patted her hand. 'Of course, darling. Do you feel up to the long drive, or shall we stay over another night?'

'No, I'm fine. Let's just get out of here.' Her attitude was dismissive and blunt. Naturally, he assumed it was her way of dealing with the worrying news.

Most of the journey was spent in silence. Whilst Justin was trying to comprehend the seriousness of the possibility of his son being born with problems, Lucy was planning her next move. The game of takeover was becoming somewhat boring, and she was even contemplating the prospect of returning to her former life. Performing the next trick and getting a buzz out of being the best dominatrix in the business versus a respectable home with Justin, a baby, and a life free from worry for ever after – it was proving to be a very tough decision.

The window wipers moved back and forth as the heavens opened. The constant noise was annoying, and Justin's silence was even more irritating. He was anxious about the baby, but she couldn't care less about it. She just didn't want to think about the child or the fact that he could be disabled. Having a kid was bad enough, let alone one with problems.

'Do you want to stop for a break, grab a coffee, or something?

'Is there anything I can do to make the journey more comfortable?' asked Justin, now in obsequious mode, which, on occasions, he was prone to do. It made Lucy want to punch him. Sometimes, Justin was the antithesis of hardman Carl. She needed to add that to her list of plus and minus points before deciding whether to ditch her husband or keep him.

'I'm okay,' she responded through gritted teeth.

Justin's mobile phone interrupted their thoughts.

She stared at the centre console where he'd left his phone and noticed the word 'Mum' flashing. Justin glanced down and sighed. 'I'll call her back.'

Lucy had a gut-wrenching feeling that his mother had gone to the trial and had news to tell. She decided not to say a word.

A few moments later, his phone rang again. Perturbed, Justin forced himself to concentrate on his driving while he came up with a plan. It wasn't like his mother to call twice like that. The rain poured, and the skies became so dark that he decided to stop at the next service station. He was tired, and the rain was making it impossible to drive safely.

'What are you doing?' she snapped.

'I'm going to get a coffee. I feel too drained to drive. I need a break, before I fall asleep at the wheel.'

She knew he was lying. *What a wimp*, she thought. *He wants to speak to his mummy. Add that to the list too.*

'Would you like a drink or something to eat?' he asked, less attentive now.

'No, I'm fine. I just want to get home, Justin!'

'Lucy, I *am* taking us home, but we want to get there in one piece. Besides, what's the rush now? Presumably the court case will be over, and I'm in no hurry.' He snatched the phone.

She knew his mind would be back on Kara, and in a flash, she nearly bit his head off. 'Christ, our baby could be damaged, and all you care about is that fucking ex of yours.' As soon as he appeared to be concerned over Kara, she felt an overwhelming urge to complete her plan. Just saying the bitch's name was sending Lucy into an angry place.

Justin was half in and half out of the car when he shot her a look of death. His eyes narrowed, and his face looked spiteful. 'That's enough!' he spat, as he slammed the door shut and marched towards the food hall.

* * *

He'd tried his best to be kind and caring, but for the last two hours, she'd been cold and distant with one-word answers. Had she forgotten he would also have feelings? It was his son as well, and yes, he was worried about Kara; he'd promised he would be there as a witness, if need be, and besides, he'd let her down big-time. This wasn't who he was; he could never be so callous.

The rain lifted, allowing him to reach the food hall almost dry. Once inside, he called his mother. As if she was sitting by the phone, she answered, 'Oh my God, Justin, where are you? Lucas called me to say you were supposed to be in court, so I hurried there myself. I've been trying to call you for hours!'

He had left his mobile in the car whilst he was in the hospital. 'Sorry, Mum, I had something else to deal with.'

'Do you know what, Justin, you may be my son, but I don't know you anymore. That poor, poor girl standing in that dock, sobbing she was. Justin, she was beside herself, and I couldn't even go and console her ...' Her words broke off and it sounded like she was trying to hold back a sob. 'She was so alone. She had no one, Justin, the girl had no one. And to see her little sweet face trying to take it all in, she was terrified, Justin, bloody terri-fied.'

A cold chill swept through his body as he pictured her there, standing in a grand but intimidating courtroom. 'Did she get sentenced?' was all he could ask in a pathetic schoolboy voice.

'Yes, Justin, she *did* get sentenced; she got four damn years

255

and six months. Four and a half years, Justin. That poor girl doesn't deserve it. You should have been there, to show support, or talk with the solicitor, or to do *something*. What could be more bloody important than that, eh …?'

There was silence. He tried to digest the news; it seemed unreal.

'Well, Justin, do tell me, what on earth was so much more important than being there? I would love to hear it.' Her sarcastic tone rang in his ears. He hated it when his mother used that tone.

'Well, actually, Mum, Lucy had to go to the hospital. We thought she was having a miscarriage, and they found that there is something potentially wrong with our son. He is not developing as he should.' He hoped that would change his mother's attitude and she would be more forgiving, but he was wrong.

'Well, Son, you made your bed, you lie in it.'

'Mum, how can you say that?'

'I am sorry about your son, truly I am. But while we're on the subject of babies, there is something else you should know. Not only is Kara locked away terrified in some prison, with not a soul to support her, but she's also having a baby. She looks to be about five or six months pregnant, so I can only assume you now have two babies on the way.'

'What?' It was too much to take in; he couldn't comprehend it, and his voice trembled under the emotional strain.

Mollie softened her tone. 'Yes, Son, our Kara is expecting, and no doubt, she hasn't told you because, well, I suppose she assumed you didn't want her, since you ran off with another woman, plus she probably wouldn't want you to worry. So, Son, as much as I could be sympathetic to you regarding this other woman's baby, I have too much sympathy for Kara, right now.' Once again Mollie's thoughts returned to her own husband's infidelity and how he'd supposedly fathered her best friend's child.

Unexpectedly, his phone died; the battery had run out. He stared at the blank screen for ages. Kara pregnant, his Kara and their baby stuck in a prison, and it was all his fault. His hands began to shake, and for a moment he needed to sit down. The food hall was huge and filling up with customers. A bright green plastic chair by a small table was empty. Justin eased himself onto the hard surface and held his hands together as if he was about to pray.

The background noise of people coming and going was like a swarm of bees. Everything seemed to be detached, as he absorbed his mother's words, and try as he might, he just couldn't get his head around it all. For a while, he sat in deep thought until an elderly lady plonked herself down opposite and smiled. He snapped out of his trancelike state and smiled back, before getting up from his seat. He needed a coffee; his body and his mind felt drained.

'Sir?'

He looked at the assistant, who was chewing her gum assiduously.

'What would you like?'

'Oh, yes, sorry, a double espresso, please.'

Back outside, not only had the worst of the weather moved south but there were also glimpses of sunshine. Unfortunately, this had no positive effect on his downcast mood as he hurriedly returned to the car. A glance at his watch showed he'd been ages, but this didn't seem to register with Lucy, who appeared to be lost in her own thoughts, staring out of the window with a totally empty expression.

He took two large gulps of the coffee, placed his phone on charge, and pulled away. As he reached the roundabout, to join the motorway, he glanced at Lucy, and for the first time, all he saw was ugliness. Her sour, moody face was really beginning to annoy him now.

It should have been Kara sitting there after their honeymoon. She would have worn a pleasant and pretty face, probably with her head in a book reciting something fascinating, with her hair pulled up in a messy ponytail, and her glowing, flawless skin. She would be holding his coffee while he drove and passing it every few minutes for him to drink. Or they would, as they often did, listen to an old Eighties CD and sing along together. But it wasn't Kara sitting there: it was Lucy with a face like a smacked arse.

* * *

Kara arrived back at Larkview. It could have been worse – she could have been on her way to Durham, reacquainting herself with Esme. She had been horrified when the judge had said four and a half years, but when Stuart explained that with good behaviour she would only serve two years and three months, she showed relief. It could have been worse, so much worse.

Vic and Deni already knew the outcome because Vic had called her brother and he gave her the run-down. As soon as Kara appeared back on the wing, she was greeted with hugs and a pat on the back.

Deni had paced the floor all day and was particularly relieved that they had sent Kara back to Larkview. The alternative would have been a blow to them all.

'So, Posh, it looks like you're stuck with us for a while, then?' Julie laughed.

With a chuckle, Kara nodded. She was overwhelmed by the fuss they'd made.

'Vic, your brother was there. Gosh, he must have thought me a right baby, blubbering the way I did.'

'Nah, babe, he said you were like a fish out of water, but that's a good thing. It probably saved ya arse.'

'It was tough. I mean, Stuart said I had to tell the court I didn't remember lighting the fire.'

'And?' asked Deni.

'Well, I swore on the Bible to tell the truth, but I lied. I do remember starting the fire. I mean, I remember every bloody detail.'

For a second, Deni frowned, but then she thought about things. 'My girl, there ain't no one in this fucking shit-hole that ain't lied to save their skin.' She rolled her eyes. 'Anyway, a lie like that will save you ten years inside, so come on, you must think of the baby, now.'

They all went into Julie and Kara's cell. Vic was bursting to get something off her chest. 'Listen, you need to start making arrangements. The social services will be wanting to have a word, so you need to have a plan in place or those no-good fucking busybodies will be making a plan for you. Get my drift?'

Kara nodded. 'Well, I guess Justin will have heard that I'm expecting. His mother was there in the courtroom.'

'What's she like, the mother-in-law from hell?' scoffed Julie.

'No, actually I was closer to her than my real mum ... well, what I mean is, I saw more of her while my mum was in Australia.'

Deni had her back to Kara, pouring her a hot chocolate. 'Listen, babe, about this Justin. You say he's a good bloke, although he fucked up. Now, mistakes aside, you do know he'll be the best person to care for the baby for a while, don't ya? 'Cos, as much as you'll love the little one, Justin will too, and at least for the time until you're released, you'll know she'll be in safe hands.'

Kara took the hot chocolate that was handed to her. 'Yes, of course.'

At the end of the bed, Julie was giving Kara a knowing look. Never thinking before she spoke, she said, 'Ya just wanna watch his bird. Don't let him favour her baby over yours.'

'Jue!' hollered Vic.

'Well, I was only saying.'

'Well, don't bleedin' bother! Keep that mouth of yours firmly shut. You only make matters fucking worse.'

Vic took a deep breath. 'This bird of his may well be a nice woman. We don't even know her. She may have so much guilt for what she did, that she may see fit to care for your baby until you get out. After all, look at it this way. She'll have all those mothering hormones floating about, and it's my guess, the babies won't be too far apart in age. They'll be company for each other.'

Kara looked up over her hot chocolate. 'I know you're right. It's just the thought that *that* bitch took everything from me, and it looks like she'll have my baby too.' A large tear plopped onto her cheek.

The room fell silent for a few seconds, each woman feeling their friend's pain.

'You said this Justin left you because he got this bird up the duff, and he said he still loved you, but he had to do the right thing. Silly bastard, if you ask me, but the point is, now he knows you're having his baby, he'll no doubt be running back, maybe begging forgiveness,' said Deni, eager to stop Kara from breaking down into uncontrollable sobs.

'He can beg and plead all he likes, but as far as I'm concerned, he can fucking do one.'

Julie giggled. 'Go on, my girl, that's it, you fuck him off, the dirty bastard.'

'Julie, shut up!' ordered Vic again. It may have been funny hearing Kara talk like them, but that wasn't Kara speaking.

'But she's right though, Vic. I was in that courtroom, hoping in some way that he would be there, but he wasn't. But your brother was, and he doesn't even know me, and …' she looked down at her dress '… he still made sure I had a beautiful outfit to wear *and* he sat there through the whole case, encouraging me. So, yes, if Justin ever tried to get back with me, I would, as Julie said, fuck him off.'

Vic listened intently. 'Er, Kara, I know me brother is a bit of a handsome man, and he's done good by you, but …' She looked at Julie, who now had her head down. 'But – and as much as I hate to say it, 'cos I love me brother – he ain't right for you, babe. You are refined, ya know, posh and sweet. He's a fucker, really. He comes from a different world. All right, he says he's knuckling down and going straight, but his past is dark.'

Kara placed her hot chocolate down and sighed. 'Oh, Vic, I'm not blind or deaf. I know Rocky is a bit of a lad and has lived on the other side of the law. I know to him this is probably just a bit of fun, but the truth is, I'm a jailbird now, so what does it matter what he did in the past?'

Vic shot a look at Deni. 'You tell her, Deni.'

With that, Deni went and sat next to Kara. 'You may be in this shit-hole, but inside you, you are still Kara. You ain't lived a life like we have. As much as we love Rocky, he lives a life you would never comprehend.'

'Try me,' said Kara, feeling out of the circle.

'Okay …' She looked back at Vic, who nodded for her to go on.

'I know Vic and Rocky because, as you realise now, I ran a brothel. I don't hide the fact. Rocky was into many scams, ya know, drugs, organised crime, and that kinda thing. I met Rocky before I ever knew Vic. He was good to me. He would rough up a few punters, if they got too much for me girls and too much for me to handle. But I have to be honest. He liked a freebie.'

Kara screwed her nose up. 'Freebie?'

'A free bunk-up off me prettiest girls.'

'Oh, I see,' replied Kara, now rather deflated. 'And did his girlfriend know?' she asked innocently, to the amusement of the other three women.

'Girlfriend! Our Rocky loves himself too much. Nah, he's never had a girlfriend, the flash fucker,' roared Julie, who was now falling off the bed in stitches.

'So, why are you concerned about me, if he doesn't want a girlfriend? I mean, I get the picture. He has everything he wants on a plate, if you like, doesn't he?'

Vic stopped chuckling. 'It's because I've never seen him or heard him go on about a woman like he does with you.'

With her cheeks blushing, Kara replied, 'So, what's so special about me?' She looked down and ran her hands over her belly, feeling her baby kicking.

Julie laughed. 'He probably fancies a bit of posh.'

Vic whacked her arm. 'Ya know what, Julie, you can be right vile sometimes. Just shut up! Anyway, Kara, to answer your question, that's how I know he really thinks you're something special, because I know for a fact, he don't want kids. He hated seeing me mother pregnant and popping out babies, year after year. But it ain't put him off you. So, this is the thing. When our Rocky has his heart set on something, he'll do everything to get it, and right now, babe, it's you. So, if you ain't sure about him, or he's just a man passing the time with you whilst you're locked up, then, I think it's best you put him straight, either way.'

Kara nodded; she understood completely what Vic was saying.

That night in bed, she lay awake whilst Julie snored her head off. She tried to think of the good times with Justin. Did she still love him? But it was marred by what he'd done to her, and then her thoughts drifted to Rocky. In reality, could she live that life? But then, what had life in store for her, now she was branded a convict, an arsonist? And there was no way she would ever get a decent job when she was released. And, there was her baby. What life would they have in a flat with no money?

* * *

After the silent drive to their flat, Lucy got out and headed for the front door. She looked behind her to find Justin still seated. She pushed the door open and glared at the cold, uninviting home. Quickly, she spun around; she could lose all her future plans, if she didn't do something soon. She could feel Justin pulling away from her. She hurried back to him in floods of tears; instantly, she opened the car door and sat back down, sobbing like a baby. She couldn't lose everything she'd planned for.

'What the hell's the matter?' He wasn't like before, wrapping his arms sympathetically around her. He leaned back against the driver's door and stared.

'Oh my God, Justin, our baby, our little boy. What are we going to do?' she wailed and covered her face.

He sighed because he knew he should be comforting Lucy. Perhaps the shock had just hit her, and her solemnness throughout the journey home was disbelief, and now she was inconsolable. Yet for the life of him, he could not get the vision of Kara standing all alone in the court like a lost child out of his mind.

'Come on, Lucy, let's go inside. I'll make us a hot drink and get you comfortable before I go out.'

'What!' she shrieked.

'I need to go and see my mother. She wants to talk to me.'

'But … I need you, Justin, I don't want to be alone. I've had a really bad scare. Our baby could have something wrong with him … or worse, could die.'

He knew she was right, but he wanted to see his mother. He couldn't talk it over with Lucy; she was too absorbed in her own pain.

'I won't be long, love. Look, let's go inside, get the flat warmed up, and you settled down. It's been a long day, and I'm sure you must be exhausted.'

For a second, she wanted to claw his face. His mother must have gone to the court, so now she would try and persuade him to get back with Kara. She didn't have enough time to think of a plan to stop him from going to his mother's. As soon as he turned on the heating, the lights, and the kettle, he was up the stairs and getting changed.

'Justin, please stay!' she called up to him.

* * *

Justin heard Lucy, but he didn't answer; he had to get away, even for an hour, to think things over, out of Lucy's way. He felt as if

263

Lucy could read his thoughts. He pulled a cable-knit jumper over his head and smoothed back his hair.

Within a few minutes, he'd made a pot of tea and handed her a cup. 'I won't be long, Lucy, I promise. I just need to talk to my mother, tell her what's going on.'

Lucy smirked. 'And will you let her know that we're married?'

Ouch! He felt his throat tighten. He looked at his wife, sitting with the cup of tea in her hands and a cold sneer on her face.

He didn't bother to answer her sarcastic comment but headed for the door.

'It's wicked, Justin, what you're doing to me and our baby!' she spat back in anger.

Pausing at the door, he didn't know whether to fly back into the living room and scream at her or walk away and face another kind of music from his mum. He had to start doing the right thing. He would tell his mother that he was now married and …

He stopped before he opened the car door. He should tell Lucy the truth too.

Lucy was crying and in a foul temper, when he burst back through the door. 'Right, listen to me. I'm going to see my mother because …' he paused '… you might as well know …' He faltered, almost disbelieving what he was about to tell her.

Holding her breath, Lucy assumed he was going to tell her he was leaving her.

'Kara is pregnant, with my child.'

As if someone had slapped her across her face, every emotion ran like a fast-flowing river through her head. Kara had won. She would have her life back with Justin in their big house and holidays abroad, the baby's room all perfect for their newborn. Lucy, on the other hand, would be stuck in this poky flat, with a kid who could have special needs, restricting her freedom. She would be trapped.

'But how could she be? She's in prison. How do you even know it *is* your baby? You've been with me.'

Justin glared back with narrowed eyes. 'Because, Lucy, she is about five or six months pregnant, so my mother informed me. That's why I need to go and find out exactly what's going on, and I don't want to do it over the bloody phone.'

Her temper was rising, and Lucy was about to explode. She tried to keep a lid on it, but she couldn't. 'See, Justin, do you see what she's really like? She never even let you know she was having a baby. How selfish is that? At least I told you right away. It's wrong to keep you in the dark, the selfish bitch. Oh, Justin, you must feel awful, knowing she didn't want you to know. She probably planned to bring the child up away from you, not even letting you have the pleasure of knowing your own child.' She was on a roll, digging the knife deeper into his chest. But she wasn't ready for what came next.

'Shut up, Lucy, just shut the fuck up! You don't know Kara, like I do. She would only have kept it a secret so as not to complicate matters. I went off with you because you are expecting my child. Kara is not the type of woman to use her child to get me back. She has a sense of values and class.'

Lucy jumped up from her seat. 'Class? Class? She burned ya fucking house down, nearly killed the neighbour, and hid your own child from you! How the fucking hell is that classy?'

Justin looked her up and down and shook his head. 'She wouldn't have sworn like that or behaved the way you just did.' He turned to leave.

'Don't you dare compare me to that stuck-up bitch!'

Spinning on his heels, Justin gave her a penetrating glare. 'And how the hell would you know what she's like, eh?'

Lucy recoiled, realising she'd just dropped a major bollock. 'I, er, just get the impression she is like that, that's all.'

'Based on what?'

'Well, the way you go on about her.'

'That's odd, Lucy, because I never talk to you about Kara, do I? I would never be so insensitive. I'm going to my mother's. I suggest you calm yourself down and get some rest. We can talk about this tomorrow, when we're both a little more clear-headed.'

She watched him walk away, thinking about those words: 'I would never be so insensitive'. *Did the man have no gumption?*

* * *

The cold air bit at his face as he wandered up the garden path, but he couldn't feel it; he was numb with shock.

Mollie saw him from the window and hurried to the door. 'Oh, Jesus, Son, what the hell is going on? The phone went dead, and I never heard anything. I was worried to death.'

His face was worn down with anguish and Mollie didn't have the heart to lay into him.

'Get inside, you look awful.' She ushered him into the living room. He flopped onto the sofa and leaned forward with his head in his hands.

Mollie sighed. 'Right, my boy, we need to get this mess sorted out, so I'm not going to have a go at you. There's no point. We need to move forward.'

Justin sat up straight and shook his head. Mollie noticed his eyes were moist with tears. He sniffed them back and took a deep breath. 'Oh, Mum, what the hell have I done?'

'I suppose you were doing what you thought was best. You weren't to know Kara was expecting.'

He jumped up from the sofa and gripped his hair in frustration. 'I married her, Mum. I got married three, no, four days ago. I thought I was doing the right thing, but now Kara …'

Mollie felt sick at the thought, but then she realised that Justin would probably be feeling a great deal worse. She clocked the worry lines on his forehead.

'Justin, it now comes down to what you want from your life, and, of course, what Kara wants.'

He stopped pacing and scowled. 'What do you mean what

Kara wants? You said she was sentenced to four and half years. My baby can't grow up in a prison – it's not right. She will have to give the child to me. She can't look after it in there!'

Mollie's eyes widened; she'd never expected that reaction. 'Are you that bloody cold-hearted, Justin? What about Kara? What the hell do you think she's going through? And now you want to take away her baby too!'

He looked at his mother, as if she were mad.

'I would have thought the first thing on your mind would be how you can get her out of prison with appeals and stuff, not taking the baby from her,' spat Mollie. White-faced and fuming, she left the room to make tea, leaving Justin to think about what she'd said. It crossed her mind that her new daughter-in-law had cast some spell over him. It was either that or he was on drugs because she was listening to a stranger. Her son was a kind-hearted man, who would give a homeless person his last pound. She stood staring at the kettle as it boiled, allowing a tear to run down her cheeks. Her son, her only child, had changed beyond recognition.

She returned with a tray of tea and biscuits in her hands and a look of grief on her face.

Justin was seated once more and watched his mother place the tray on the coffee table. 'Mum, don't you think Kara was wrong to deny me my child? She didn't even let me know she was expecting, and she burned my house to the fucking ground. What sort of woman was she, really?'

With a piercing expression, Mollie replied, 'I hate to hear your wife's words out from your mouth.'

'What?' he snapped.

'Justin, those are not your words, are they? You would never speak like that, or, for that matter, think like that. So, I can only assume your wife is egging you on.'

Justin had forgotten how well his mother knew him. His shoulders slumped; he didn't want to argue.

'You and I are all Kara has because Joan is sick on the other

267

side of the world. I assume poor Kara hasn't even told her about what's happened because she wouldn't want her to worry. As I said to you earlier, that's probably the same reason she hasn't told you about the baby. Also, she probably assumed you wouldn't want her now you have a hunky-dory life with your new wife, who, I might add, was the reason she burned the bloody house down.' She noticed the uncomfortable expression on her son's face; he looked to be squirming. *So he should,* she thought.

'Mum, I also need to tell you that Joan died.' He waited for a response.

Mollie stared in disbelief. 'What! Oh my God, poor Kara! Dear me, can it get any worse?'

'Yes, Mum, it is worse. Apparently, she died about six months ago now. Lucas told me he thinks it's a bit fishy because Kara claimed she spoke with some carer who never let on she was dead.'

Stunned into silence, Mollie sat with her hands over her mouth.

'How the hell did Kara *not* know?'

'She didn't phone her all the time, like you phone me.' He realised that sounded sarcastic. 'I'm so sorry, Mum, I know you were friends.'

'I wasn't really friends with her as such. I just stayed in contact for Kara's sake. The truth be known, I didn't much care for Joan. She had a selfish side ...' She paused, staring off into space, with something preying heavily on her mind.

'What are you talking about?'

Mollie slowly turned to face him. 'Oh, nothing, I just found her a bit self-centred. She couldn't wait to go to the other side of the world. I mean, Kara hardly got her foot in your door when Joan had her plane ticket booked. She didn't wait around to see if Kara was even settled. It wouldn't surprise me if Joan had other intentions, like some bloke over there. Anyway, regardless of their relationship, she was still Kara's mother and Kara will be out of her mind, if I know that girl.' She drifted off, staring into space again.

'I'm so sorry, Mum.'

Instantly jumping to her feet, Mollie's shock turned to hurt. 'Hang on a minute. You knew this, Justin, and yet you damn well came into my home having a go about Kara and wanting to take her baby. How could you be so flaming wicked, eh, how could you? I was trying to think of it from your point of view, but even knowing Joan is dead, your attitude still hasn't changed.'

Justin was stunned to the bone; his mother had never spoken to him like that before, and it hurt, like a knife through his chest.

'I'm going to write to that poor girl, and you will not dare to try to take that baby from her, because, Justin, if I get an inkling that you have tried to, I won't stand back and do nothing. Do you understand me?'

Exhausted and angry, Justin, for the first time in his life, had a go back. 'My wife has just been through a tough time finding out that there may be something wrong with our son.'

Mollie's chest heaved up and down because her only child was winding her up. 'Your son? How are you so sure he *is* yours? You don't even know the woman. You ran out on Kara because you couldn't keep it in your bloody pants, and then a stranger tells you this baby is yours. Oh, Jesus Christ, Son, are you really that bleeding stupid? All I can say is, once that baby is born, you should get a paternity test done.'

In defiance, he retorted, 'Well, she is my wife now, and so whether the baby is mine or not, I will still bring him up as my son.'

'She really has got her claws into you then, hasn't she? Don't slam the door on your way out, Justin.'

Mollie heard Justin rev up his engine and tear away. The house fell silent and a buzzing sound rang in her ears as she tried to calm her raging heart. Justin had never made her so angry, and to think she had been considering helping him to sort out his mess. She looked up at the large photo of Kara and her son, his face golden bronze, his eyes wide and fresh, and his beaming smile. They looked so happy and so well. A perfect couple, in every way.

To think only a few months ago, he was planning to marry Kara, and now her dream for them both had been blown apart. Not only had her son aged ten years, with a look that was dull, lifeless, and cold, but she wondered what her own future would hold for her now. Allowing the tears to stream down her face, she sat at the dining-room table and began to write a letter to Kara.

Chapter 17

Lucy was sleeping in their bed, so Justin crept into the spare room and fell asleep, still fully clothed. The morning traffic caused him to stir, but his eyes were too sore to open, and his body ached from stress. He sensed Lucy at the door; perhaps it was her breathing or sighing, but he kept his eyes closed and remained motionless, nevertheless. He didn't want to talk just yet; really, he didn't have the energy. Then he heard her go down the stairs. Ignoring the inevitable, though, would prove counterproductive.

He sneaked into the shower and allowed the hot spears of water to liven him up before he washed his hair; it felt wet and heavy, resting on his shoulders. He hadn't been looking after himself lately. His locks needed a good cut, and as he ran his hands over his head, he thought perhaps with fatherhood rapidly approaching, he was too old for the surfer look. He knew the young girls liked it, although, apart from Lucy, he'd never flirted with another woman; he just enjoyed looking good.

It was different now. He'd let himself go, which was another worry to add to a very long list. The thought again overwhelmed him, and he shook his head to dismiss all the concerns circling like a pride of lions around in his head.

His body was still aching from tiredness, and so he slipped

into a grey tracksuit and went to face Lucy. With her dark eyes and dishevelled hair, she was not looking so good herself this morning. She offered him a cup of coffee and nodded. 'Here, Justin.' Even her voice sounded deflated.

He took the drink and gave her an awkward smile.

'Can we sit down and talk about all this?'

Lucy felt her throat tighten. Was he going to leave? 'I'm sorry about yesterday. I didn't mean …'

He held up his hand for her to stop, as he slid onto the kitchen chair. 'No, forget yesterday. There is something I need to tell you, and to be honest, I don't know myself what to think and for that matter what to do.'

Lucy held her breath and sat opposite. She was witnessing a new expression, one she'd never seen on Justin's face. He looked serious rather than angry.

'Kara got sentenced to four and a half years, and as I told you, she is pregnant, about five or six months, so my mother reckons.'

He waited for a response, but Lucy turned to stare out of the kitchen window.

After a few moments, she replied in a flat tone, 'She will only serve two and bit years.'

'What?' asked Justin, seeming surprised at her reaction.

'I said she will only serve two and a bit years. A non-violent crime – she will only serve half the sentence.' Realising she'd said too much, she quickly said, 'Excuse me, I need the bathroom.' In a flash, she was up and gone.

Justin didn't know what to think or do. He remained seated and waited for her to return, but she didn't appear. He knew it would be a shock, but she had to be told. He contemplated going out and leaving her alone to digest the information, but it was all his doing, and he had to face the music. Stupidly, he'd assumed that Lucy was on the same page as him, thinking about what was best for the child, and since he must be the father, then naturally, he would be the one to care for it.

Sitting on the cold bathroom floor, Lucy was silently screaming, and then racking her brains. Was Kara really pregnant? Was it a ploy to get him back? She got up from the floor, wiped her eyes, looked in the mirror, and snarled, 'Kara Bannon, you will not win. I will make sure you don't get your hands on what's rightfully mine.' Then an evil smile crept its way across her face. Two years inside, Kara would go insane, especially once the social services took her baby away from her, and then she would have nothing.

Justin wouldn't go running back to her. She was in prison. What sort of absurd relationship was that? Her knock in confidence now having receded, she was on top again, and by hook or by crook, she would remain there. She took one last look in the mirror and sadistically grinned to herself.

Eventually, after washing her face, she reappeared in the kitchen with a sheepish smile, knowing he liked her when she was at her most vulnerable.

'Sorry, Justin, I just needed a moment to process everything.' She lowered her head and gracefully took a seat.

He reached for her hand. 'I know, darling. I've been doing that too.'

'Yes, of course, Justin. All those questions, and to think for this length of time you've been feeling guilty about us and she was at it with someone else.'

Angry and frustrated, he snatched his hand away. 'What do you mean? No way was she. That baby has to be mine. I was with her six months ago.'

Lucy sighed. 'Oh, babe, of course it's not your baby. She would have told you right away, like I did. Let's face it, she was probably planning to leave you, and because you got in there first, she burned the house down in spite.'

'Well, Lucy, either way, I need to see her to find out the bloody truth. I can't have a child of mine being brought up in a prison. Jesus, I'll go for custody. They will have to let me have the child. It has to be better than prison.'

Stunned into silence, Lucy glared with venom in her eyes. She never expected Justin to take on the child, but then, perhaps it shouldn't be such a shock. He loved to do everything the right way. Without thinking, she blurted out, 'And what about me?'

He studied her, with confusion across his face. 'What do you mean?'

'Well, you want to take on her baby. Who will look after it, and what makes you think I want hers? We have our own son to think of, and for all we know ...' her eyes glistened '... he may have special needs. Or is that why you want her baby – because no doubt it will be perfect and not like ours.' She began to cry, leaving the fat tears to roll down her face. *Christ, I should go into acting*, she thought. She could almost believe her own sad words.

She was right. He hadn't thought about Lucy and her needs, but he wanted his baby with him, not in prison. The urge was stronger than Lucy's feelings right now. 'Don't be stupid, Lucy. I will love both the children equally, and if need be, I will get a nanny to help.'

She noticed his firm words and manly expression; it made him distinctly more attractive and her more resolute to keep him.

'How will you see her, if she doesn't want to see you?' she asked, forcing herself to keep her tone even.

'I'll go to the prison.'

'She will have to send out a VO. She's not on remand now, you know.'

Alarm clearly showing across his face, he said, 'How do you know so much about all of this, Lucy?'

'Being in children's homes, I heard and saw more than most as a youngster,' she replied, evenly, grateful she was on the ball this morning.

274

With a huff, he got up. 'I'm popping into the office to collect some paperwork. I can work from home.'

Lucy was hoping he would stay at the office. She needed a drink, and with him around, it was nigh on impossible. 'Babe, you don't have to come back. You stay there, I'm fine. I'll probably go back to bed, as I didn't sleep well, you know, worrying about our baby.'

He nodded, kissed her on the forehead, and left.

* * *

Watching Justin leave the flat, Carl smiled to himself, thinking *what a mug*. Yesterday's downpour had almost flooded the streets and the elderly lady in the flat below Lucy's was struggling with two black sacks of rubbish because her slippers were sodden and falling off her feet. Carl jumped from his car and relieved her of the heavy bags. 'Where do these go? In the green bin?'

'Oh, me darling, thank you. Yes, just chuck them in there for us, will ya? It's a job, ya know, to lift anything up these days, and those bins are so tall.'

He looked the dainty woman up and down. 'Why don't you leave them on the ground, next to the bin? I'm sure that Justin, your neighbour, would help you with them.'

She gave Carl a sad expression. 'He would, bless him, a lovely young man, but his missus, Lucy, would go mad. The last time I dropped rubbish, she shouted at me in the street. I thought, crikey, I'd best not upset her again.' She stopped and stepped back. 'Oh, I'm sorry, I'm speaking out of turn. She's probably a lovely lady, really.'

Carl put his arm around her shoulder. 'Nah, me darling, she's a bitch. Do you need anything else doing, sweetheart, while I've got a bit of time on me hands?'

She looked up and her eyes watered. 'Well, there is a job ...'

'Go on, what do ya need doing?' He chuckled.

'My husband died, six months ago, a tall man, twice my size, and well, all our memories, photos, and things, are on top of the wardrobes, and I can't reach them. I keep looking at them, and it breaks my heart that I can't get my hands on them.'

Carl squeezed her shoulder. 'Well, then, let's get those memories back for ya, shall we?'

He followed her inside and straight into her bedroom. 'There, see?' She pointed to the 1920s suitcases stacked neatly above the wardrobes.

He carefully pulled them down and laid each one on the bed. 'There you go, love.' He smiled, as he saw the pure delight on her face.

'Oh, I have longed to get them back. Every night, I sit in that bed and stare up at them and pray one day, well, you must be that angel I longed for. Thank you, my dear. By the way, my name's Lillian, Lilly for short.'

Carl nodded but didn't introduce himself. 'Anything else, while I'm here?'

She blushed, and all the creases, hiding a lifetime of marriage, lit up her face, making her look years younger. 'Well, yes, if you wouldn't mind. On top of the kitchen cabinets is my cake mixer and a few cooking bits. I love making cakes, but arthritis in my hands won't let me do it without that mixer. My Harry used to put everything away, Gawd rest his soul. I didn't think he was going to die when he did.'

After removing all the cooking pots and cake mixer from above the units, he placed them on the kitchen side and shivered. 'Is your heating not working, love?'

Lillian shook her head. 'No, my dear, I have to put the gas fire on in the living room.'

Carl looked at the boiler on the wall and noticed the switch high up just above the cabinet. He pressed the button and at once the boiler began rumbling. Lillian clapped her hands together.

276

'That's it. Oh my goodness, what did you do? I've been fiddling with the dial and couldn't get it to work.'

'I pressed a button next to it. Ya ol' man must have turned it off. Look, up there.' He pointed to the partially hidden time clock.

'Oh, you are a good boy. Well, I bet your mother is proud of you.'

Carl shook his head. 'I doubt it, but then, I ain't too fond of me mother, to be honest. She's not a nice person.'

'Ahh, that's a shame. I don't have a lot of money, but let me give you a few pounds because you've made an old lady very happy.'

He rubbed her shoulders. 'Well, that's all the payment I want, to see that smile on ya face.' With that, he pulled a card from his pocket. 'Take this, it's got me phone number on it. Call me, if you need me.'

She took the card, and as he was about to leave, he saw her eyes moisten. A soft glow emanated from her face. 'I never had children, but if I'd had a son, I would have loved him to be like you.'

'And, Lillian, I would have liked a mum, like you.' He kissed her on the cheek and was gone.

* * *

As Lillian returned to her bedroom, excited to look through her photo album, she heard Lucy shouting. Lillian thought about calling the police, when she heard the words, 'Fuck off, or I will call the Ol' Bill'. But she didn't. The young woman had a nasty side to her, and if it was that nice young man at the door, he didn't look like any threat to anyone.

She opened the first suitcase and fingered her beautiful gowns and the precious dresses and jewels her mother had left her. She'd pretended to her husband that they were costume jewellery, but they weren't, they were real. Then she pulled a photo album from under her bed. Flicking the first page over at her husband looking back at her, she smiled. He was deathly white in his sick bed, days before he died. 'I will get this photo enlarged, Harry, and drink to you dying, ya nasty 'orrible bastard.'

Not only had Lillian been violently bullied all her married life, she'd been left with nothing at the end of it. He'd spent their money, and when he went out on the piss, he would turn the heating off. He never told her where the on-off button was. She'd been struggling to keep warm next to the small gas fire in the flat, that day he came home drunk. It was the day he crushed her hands and broke her fingers, leaving her, years later, riddled with arthritis.

* * *

Lucy was desperate to get Carl out of the house, still unsure if Justin was going to return with the paperwork. 'You can't just turn up here whenever you fucking please. I've already told you once – I'll call the Ol' Bill,' she bellowed. 'Now, get out!'

Carl mocked her again. 'Lucy Lou, don't get so lairy. You always have been a cocky little prat. Now, shut ya mouth.'

Her eyes narrowed, and her spiteful glare might have been enough to scare some men. But not him.

He smirked. 'Your shitty past is your past. Quite frankly, I don't give a toss, but you owe me twenty fucking grand.'

'You're fucking loaded, so what's twenty grand to you?' she spat, with her hands on her hips and defiance plastered across her face.

'Yeah, you're right, I am doing well for meself, and doing it honestly and fairly now. Unlike you. I know your game, Lucy, but it won't work. Taking up with a decent fella won't change *who* you are.'

His arrogance and clearly defined words, with no hint of anger, infuriated her. She wanted him, not Justin, or anyone else, just him. 'Well, you can whistle for your money. You owe that to me, anyway.'

He leaned against the doorframe and laughed. 'And what for, Lucy? Tell me how the hell do I owe you twenty grand?'

She flared her nostrils. 'Lots of fucking reasons. You raped me as a kid, you had me working for ya sitting on that banker's lap, and you used me as a fucking hooker. I earned you money and what did I get, eh? Fuck-all, that's what.'

He shook his head. 'I would have thought, Lucy Lou, by now you would have grown out of your mad illusions. You've always been a pathological liar, a totally warped headcase. You only saw what you wanted to see, and deep down in that disturbed brain of yours, you know damn well I never fucking raped you—'

Before he could finish, she ran at him, clawing at his face, but he grabbed her wrists and pushed her down onto the sofa. 'Leave off, Lucy, don't start getting violent with me. The problem is you believe in ya own lies. Tell me, Lou Lou, did you ever go back and see your shrink?'

Her anger was rising, her face bright red. 'I never needed a shrink, you bastard!'

'Come on, your dear ol' farver—'

'Yes, me ol' man fucking sold me to you to pay off a debt.'

He shook his head again, not shocked to hear those words. 'You need to go back and see that psychiatrist of yours. There was no debt!'

Lucy leaped from the sofa, screaming at the top of her voice, 'You and me farver were the fucking reason I needed a shrink!'

He could see she was apoplectic with rage, just by the expression on her face and the fact that the veins in her neck were bulging. 'Calm down, Lucy, you're expecting a baby. You need to settle yaself. I'm going before you pop that baby out. However, I will be back, and I do want me money.'

He turned to leave, but she grabbed him by the arm. 'You

know what you did to me,' she cried. 'You raped me when I was fucking fifteen. I owe you nothing.'

He knew then he had to leave. The tears were falling down her cheeks, snot bubbled from her nose, and she looked deranged. 'Get off me, Lucy, I'm going, and I won't be back until you have the baby, and then I want me money, but I'll not upset you again.' He looked at her hand clutching his arm and then at the swollen belly.

She let go and screamed, 'I hate you, Carl. I fucking hate you.'

He looked back at her, as he headed for the front door and felt guilty. He knew she loved him, she always had. But he could never be with her. She was just not his type. He was doing her father a favour but he wished now he'd never got involved.

Lucy was hysterical and grabbed him once more. 'I will pay you your fucking money, and then, I never want to see you again. Wait there!'

He stopped and waited, as she tore up the stairs. He hoped she did have the money; it would save him from having to lay eyes on her again. She appeared like a bat out of hell, angrily hurtling down the stairs. 'Here, fucking take this, it's worth ten grand, and you will get the other half when I have it!' She slapped a ring into the palm of his hand.

He didn't bother to look at it, too intent on getting out of the flat and away from the psycho bitch. The look in her eyes said she was out of her mind, and knowing Lucy, she could easily have pulled a knife on him. Besides, she had done so once before, leaving a nasty scar on his leg. He wasn't about to make the same mistake again.

* * *

Lillian was in her element trying on the silk dresses and parading around in her mother's jewels whilst enjoying the warmth of the flat, when something caught her eye. She peered down, and there on the floor was a wad of notes held together by a diamond and gold clip. The young man must have dropped it. She flicked the bundle of notes and her heart skipped a beat; there was enough money in her hand to fill her larder and pay the gas bill.

Then she felt guilty for even thinking it. She had his number, so there was no excuse; but for a while, she continued strutting in front of the mirror in her expensive gown, with the rows of pearls and diamond bracelets, fanning herself with the fifty-pound notes.

* * *

Carl made it to his car, thankful he was still in one piece. That girl was totally out of control. He sat and sighed and then opened his hand to find the ring. He held it up to the light and noticed it wasn't a diamond but an unusual beige-coloured gemstone; the band itself was quite thick for a lady's ring. He was attracted to the piece and slipped it on his little finger. Knowing Lucy, she would have nicked the ring from one of her punters, so it could be worth a few quid.

He looked back at the flat and decided it was better to leave Lucy alone. Not that he wanted to write off the money, but never seeing her again was worth forfeiting twenty grand. His stomach churned over at the very thought of her and the sick games she played. He had better things to think about. He could leave and never look back.

He drove along Chislehurst High Street and headed for home. As he stopped close to the crossroads, he thought he saw Justin. He shuddered; the poor man had no idea what he'd let himself in for.

* * *

281

Justin had decided to take his paperwork home. He was too tired and drained to deal with any customers. Some of the lads were busy positioning cars in the showroom using car wheel dollies, so all he needed to do was to update the company's expenses. Holding three heavy files, he tried to manoeuvre his way up the path, dodging the pools of water from the recent flooding.

Back home Lillian was on her way to the phone box to call Carl, when she saw Justin struggling. 'Oh, my dear, can I help you with those?'

Justin straightened the files that were about to slide from his hands. 'I think I have them balanced but thank you.' He smiled and was about to continue into the flat.

'Oh, um … your wife's friend was here earlier. I was just about to call him from the phone box. He left something behind. Would you let him know?' She suspected he wasn't still at Justin's flat, but even if he was, she didn't feel inclined to knock on the door herself, after all the screaming and shouting.

A deep frown was etched across Justin's brow. 'Sorry, who did you say was here?'

'I didn't, but he seemed such a lovely man, a real gentleman. Anyway, would you let him know I have his money?'

Justin was trying to absorb her words. 'I'm sorry, love, I don't know who you mean, but if he is still here, I'll tell him.'

She gave him a quizzical look and left him there.

He didn't bother to dodge the puddles but angrily marched up to the front entrance.

* * *

The noise of the door slamming shut made Lucy jump, and she hurriedly hid the bottle of brandy inside her secret box, which she kept out of sight under the bottom shelf of the wardrobe. No one would even suspect that inside that concealed compartment were all her darkest secrets. God help her, if they were ever

282

discovered. She rushed to the bathroom to clean her teeth and then waited for Justin to call out. The sound of him banging and crashing rang alarm bells. Something was clearly wrong.

She joined him in the living room where he was sitting at the small dining table, staring at a pile of folders.

'Are you okay, love?' she asked sheepishly.

Assuming he was annoyed about Kara being pregnant, she was taken aback when he shot her a look of disdain. His top lip curled like a dog's, his eyes narrow.

'What's the matter?'

'Who was the man you had in the flat earlier?' he growled.

She stood like a rabbit caught in the headlights. 'Are you spying on me?' she spat back.

'No, I'm not fucking spying on you, but that comment is a strange one, Lucy. What do you have to hide?'

She realised she'd asked the wrong question and tried to hold back her temper. 'It was Carl, if you must know, but I sent him away.'

Justin stood up and ran his fingers through his hair. 'What does he want? And cut the crap, Lucy. There's more to this man than you're telling me, so spit it out, because I've just about had enough. I want the fucking truth.'

Her eyes flicked from side to side, as she grappled to find a plausible story. 'Carl is infatuated with me, and somehow, he's found out where I live and ...' she stalled.

'And what, Lucy? What does he fucking want?'

'Oh, for God's sake, Justin, the man's in love with me. He always has been and wants me for himself.' Her lie was believable ... to herself. 'He tries everything to get me back.'

'What do you mean "to get me back"? I thought you said he raped you when you were a kid?'

Her face reddened. She'd forgotten she'd told Justin that.

'Yes, he did, and then he treated me as if I was his girlfriend. You know, buying me stuff, sending flowers.'

'No, Lucy, you said he wants you back, as if you were dating him,' shouted Justin.

'Please, Justin, you have to understand. I was a kid, a desperate kid, and I knew no different. He did take me out a few times, but I went out of fear. I was terrified of him. He stalked me; he wouldn't leave me alone. The man was obsessed. I managed to get away, and now he has found me, he's trying it again.' She allowed her voice to waver, giving the impression she was afraid and upset.

With so much anxiety now playing with his emotions, he realised he was taking it out on her and it was wrong. He sighed. 'Sorry, love, it's just I've a lot to contend with at the moment.'

She approached him, putting her arms around his waist. 'I know, babe, but Carl is nothing to worry about. I sent him packing.'

'He may be back. The old lady downstairs said she had something of his. I think it was some money.'

'What? Why would she have his money?'

Justin shrugged. 'I don't know, but anyway, I need to get these expenses sorted. Do me a favour, would you, please? I need a cup of coffee.'

As Lucy went to make the drink, she noticed Carl's car parked up outside, and then she saw him walking up the path. Her heart was in her mouth, yet he didn't knock at their door. Presumably, he went to the old lady's, downstairs.

* * *

Lillian was pleased to see him again. He did remind her of Harry in his younger days, when Harry was full of charm and smiles and treated her like a princess.

'Son, sorry to call you back, but you left this. It must have fallen out of your jacket pocket.' She held up the money.

'Like I said on the phone, Lillian. You have the money, love, I

284

only wanted the clasp. It belonged to a dear friend of mine.' He winked.

'Oh, I couldn't, my dear.'

He chuckled. 'Most people, me included, would probably have kept it anyway. So, you have the money.' He looked around the tired flat and knew her need was greater than his. 'Honestly, I insist. I have plenty.'

She looked at the wad and smiled. 'Well, if you're sure. I mean, I can pay the gas bill and fill me larder.'

'Well, then, me little treacle, you do that.'

He took the gold clasp, kissed her on the cheek, and left as quickly as he arrived. 'Keep me number, Lil, and if ya need anything doing, you call me.'

She waved goodbye and was overcome with a warm feeling of such happiness. She closed the door and counted the money.

Chapter 18

The last three months had been as comfortable as the inmates could make it for Kara, under the circumstances. Her pregnancy had gone along with no hitches, and she had more room since Julie had been released from prison and Kara now had the cell to herself. She waddled to the shower, her feet now swollen and her bump heavy. Vic hurried along the wing to catch up with her.

'Oi, what are you doing, wandering off on ya own? You're ready to drop that little one. You could slip in the shower. Gawd, girl, you should wait for me or Deni.'

Kara giggled. 'Vic, I'm only having a shower. I'm fine, honestly.'

'How are you feeling?'

'Well, the twinges are getting more regular. The personal officer has alerted the hospital wing, so I thought I would get showered and sort out my stuff before they take me off.'

Vic placed an arm around her shoulder. 'Cole has said that she thinks Deni would be better to be your birthing partner 'cos she's feeling queasy, the great big lummox.'

Kara chuckled again. 'I guessed as much. She said yesterday she was nervous and felt she had the world on her shoulders. She takes the responsibility so seriously that it's really worried her. I said Deni can take her place.'

'Her heart's in the right place, though,' replied Vic, with a warm tone in her voice. 'You can call that Justin, if you want him there, ya know, because they can't stop him being at the hospital.'

Kara stopped in her tracks and turned to face Vic. 'No! He has his son. He married this Lucy woman, and just because he sends me letters every bloody day, it changes nothing. I read them when I'm bored, but I've never responded. He thinks he has some kind of right to my child. I've a good mind to write back and tell him my baby is not his, she's someone else's.'

Vic gave her a cheeky smile. 'And would that someone else be our Rocky, by any chance?'

With peachy cheeks, Kara chuckled. 'That would be difficult. We haven't even … well, you know.'

Vic nodded. 'Yeah, kiddo, but I bet you can't wait to do so when you get outta 'ere.'

'I do love him, Vic. He's so kind and caring. I just hope he waits for me. I still have nearly two years to serve, and I just hope he will stick it out. That's selfish, I know, but I've fallen for him.' Caught unawares, she gritted her teeth. 'Ohh, that was painful.'

Vic smiled. 'Well, she's on her way. You quickly get in the shower. I'll call your personal officer with an update. I think it's time, love.'

By the time Kara had showered, she'd had two contractions and was feeling overwhelmed with excitement and fear. Officer Melanie Brent arrived and helped Kara back into her oversized tracksuit.

'Right, my lovely, let's get you over to the hospital wing.' She looked down the landing to find Deni panting and puffing. 'Take your time, Deni. Kara is not about to drop the baby just yet.' She laughed.

'Gawd, I need to get fit,' she choked, in between gasps of air. The officer smiled. 'Right, are we ready?'

Deni was fussing. 'Hold me arm, babe. Take ya time.'

Kara felt relieved that Deni was by her side. Unexpectedly, Vic grabbed Kara's hand and squeezed it. 'You will be fine, love.' Her voice was gentle, unlike her usual harsh words. It was at that point, Kara could see her as a sister, and it warmed her heart.

The hospital wing had a private room where Kara lay on the bed. The midwife, Gina, checked her over and concluded that everything was going well. Gina had been assigned to Kara and had regularly visited, ensuring that the pregnancy was going to plan. The scans had shown that the baby was healthy and full-term. Kara was now listening to the baby's heart rate through a monitor strapped to her. The sound made Kara smile. 'Ahh, is that her?'

Deni watched the midwife, looking for any expression on her face that would show if there was anything wrong.

Rubbing Kara's shoulder, Gina nodded. 'Yes, she has a strong heartbeat too.'

Gina asked if Kara needed pain relief, but she shook her head. 'No, I want to try to have her without analgesics.'

Deni looked at the midwife and rolled her eyes. 'I bet they all say that.'

Gina laughed. 'Yep, and would you believe it, the mums who say they will want all the painkillers you have, are the ones who don't need them.'

Kara's face was flushed with a few beads of sweat dampening her hairline. Deni could tell the contractions were closer and stubborn.

'Babe, if it's too much, Gina can give you something.'

Kara shook her head. 'No, I'll try on my own for a while.'

'Well, Gina, what she don't use, can I have?'

They laughed and tried to make light of the situation to make Kara's experience as pleasant as possible.

An hour passed, and everyone could tell Kara was struggling. Gina looked at the monitor, with some concern. She could see the baby's heartbeat was dropping below what it should be. Jumping up, she reached for the phone and called George. 'We need an ambulance, quickly. Kara has to go to hospital.'

Kara was sucking on the gas and air and Deni was biting her lip; she didn't like the look on Gina's face. Luckily, Kara was in too much pain to notice the panic in the air.

'Kara?'

She pulled the gas away from her face and tried to focus.

'Kara, the paramedics will be here in two minutes. We'll take you to the hospital. There's nothing to worry about. I just want to be sure, that's all.'

Gina looked at the fear across Deni's face. 'It's just a precaution. Don't worry, Deni, this happens a lot. The baby is tired.'

Deni, white-faced, nodded and stroked Kara's hand. 'Babe, you go with Gina. She'll look after you.'

Kara felt panicky and clutched Deni's arm. 'No, I need you, Deni; I can't do this alone. Please stay.'

Deni looked at Gina for guidance.

Gina then completely took over. 'Kara, I will not leave your side, okay? Everything will be fine. You just breathe in that gas and air, and it will all be over very soon.'

The paramedics strapped Kara to a stretcher and hurried her into the ambulance. Gina, as she promised, was by her side, yet Kara was reluctant to let go of Deni's hand.

'Come on, babe, you'll be fine, I promise.' With a kiss on her cheek, Deni stepped away, leaving the paramedics to get Kara out of the prison.

* * *

As the ambulance rushed along the bumpy lane, Kara stared with terror in her eyes. 'I can't lose this baby, Gina. She is all the family I have, now.'

One of the paramedics, a young man with huge hands and no neck, took the details and her vitals. Kara was sucking hard on the gas and air and staring at the young man.

At that point, the ambulance speeded up, and Gina realised

then that the baby was under stress. She should have called the paramedics earlier and not waited so long. Her heart raced, and sweat covered her brow. *Please make it,* she prayed.

* * *

Melanie Brent and George followed behind in a car because Kara was still a prisoner.

As soon as they reached the hospital, Kara was taken directly into surgery. They had no time to give her an epidural; instead, they gave her a general anaesthetic, and within ten seconds, she was out cold.

Gina, Melanie, and George sat in the waiting room, all too stunned to speak. Gina stared at the door, watching doctors and nurses going in and out. Her heart ached because she feared the worst, until, finally, a nurse came over, projecting a generous smile. 'Both mum and baby are doing great.'

Tears welled up in George's eyes and he quickly blinked. Melanie burst into tears. Gina sighed with relief, having felt so guilty; all her visions of being sacked or shunned vanished as quickly as they appeared.

* * *

Still groggy from the anaesthetic, Kara stared at her baby in the crib next to her bed, unable to believe that the beautiful child was actually hers. She tickled the baby's cheeks and stroked her thick mop of black hair. Melanie and Gina, too excited to wait for the okay, crept into the room.

'Aw, look at her. She is so beautiful,' whispered Melanie, as she looked over at Kara and smiled. 'Does her dad have black hair?'

Kara thought about Justin and an unexpected tear trickled down her face. 'No,' came the curt reply.

Gina ran her hands over the baby's thick mop of locks. 'Ahh, it's a shame because all that luscious hair will probably fall out and she will end up as blonde as you.'

The baby opened her eyes. 'Look at that! She has huge eyes. What a stunner. She looks like you, Kara,' said Melanie, still cooing over the tiny bundle wrapped in a pink blanket like a seashell.

Tears worked their way down Kara's nose, thinking about Justin. Was it really fair to deny him his right as the father? She wiped away her sodden cheeks. 'Melanie, would you call someone for me?'

With a sympathetic smile, Melanie nodded. 'Justin?'

'Yes, I think he should know, or rather I think my baby should know her father.'

Melanie pulled out her mobile and rang the number Kara gave her. It sounded four times before Justin answered. Melanie covered the phone with her hands. 'Do you want to speak to him, Kara?'

She shook her head; she wasn't ready just yet.

Melanie left the room. 'Is that Justin Fox?'

'Yes.'

'Hello, I'm Melanie Brent, one of the officers from Larkview Prison. Kara Bannon has asked me to call you. She gave birth to a baby girl, an hour ago.'

'Where is she?' came the panicked voice.

Melanie wasn't sure whether she was supposed to tell him or not, but Kara had said she wanted the baby to know him. 'Sutton Hospital.'

'Okay, I'm on my way.'

'Er, sir, no. I don't know if she wants you here. I mean, she wanted me to let you know—'

'Excuse me, Melanie, but I want to see my daughter, so I'll be there in an hour.' With that, he cut the connection.

* * *

Looking surprisingly well for a woman who had given birth only few weeks earlier, Lucy shot a look at Justin. 'What? Who was that?'

Justin's dismissive attitude lately was getting worse by the day. 'Someone called Melanie, from Sutton Hospital. Kara has given birth. I'm going to see her now.'

Without thinking, she snapped, 'And what about our baby? Are you going to visit him too?'

Justin looked her up and down. 'Lucy, I visit him every day. It's about time you did as well. You're his mother,' he growled, with tight lips. His eyes were heavy, and during the last few months, he'd found himself overloaded with thought, with the worrisome time over his son and the concerning issues around the baby's health. The rebuilding of his house and of course his work, not to mention his concern over his unborn baby and the prospects of her being brought up in a prison cell, were also draining him.

'You know how hard it is for me. It breaks my heart to see him wired up with all those tubes and monitors. I'm doing my best, to have the house ready for our son when he comes home. And what you expect to do when you get to the hospital, I don't know. She won't let you have the baby, and it's just going to torment you, knowing that your other child is being brought up in a prison, and there's fuck-all you can do about it. But our baby needs us, and I'm going to make sure, when he comes home, he has a beautiful room and a nice environment. So, Justin, don't think for one minute I'm neglecting our son. I'm making a brighter future for him.' She tried to sound convincing; whether it was to ease her own guilt or dupe Justin, it didn't matter.

Disappointed and exhausted, Justin snapped back, 'Sometimes, I wonder if you care more about the bloody house than our son.'

Lucy had learned to bring on the tears at will, and she did so to make him feel guilty. 'How could you, Justin! Twenty-four hours I was in labour, and for two weeks, I prayed by his cot. You have

292

no idea what it's like for me. I'm doing my best to make sure he has everything he needs ...' She broke off in floods of tears. 'I find it so hard to see him there, and I feel guilty because it was my womb he grew in. How do you think that makes me feel?'

He rolled his eyes because she came out with the same whining words. He'd stopped holding her and comforting her because his affection was for his son, that little boy fighting for his life. He knew that the baby might never make it to the house, and it infuriated him even more that his wife wouldn't accept it. Ben was born with various problems and most concerning was that his lungs were not as developed as they should be, so even with the proper care, he could still die.

'I'll call at the hospital on the way back from seeing my daughter, and hopefully, I'll be able to make Kara see sense.'

Lucy gave him her death stare. 'You only want her baby because hers is probably perfect and not damaged like ours!'

Justin wanted to throttle her. Mad as a hornet, he lunged forward and stopped an inch from her nose. 'Don't you fucking dare say that to me. I love my son.'

His eyes burned into hers. She stepped back. 'Go on, then, see your precious daughter.'

He didn't bother to argue any more; slamming the door behind him, he passed another deliveryman carrying more boxes. He looked back at the house and shuddered. His home with Lucy was now brand-new, complete with a redesigned front garden – all Lucy's ideas, of course. His mood was drained along with his bank balance. She was spending money as if it was going out of fashion.

* * *

Kara was well enough to sit up and hold her bundle of joy; she didn't want to put her down, but the nurse insisted they both rest. 'Can't I hold her for just another minute?'

The young nurse, Alison, smiled and nodded. She admired Kara for how well she was recovering from her caesarean section. She was now sitting upright, her eyes alive and wide. Alison hadn't experienced caring for a woman prisoner admitted to hospital to have her baby. She tried to put herself in Kara's shoes, knowing that as soon as she was better, she would be back in a place that the nurse herself just couldn't imagine. Quickly, she left the room, allowing the mother to spend time alone with her daughter.

Seconds later, the door opened, and there, looking older, thinner, and washed out, stood Justin. Kara felt her hands shake and she gripped her baby tighter. 'What are you doing here?'

He appeared awkward and slightly dazed.

It had been months since Justin had laid eyes on the one woman he truly loved, and seeing her looking so sweet and yet flushed, holding their child, made him want to run to her and throw his arms around her and beg her forgiveness. But the cold glare she gave him put paid to that thought.

'I wanted to meet our baby and see if you were okay.'

She looked down at her sleeping daughter. 'Well, here she is.' Her words were cold, and her expression held no warmth for him.

He ventured towards the bed nervously, and then, when he saw the perfect bundle, he felt a lump in his throat and swallowed hard to stop his emotions showing.

'She's beautiful, Kara. She looks so like you.'

Kara sneered at him. She'd thought that seeing him would have her in knots, and all the love she had for him would come flooding back, but she felt nothing, not now, not after everything.

'Can I hold her?' He held out his hands.

She pulled her baby closer. 'No, she's sleeping.'

He winced, as if she'd pricked him with a fork. The rejection seemed to anger him.

'We need to talk. It's not right for our daughter to be brought up in a prison. I can give her a good home.'

Those words were like a red rag to a bull. 'Get out, Justin, get out!'

He held his arms out in a gesture of supplication. 'No, listen, please, I don't want to upset you.'

She continued to glare, but the stress of seeing Justin caused a sharp pain through her middle, and just then, she could feel every stitch.

'Please, Kara, what sort of life would she have locked up in a prison cell? No walks to the park, no fresh air, no toys to play with. Is that what you want for our daughter?'

'She will have me, Justin. She will fucking have me!'

He jolted with shock. Never having heard her talk like that before, he could only assume prison had changed her. 'Kara, don't make this difficult. I can get full custody, you know. Let's face it, what judge would award you custody?' There, he'd said it, and he could have kicked himself. But there would be no appeasement now. Both of them had laid their cards firmly on the table.

Kara looked at her perfect baby and a tear ran down her face. 'You know, you are such a bastard, Justin. You've ruined my life. You let me love you so much, and then you went off with another woman. You sent me that letter demanding that I must vacate the house, and when I set fire to our home and got locked away on remand in prison, you didn't even turn up in court for the trial. You destroyed me, Justin, but I won't let you ruin this little one's life. You may visit her, but you will never have custody. I will appeal and appeal, until I'm released, and then you will have no grounds for custody.'

'I've spoken with a lawyer and you have to send her out to me while you serve the remaining months of your sentence,' he said, with a cockiness carved on his face.

She smirked. 'No, I don't have to send her out to you. I may not be able to keep her with me, but she doesn't have to go to you. Oh, come on, Justin, don't look so shocked. You fucked me over, and by Christ, I will make sure I return the favour.'

His eyes narrowed and he frowned at her anxiously. 'I don't understand.'

'No, of course you wouldn't because I assume it's all a shock to you that I could have any friends on the outside now. I have no family, yes, that's true, but I have friends.'

She was right; he'd assumed she had no one, and he also believed she had no option.

'But I'm her father. It makes sense for me to have her. I'm her blood.'

'So is your mother,' she snapped back.

Justin cocked his head to the side. 'My mother? Have you been in contact with her?'

'Yes, Justin, she visits regularly and writes every day. She's even sent in baby clothes and blankets. She's been an absolute godsend. It's a pity that you don't take after her.'

Biting his bottom lip, Justin felt his stomach churn over. He hadn't spoken with his mother since the day he stormed out – no, make that was kicked out. He'd taken too much for granted, assuming Kara would be only too pleased to have him to look after their daughter. He was totally blind and stupid. Of course, his mother wouldn't have stood by and let Kara rot in hell; she was too kind and caring to do that.

He knew Kara was right. She could hand the baby over to his mother – the child's grandmother – the lawyer had said as much. Lucas, his long-term friend and lawyer, had refused to see Justin again after his no-show in court. So, he'd had to find a new and expensive solicitor. Justin looked at his empty hands: he'd not even brought a card or flowers for Kara. Instead, he'd behaved like a bully. Whatever was he thinking?

'Okay, Kara, I'll leave you in peace, but please send a visiting order so that I can at least see her. What's her name?' he asked, solemnly.

She looked down at her baby and smiled. 'Denise Rose, after my friend.'

296

He paused, surprised that she hadn't named the baby after her mother. 'Aw, Kara, I'm sorry to hear about your mother. It must have been a terrible blow for you.'

'Yes, I guess you could say it was the final nail in the coffin. Anyway, it's still under investigation as to what really happened, but I'm stuck inside, and all I can do is hope that my lawyer eventually gets to the bottom of it. But that's not your concern.'

He knew that was another dig at him.

'What do you mean, your lawyer's getting to the bottom of it? The bottom of what? Is there anything I should know?' He tried to sound concerned but at the same time empathetic, although even that seemed to come out wrong. The scowl on Kara's face said it all.

He left before he said anything else that he would regret. *What a mess*, he thought. Not only had he handled the conversation badly, but he'd come out of the hospital with a raging headache and feeling totally rejected as well. He'd anticipated an emotional reunion, with Kara being needy and begging to have him back; however, he'd been so riled up, due to his pride and disappointment, that he'd said all the wrong things.

* * *

Watching Justin walk away, Kara thought her heart would be shattered all over again, but it wasn't. A broad smile stretched across her face, as she kissed her baby on the top of her head. It was a relief that she felt nothing; it was certainly one less worry to contend with.

* * *

During the drive back Justin was consumed with thoughts of Kara. He'd expected her to look rough, but she appeared the same fresh-faced woman he remembered. She was so different from his wife, someone he was beginning to resent. Perhaps when little

Ben, their son, came home, if he ever could, then he would witness Lucy being the mother she was supposed to be. He suspected she hadn't bonded with their child.

Before he made his way to the hospital to see his son, he stopped at the flat to collect a few more boxes. Two weeks had gone by since they had returned. Lucy was so excited to get her foot in the door of his newly renovated house, she hadn't even bothered packing her old things, simply preferring to buy new. However, he still had to clear the flat before he could hand over the keys.

As he approached the steps leading up to the front door, a smell hit him, a sour metallic odour that made him gag. He naturally assumed it was the drains chucking up that pungent stench. He would have to get it sorted out before the agents checked over the flat. He needed to see the old lady downstairs because it may well be her drainage that was the problem. He had his hand over his face, as he wandered around the side of the building where her front door was. The smell was stronger here, and he had to hold his nose.

After banging three times, he waited. There was no answer, so he peered through the letterbox and jumped back; the heat and the buzzing of flies hit him. Then it dawned on him, the disgusting odour was coming from inside the old lady's flat. The flies and the fact that the heating must still be on in this hot weather told him all he needed to know. He rushed back to his car and called the police.

He waited patiently by his car as instructed by the policewoman on the phone. It wasn't long before a police vehicle arrived. Two burly officers clambered out and nodded in his direction. He walked over to them.

'Are you Justin Fox who called the station?' asked the larger of the two officers, who then introduced himself as Larry Bart.

'Yes, I was going to collect the rest of my belongings from my flat when I noticed the smell, and, well, when I lifted the neighbour's letterbox … perhaps you should check it for yourself.'

Bart walked off to investigate, whilst Conroy Matthews, remained with Justin, taking down a few details. They heard the sound of breaking glass and Matthews was quickly radioed through.

Justin could clearly hear the conversation.

'Conroy, you need to keep Mr Fox there. I'll call the sergeant,' said Bart, his voice shaking.

Matthews walked a few feet away to get out of Justin's earshot. 'What's happened, Larry?'

The radio crackled but Justin could still hear. 'It looks like the old lady has been hit around the head. Jesus, it stinks. I'm coming out … I don't want to tamper with the evidence. It looks like she's been murdered. Fucking poxy flies.'

Matthews looked over at Justin. 'Mr Fox, please stay where you are.'

Feeling nauseous from the news, Justin nodded compliantly.

As they waited for the coroner, Bart walked back, looked up at the flat, and then studied Justin. 'So, you're moving out, then?'

'No, well, sort of. We moved out two weeks ago. I was just about to collect more boxes when I thought the drains were blocked because of the smell.'

Chewing the inside of his lip, Bart gave Justin an enquiring look. 'Two weeks, you say?'

An uncomfortable feeling swept over Justin. 'Yes, why?'

'The deceased woman must have been dead a good few days, maybe weeks. I'm no expert, but she didn't die yesterday, judging by what I saw.'

A sudden chill ran down his spine. Bart's studied expression and the pointed observation made Justin feel uneasy. 'What are you saying?' he asked, shifting from one foot to the other.

'Did you notice anyone hanging around, any strange noises, anything unusual?'

Justin shook his head. 'I never really knew her. I only spoke to her a couple of … Hey, hang on, yes, a month ago, this man,

Carl, his name is, was in her flat. He'd left some money behind, and the old lady asked if I would let him know if I saw him.'

Bart narrowed his eyes, as he said, 'So, this Carl is a friend of yours, then?'

He shook his head. 'No, she assumed he was because he came to see my wife.' He stopped and realised it was going to sound odd. 'This Carl guy is stalking my wife. He raped her when she was a kid, and for some reason, he's infatuated with her. I don't know why he was in the old lady's flat.'

'Where does this Carl live? Do you know any more about him, or could we speak with your wife?'

Justin tried to think if she'd mentioned where he lived. Then it dawned on him. 'I know where you'll find him. He owns Desperados, up the road.'

Matthews closed his notebook and curled his lip. 'Ahh, I know who you mean, now.'

Justin gave a confident smirk. 'I'm not surprised. I guessed he was known to the police.'

'And you say he raped your wife?'

With a serious nod, Justin replied, 'Yep, when she was a kid.' He then thought perhaps he'd said too much. Besides, it was his wife's business, not his to discuss.

'And your wife's name, Mr Fox?'

'Look, I'd rather not get her involved. I think the rape was something she'd prefer to forget.'

Bart, with a deadpan face, repeated his colleague's question. 'Her name, sir?'

'Lucy Fairmount, now Lucy Fox.'

The two officers looked at each other knowingly, and Justin could sense they were mocking him by the half-smiles.

'Lucy Lou Fairmount?' sniggered the younger officer.

A cold uneasy dread ripped through him. That name – Lucy Lou – and the jeering look. 'How do you know my wife?'

Before Matthews could answer, two other police cars and a

300

black Lexus pulled up. The officers turned away from Justin and welcomed the detective. Justin was still eager to know how they knew his wife and tapped the younger officer on the shoulder. 'How do you know my wife?' he demanded, but his firm words were ignored.

Then Matthews turned around to face him. 'Sir, what's your address?'

Justin reeled it off and asked again. 'Look, tell me how you know my wife!'

The officer could see he was frustrated. 'Mr Fox, your wife was known to us a few years ago.' He held his hand up. 'She's not wanted, but let's just say she has a history. Look, mate, we have your details. Don't leave the country, and we'll be in touch.'

'A history?' questioned Justin.

'Look, ask your wife. I'm sure she'll explain.'

'And what about this Carl fellow? Are you going to question him?'

With a look of annoyance, Matthews replied, 'Yes, I will, but I want you to know this. We don't like anyone taking the law into their own hands. I would be very careful about accusing Carl Meadows of rape.'

'Why, because he is dangerous? Violent?'

Matthews sighed deliberately and shook his head. 'No, that's a serious accusation, sir. Look, maybe you need to have another conversation with your wife and get your facts straight.'

'So, officer, why would Carl be in the old lady's house? Do you think he killed her?'

With a look of frustration, Officer Bart replied, 'Leave the investigation to us, sir. Now, if you don't mind, we need to clear the area.'

Justin left, with his shoulders slumped and a lot on his mind.

* * *

After a few hours of sleep, Kara woke up to find the nurse holding Denise Rose. 'How do you feel?'

With sleepy eyes, Kara replied, 'Yes, I feel much better. May I hold her?' She held out her hands and winced as she tried to sit up.

'It will take time to heal, but I can top up your painkiller.' The nurse smiled.

'No, I'm fine. It's just uncomfortable.'

'Oh, there's a gentleman outside, waiting to see you.'

Kara assumed it was Justin, ready to have another attempt to talk her round. 'Tell him, I don't want to see him again.'

The nurse handed Kara the baby. 'Again?'

'Is it the man who was here earlier?'

The nurse shook her head. 'No.'

'Oh, okay, please send him in.'

The bouquet of artificial flowers was almost as big as the person carrying them. With a beaming smile and a twinkle in his eye, Rocky entered the room. He placed the flowers on the cabinet and stared for a while. 'Ahh, my treacle, look at you. Ya look beautiful, babe. Motherhood suits ya.' He leaned over the bed and kissed her on the forehead and then kissed the baby. 'Cor, a real living doll, ain't she? Hang on a minute ...'

Kara watched the excitement on his face as he hurried from the room, only to return with a huge basket filled with pink baby gear. He struggled to carry it in. 'There ya go, babe. Apparently, that's everything ya need, well, so they told me in Mothercare. I'm new at all this.'

He smiled when he saw her reaction and felt overcome with an emotion that was unfamiliar to him.

'Oh my gosh, you're so generous, Rocky. Thank you.'

'Let's have a cuddle.' He giggled like a child, as he held out his hands to take the baby. Kara held her out to him, proud of her tiny bundle.

'Ahh, she is a beauty, treacle, like her mum. What's her name?'

She watched him walk around the room, staring down at the baby with such a loving look in his eye.

'It's Denise Rose. I named her after Deni.'

The baby started to stir and make a noise, and instantly, he handed her back. 'She wants her mum.' He laughed again.

Sitting boldly on the bed with Kara, he took her hand, and his eyes turned serious. 'Ya know I like ya, babe?'

She blushed.

'I know you've got to serve a couple of years, but that's okay, see, 'cos I don't mind waiting. The thing is, Kara ...' He stopped and looked at the door checking no one was there. 'I, er, well, I have grown kinda fond of ya. I mean, I know it's early days. I've only started to visit ya in the last four months. Oh, Christ, what I'm trying to say is, I love ya, yeah?'

Listening to him, Kara felt joyful tears well up in her eyes. She'd grown fond of him too and had longed to hear those words. She smiled and nodded. 'I love you too, Rocky.'

'Do ya, babe? I mean, do ya really love me, or am I just someone to make ya incarceration easier?'

She looked down at her baby and then up at him. 'No, I have your sister to help me do that. I do love you, Rocky. I never thought I would ever love anyone after Justin, but perhaps I never loved him at all, and I just went through the motions. I was young when I met him, and the relationship just took a natural progression. I didn't know anything else, but I do now. Funny, really, because you and I are so different.'

He stroked her face. 'I know, and to be honest, it does bother me. You're probably used to middle-class people all talking a different language, and I'm not like that, am I? I'm more spit and sawdust, like an old pub, whereas you're more wine bar.'

She laughed at his analogy. 'No, I'm not like that. I don't come from money. I just went to a good school, so that's why I have this posh accent, but as for knowing the difference between a good wine and a bad one, I have no idea. Yes, we're different, but I like our differences. It's not such a bad thing, you know.'

He soaked up her words. 'So, do you think, Kara Bannon, you would want me when you come home?'

'Yes, more than anything.'

He moved the loose strand of hair away from her face and examined her eyes for a while. 'I want to know because I have this nice house. I rent it out, but the lease is up soon. I was gonna get it all done up nice, ya know, for us and little Denise Rose and do the baby's room up in pink and stuff.'

Kara could feel her heart beat faster; she held her breath.

'So, if ya still love me when you get out, I thought me and you, girl, and little Denise Rose, here, could make a go of it.'

A tear left her eye and fell to meet her huge smile. 'I want nothing more, but I'll try not to get too excited because two years is a long time, and you may change your mind, like Justin did.'

Placing a finger over her lips, he said, 'Now, you listen, babe. I don't make promises I can't keep. Ask me sister. I've never had a bird live with me either, so you can get as excited as you bleedin' like because as far as I'm concerned, you're my girl, now, and I will treat you like a fucking princess.'

Kara looked down again at the baby.

'Oh, and little Denise Rose – I will love her as if she were me own, even if she is our only baby,' he said, as he planted another kiss on the baby's head.

Kara felt safe and warm in his presence, and she hoped beyond hope that he would wait for her.

'I have a scar now, Rocky. Denise Rose didn't come out naturally.'

He threw his head back and laughed. 'I wouldn't care if ya had no legs. I'd still love ya.' A twinkle in his eye and a raised eyebrow made Kara redden.

'I can't wait to see that scar.'

She felt bold and daring. 'I can't wait to show it to you.'

The gentle kiss became more passionate and was only stopped when the nurse walked in.

Rocky squeezed Kara's hand, winked, and said, 'I'll be back tomorrow.' He wanted to make the most of the time he had with her, and the officer outside the room couldn't and wouldn't stop him. Melanie Brent was allowed to stay at George's request. As Rocky closed the door, he looked her over. 'What's ya favourite drink, love?'

Melanie was slightly embarrassed and blushed. 'Oh, no, it's fine. I want the best for that woman. She's a good person.'

'Yeah, she is, ain't she – a real gem. Did you want a sandwich or something? Coffee? I can grab ya something, while I'm 'ere.'

Melanie shook her head. 'No, honestly, I'm good, but thank you.'

He winked, and she watched him take confident strides down the corridor. For a moment, she wished she had someone like him – a broad-shouldered man, with a sexy magnetism that oozed charisma. Kara may be posh and sweet, but she could do a lot worse than Rocky. She sighed and went back to burying her head in her book.

* * *

Justin drove like a madman back to his home. He didn't know who he was angry with the most: Kara for not falling into his arms, or Lucy and her unknown history, or even, of course, the two officers who appeared to have mocked him. Then there was Carl, the so-called hardman, arrogant to boot, thrown into the mix, and Lillian, his sweet neighbour, found dead, hit around the head.

He could only conclude that Carl was far more dangerous than anyone was prepared to admit. He was convinced that Carl was the culprit, and there he was, being allowed to walk around free. He thought about setting up CCTV cameras in case this rapist and murderer should come calling. It niggled him that Lucy didn't seem afraid of the man, and it concerned him more that there was another side to her that he'd yet to meet.

He reversed into the drive and slowed his irate breathing down. It was ridiculous how his life seemed to be spiralling downwards. What was supposed to be a happy marriage was now filled with constant jibes and tensions.

Lucy was holding a roll of wallpaper covered in bright in-your-face swirls of black and silver feathers.

'Now, don't you think this will look lovely in the living room?' She smiled, as she turned to greet him.

He stood with his hands on his hips, his hair flopping forward, and his lips pulled tight.

'What's the matter, Justin? I thought you would have a smile on your face, seeing you've just met your daughter.'

He wasn't sure if she was being sarcastic or not. 'Put the bloody wallpaper roll down. You and I need to talk and no more fucking bullshit, or that paper and you will be out that bloody door.'

Instantly, Lucy dropped the roll and flopped onto the new grey velour sofa. Something was seriously wrong. Racking her brains, she couldn't imagine what was going on in his head.

He didn't sit down but stepped closer and looked at her squarely in her eyes. 'I want to know about you, about who the fuck you really are!'

As she dropped her fake smile, Justin continued. 'Straight talking or fuck off!'

She knew then she couldn't put on the tears; he was definitely not going to comfort her.

'What do you want to know, exactly?' Her tone was just as sharp.

'Why the police know who you are, for starters.'

Her eyes widened, and her brain raced through every possible explanation as to why he would know she had a past. She wasn't about to admit that to him, not a man with a high and mighty moral standard.

'I told you I was in foster care. Well, I was left pretty much to my own devices, and as teenagers do when they have no family to guide them, I shoplifted, and I got caught a few times.'

Justin paced the floor, running his hands through his hair. 'No, Lucy Lou, it wasn't for shoplifting, was it?'

Her hands trembled as soon as he said her nickname. What did he know? Had Carl spoken with him? She had to hedge her bets.

'Oh my God, you haven't been talking to that bastard rapist Carl again, have you? Because he will string you a long line of bollocks!'

Justin gave her a weary smile and shook his head. 'No, not Carl.'

'Then, who has said what?' she demanded, her eyes searching his face for a clue.

Justin changed tactics. 'Look, Lucy.' He tutted and sat down in one of the new armchairs. 'We all have a past, some more troubled than others. I'm not bothered about what you did in your previous life, but I want to know, so that it's not a shock to me, when, like today, the police told me they knew you. So just tell me, love. I won't hold it against you. I'm more broad-minded than you think.'

She tried to gauge if he was genuine or not, but even if he was, how could she tell him the truth? She had to tell him something or she would be out on her ear. Or would she? They were married now; she owned half of everything, and she was the mother of their baby, so she would get the house.

'Do you know what, Justin? I'm fucking sick of you judging me. It's the way you look at me with disgust sometimes and the way you treat me like you have to question everything. Well, for your information, my past was not pretty because, unlike you, I didn't have a fucking family, so either we move on and you allow me to put my miserable past behind me, or I go my own way, with my child, I might add, because I'm not going over that sad ground again.'

Just for a moment, Justin felt that he wasn't looking at Lucy; he was probably facing this other woman, Lucy Lou, whoever the hell she was. 'So, I take it, Lucy, if you won't tell me about your past, then I'll have to find out for myself, because I also want to know who you really are. At the moment, though, I don't flaming well know you at all.' He jumped up to leave and then turned to face her one more time. 'Oh, by the way, the police want to talk to you. The old lady in the downstairs flat is dead.'

For a split second, Justin discerned panic on Lucy's face. 'What's the matter, Lucy?'

She shook her head. 'Nothing. Why do they want to question me? I mean, I never went down to her flat, so it couldn't have been me.'

'I never suggested that the police are regarding this as suspicious. I just said they want to question you about whether you saw anyone coming or going.' He raised his eyebrow and sneered.

Unexpectedly, the phone rang, to Lucy's obvious relief.

It rang again but Justin made no move to answer it. Lucy got up from her seat and placed the phone to her ear. An exaggerated gasp left her lips. Justin snatched the phone from her. 'Hello!' he said, rudely.

The nurse from the intensive care unit answered. 'Your son has taken a turn for the worse. I think it's best that you both come along as soon as possible. I'm very sorry.'

As he replaced the receiver, he studied Lucy's grief-stricken expression and immediately felt the need to place an arm around her shoulders. 'Come on, let's go.' His voice cracked, as he held back the cry waiting to escape. None of the past mattered now. Lucy was right: they had more pressing issues to deal with.

* * *

The neonatal unit was immaculately white, bright, and clean, and set up with state-of-the-art facilities. There, lying in the see-through acrylic cot, with every tube and wire imaginable, was their frail, sickly baby. Justin peered down and allowed a tear to trickle down his nose and land on the baby's bare arm. He wiped it away and stroked the soft dark down on his son's head.

Dr Khalid, the child's paediatrician, who had been overseeing his care, pulled Justin away and allowed Lucy a moment alone with her son.

'He has a lung infection and we have given him antibiotics, but I'm afraid he's not responding as he should.' His eyes looked downcast, as he waited for Justin to speak.

'It may be that he will pick up, but he may not, and it's only right that you know the situation. A cuddle always helps.' He looked over at Lucy staring out of the floor-to-ceiling window with a view across to the park. 'I know she's taking it hard and finds it difficult to see him like that, but perhaps you could encourage her to hold him.' He patted Justin's shoulder and returned to the cot to check the baby's vitals.

Justin looked at Lucy and saw an expression he'd never seen before. Her face was pale and her eyes were pulled down at the sides. She was sad and lost.

He felt an overwhelming sense of sorrow for her and decided to let the past be just that – the past. He pulled her close, as they both looked down at their helpless little boy. Justin felt her body trembling and her silent sobs building up until she became weak in his arms and cried uncontrollably. 'No, no, please, not my baby, he is all I have,' she wailed.

'It's okay, babe. Come on, we'll get through this together and be strong for him.'

She slowly stopped the tears and wiped her nose with a tissue, leaning in to his chest. 'Oh, Justin, I couldn't bear it if he died. I feel terrible. I just couldn't keep visiting him, not seeing him like that and me helpless. But I know it was wrong. I can't forgive myself.'

'Hold him now, Lucy. Let him know you love him.' His voice cracked again, and he coughed, unable to speak. The nurse lifted the baby from the cot and gently placed him in Lucy's arms.

Justin watched with a heavy heart. Of course, Lucy must have been hurting as much as him; she was the baby's mother, after all. As Lucy rocked him gently, she turned away from Justin and whispered to her baby, 'I'm so sorry, little one. I do love you so much. I guess I just never knew it before.'

The door opened and the woman standing there caught Justin off-guard. His mother's arms dropped by her sides. 'Justin, I didn't expect …'

The nurse smiled. 'Hello, Mollie.'

Justin blinked hard. *How did the nurse know her name?*

She approached her son. 'I come at this time most days. I don't like to get in the way.'

'You've been visiting my son?'

Tears welled up in Mollie's eyes. 'Yes, I know we have our differences, but that isn't the baby's fault.'

Her face expressionless, too consumed in her own world of despair to care, Lucy slowly turned to face her mother-in-law.

'He's very sick, Mum, he may not …' He couldn't bring himself to speak.

Mollie grabbed his arm. 'Now, you listen to me. You need to be brave and positive. It will do him no good to give up on him now.'

Justin nodded. He needed his mum; she always knew the right thing to say.

'Go on, Son, give your wife a break.' She smiled at Lucy who was still glazed over.

Justin tried to take the baby, but Lucy pushed him away. 'No, leave him,' she whispered.

Mollie winked at her son, letting him know it was okay. 'Let's get a coffee.'

Lucy was still in a trance and didn't even notice them leave.

Outside in the corridor was a coffee machine. As Mollie searched in her purse for change, Justin asked, 'What are you really doing here, Mum?'

She straightened up and gave him a resigned look. 'I've thought about you a lot lately and this awful situation. That young nurse in there is my friend's daughter. She told me about little Ben, and so I asked if I could visit. She said you always come in the mornings or afternoons but never in the evenings, so I come at night, just to give him a cuddle. I know what I said, Justin, and it was all in the heat of the moment, and what with Kara having a baby too, I just think it's unfair that I only see Denise Rose. I just want to treat both little Denise Rose and Ben the same.'

'You know, then, she had the baby?'

Mollie nodded. 'Yes, love, she called me straightaway.'

'I went to see her in the hospital. She wouldn't let me hold her. She doesn't want me to have the baby.' His eyes narrowed. 'She said you would have her for the last few months of her sentence.'

Mollie averted her eyes, clearly embarrassed that her actions had caused friction between herself and her son. 'Well, yes, she asked me, and of course, I accepted the offer. After all, she is my grandchild.'

Justin sighed heavily. 'But she is my daughter. I can't have her brought up in that bloody prison, not when I can give her a good home.'

Mollie looked shocked. 'What do you mean?'

He paced the floor with his jaw set and his hands clenched into fists. 'You just don't get it, Mum! She burned the house down because she was angry! What would she do to my daughter, if she lost her temper? And another thing. She's not the sweet, innocent Kara you once knew. She even talks differently. She swore at me.'

311

'After what you've done and said, and yes, I know what you told her, do you honestly expect her to let you take her baby – the only real family she has – because *you* think you're a better person to look after baby Denise Rose? I know she lost her temper and damaged your home, but I don't believe she'd ever hurt her child.'

'I think, Mum, it's better that you leave. You really don't understand, and I won't allow my daughter to grow up in a prison. I have a home, a wife, and a son. Denise Rose will be better off with us, in a loving, safe environment. End of.'

Mollie shook her head. 'What's got into you? This isn't you, Justin, you would never do this.'

'She looked at me as if I were dirt. She hates me, and …'

'I know she may have hurt you, Justin, but that's no reason to want to take the baby, really, is it?'

With flared nostrils, he growled back, 'If you are not going to help me fight my case, then go and leave me in peace to see to my son.'

As Mollie went to walk away, she stopped and turned to face him, and a bitterness swept through her body, making her cringe. 'A loving home, eh? What with your wife who never comes to visit her own son? I don't think so.'

'Yes, she does. Not often, because she can't handle seeing him, but she does occasionally,' he snapped back.

Mollie shook her head again. 'No, Son, she doesn't. She hasn't been here for two weeks. I know this for a fact because I have been here almost every night.' As soon as she said it, she regretted it. This wasn't who she was, but it was certainly what her own son was turning her into.

'It's better that you leave and don't come back. We don't need you.'

Heartbroken, Mollie left, with the fervent wish that her son would see sense and soon. How he had changed. She'd once been so proud of him, with his boyish fresh looks, which she knew turned many a head, and his polite sweet-natured ways. To see him like this – a broken and almost unkempt man with a bitterness in his words –was a travesty of Olympic proportions.

Chapter 19

Three weeks after Kara had settled into her new cell, in the baby unit, a letter arrived from Justin. She stared at it, with her hands trembling, in total disbelief. Denise Rose began to whimper, and in a flash, Deni was there, lifting her from the cot. 'There, there, little one,' she whispered, as she rocked the baby back to sleep. 'What's it say, babe?'

Kara shook her head. 'He's going to court to get custody, and he will win, Deni. There's nothing I can do.'

Deni gently put the baby back in the cot. 'Don't give up, just yet. That Stuart fella, surely, he can help?'

Slowly, looking up from the letter, Kara gave a desolate smile. 'I've already spoken with Stuart, and he said that I don't really stand a chance, but he'll work away to assign temporary custody. He says he wants to help because he feels he has let me down with regards to my mother's death. They can't seem to find any other leads. I don't bloody understand it. They should be out there trying to find this Lucille woman, who was supposed to be my mother's carer. She has obviously stolen my mother's money and probably killed her in the process.'

Deni could feel the woman's pain and sat next to Kara, placing her arm gently around her shoulders. 'Don't let all this business about ya mum get in the way of making a clear decision. I know it's hard to think of anything but holding on to your baby. Maybe this Justin and his wife will be a good option? I mean, she has a baby, and so she will be very motherly. Little Denise Rose will obviously want for nuffin.'

'I just can't bear the thought, Deni. He has changed. The way he spoke to me and that cocky look in his eyes – it's like he's turned into a stranger.'

'Why don't you send out a VO and talk to him? This letter business can be so cold. Maybe in person, he can put your mind at rest? I mean, babe, he loved you once, and you did him no lasting harm.'

Kara put her hands to her face and sobbed, her heart breaking.

'Now, now, babe. Come on, you'll have a lifetime with ya girl. It's something I never had.'

Kara swallowed back the tears and remembered the story of Deni's daughter and accepted the fact that if Justin did get custody of their baby, it would only be until she was released from prison. Maybe she would have to sacrifice a few months of seeing her baby grow up. But then after that, she would always be there for her.

'What's Rocky say about it all, anyway?'

Kara smiled. 'Look in that drawer. There are photos of our new home. He's even had a castle bed built for Denise Rose. It does look lovely. He's been a rock ...' She laughed. 'Rocky the rock, eh? Who'd have thought it?'

Deni patted her knee. 'A right decent fella. So that's good for you, 'cos you'll have a lovely home for the baby, and there'll be no reason why the judge won't grant you custody when you get out.'

Kara nodded. 'That's what Rocky said.'

'Kara, Deni!' called Vic, who was nearly out of breath, running down the corridor.

Jumping to her feet, Kara went to the door and peered down the wing. 'In here!'

It was obvious to anyone that Vic was about to announce good news. Her face was beaming with excitement. 'They've only gone an' fucking granted my parole!' She jumped up and down like a child. 'I'm going home!'

The three were like girls in a school playground, hugging and hopping around with excitement. Denise Rose cried, the noise having woken her, and all three rushed to her side. Vic held the baby, and Kara wanted to cry again; her new-found sister was leaving, and all she would have was Deni, and her baby of course.

'We are going to miss you,' Kara said, in a sad tone.

'I'll come and visit a lot, if Rocky lets me. I know he likes to have you all to himself. Talking of which, we have a double visit on Wednesday. I need to 'ave a word about me flat, and, of course, I need a job.'

Kara slid the letter from Justin into the drawer. She wanted Vic to be excited about her news, not dragged down by her own tales of woe.

* * *

Wednesday morning arrived and Kara was brushing her hair. She looked in the mirror and tried to smile, but even her face muscles hurt. She was not in the mood to be happy. Justin was coming to visit her, and it would be a conversation that would fill her heart with endless grief.

Vic came bounding into the room. 'Right, babe, are ya ready for the visit?'

Kara gave a short gasp. 'Oh, no, I can't. Only Justin is coming to discuss the baby. I didn't tell you, Vic. You were so happy about your parole. But Justin's going for temporary custody and will no doubt win. He has agreed to talk with me first, though, as you can see from this letter he sent me.'

316

Vic studied it, and her eyes flashed with anger, as she turned to face Kara. 'Okay, babe, but I may have to hold Rocky back because he'll probably want to give this ex of yours a good pasting for what he's done to you.'

'No, no, please tell him not to do that. It'll only add fuel to the fire, no pun intended! Besides, Justin is bringing his wife. It's so hard, Vic. I don't know how I'll feel. I mean, I've never met the woman. That woman who took my Justin … well, she can have him.' She grinned at Vic. 'I have a decent man, a better man. I have Rocky.'

Vic nodded. 'Don't worry, babe, I'll take care of Rocky. Decent, eh? I wouldn't go that far. A little fucker at times, yes, but, nevertheless, he loves the bones of you.'

* * *

The weather had changed dramatically from bright blue skies to torrential rain. Justin called up the stairs to hurry Lucy along. She stared at her wardrobe that held her orderly collection of coats; she wanted to look good to show Kara that she had what that bitch used to have. She pulled the Burberry raincoat from its hanger and slid her arms inside. It hung a tad loose where she'd lost her baby weight. She hurried over to the mirror and looked at herself, and then she smiled – perfect.

'Lucy, we have to hurry, or they may not let us in.'

She rolled her eyes and took a deep breath before descending the staircase.

'How do I look?'

He nodded approvingly. 'You look great, love.'

Lucy knew her skin was glowing, and her eyes appeared large, with her new make-up coating her eyelashes. She'd been to the beautician's and hairdresser's that morning, to ensure she would look the quintessential wife and mother. Justin had questioned her, but she said she needed to look fresh and attractive, to give

Kara the impression that she would be a suitable parent for Denise Rose. Although the thought of having Kara's screaming child in the house was not in itself appealing, at least Justin had promised a live-in nanny.

The chaos of flash floods had caused the roads to be gridlocked in parts, and so they arrived after everyone was inside and seated. By the skin of their teeth, they were allowed through to the search room. With a bolshie female officer on their heels, reading the rules on punctuality, Justin looked annoyed. He was not prepared for the arrogance of the officer asking him to remove his shoes and belt. A huff and puff, followed by him rolling his eyes, was not missed by her, and she swiftly took him to task. 'Sir, it's your choice. Either follow the instruction or abort the visit!'

* * *

Inside the visiting room, Vic was already in the middle of her visit with Rocky, yet his eyes kept darting everywhere, looking for Kara. 'Sis, I don't reckon that Justin guy's gonna show. I bet the weasel has backed out of taking Kara's baby.'

'No, he's determined. I read the letter, the poor cow. But listen to me, Rocky – when he shows his face, don't you do anything, 'cos you'll only make matters worse.'

Rocky was shaking inside. 'I won't do anything, Vic, I promise.' He was also interested in what Justin looked like; not that he was competition, but still, he was intrigued.

'I can go and give her a hug, though. I mean, this bloke knows she has me now, don't he?'

'I don't know what she's told him, but just play it by ear. She may call you over, anyway.'

Vic looked around the room and noticed the only table and chairs available were behind Rocky. 'She will be right there behind you, anyway, I'm guessing.'

Rocky beamed as he saw Kara enter from the back of the room towards where he was facing.

She smiled back and mouthed the word, 'Hello.' Then, she looked straight ahead, and Rocky could see her expression sadden. Vic grabbed his hand and whispered, 'Don't look around.'

His heart was thumping, yet when he saw the concerned look on Vic's face, he knew something was not right. Her eyes were intent on whoever was behind him.

'Sis?'

She leaned forward and whispered, 'I want you to say nothing. Don't look their way, just listen, okay?'

'Do I know him?'

'No, but, look, hide ya face a bit.'

Rocky was desperate to look, but whatever was going on was serious, and so he tilted his head away.

* * *

Kara remained seated and made no attempt to stand and greet the couple. She looked Lucy over, and for a moment, she thought she had seen her before, but she couldn't place her. Justin looked tidier than he had the last time she'd seen him; his hair was cut short, and the golden waves were mousy, with perhaps a few grey strands weaved in there too. He wore jeans and a smart leather jacket, so different from the Justin she knew. But the generous smile and the glossy eyes – such hallmarks of his appearance – were absent.

'Hello, Kara, this is my wife, Lucy.'

Kara's eyes widened, as she glared at her. She'd waited a long time to meet this Lucy creature. She imagined her with darker hair and dark eyes, almost her polar opposite. She was, however, very attractive, although taller than she'd imagined.

Lucy didn't smile; she smirked, as if she were mocking the younger woman.

'It's nice to meet you,' said Kara, although she had to almost unclench her teeth to say it.

'You too, Kara,' replied the familiar voice.

* * *

Rocky felt his hands shaking. His heart racing, he glared at his sister and flared his nostrils. Vic knew then he'd guessed. Quickly, she gripped his knee under the table and hissed, 'Don't. Do. Anything.' But Rocky's mindset was not functioning on her wavelength. Slowly, he turned his head, and there, to his disbelief, was Lucy and her fella, Justin, the college boy. Was this more than a coincidence? Either way, he had to say something.

'Well, well, Lucy Lou.' He didn't raise his voice but kept it at a low and cold tone.

Instantly, her eyes were like a bush baby's, her face flushed crimson. Justin was taken aback, staring at the man who had recently caused a rift between himself and his wife.

'Well, hello, Justin. Small world, ain't it?' He smirked.

Kara shot a look at Rocky and then one at the couple. 'How do you know each other?' Her eyes were full of fear.

'Now, this is a funny coincidence, don't you think, Lucy Lou? And while we're here all nice and cosy, like, why don't you tell this lovely young lady just how exactly you know me? Since you and drippy bollocks there' – he pointed to Justin – 'want to take charge of Kara's little Denise Rose.'

At once, the room went very quiet. Visitors, inmates, and prison officers looked across to see an altercation was about to kick off big-time. Most of those present either knew Rocky or were aware of his reputation. After all, he was a Face. Lucy and Justin were shocked into silence.

Kara's mouth dropped open. Her mind was all over the place, watching what appeared to be a *Coronation Street* drama unfolding before her very eyes.

320

'Rocky, how do you know Justin?' she asked again, searching his face for answers.

With the biggest grin on his face, he replied, 'Babe, I don't really know him, but, see, Lucy Lou, I know only too well, don't I, Lucy?' He faced her, smirking. 'Go on, Luce, tell Kara how you know me. 'Cos, girl, I think it's about time your husband and my girlfriend know exactly who the fucking 'ell you are, and, more importantly, *what* you are.'

Lucy heard the word girlfriend and glared back at Kara. 'She's your girlfriend? How can that be, Carl?'

He sniggered. 'That, my dear, is none of your business, but don't change the subject. Go on, Lucy, tell them how you really know me? I think, considering that Justin wants to take away Kara's baby to live with you and him, it's only fair you tell them a bit about yourself. I mean, as your ex-boss, I could run up a CV, if ya like?'

Lucy's humiliation, shock, and horror were all too much. She turned to Justin, her only ally among them. 'Will you say something? I told you what he's like,' she growled, through gritted teeth.

Justin faced Kara. 'I think, under the circumstances, I'll go for total custody. You, Kara, are mixed up with a nasty, dangerous man who raped my wife when she was fifteen years old. I will never let my daughter anywhere near someone as vile as him.'

Kara trembled, thinking this was like a car crash, with her stuck right in the middle of it. She looked at Rocky, and her face appeared crushed. Yet Rocky wasn't in the least fazed by the events unfurling. In fact, he seemed to be enjoying the whole experience. Grinning and nodding his head, he said mockingly, 'Oh dear, dear me, ya never stop lying, do ya, Lucy Lou? Well, Justin, I was gonna let you carry on living a lie, 'cos you are no one to me, but it's time ya knew the fucking truth about your wife.'

Justin jumped up from his seat. 'I'm not listening to this bullshit.'

Rocky laughed. 'That's as may be, but you may want to hear this.'

Lucy was up on her feet, ready to leave. She knew he held her secrets, and right now, the only way was to get out of there and fast.

But it was Vic who spoke up. 'I would listen to him if I were you, before you make the biggest mistake of your life.'

Justin threw a spiteful glare at her. 'And you are?'

'I'm the teller of the truth, his sister, and that skank there is not who you think she is.'

'Are you threatening me?'

'Justin, I'm not threatening you, I'm warning you for the little one's sake. I would steer well clear of her, for your own sanity.' She pointed to Lucy. 'And I definitely wouldn't have her anywhere near my baby, if I were you.'

'Well, it's none of your business.' He looked at Carl and shook his head. 'And it's none of yours either, so stay away from me and my wife.' He turned back to Kara. 'I would suggest you pick your friends more carefully. He is a rapist.'

The uncomfortable expression on Kara's face was telling another story.

'Wait a minute, Justin …'

'No, Kara, you've changed, and I can see why, mixing with scum, but, mark my words, I will have custody of Denise Rose, for her safety, if nothing else.'

Rocky knew then he had to do something fast before he made matters worse. He was now beginning to think his sister was right, and perhaps on reflection he'd been unwise to go for a full-on confrontation. But he had, he hoped, an ace up his sleeve, or in this case on his finger. The ring. 'Wait, you may want this ring back, Justin. I'm assuming this little beauty was a gift from you to her, but she owes me a lot of money, and this was given to me in part payment.' He pulled the ring from his finger and held it up, showing a beige-coloured gemstone.

Justin stared for a while. 'Good try, but I've never seen that ring before. Perhaps it belonged to the old lady who was murdered in the flat below us.'

Slowly, Rocky turned to Lucy and stared, shaking his head. 'The old lady is dead? What, that sweet old dear in the flat below yours?'

'Yes, and the police will be questioning *you*!' spat Justin.

Rocky stared at Lucy, flaring his nostrils.

But it was Kara who snatched the ring from Rocky. 'Oh my God. This ring!'

They all turned to face Kara, puzzled by her outburst, her expression, and particularly by the desperate tone in her voice. 'Did she give you this ring?'

Rocky frowned. 'Yes, babe, why?'

'This was my mother's ring. Look, see inside. It has my name engraved. She was leaving it to me. It was her mother's ring, to be handed down, and my mum had my name put inside.'

Vic grabbed the ring and read the name. 'Where did you get this ring, Lucy?'

Lucy was literally on her feet, heading for the exit, but Justin caught her and brought her back to the table. 'Where did you get the ring?'

'I, er … I never had that ring. I've never seen it before in my life. He's lying. He probably stole it. That's him all over, a proper villain.' Her words were tripping over themselves. But her mind wasn't on the *faux pas* – her deep-seated anger was now directed at that bastard Carl and the bitch Kara. Like a raging fire tearing through her body, she saw Carl leave his chair and comfort Kara. She'd never seen him so affectionate and it ripped her in half.

Rocky whispered in Kara's ear, 'Babe, listen to me, call your lawyer to inform the police.'

She snapped out of her state of shock and slowly turned to him. 'You've never been to Australia, have you?' Her words begged him to tell the truth.

'Australia? No. Babe, I ain't been north of Watford. I don't even 'ave a passport. Why?'

She looked at Justin and then sneered at Lucy. 'Because this ring was on my mother's hand, wasn't it, Lucy? The last time I saw my mother, she was alive and well, living in Australia.'

'Kara, love, me brother hasn't got a passport, 'cos as tough as he is, he's too scared to get on a plane.'

She knew then he was telling the truth: Vic would never lie to her.

Lucy began to panic. 'Justin, let's get out of this shit-hole. I can't breathe.'

With so much confusion, Justin also needed air, and without another word, he grabbed Lucy's arm and marched her out of the visiting room. But he didn't get far.

Rocky managed to catch him, just before he was out of the door. 'I'm gonna make sure your wife comes back here for a very long time, because I know what she's done, and by Christ, I will make her pay, and you, ya fucking prick, will be done as an accessory. But remember this, Justin. You hurt that girl in there, and I will see to it you never fucking walk again, and that is a threat!'

'Get ya hands off me! You won't need to call the police because, when I get home, I'll be doing exactly that, and you'll be the one serving time.'

Lucy stood in silence, the anger still eating away at her. 'You, Carl … you just fucking wait. I hate you, I fucking hate you!'

The venom in her words made Justin wince. He'd never heard that tone and felt his stomach churn over. Yet he wasn't going to back down to Carl, the common-or-garden gangster who had somehow wormed his way into Kara's affections.

Barbara was watching and grinning. This was actually better than any soap opera. She should, by rights, have escorted the confrontational visitors off the visit, but she was hoping for more fireworks. And, of course, she was bored. Her colleague, a new officer, went to approach them, but Carl held his hands up. 'It's okay, miss, they were just leaving.' He winked and headed back to Kara, who was now being comforted by his sister.

She was holding the ring tightly in her hand and tears were falling like Niagara Falls. He moved his sister away and pulled Kara into his arms. 'Listen, babe, I love you, and I won't let them get their hands on the baby, not while he is with that bitch.'

She felt his heart beating fast in his chest and allowed herself to be held and calmed by him.

Barbara could see the situation was quietening down and decided to add fuel to the flames. 'Right, Bannon, your visit is over. I'll take that ring, thank you.' She held out her long witchy fingers.

But Kara gripped the ring even tighter, and then she placed her hand over Rocky's. 'Take this. I only trust you with it, and please, let the police know ...'

Barbara roughly grabbed Kara's arm. 'Come with me. I said, visiting for you is over.'

Vic jumped up and stood in the way. 'Barbara, you are manhandling an inmate for no reason. Kara hasn't said or shown that she's not going back to the wing. You're a fucking heartless bitch.'

Kara held up her other hand. 'It's all right, Vic, I have some calls to make.'

Rocky quickly stole a kiss, before Barbara frogmarched Kara away. 'I'm on it, babe,' he called after her.

He watched until she was out of sight, and then sighing heavily, he flopped back down on the chair. Anxious to ensure his sister didn't become embroiled in this saga, he said, 'Sis, you need to keep ya nose clean. No bashing the life out of anyone, 'cos I need you on the outside, all right? So, no fucking up ya parole.'

Seeing the look of concern on her brother's face, Vic placed her hands over his and smiled encouragingly. 'I will be the perfect angel.'

'Good, 'cos I will need help to get Lucy locked up, the double-crossing whore.'

'What does she have on you, though?'

With his arms stretched wide and his chest puffed out, he gave a full teeth-baring grin and shook his head. 'Absolutely fuck-all.'

Sighing deeply, Vic went on, 'Well, I feel sick to me stomach. The girl saved me life. I like her. Are you sure they've nothing on you?'

'As if! Christ, girl, you know me, by now. On the outside, I'm fucking squeaky clean. I leave no stone unturned, but that's where me and Lucy are different. She's distracted by her emotions, the thick prat. Well, she has marked her own grave now.' He looked at the ring. 'And to think, the fucking div gave me this. She has a wedge that belongs to me, and I want it back.'

A sudden feeling of unease shrouded Vic. 'Look, Rocky, Lucy is dangerous. You know that and so do I. If you threaten her with the police, it will have her running, and you'll never get your money. It will certainly have the Ol' Bill delving into your affairs and they will find something.'

'Vic, I ain't gonna call the police, and I bet ya bottom dollar that she won't let Justin do it either. I mean, she's a muppet at times, but she's the best manipulator I know. Why do you think I had her on me books for so long? Well, not anymore. I will have her inside or buried, 'cos she's taken a serious liberty with me.'

'Maybe it wasn't the best of ideas to confront them both in here. It's all a bit messy.'

'Ahh, see, that's why I did it. I *wanted* to provoke a reaction. I know Lucy will be panicking now. In fact, she'll be shitting herself, and that's how I want her. Let's just see what she does next.'

Vic was still feeling uneasy, as if the devil himself was watching. 'Do you think Lucy killed Kara's muvver?'

The officer called out, 'Visiting time is over.'

'Without a doubt, but I will get my money, and she'll get her comeuppance. I still can't get my head around Justin leaving Kara for that nutter Lucy Lou. He's no bleedin' idea, not a fucking scooby, unless there's more to him than just a wealthy businessman. But my guess is that he's a gormless prick who's been sucked in by her.'

Vic tried to muster a smile, but her heart was still heavy.

* * *

Justin was so angry, he marched ahead, leaving Lucy scurrying behind him. Entering the car and slamming the driver's door, he smashed his hands hard on the steering wheel. Lucy had crept into the car, wondering how she could put a massive spin on events to exonerate her past history and blag her way out of this one. There was no way she could have predicted what she'd just witnessed inside Larkview. It was a fucking disaster, a monumental fuck-up.

After a few deep breaths, he turned to Lucy. 'What the fuck was that all about, in there?' His words were slow and precise. She saw the burning in his eyes, as if they could fire lasers at her.

'I have absolutely no fucking idea. But I told you he was full of lies.' She tried to keep eye contact; it was her feeble attempt at getting him to believe her.

He grabbed her wrist; *not a great sign,* she thought.

'You may take me for a fool, but don't you fucking dare expect me to believe that you are so estranged from the man. You'd better start talking, or, by Christ, I will fucking use everything I have to make you talk.' He gulped back air and she could see the anger in his eyes. 'My daughter's future is on the line here, so you'd better tell me what the hell he was on about.' When she didn't immediately respond, Justin shouted, 'Well, go on, I'm all ears.'

Her pulse raced, her mouth went dry, and she was sure, if she didn't come up with an explanation soon, he would hurt her. 'I told you he is stalking me and will stop at nothing to get me.'

She was drained and surrendered. As she slumped her shoulders and sighed, Justin's anger softened slightly. 'Tell me, Lucy.'

'There's absolutely nothing to tell except, right now, Justin, I have lost faith in *all* men. Carl, my foster dad, you, and a string of others along the way, have all used, abused, and treated me like a piece of shit. It's like a constant repeat of history. I've never been believed, ever, and now you're the same, the one man I truly love. Instead, you believe a man who stole my virginity, stalked me, and beat me, and for what, eh? All because he wants me.'

Without another word, she got out of the car and marched away, leaving Justin more confused than ever. He hated Carl with a passion and for more reasons than before. Seeing him comforting Kara was the last straw, and now he himself was taking it out on Lucy. He ran after her, grabbing her by the arm and spinning her around, to find her face tear-stained and shiny. She looked so lost and vulnerable.

'Stop, Lucy, I'm sorry. Look, let's go home and talk about this. I think we need to call the police and get this bastard locked up once and for all.' The rain lashed down, and in an instant, Lucy was drenched; her make-up ran down her cheeks and her hair stuck to her face. She didn't move.

Justin tugged her arm. 'Come on, Lucy, I'm soaked. Let's get back in the car.'

She remained almost immobilised. 'You go on. I need time alone.'

'What? Don't be stupid, come on, get in the damn car.'

She shrugged him off. 'No, Justin, leave me alone!'

'Lucy, listen. I'm sorry for doubting you. I'm just confused and a little upset. I'm sorry, really sorry. Now, will you get in the car?' He let go of her arm and pulled his jacket closer and lifted his collar. The rain was soaking him through to the skin, and yet Lucy just stood motionless and seemingly preoccupied.

'You go, Justin – I'll meet you at home.'

He looked down the road to the car and then back at his wife, who was now acting very peculiarly. 'Wait here,' he said. With a resigned sigh, he returned to the car to retrieve her handbag. Before handing it over to her, he said, 'You're acting stupidly. If you won't get in the car, then I'll leave you to find your own way home.'

She took the handbag and nodded. 'I just want to be alone, Justin. I'll see you back at the house. I'll get a cab.'

The surface water was now like a stream as it made its way along the kerb.

A crack of thunder made him jump, and Lucy, unexpectedly, began to sprint away.

'Lucy!' he called after her, but she didn't stop.

He pulled open the driver's door and hopped in. His hands were shaking as he placed the key in the ignition. Trying to set off was impossible. The inside was full of condensation, and it took several minutes for the interior to clear. He cursed and bashed the steering wheel again. By the time he could see enough to pull away, Lucy had vanished.

The rain stopped as suddenly as it started, and the sky was bright blue. He looked at the main prison gates and then ahead. Kara, the woman he loved so much, was inside and also in a relationship with the man who had raped his wife. His anger and frustration were climbing to a dangerous pitch, so much so, that he had to take a few deep breaths to concentrate.

That's when he saw the bastard.

Carl, with his broad shoulders and arrogant gait, looked as if he hadn't a care in the world; it was the final insult of the day and it needed sorting. With his heart racing and his head about to explode, Justin visualised Carl rocking his child, kissing Kara, and then mocking him, laughing in his face. That man had raped his wife and was muscling in on his Kara. The veins popped out from his neck, as the blood rampaged around his body. He couldn't stand it.

Something inside his mind took control of his actions. It was as unexplainable as it was scary. Somehow, his foot hit the accelerator, and in a blind fury, he tore along the road and mounted the pavement.

Carl heard the roaring of the engine and instinctively threw himself against the fence out of the way of the speeding car. But he didn't manage to escape entirely; the bumper of the car drove his legs into a metal post. The shock left him numb as he hit the ground in a crumpled mess. Both legs had taken the hit and his trousers were completely covered with blood. So much so, that it was gushing from Carl's legs and joining the rivulets from the recent storm into a nearby drain.

A few other visitors had witnessed the scene and ran to help Carl. He was now slumped on the floor, lying in an unnatural position. Surprisingly, he was still conscious, and the agony was creeping in as the shock was wearing off. He stared at Justin who was doing likewise at him through the windscreen, in total disbelief at what he'd just done.

Justin couldn't believe he had done this. Him. What the hell had he been thinking? He jumped from the car and pulled away the people who were now gathered around the injured man. The terrified look on Carl's face was something he knew would live with him forever.

He shook his head. 'What have I done?'

The blood loss and pain were too much for Carl and he lost consciousness.

Justin could hear sirens in the background and stared on in disbelief, with his hands over his mouth. The onlookers glared at him, each mumbling under their breath. The ambulance pulled up at the roadside and the paramedics moved him away, as they hurried to see to Carl. Placing his neck in a brace and carefully lifting him onto the stretcher, they put him inside the ambulance. One paramedic came out and tapped Justin on the arm, totally oblivious that Justin was responsible for the incident. He said, 'Do you know this man?'

Justin couldn't speak; he just nodded.

'Sir, would you like to come with us?'

He nodded again and followed the paramedic inside the ambulance. The doors were closing just as a police car pulled up.

'We can't wait. Nigel, put the blue lights on.'

Nigel didn't waste time and they sped away.

The other paramedic cut away the blood-soaked trousers, revealing a gruesome sight. Two compound fractures. Both shins were gaping through the broken skin. Justin gulped back the vomit that instantly rose to the back of his throat. The paramedic placed heavy compressions around the wounds to stop the blood.

The horrendous sight didn't stop Justin from staring. He had to see what he'd done; he had to take responsibility. And he needed to feel the guilt, as if in some way it would exonerate him.

Within minutes, they'd arrived at the hospital. The paramedic asked the name of the injured man. Justin could only answer, 'Carl.'

'And his surname?'

'I, er, don't know.'

The paramedic seeing to Carl gave him a frown and stopped what he was doing. 'You *are* a friend of this man, aren't you?'

'I, um, well, I know him, that's all.'

An alarm bleeped from the heart monitor, and Justin was almost shoved out of the ambulance, as they hurried to get the injured man inside the hospital. Two doctors appeared and wheeled him into surgery with Justin on their heels.

He was all alone in the corridor, which was quiet and eerie; the smell of the hospital hit him, and he sank down on one of the plastic chairs that was mounted to the wall.

Holding his head in his hands, he felt his eyes burning, ready to cry. Then he heard voices, and as he looked up, two police officers, one a sergeant, along with the paramedic, were standing in front of him.

'Sir, what's your name?'

Justin rubbed his face. 'Justin Fox.'

'Is your car a black BMW, registration FOX 132?'

He nodded.

'Did you run down a man on High Down Road?'

Justin got to his feet. 'I, er … yes, but it was an accident, I didn't mean to.' His mind was going into overtime, as the reality of the consequences hit him. 'I was going to give him a lift, and for some reason, my foot slipped on the accelerator and I mounted the pavement … I never meant to hit him.'

The grey-haired sergeant who was busily writing notes in his book stopped what he was doing and looked up with a raised eyebrow. 'But the paramedic said you didn't know your friend's surname.'

Justin shuffled from one foot to the other and looked at the floor. 'I, er, haven't known him very long, but his first name is Carl.'

'Right, Mr Fox, will you accompany me to the station? I think you need to make a statement.'

'Yes, of course, but please can I wait to see if Carl is okay? I mean, I feel dreadful.'

The sergeant looked at the paramedic.

'I think they must be friends. He wanted to join him in the ambulance.'

Sitting down, the sergeant indicated for Justin to do the same. He took all the details and then said, 'We'll be in touch, after we've interviewed the injured man.'

Justin could feel his palms sticky with sweat, as he watched the two officers walk away, knowing that once they spoke with Carl, he would find himself in prison. *Why, why, why, did he do it?*

Chapter 20

Justin paced the floor for an hour, going over and over what he'd done. What on earth had pushed him to try to kill the man? The stress of the last few months could be a reason, but one thing he was sure about was he would say he was sorry to the man he almost killed. A doctor appeared in the corridor. 'Are you friends with Carl Meadows?' He was dressed in green scrubs, and his hair was still in a net, tied tightly back. His black eyebrows were prominent against his pale skin, and his features were so sharp, they looked almost spiteful. Justin straightened himself and nodded.

'We have taken him to Harvard Ward. Perhaps you would let his family know? Only, he mumbled something about his phone being lost. I would suggest you return in a few hours, when he should be up to talking to you.'

Justin felt his hands trembling, as he nodded again. The hospital canteen was slowly emptying. Only a few people remained, some still in their hospital gowns, each dragging around an attached drip on wheels. After two cups of coffee, and reading through the newspapers, he peered up at the clock. It was seven o'clock. Where had the time gone? He brushed himself down, swallowed hard, and went in search of Harvard Ward.

Finding the ward was a feat in itself, but eventually, he stood outside the double doors, reluctant to go in. After all, what was he going to say? After a few deep breaths, he wandered through and found Carl, just off the nurses' bay, on the left, in a single room. He was looking extremely well for a man who had just had his legs reshaped. Tentatively, he entered the room and stood at the end of the bed.

'Pour us a drink of water, will ya?' asked Carl, coldly.

Justin searched the room and found a sink with elbow taps, and on the cabinet, next to the bed, there was a plastic cup. He hurriedly filled it, almost spilling the contents, as he handed it to Carl.

After a few large gulps, Carl coughed. 'Fucking anaesthetic dried me throat up.'

Justin pulled over a chair and warily sat down. 'Look, this is madness. I'm so sorry. I don't know what came over me …'

Carl let out a laugh. 'Oh, I see. Ya don't want me to press charges. Ya want me to say it was an accident?' He placed the cup back on the cabinet.

Justin shook his head and looked to the floor. 'Of course not. I came to apologise. I just wanted you to know, I feel really bad, and … well, I don't know what else to say, and no, I will not talk you out of pressing charges. Jesus, I deserve all I get. For fuck's sake, I could never forgive myself, if you couldn't walk again.'

'Are you angry 'cos you really believed I raped Lucy or was it because I'm seeing Kara?'

Justin looked up and rubbed his face. 'The truth … probably both.'

'Well, Justin, you're one stupid fucker. I didn't rape Lucy, and as for Kara, you threw her away. I mean, let's be honest and have a man-to-man chat now. You want *both* women. Why you would want Lucy over Kara is still a bleeding mystery to me, but one man's love is another man's poison.'

A frown spread its way across Justin's face. 'You mean one man's meat is another man's poison.'

Carl grinned. 'Everything has to be correct with you, don't it, college boy? No, I mean love, not meat. I bet you're even wondering what Kara sees in me? I know what I am, Justin, a little rough around the edges, and yeah, I have a shady past, but I've good intentions. See, that's where me and you, me old son, are so different. You are educated, ya speak well, ya look clean, yet ya can't see the wood for the trees.'

Justin looked Carl over. The man must be superhuman. There he was, sitting up after a serious operation, cocky and carefree – not quiet, timid, and afraid, as he would have been.

'Why would Lucy say you raped her? Because that is a serious accusation and I just cannot imagine anyone making that up.'

Carl smirked. 'No, you're right. It's hard to imagine any genuine, sane person saying that, but ya see, Justin, Lucy *ain't* fucking normal, by *any* stretch of the imagination. She's a first-class manipulator, a right evil bitch.'

Like a coiled spring, Justin jumped up from his seat. 'Now, hold on a minute, Carl—'

No sooner had he got those words out than Carl put his hands up. 'No, Justin, you hold on a fucking minute. Lucy is a dangerous woman, and before you run to her fucking defence, go and get a piece of paper and a pen. I'm gonna give you an address. You go and speak to the man that lives there, and he will tell you exactly who you're married to.'

'What? Who?'

'Her father, Les, a good man. Well, he was until Lucy drove him around the bend.'

'Her foster father?'

Carl laughed. 'So, she spun you that one as well, did she? No, Justin, her *real* father. Lucy was never fostered.'

As if a cold chill swept through him, Justin felt his legs go weak, and he stumbled back against the chair, allowing himself to sit down. 'No, surely, you have it all wrong?'

'That's how I met Lucy. Her father worked for me. Such a

good, honest, and kind fella, I owed him a huge favour, 'cos he saved me life. I was taking a right good kicking from five geezers trying to rob me, when Les came from nowhere and saved me. But he took a nasty knife wound in the process. So, I gave him a job as a bouncer. Believe me, I know for a fact, he ain't her foster father, he's the real deal. But, hey, listen, if you don't believe me, go and see him. He will tell you the truth, and when he does, I want you to come and see me because I can guarantee you'll want to.'

Justin pulled his mobile from his pocket and asked for Lucy's father's address, which he tapped into his phone. He walked to the door and looked back. 'Did you really get that ring from Lucy?'

Carl gave Justin a sad and almost sympathetic expression. 'Yes, the truth is, Justin, Lucy owes me a lot of money, and she gave it in part payment.'

'Money for what?'

'She stole twenty thousand pounds from my safe and buggered off to Australia.'

'Australia? Are you sure?'

The pain was starting to set in and Carl winced. 'Yeah, she rented one of me flats. A letter arrived, which I opened when I was cleaning her flat, and it was the receipt for the airline ticket.'

Justin held up his hands. 'Jesus! Look, Carl, if what you're saying is true, then I deserve all I get, but before you tell the police, please will you give me time to get to the bottom of this?'

'I ain't gonna tell the Ol' Bill the truth. It was an accident, right, but you promise me, you won't take Kara's baby.'

Of course, Carl had an ulterior motive for allowing Justin to sit and talk without screaming blue murder, and he held all the cards. Justin knew when he was beaten. 'I'm still the baby's father.'

'Yeah, mate, and if you don't drop this fucking custody battle, you'll be writing Denise Rose's letters from inside the nick. It's your choice.'

'All right, I'll drop the case.'

'Good boy. I knew you'd see sense.'

* * *

It was late by the time Justin reached Lewisham; the cab took forever to get back to the prison. After his visit to see Carl, so many questions were going through his head, he needed answers, PDQ. He had to know the truth, wherever that led him. He circled his car and looked at the slight dent in the bumper and then at the blood on the ground. The darkness made it appear like black tar. At first, he didn't want to drive because his car was now a death machine. He tried to rid his mind of a searing migraine that had just developed and turned on the ignition. Taking a deep breath to control his nerves, he drove away, in search of the truth about his wife.

The house was in darkness except for a lamp on in the living room. Justin looked up and down the road before he slipped through the garden gate and along the short pathway to the small three-bedroom semi-detached council house. A sensor light flicked on, and he could see the front door more clearly; the paint was faded and peeling, and the stone step was crumbling with grass growing through the cracks. He paused for a moment, gathering his thoughts before he rapped on the door. As he stepped back, the door opened and there stood a large man, roughly sixty years old, with a prominent belly and bloodshot eyes.

'Are you Lucy's father?' was all Justin could think to ask.

The man, dressed in dirty jeans and a grey grubby-looking vest, slowly nodded, with a deep furrowed brow. 'What's happened?' he asked, in a hoarse voice.

Justin sighed. 'Nothing, but … I know it's late. Could I come in and talk?'

Les stepped back and looked Justin up and down. 'Who are you?'

'I'm Justin Fox, Lucy's husband.'

A slow snigger escaped Les's lips and he shook his head. 'Her husband, eh?'

'Yes, I am.'

Les laughed again. 'All right, then, you'd better come in.'

The ambience was hardly conducive to a non-smoker. The air was thick with stale smoke, and the place looked unkempt and uncared for, with wallpaper that was coming off in places and carpets that were threadbare. Justin followed the man as he made his way into the living room. It was sparse: a sofa, one armchair, a gas fire, and a battered-looking television set were the only items of note. And, also strange, the room was devoid of photographs. You could be forgiven for thinking Lucy never lived there. Les flopped into the armchair. He snatched a packet of cigarettes from the side table and politely offered Justin one.

'Er, no, thank you.'

Les sucked hard until the end of the cigarette glowed. He blew out a huge cloud of smoke.

'So, Justin, what did you want to see me about?'

Sitting himself on the sofa, Justin clasped his hands together. 'The truth about my wife.'

'Now, that's a hard one, see, because I never knew if she was ever honest with me. The girl lied through her back teeth on a daily basis, so what exactly did you want to know?'

Looking around him, Justin felt uneasy; the room was cold and depressing. If his wife had grown up here, then no wonder she pretended she was fostered. Her father looked like a fat slob.

'She told me she was fostered, that she didn't have parents.'

Les laughed sarcastically. 'Oh, yeah, I bet she said she was used, abused, beaten, locked in a cupboard, raped, tortured and, oh, the list goes on.' He sighed heavily and took another deep drag on his cigarette.

'Yes, she did say something like that, so why should I not believe her?'

'You do what ya like, mate, she's no concern of mine now. I ain't seen her in a couple of years, and to be quite honest, it's done me a right favour. At least I can live in peace and quiet. So, Justin, if we're done, you can see yaself out.'

As Justin got up to leave, he said, 'Oh, you might like to know, you have a grandson.'

Les sat up straight at that remark, shooting Justin a concerned look. He stubbed the cigarette out and jumped to his feet. 'You what?'

Stunned at the sudden change in Les's laid-back manner, Justin tilted his head to the side. 'Why do you look so shocked?'

'Fuck me, mate, where's the baby now? Is she with him?'

'No, he's still in the hospital. He's a very poorly baby. Why?'

'Christ alive, you'd better sit ya arse back down. There's a lot you need to know.'

The look of horror on Les's face told Justin he wasn't lying; no one was that good at acting.

Sitting down again, Les looked crestfallen. 'Lucy has problems, as did her mother. She, the poor cow, ended up in a nuthouse, and I was literally left holding the baby. Try as I might, I did my best for that kid, but she wasn't normal. She's got an evil streak in her.'

Justin was now on the edge of his seat. 'But why are you so concerned about our son? She wouldn't hurt him, surely to God?'

Les's eyes widened. 'Yes, I believe she would. She had a baby a few years ago.'

'What!' cried Justin.

He could see Les's eyes becoming sorrowful and the tears beginning to form.

'A dear little thing, she was, such a pretty baby …' He broke off and stared into space. 'When the coroner said she'd died through suffocation – she'd got her face caught up in the blankets – I knew then …'

339

Justin had his hand over his mouth, gulping back the gasp ready to escape. 'She didn't kill her own baby, did she?'

Les allowed the tears to tumble down his fat cheeks. 'They may have believed it was an accident, but I'm not convinced. She has a side to her that scares the shit out of me, and I'm a grown man. There is more to that girl than even I know about, but please believe me, for your son's sake.'

Justin turned away and racked his brains, going over and over the odd behaviour over the past few weeks. He recalled his mother's words in the hospital, telling him that Lucy never visited the baby, yet she'd told him that she went in the evenings. What other lies had she been feeding him?

'Has she ever done anything else? I mean, her little girl may have suffocated. Why would you assume she had something to do with it?'

With a distant, vacant expression, Les remained silent for a few seconds, and then he slowly turned to face Justin. 'Because she tried to kill her own baby sister, on more than one occasion.'

'Jesus, what happened to her?'

Les wiped his narrow eyes. 'I sent her mother-to-be and the baby away, for her own safety.'

Justin was more confused than ever. 'But, didn't you say her mother was in a nuthouse?'

'Yes, she is, but I met another woman, such a beautiful woman, willing to take on Lucy and the baby. Lucy was five years old, and as soon as she held her little sister, she hated her. I saw it in her eyes. When I caught her trying to suffocate the baby, I knew then that I could never live with anyone, so I sent my lovely partner away, bless her heart. She adopted my baby and promised to give her a good life. Lucy was my responsibility, and so it was best all round.'

This was like a sick, twisted film and Justin shuddered. This could not be right, not Lucy. He was finding out a different side to his wife. As for harming a little child, her *own* child, it wasn't possible. She could be difficult, but she was sweet at times. He could picture her, holding their son. Hearing all of this was proving to be quite an unnerving experience. It drove him to get up to leave. 'Look, I have to go. I need to get to the hospital.'

Les struggled from his seat to show Justin to the door. 'Yes, mate, please make sure she's never alone with him.'

As Les turned on the hallway light, Justin was drawn to the pictures that were evenly placed up the staircase. He hadn't seen them before. One particular photo showed a woman holding a baby.

Les followed his eyeline and noticed the photo that had grabbed Justin's attention. 'Yes, that was the love of my life. I still miss her and my other little girl, to this day. Shame, I only put that photo up last year. Lucy smashed the frame years ago, so I hid it in a drawer.'

With a dry mouth, and his heart beating like a bongo drum, Justin slowly turned to Les. 'Is her name Joan, by any chance?'

Les's eyes widened. 'Yes. Why, did Lucy tell you about her?'

Justin swooned, and his face drained of colour. Les grabbed his arm. 'Are you all right, mate? You look like you've seen a ghost.'

Gasping for breath and reeling from the shock of what he'd just learned in the house, Justin collapsed onto the bottom step of the stairs. Taking his time to get his breath back and clear his head, he asked, 'Is your other daughter Kara?'

Les's face visibly crumpled. 'Yes, why? What's the matter?'

With the pain, worry, and fear evident across Justin's face, he felt his world had been jolted like a meteorite smacking him in the head. *It was that karma thing: it had returned to kick him in the balls.*

'Jesus, Les, Kara was my girlfriend for years before I had to leave her because I got Lucy pregnant. I had no idea …'

All of a sudden, he remembered accusing Lucy of hating Kara

some time ago. Everything was falling into place. Les was stunned into silence, just staring at Justin, as if he was dreaming.

'What the fuck is going on, Les?' He choked on the words.

Les pulled Justin to his feet and guided him back to the living room. 'Let me get you a drink. Would you prefer brandy or tea?'

'I think I need a coffee to wake me up. This is all like a fucking nightmare.'

As Les left the room to make the drinks, Justin called the hospital to make sure his son was all right and to warn the nurses to keep a close eye. He was convinced now that his mum was right: Lucy had been lying to him about her visits to Ben. Luckily, the nurse on duty assured him that little Ben was fine and that Mollie was there for her nightly visit. Justin should have been angry because he'd told her to stay away, but now, he was relieved. He had to know the truth. 'Do you know if my wife ever visits Ben?'

There was a short pause. 'Sorry, Justin, but she doesn't. It's been a concern and I was going to have a word with you about it.'

'Thank you,' was all he could say before he ended the call.

As he absorbed his surroundings, he thought his initial feeling of the house being too depressing for a child to live in was ill-judged. He realised that the house's empty, loveless soul was not the fault of Les, but of his daughter. That same daughter had drawn him in with her web of deceit. He wandered back to the hallway to look at the other photos, and there, sure enough, was Lucy as a little girl, dressed in beautiful frilly clothes and playing happily with her toys. There were no pictures of her living in a sad, destitute home. He looked around again and realised that although the house was worn and tired it was, in fact, clean. Les was obviously just skint. The television set was such an old model, he would be surprised if it even worked.

Les returned with a mug of coffee and gave Justin a sorrowful smile. 'Take the weight off ya feet, mate. Let's get this cleared up, shall we?'

Justin sighed. 'It's all a bloody mess, Les. I was with Kara, and then, stupidly, I ended up with Lucy. Now, it appears, I don't even know her.'

'What's Kara like, Justin? I haven't seen her since she was a baby. Her mother still wrote to me every so often, until she moved to Australia. After that, I never heard much from her.'

An unexpected tear escaped Justin's eye. 'You've no idea, Les. She is wonderful, so sweet and gentle, so kind and loving, and beautiful, I mean naturally beautiful, but she is clever too, a real brainbox … Christ, what have I done?'

The look on Les's face said it all. His smile broadened, and that expression transformed the man into someone thirty years younger. In fact, he could see where many of Kara's attractive features came from. He'd been a vibrant, handsome man in his day, no question.

'You still love her, then?'

'I never stopped loving her. I just had to force myself to … fucking hell, Les, I got angry with her, when I saw her in the hospital. All because she didn't care for me anymore. What a tosser, I've been.'

'Hospital? Is she all right?'

'Yes, she is. Well, actually, no. I mean, she's in prison for burning the house down, but she was in hospital because she had our daughter, little Denise Rose. My God, she's been to hell and back, and then, having to deal with her mother, who sadly …' He paused for a moment, realising he was going to deliver bad news. Accordingly, he softened his tone. 'Les, I've some dreadful news for you, I'm afraid. Joan passed away several months ago.'

Les placed his mug of coffee on the small side table and covered his face. Justin watched the heavily built man's shoulders move up and down, as he quietly sobbed. Feeling his own world completely crumbling around him, with so much pain and misery, he conceded that it was all connected to him. For a second, he wanted to run and leave the man to cry alone because he couldn't bear to watch anyone hurting. These last months, he'd seen enough pain to last a lifetime. However, he had to know more about Lucy. Who the hell was he married to, and, more to the point, what was she capable of?

'Les, Lucy said you locked her in a metal cabinet. Why would she say that?'

As Les moved his hands away from his face, Justin could see his eyes were locked in sadness.

Without a word, Les rose from his chair and beckoned with his head for Justin to follow. They went through the kitchen to a door on the side that led to the garage. Les fiddled with the keys and pushed open the door. There on the back wall of the garage was indeed a metal cabinet, although it was too small for even a child to be shoved inside. Justin looked enquiringly at Les, who just shook his head. He opened the cabinet door and pointed to the doll that was there. 'She even had the social services check me out, saying that I would lock her in there. I never did, but when she was bad, and believe me she was bad, I would lock her toys away.'

'Tell me, Les, what about this Carl guy? She convinced me he raped her.'

'Carl rape her? No way! Carl was her saviour. By the time she was fifteen, she was sleeping around, and then she got hooked on drugs. I didn't know much about drugs meself, see, but Carl did. I was at my fucking wits' end. I was working for Carl at the time. One night, we were all playing cards, as we did most Wednesdays, a regular poker night, when in she came, dressed like a fucking hooker and with make-up slapped all over her face. She was acting like a tart, flirting in front of Carl. It was embarrassing. I remember Carl shaking his head. He said it was such a shame. I suppose he was fed up with seeing me out of my mind with worry.

344

'I remember he dragged her upstairs and gave her a good talking-to. Ya see, Carl wasn't a paragon of virtue, not by any stretch of the imagination. On the contrary. If the truth be known, he used to run a whorehouse, but it wasn't like you would imagine. He took girls off the streets and put them in his flats. Sounds bad, doesn't it? But, ya see, he wasn't a cruel fella. Anyway, he told her that she would end up dead, if she carried on. The little bitch never listened, though. She would dress up like a real slapper every Wednesday and skip around him like a dog on heat. In the end, he stopped coming around to play cards.'

'But she said she was fifteen, when he raped her,' retorted Justin, not wanting to believe Lucy had lied.

'It pains me to say it, Justin, and it still turns my stomach to this day, but when Lucy was fourteen, the police dragged her home. She was caught selling herself like a common tom on the streets. I asked myself every day what the hell I'd done wrong. How could my little girl become so bloody wayward? I mean, she never went without. I took her to school every day, I did my best, but it wasn't good enough. She stole from me; she would lay into me with her fists and call me disgusting names. I should have told the truth back then and had her locked away.

'But Carl came to the rescue. He offered a flat of her own, away from me. She was older then and had got herself into all sorts of bad stuff. She was making money on the streets. I knew she wouldn't stop, but Carl was always keeping an eye on her. So when she took up escort work, Carl spoke to the agency without her knowledge because he wanted to vet all her punters. I know that sounds bad, but it was either that or have her standing under some lamppost in London for any old Tom, Dick, or Harry to take her away and do God knows what.'

Justin let out a long, deep sigh and looked up at the ceiling. 'Fuck me! So my wife is a prostitute? My son probably isn't even mine.'

'You weren't the first and you won't be the last.'

'She's done this before?' gasped Justin, incredulously.

'Yes, she claimed that the little girl of hers was the result of having sex with Carl. But he's adamant that Lucy drugged him the night he was with her. He told me himself. She gave him Rohypnol, or whatever it's called, but he was unaware of this when he woke up in the morning, after she'd boasted about a night of passion they'd enjoyed. Then, a month later, she announced she was pregnant.'

Maybe Lucy did the same to him. She could have drugged him and led him to believe he was the one who came on to her, and like an idiot, he fell for it. But the guilt veiled his mind like a black demon sucking the energy out of him. How could he tell Les, who obviously cared for Carl, that he'd run him over and nearly killed him? Justin jumped from his chair. 'I have to go, Les. I have something to do.'

Before he was out of the door, Les grabbed his arm. 'Are you going to see if that boy of yours is really your baby?'

Justin couldn't have felt more hurt, if he'd tried. 'Of course.'

'And tell me, Justin, do you love that boy?'

Justin nodded. 'Yes, I really do.'

'So does it really matter, then, if he's your own flesh and blood or not?'

It was a leading question. Justin knew then that the chances of Ben being his baby were next to zero. He would go and see for himself.

346

Chapter 21

As Justin drove towards his home, his stomach was in knots and his hands trembled. Not being hard himself, he never liked violence and had never fought before. He had been living with a real nutcase. Dark images of a scene from *Fatal Attraction* came to mind, and he visualised Lucy standing behind the door holding a knife. He shook himself out of the thought.

There was no reason to doubt Les and that photo on the wall of Joan and of Kara as a baby certainly gave him so much to think about. He cast his mind back over the past few months and tried to see things more clearly, but so much tainted his thoughts. As he pulled up at the traffic lights in Chislehurst, he impulsively took a detour back to the flat. The keys had still not been handed over, and there were boxes that needed to be taken home.

As he approached the stairs, he could see the remnants of the police tape that had sealed off the old lady's flat. A chill froze him to the spot. He stared for a while, recapping what the officer had said, that they would question Lucy. At the time, he took it to mean if she knew of any comings and goings, or if she'd seen any strangers lurking about. The police, however, hadn't been to the house to question her, at least not while he was there.

As he went to put the key in the lock, he shivered, as if there was a monster hiding behind that door. To add to the eerie atmosphere, the wind encircled him, and he shuddered again. Once inside, he instantly switched the lights on. It then dawned on him that he really was a weak man. The mirror in the hallway showed his face; he looked closer, and for a second, he didn't recognise himself. It wasn't the grey flecks in his hair or the lines around his eyes but the sad, pathetic expression. And his gaunt cheeks and shorter dull lank hair didn't help either.

He could almost feel Kara running her hands through it, smelling of her favourite tropical scents. So much had changed, including himself. It was such a difference from his former self that he felt ashamed, guilty, and worthless.

He pulled himself away from the reflection and headed upstairs where the remaining boxes were. Two smaller cartons belonged to him, and there, in the corner, alone and in the darkness, was an even smaller one belonging to Lucy. On closer inspection, he noticed just how many times she'd sealed it with tape. He turned his eyes to the others that seemed to be marginally sealed and then back to hers. After finding out so many secrets in such a short time, his brain was now in detective mode, and he wanted to search the flat. But for what? He didn't know, but he needed to make sure there were no other secrets like the one that burned away in the back of his mind, a secret that if true would make him explode with fury and want to kill Lucy himself.

He ran back down the stairs to search for a knife, but they had cleaned out the kitchen cupboards beforehand. He would have to use his keys and painstakingly open the heavily taped box. As he kneeled down beside it, he noticed the wardrobe door open, and at first, he thought the base seemed higher than the door. He looked more closely and realised that what should have been the baseboard that held the wardrobe in place was in fact a loose shelf. He lifted the board and noticed the large space under it was not dusty with cobwebs as he expected but it was clean and tidy. Inside were two empty wine bottles. His eyes were then drawn back to the box he was about to open.

Five solid minutes it took to cut through the tape, but finally, he was able to lift the lid. He stared at the papers, letters, and silly love notes, and then his eyes widened as he spotted paperwork with his name on it. It was his company annual report for the last tax year, showing how much money his business had made. In a manila folder was a copy of the deeds to his house. As well as a notebook, a valuation report was included, showing what appeared to be all his assets and their current value. Underneath the sums was a division figure of fifty per cent. Also enclosed in the folder was a copy of their wedding certificate and their son's birth certificate.

Slowly, the picture was coming together. He sat back and stared in disbelief. It was there in black and white: everything Lucy needed to claim half of all his assets. She was his wife and the mother of his child; if she wanted a divorce, she could easily be awarded these holdings by any court of law. 'What a fucking bitch,' he mumbled to himself, still in shock.

As he moved the papers aside, his eyes rested on a phone and the charger. He'd never seen the mobile before. Perhaps it was broken or an old one from an upgrade because Lucy had her Swarovski-crystal-encrusted phone on her all the time, playing Candy Crush Saga. Something told him to plug it in. While he waited for the phone to charge up, he continued to search through the box.

He pulled out what he initially thought was a notebook only to find a diary. On closer inspection, he saw it was Lucy's diary. The first few pages seemed confusing. They were written by a Dr Spinks, asking her to recall significant events, her motivations for her actions, and her feelings at the time. Justin's hands trembled as he was about to enter the world of Lucy Fairmount, afraid of what he might discover.

From just a few scribbled notes he established that his wife was one very mixed-up woman. She was angry with the world and everyone in it. She believed no one loved her, her own mother had abandoned her, and so she continually reinvented her life to escape reality. He flipped through hundreds of pages, and near to the end, he was startled when he saw Kara's name. His stomach turned over at the vile hateful words. *I wish Kara was dead – I deserve her life and everything that goes with it – Justin – the house – money – the life. And you, Mother dearest, are such a fucking sucker. Really, Joan, I should hate you the most. Shame you had to die. I was quite enjoying sunny Australia.*

As he glared at the words, a sudden bleep made him jump. The phone was charged. Moments later, the phone bleeped again and then bleeped a few more times. He checked the screen. For a second, he was puzzled, until he realised there were several unopened text messages.

As he opened the first text, he almost dropped the phone. It read: *Hello, Joan, I hope you are well. I haven't heard from you in a while. Text me when you can, love Mollie.*

The next text read: *Hi, Mum, I am in Papua New Guinea, will call when I get home, missing you, love Kara xx.* It was sent the day Kara left Papua New Guinea, when her mother was already dead and buried.

Justin felt choked up, as tears streamed down his face. *Oh, what have I done, Kara? You poor thing.* His eyes were still gaping at all the messages, when, suddenly, a noise from downstairs startled him, and for a second, he froze. He hurriedly placed the phone back into the box and quietly went to the bedroom door to listen. He could feel his bowels stirring. Why should he be scared? He was more than capable of handling himself, and if it was Lucy, taking her on, one-on-one, would be a doddle.

The footsteps were now trudging up the stairs, but they were heavy, not light like Lucy's. He waited nervously and unarmed. Coming into view was a man he didn't recognise, but in a state of shock and confusion, Justin remained glued to the spot as if his legs were welded to the floor.

'Justin Fox?' asked the man, who waited a good ten feet away.

Justin looked the man over, trying to recall if he'd ever met him before. He seemed harmless enough, but, reassuringly, he also had an air of authority about him.

'Yes.'

'Right, I'm Bruce Williams, a private investigator for Kara Bannon. Actually, her lawyer engaged my services, and today we had a call that indicates that your wife, Lucy Fairmount, may have been the carer for Kara Bannon's mother, Joan Bannon. Do you know anything about this?'

'How did you get in?'

Bruce looked over his shoulder. 'The door was open. I hope you don't mind?'

Feeling a little spooked, Justin stepped back. 'Do you have any ID on you?'

Bruce smiled. 'Yes, I do.' He rummaged inside his tweed jacket and pulled out a card. 'I was a detective for the Met, but now I do private work.'

Justin snatched the card, but his trembling hands didn't go unnoticed by Bruce. 'Hey, look, are you okay, mate, because you look a little out of sorts?'

Justin slowly nodded and relaxed his shoulders. 'Well, Mr Williams, I've been doing some digging myself, and I think you may have everything you need in that box over there.'

Bruce tilted his head to the side. 'What's going on, mate? By the way, call me Bruce.'

'Bruce, I've discovered that my wife, Lucy, is nothing but a dangerous psychopath who probably needs fucking locking up.'

'Where is she now?'

A good question. Justin realised he had no idea. 'I left her at the prison. Christ, that was hours ago.' He looked at his watch and raised his eyebrow. It was four o'clock in the morning.

'I know a café that serves a good coffee. Why don't you and I get a drink? You can tell me what you know, and let's see if I can help.'

'No, I'm fine.'

Justin grabbed the box and handed it to the detective. 'I haven't been through all of it, but there is enough in there to tell me that the bitch married me for my money and she was Kara's mother's carer. What the hell she did to her mother, God only knows, but I wouldn't be surprised if there was foul play, not after hearing about Lucy's antics from her very own father's lips and then reading her diary and the phone messages …'

Bruce peered inside the box. 'Do you mind if I have a look?' As he lifted the lid, he looked sideways at Justin. 'We received a phone call from Kara, you know. She said that your wife handed Carl Meadows Joan Bannon's ring.'

Justin's face was drained as he nodded. 'Well, so he says, and right now, Bruce, I think I believe him.'

Bruce was tired himself. He'd taken on the task on Stuart's behalf, and yet, hitting constant dead ends was making him feel like retiring completely. Perhaps the Met had been right, and he'd outlived his role. 'Shall we take this to the kitchen? My eyes are not as good as they used to be.'

Justin felt his eyelids droop and would agree to anything, providing he didn't have to think anymore. The kitchen fluorescent light livened him up, though, and he watched like a kid as the detective carefully removed the contents of the box. He set aside all the paperwork, and then he rifled through Lucy's diary, pausing at intervals, as he scrutinised some of the entries. He was very careful handling the mobile phone, using a cloth to hold it at the corner to ensure his prints weren't on it. Then, at the bottom of the box, he found a small yet exquisite jewellery case. He looked up at Justin. 'Was this Lucy's mother's or grandmother's?'

Justin stepped closer to get a better look. 'I wouldn't know.

I've never seen it before, but, to be perfectly frank, there's very little I know about my wife.'

Bruce sensed the anger as Justin spat out those cold words.

As Bruce opened the lid of the nineteenth-century wooden inlaid case, he frowned. There, inside, was a pill bottle, the label clearly showing the name of Joan Bannon. Beside it was a bracelet. From Bruce's knowledge of jewellery, he guessed it was also nineteenth century. A little hobby of his was antiques, and, in particular, he was fascinated with jewellery. He was a collector of pocket watches and thought jewellery from around 1700 to 1800 rather interesting and especially how they were hidden and protected through the wars.

'Well, Justin, this is certainly evidence that Lucy had been in contact with Joan Bannon.' He pointed to the empty pill bottle. 'It also seems that she acquired a very valuable bracelet. That's not to say, though, they weren't passed down to her by someone named Lilly.' He pointed to the inscription on the bracelet.

'I wouldn't know. As I said, I never really knew her at all.' His distress was written across his face. It was clear that Justin was fraught with worry. Bruce noticed how the man's hands were still trembling as he ran his fingers through his hair. Then, Justin gasped. 'Oh my God! Lilly! The lady downstairs who died was called Lillian, so I guess Lilly was her. I bet Lucy murdered her and stole that bracelet!'

Bruce gripped Justin's shoulders. It was all too much for Justin to absorb. 'Listen, we don't know that for sure, do we? You're tired. Don't get carried away. It could be a coincidence.' Bruce was more interested in the phone. 'Tell me, what do you know about the phone?'

Justin painstakingly repeated everything he'd read from the messages and then broke off. 'Christ, Bruce, I really have fucked up. Do you know, I've been living in a bloody trance. My work is going down the pan, I can't concentrate, and yet, for some idiotic reason, I've gone along with this woman's ideas, plans, and lies. What a fool I've been.'

'Well, mate, from what you've said, this Lucy is a master of strategy. Some women are, and we as men can be blinded by their real intentions. I know my wife has me doing stuff – you know, decorating and such like – somehow making me believe it was my idea. I still fall for it. Anyway, mate, that doesn't help your problem.' He lifted the jewellery box, only to find another one inside which was not so ornate. He lifted the lid and shook his head. 'Fucking Rohypnol!'

Justin snatched the packet and held it to the light. 'That's the date rape drug, isn't it?'

'Yes, it is, although it's not just used for that. In smaller doses, it's like having a drink. It's used for recreational purposes, but why she would have it, I don't know.'

With his throat now tight, Justin gasped for breath. 'Tell me, Bruce,' he asked, agitatedly and taking a deep breath, 'if a man was given this, could he perform? I mean, could he have sex?'

'I doubt it very much. Why?'

'Because I woke up in her bed. Twice. In fact, having not remembered a bloody thing. I reckon Lucy drugged me … Oh, Christ, if she did, then everything is a lie.' Justin appeared shell-shocked from his discoveries. He staggered back against the wall and his body slid to the floor until he was sitting with his head in his hands.

Bruce replaced the box inside the larger one and sat next to Justin. 'Listen, mate, you are tired, you need to get some rest. I'm going to call the police, let them take this up, because, right now, we can't do much else. Let's hope they find something in that box to unravel this mess.'

'I fucking hope they lock her up.'

Bruce looked at the box and sighed. 'I'm not sure there's anything that they can use to confirm any offence. Let's take this one step at a time, Justin. I need to make a few calls.' He stood up, and with his notebook and pen, he carefully wrote the name of the drug and dosage that was written on the pills for Joan Bannon. 'Firstly, I need to call the coroner in Australia to see if there were large enough doses of this drug in her system to kill her. The authorities over there are taking this very seriously, let me tell you, and apparently, they are sending over some report from a second coroner. He's looked over the blood samples taken at the post-mortem. So, look, you go and get some rest, and hopefully later today, we will have a clearer picture as to what is actually going on here.'

Removing his hands away from his face, Justin frowned. 'How can they know for sure? Joan was cremated, by all accounts.'

Bruce nodded. 'Yes, she was, but they would have taken blood samples from the autopsy and kept the results on file. It's just routine.'

'I can't believe I was living with a real-life nutter.'

'Hold on a minute, Justin, we don't know that yet. It could all be innocent, well, perhaps not innocent, but there may be an explanation for all of this. Look, we can't be sure that your wife was even in Australia.'

Justin's eyes met Bruce's. 'Oh, yeah, she definitely was. It's all there, in the diary. And Carl Meadows has just told me he found an airline ticket receipt in her old flat, showing that Lucy had recently been there.'

'Where do you think Lucy would go?'

Justin looked up. 'I'm afraid I don't know. It was strange. I took Lucy to see Kara in prison to discuss custody of our daughter. When I got there, I found out that Carl, who also goes by the name of Rocky, was visiting his sister. But this guy confronted us and an argument started. If Lucy has disappeared, it might have something to do with a ring that Lucy gave him in part payment over a debt she owed him. When Kara recognised that ring as her mother's, Lucy looked mortified. She was out of that visiting room like a bat out of hell.

'Anyway, outside the prison, she stood there in the pouring rain and refused to get in the car. Then, inexplicably, she took off. I don't think for one minute she will return home, well, to my house, knowing how much trouble she's in. I hate to admit it, but I'm a bit nervous of going back there myself. These last few hours have given me the right creeps ...' He paused and sighed. Bruce could hear his voice crack. 'I'm just so tired, I can't even think straight. Christ, I feel like a fucking sissy.'

'No, no, Justin, let me tell you this. If half of what you believe is true, then it would be better for you to stay elsewhere, until we find her.' Bruce could completely understand because the idea of Lucy pretending that Joan was still alive weeks after she'd died was eerie to say the least, and finding the Rohypnol and the diary made matters worse. He concluded that on the face of it, Lucy was a dangerous woman and possibly a psychopath, with devious goals in mind.

'Right, Justin, have you got anywhere to go?'

Slowly, he got to his feet. 'Yeah, my mum's, if she'll let me through the door after how I've treated her lately.'

Bruce patted Justin's arm. 'Mums forgive anything. Go on, get yourself some rest. I'll have a word at the station and see if we can get this shit cleared up.'

Chapter 22

Deni shuffled into Kara's room, her hair sticking up in all directions, and her face looking withered. 'I couldn't sleep. How about you, babe?'

With a shake of her head, Kara replied, 'No, not a wink, even the baby was restless. Why is it all taking so long? I'll wear the floor out, if I pace this cell one more time. It's been more than three days since I called Stuart, and I've heard nothing, not even a letter.'

'Now, now, don't get yaself worked up. He's probably looking into it all, and ya know the police can take forever. It will all come good in the end. That Stuart is pulling out all the stops. I mean, I've never heard of a barrister going to all this trouble at his own expense to help an inmate the way he's helped you.'

Kara wasn't listening. 'I just can't believe it, and furthermore, I don't understand it, Deni. I mean, how was Lucy caught up with Justin, if she's as bad as Vic said?'

Deni sat heavily on the bed and slowly removed the baby from Kara, gently rocking her. 'Well, look on the bright side. No judge in the poxy land will let Justin have the baby, not while he's with her. Fuck me, whatever possessed the man to take up with someone like her, when he could have a diamond like you?'

357

'I was so upset, after that visit, Deni, I can't remember half of what was said. Tell me, did you know this Lucy well?'

With the baby in one arm and using the other hand to push herself off the bed, Deni gently laid Denise Rose in the crib. 'There, she has gone off.' Deni sighed heavily, and the corners of her mouth turned down. 'Yeah, babe, I'm afraid to say, I knew her all too well. She was a fucking trollop and no mistake.'

'They won't get custody of my baby, will they?' Her eyes were full of desperation.

Deni folded her arms under her breasts. 'Cor, blimey, no, not once they find out about her criminal record. I mean, it's as long as a fireman's hose. Even one of my own girls had her nicked, and that, in my line of work, goes right against the grain. Mind you, I couldn't blame Manda.'

'Tell me, Deni, what you know.'

'Little Manda, we called her, stick-thin she was, but she had this really pretty face, you know, like a china doll, with rosebud lips and huge blue eyes. The poor cow was wandering the streets, refusing point-blank to go back home. She was a wreck when Rocky brought her to me. He said she was too young to be streetwalking. Anyway, the little lass was streetwise, and no matter how much I tried to talk her out of selling herself, she was adamant. Rocky took a shine to her – not in that way – but he wanted to help her, ya know. He took her to the flat he'd put Lucy in. A right nice pad, that was.

'Well, anyway, Lucy was up in arms and made it quite clear she wasn't happy. That's when Rocky told her, if she didn't accept little Manda, then she would find herself out on her ear. The cunt played them both, pretending she would accept her, and for a few weeks, Manda said she was really nice. Of course, I had my concerns then 'cos Lucy was never really nice …' Deni held back the emotion that was trapped in her throat. She sighed heavily and shook her head. 'That kiddie was scarred for life, the poor little thing. Lucy had drugged her, and let a punter have his wicked way with her.'

Kara gasped, and her eyes widened. 'No!'

'Yep, she'd drugged the kid and told the police that Manda had men in and out and anything could have happened. Lucy said she'd gone out for the evening, yet Manda, in her half-conscious state, only remembered bits and pieces. But the poor cow was too doped up to do anything about it ...' She shuddered and wiped her brow. 'What she must have gone through was pure terror. The fucking nutjob of a man beat her black and blue. You know, what makes me sick was the police didn't charge Lucy because she was fucking the detective.'

Her eyes fell on Kara, who was open-mouthed with horror. 'My God, and Justin expects me to leave my baby in the hands of that basket case?'

Deni threw her hands in the air. 'Well, it's all on record, so you can have your solicitor pull that as the trump card.'

Kara looked over at her sleeping baby and slowly nodded. 'I will insist they dig out her records because I'm sure they'll find more.'

'Oh, there is! So much more. Anyway, you can talk it all over with this Stuart guy. I'm sure he will look after your interests. It seems to me, he's doing more than his job. I told you ages ago I thought he had a little crush on ya. Otherwise, why would he go above and beyond?' she said, with a mischievous smile.

Kara waved her hand. 'Oh, Deni, don't go there. Anyway, I have Rocky, now.'

'About that, um ...'

With a frown deeply edged on Kara's face, she urged Deni to go on.

'He is lovely, Kara, but you are worlds apart, although I know it's none of my business.' She looked outside the room, to make sure no one was listening. 'He's no angel, babe. I like him 'cos he looked out for my girls, but that's no life for you. Once a villain, always a villain, and no matter how much he thinks he's on the straight and narrow, he can never really have two feet in the law-abiding world. He'll always have a size-twelve boot in some crime venture. You, my babe, are made of finer things, and as much as you think you don't deserve better, you damn well do.'

'But I love him, Deni,' she almost whimpered.

'Nah ya don't, Kara, you love the idea of him. That's something entirely different.'

Kara changed the subject. 'I wonder if Stuart has called the police about the ring?'

Deni nodded. 'He has a legal obligation to do so, love.'

As her heart pounded in her chest, Kara felt nervous, yet excited. Her unanswered questions had kept her up for three nights, and she needed answers, before she climbed the walls. Just as Deni was about to leave the room, she was almost knocked down by Vic. 'Jesus, girl, what's up with you?'

Vic was clearly distraught; her face was crimson and her eyes were glassy.

'I've been trying to speak to Rocky about my parole, but I couldn't get hold of him. Then, when I phoned Angie, she told me. Me brother's in hospital. That fucking Justin has only gone and mown him down. His legs were crushed.'

Leaping from the bed, Kara threw her hands to her mouth. 'Oh my God! Is he okay? I mean, apart from his legs?'

Vic slumped down on the bed. 'I dunno. Angie reckons he is, but she's as daft as a fucking box of frogs. Fuck me, what on earth bleedin' went on after that visit?'

Kara was still in disbelief and shook her head. 'My God, this just gets worse. I feel so bad. If it wasn't for me, none of this would have happened. I just seem to be blighted with a black cloud following me around and raining hell on anyone who knows me.'

Vic jumped up, out of breath from the shock. 'Now, you listen to me. This ain't your doing. It's that bastard Lucy. I will bet me own sanity that she's behind it. If anyone leaves mayhem in their fucking path, it's her.'

'I just cannot imagine Justin doing something so reckless. He was never violent. Running someone down is just so hard to believe.'

Vic shot her a questioning glare.

'Oh, no, Vic, I'm not saying I don't believe it, of course I do, but it's just so out of character.'

'And he ain't pressing charges either, so Justin will get away with everything scot-free.'

The guilt overwhelmed Kara and she cupped her hands over her face and cried. Before Deni or Vic could comfort her, Barbara stepped into the cell and screeched, 'You two, get to work!'

Vic didn't argue. She was on her way home soon and needed to keep her nose clean. Deni, however, had nothing to lose, and, as was often the case, had plenty to say. Like now. 'You really are a right miserable fucking mare.'

'Don't push it, Denton!' snapped Barbara.

With a huff and a sigh, Deni waddled out of the room leaving Barbara with a nasty smirk on her spiteful face. 'You can take the baby to the nursery while you have your legal visit.' She scowled as she turned to face Kara.

'A legal visit? What? No one said.'

'What were you expecting, a gold letter handed to you on a silver plate? Just get that baby over to the nursery. Your visit is in ten minutes,' retorted Barbara.

'No, I won't. Cole can watch her for me. She is down as one of my baby's partners, since you have just demanded Deni go to work.'

It was obvious Kara had been crying and Barbara grinned even more. 'Well, you need to get used to being away from your kid 'cos you'll be handing her over long before you leave 'ere.'

Kara stood up and inclined her head to the side. 'Tell me, Barbara, why are you so cruel?' She kept her voice to a soft controlled pitch, which strangely unnerved the officer.

'What?'

'You know, Barbara, you just seem to enjoy being particularly wicked, like poison.' She stepped closer and watched as the officer backed away.

'It amazes me somewhat why no one has smashed your head to a pulp.'

Barbara was spooked. Kara's tone was low and slow, and it was said with such an undercurrent of creepiness.

Without responding, Barbara turned on her heel and walked out of the cell. This was not the Kara she recognised. The woman was clearly able to switch to a different – scary – persona whenever she felt like it and her words sent a shiver up Barbara's spine. Once outside the cell, the officer took a deep breath. Although she'd become hardened to the inmates shouting abuse, her defence mechanism seemed to have no answer to Kara, who was different and almost passive-aggressive.

* * *

As soon as Colette had arrived, Kara was ready to meet her lawyer. She brushed her hair that was now very long and added moisturiser to her face. Her skin had dried out from a lack of fresh circulating air in the mothers' unit. George himself came to collect her. He asked how she was doing and if she had everything she needed, now particularly concerned for her welfare after all that had happened to her.

The moment he opened the door to the visiting room, Kara jumped back; she was shocked to see two other men there with Stuart.

'Hello, Kara, please do come in. At last, I can introduce you to Bruce Williams, who, as you know, is my private detective, and this is Detective Inspector Hamilton from the Metropolitan Police.'

With a nervous smile, Kara gingerly took her seat, her eyes wide and full of trepidation.

DI Hamilton was a man in his late fifties, tall and thickset, with mousy hair cut close to his head. His shoulders were pulled back as he sat confidently next to Bruce Williams.

Clutching a stack of papers, DI Hamilton held them up and said, 'This, here, is a pile of notes regarding an unsolved case.'

Stuart Venables and Bruce Williams remained quiet, just watching the expression on Kara's face. She noticed how tired they both were. Stuart had a five o'clock shadow and Bruce also appeared dishevelled. His hair was greasy, and he hadn't shaved.

'We followed up the message you left with your lawyer and Bruce spoke to Justin Fox.' He placed the file back on the table. 'He informed us of his concerns regarding his wife, Lucy, and I have to say we were very alarmed. It appears that she did indeed go to Australia, and whilst she was out there, she referred to herself as Lucille, and for a time, she did look after Joan. She also had in her possession a box of Rohypnol, and as a scientist, I have no need to tell you what that is used for.'

Under the table, Kara was wringing her hands, her knees were shaking, and she stared, trying to take in the detective's words and the cold manner in which they were said.

'The second coroner that dealt with your mother's post-mortem samples—'

'What!' shrieked Kara.

Hamilton raised his brow. 'Yes, Miss Bannon, your mother died unexpectedly, and I know you are aware that a post-mortem was carried out, although initially, it was deemed as self-inflicted, a possible suicide, or an overdose of her prescribed painkillers. But we requested another coroner to reassess the blood samples and report, considering the recent concerns. The latest report confirmed abnormal swelling of her liver and lethal damage to her kidneys, again possibly caused by an overdose of her current medication, but, interestingly, on close examination, the coroner found small unusual bleeds in the liver, indicative of poisoning.'

'Oh my God! No! But you ...' She paused, looking at Stuart.

'You said she'd died and was cremated months ago. You never mentioned she was poisoned.' Her eyes frantically searched the expression on the men's faces. The anxiety curled into her stomach and clawed up her throat, as if it was choking her.

Stuart looked away.

'Stuart!' she cried.

'Miss Bannon, Stuart acted as your barrister for the crime for which you were convicted, namely, for the arson attack on Justin Fox's home. But Stuart, here, went beyond that. Out of the kindness of his heart, he employed the services of Bruce Williams, a former colleague of mine, because you had concerns that your mother hadn't returned your calls.' Hamilton's cold stare and no-nonsense manner turned Kara's stomach over and a wave of light-headedness swept through her, leaving her mouth dry. All eyes were on her. She remained speechless, almost predicting the next sentence.

'We tracked down Lucy at the hospital, nursing her son. He is very sickly, you know, and it seems he has problems brought on by a particular poison – the same poison Joan Bannon died from.'

'Oh my God! Are you saying she murdered my mother *and* tried to kill her own son?'

Hamilton shook his head. 'No, Miss Bannon. I'm absolutely *not* saying that. She never poisoned anyone, did she?'

With the realisation that the detective had uncovered so much, the blood rushed to her ears, her pulse skyrocketed, and Kara stared in disbelief.

'No, she didn't try to kill her own child because she herself had ingested the poison. Sadly, she was unaware that she was pregnant at this time.'

The tension in the air was almost palpable. Kara was too afraid to speak, as she dug her nails into her hands and bit down on her lip.

'Lucy, however, wasn't squeaky clean. It seems she did have a dark, sinister part to play in all of this, a part, Miss Bannon, you didn't see coming. Lucy, as you may or may not be aware, is your sister.'

He paused to see her eyes open wide and her pupils suddenly dilate. The blood visibly drained from her face. Kara remained motionless, still digesting his words.

'You do know she is your sister, don't you, Miss Bannon?'

'What? My sister? But ... this Lucy or Lucille was my mother's carer, wasn't she? My mother never said ...?' Stumped and totally bewildered, as if her thoughts were all suddenly glued together, Kara couldn't speak.

Hamilton continued in a stiff tone. 'Two sisters separated at a young age, both despising each other, both believing their lives would be better.'

'No, no, you've got that all wrong. I didn't know her. I didn't even know her name. I just thought ...'

Butting in, Hamilton was cold. 'You hated Joan, though, didn't you?'

Uncurling her hunched posture, Kara sat back on her chair and raised her eyebrow, with a sheer look of smug defiance. Stuart's eyes widened as he witnessed what he thought was a sweet, unassuming young woman transform into a dark, evil-eyed, and sneering creature.

With a cold stare, she thought about her mother. No, she didn't like her; in fact, she hated her with a passion. She knew all along that she had a sister and a father but was denied any further details as to where they lived or even their names. Joan wanted to move on with her life, and so when Kara was nine years old, Joan took up with Thomas Grey, a wealthy businessman, who was already married, and who kept Joan as his dirty little secret. It sickened Kara how her mother acted like some lovesick teenager, running around after him.

But that wasn't why she detested her mother. It wasn't jealousy; it was her mother's denial. She shivered, as if a ghost had walked right through her. The vision of him sneaking into her bedroom and slowly lowering himself onto her bed was almost vivid. His hands were pawing at her, his hot, sickly breath, always smelling of whisky, lingering as he buried his face into her neck. Then, it turned physical, as the biting and kissing, which turned her stomach, led to the unforgivable outrage and that unbearable pain and humiliation where she left her body to escape reality, and her mind took her to a place in one of her books as it over-compensated for the brutality she was experiencing.

Joan was there, though, outside that door, spying on her. She never stopped him, and she never came to Kara's rescue. Her selfish excuse was that she just didn't want him to run back to his wife. She would do whatever it took to keep him – even if it meant allowing the disgusting man to take what he wanted from a naive and frightened twelve-year-old child.

The day her mother sent her to boarding school was the day she planned her revenge. She had to read and study; no one would get away with murder, if they didn't have a brain.

She craved the solitary existence whilst surrounded by all the pupils at school during the day and those who were in her dormitory at night. She imagined her sister free to live a wonderful life, having her own bedroom and real friends, not friends who were thrust upon her. She pictured her sitting with her father and both of them laughing together as she told him what she'd done that day. She craved the love of her real father; it must be a joy, she thought, and so different from the cold suffocating glares Thomas Grey gave her, the man she despised, and for good reason.

Lonely, sad, and yet frightened to be at home, Kara occupied her days with her nose in a book, hiding from the bitter disappointment of life, always wondering what her sister was doing, and forever pondering why she was with her mother. As the years passed, Kara began to despise Joan. She didn't hate her sister, because she never knew her, and she was intelligent enough to realise that whatever caused her to be separated from her sister was down to their parents, including Joan. That was another reason for hating her mother. She believed that her mother had taken her from her real father and forced her to live with Thomas Grey.

By the time Thomas had returned to his wife, which was inevitable, Kara was living at home before going off to university. She tolerated her mother for the simple reason she still needed to learn about medicine and diseases. Vic was right when she said, 'She knows how to make ya better, so she will know how ta kill ya.'

She recalled that Joan had pulled out all the stops and arranged a birthday party for her twenty-first. Of course, it was all through guilt and shame, but little did Joan know that, come what may, she could never make up for the terror she'd caused her daughter by allowing Thomas Grey into their home. Joan secretly invited the girls from her dormitory and her own friend's children, one of them being best friends with Justin.

As soon as Kara clapped eyes on Justin, she fell deeply in love. She'd never loved anyone before and the feeling was over-whelming. His beaming smile, loose locks, and round open eyes had sucked her in, easing the bitterness she felt towards her mother. She never told Justin how she really felt about her mother because the truth was he was a real family man and would never have understood her hating her own mother. She wasn't brave enough to tell him or anyone about her years of sexual abuse. Too ashamed and even in some ways feeling her own guilt as a child, she struggled to comprehend it, but as an adult, she knew exactly what Thomas Grey had done and that was to take from her *her* own precious childhood.

So that was how it was for many years. And as her relationship strengthened with Justin, she assumed it did between their mothers. It was a shame, really, because she loved Mollie more than Joan.

'I never hated my mother!' she spat back, to the surprise of

367

Stuart, who had only seen the sweet, charming expression, which had obviously been a deliberate act.

'You see, Miss Bannon, initially your mother's death wasn't ruled as suspicious. Clearly, you didn't realise that your clever plan would ultimately backfire. And, Miss Bannon, if you had never voiced your concern to your lawyer, by mentioning the fact that you had tried to contact your mother, and if Stuart hadn't discovered she'd been dead for months, Joan's death would never have been investigated.' He paused and waited for a reaction, but the stillness in her eyes told him she wasn't about to confess; it was clear she was cunning and waiting to see what they had on her.

Then, unexpectedly, her lips curled to a thin sneer. 'I wasn't responsible for my mother's death though, was I? I mean, I was in Papua New Guinea, working.'

Hamilton nodded and slowly opened the file in front of him. He retrieved a photocopy of a stamped immigration form and turned it around so that she could see it for herself. Kara's eyes widened, as she saw the authorised flight list. There, clearly, was her name, along with five others, who had been on the small aircraft from Papua New Guinea to Melbourne.

Her eyes darted over the paper; it was too impossible to believe. How did she make such a crass error? There and then, she realised they had proof and there was no way out and her confident posture changed to that of a frightened child, forcing her words to tumble out. 'No, listen, it's not what you think. I was just visiting my mum. She was sick, I mean, she was dying. She begged me to visit her. I only went there for the day on a weekend. I was working hard in Papua New Guinea, really hard. We were trying to get to the bottom of the pigbel outbreak. I needed a break, I needed my mum … You have to believe me. I never killed my mother; it was her, Lucy. She was the one. It had to be. I would never kill anyone. I'm not violent. Please, you have to believe me. Ask the prison officers here. I would never hurt a living soul.'

The lawyer's mouth was open; he just couldn't comprehend that this young woman could change like a chameleon from a gentle and unassuming person to a dark and malevolent individual. For a second, he thought he had imagined her eyes cloud over with evil, but now, here she was, rambling with a sweet voice, begging to be believed. He wondered if he was going mad himself.

Hamilton nodded. 'No, Miss Bannon, you are right. You would never be violent in the aggressive sense of the word, but you weren't in Papua New Guinea fighting some outbreak, were you?'

Her eyes shot a terrified look from Stuart back to Hamilton, and a dramatic tremor forced her head to nod rhythmically, as her heart rate increased. *Surely, they didn't know the truth?*

Stuart searched her face; he wondered if Hamilton had got it wrong. Kara looked so helpless and traumatised; she didn't look capable of harming a flea. He must have imagined that creepy look. He was tired and perhaps his mind was playing tricks.

'No, Miss Bannon, you were in Papua New Guinea to retrieve the batch of drugs that had been wrongly dispatched. This was a drug that was supposed to save lives, but actually, it would have the opposite effect and with catastrophic consequences. That's true, isn't it?'

Her eyes like saucers, she didn't respond.

'You were there to mop up the mess made by the company. In fact, it was your own incompetence in the first place that led to the okay being given to that particular batch being shipped out. You were on a written warning for such a huge mistake that could have cost many lives.'

He paused and lowered his bitter voice. 'We have spoken with Professor Luken and he confirmed exactly what happened. You also knew that the drug itself wouldn't be detected after death, so a coroner would never be searching the blood samples for it. The unsuspecting culprit would have died from liver and kidney failure, and on the surface, it would have been quite plausible, particularly in a woman riddled with arthritis and having taken huge doses of all sorts to stop the pain. Apparently, her liver would have shown signs of possible failure, but, of course, Miss Bannon, you would know that.'

Kara's mind was in turmoil. The information was correct, but there was no way they could accuse her of poisoning her mother. The drugs used would kill the parasite, but the batch she had overseen – the particular one that had been filled in the wrong proportions, containing an active ingredient that had been added a hundred times over its acceptable dose – had been dispatched at her say-so.

In her rush to get home, she tested the wrong batch number. She never intended to cause harm, and it wasn't until after the weekend, when she carried the empty vials to the disposal unit, that she realised the batch number didn't match the one on the test sheet. In a fit of panic, she got to work testing the correct one, a routine analysis that lasted two days, and in that time, she held her breath and waited.

To her dismay, her world came crashing down around her. The rats that she'd administered the drug to were now all dead. Shockingly, a further examination showed that the drug contained extremely high doses of the active substance and was therefore toxic to humans. The drug was undetectable, unless, of course, the pathology department would have known what to look for, and there was no way that could have happened. The drug itself was an orphan drug not designed for the masses but just a few select patients – those in Papua New Guinea who had contracted the parasite from the pigs that would cause their intestines to swell to the size of sausages and die the most horrendous and unforgiving death. The drugs used would kill the parasite and make the patients better but only if the correct vaccine was used.

She remembered her manager looking at her in complete horror and leaping from his seat. She could still recall his words, which remained stuck in her head. He'd said, 'If just one person dies from your stupid mistake, I will personally see to it you never work in a lab again.' She was on the next flight to Papua New Guinea, and luckily for her, the box of capsules hadn't even left the holding bay. Rather than fly her back to England, the professor demanded she stayed there and work with the team for a few weeks. She thought perhaps it was a punishment, being forced to stay in a developing country rather than being allowed to come home.

'It's lucky that the coroner kept samples of your mother's blood, and with the evidence we had, he could test for that very same drug, and, lo and behold, it was there and in high doses too.' He stopped and sighed. 'There's only one person in the world who could have given it to her and that, Miss Bannon, is you.'

The silence was long, as they waited. Her eyes fell away from theirs to stare at the flight list, and his words circled her mind like a swarm of bees, pricking every means of finding a way out.

Her voice was a mere whisper, as she grappled to save herself. 'No, you've got it wrong. Lucy was there. She could have ...' Unsure of what to say, her words trickled to nothing.

Hamilton smiled. 'Ahh, yes, Lucy, and yes, you are right in so much as Lucy was looking after your mother. You see, Lucy had found out where Joan lived, and her desperate, wayward character meant that she stole money from a Mr Carl Meadows to go and visit the person she believed was her mother. When she arrived, she was horrified to find Joan so poorly, and so she spent three months nursing her without letting Joan know who she really was, and yes, she admitted that she did have revengeful thoughts towards you.'

Kara choked. 'What revengeful thoughts, though, and why me? She was the one who had a happy life. She wasn't alone, not like me.'

'Lucy remembered you as a baby and how Joan took you away, leaving her behind. She hated you, even blamed you for Joan leaving. Then she came across letters from Joan, telling your father how beautiful and wonderful you were, describing the holidays, even enclosing snapshots of you and her on a beach holiday. It sent her on a downward spiral and her hate turned to anger. She admitted she wanted your life.'

'See, she's dangerous ...'

'Miss Bannon, I went to Australia. In fact, I spent weeks there, gathering information—'

'But you're not even a real detective!' she interrupted. She decided then to shut up, realising how pathetic she sounded, gripping at any float to stop herself from sinking.

'I am a real detective, Miss Bannon, but that's not the point. As I was saying, I spent weeks there, and it is true Lucy did spend months in Melbourne. She cared very deeply for your mother. The nurses and the doctors recall how well she'd done her job. It was one that required a lot of patience. However, there was a weekend when Lucy took time out for herself and met a young man and stupidly found herself pregnant. Yes, she has admitted that her son is not in fact Justin's child. A bit like you, really, she knows about drugs, but her knowledge is confined to illegal ones rather than pharmaceuticals. Nevertheless, and this is the interesting point, when Lucy returned after her night away partying, she found Joan very poorly, lying in her bed. She assumed Joan was hallucinating because she'd said that you, Miss Bannon, had paid her a visit.'

Kara screwed her nose up. 'Yes, I did, like I said, but I never killed her.'

'She also said that on the bedside cabinet there was a bottle of cold fruit juice. Joan asked her to pour her another drink because she was burning up. The air conditioning wasn't working. It had in fact been unplugged. Lucy poured the cold juice into a glass, and before Joan put it to her lips, Lucy took a few sips herself, trying to rid herself of a dry mouth from all the drink she'd consumed over the weekend. A short time later, Joan passed away and Lucy felt ill, although she recovered. She did, however, go to the hospital and blood was taken which confirmed she was pregnant. That blood sample has also been tested, and it showed small traces of the very same drug that killed your mother. Sadly, the drug remains in the system for a very long time and would affect an unborn child.'

'But what about Lucy's part in all of this? I mean, she pretended that Justin was the father of her child. You said she'd drugged him—'

Breaking in, Hamilton leaned forward. 'Lucy never murdered anyone. In fact, Miss Bannon, without the messages on the phone, we would never have known the full truth. You see, Lucy kept the phone with all the messages – and I mean all of them. They included the ones that your mother had sent you. Lucy admitted she made phone calls to you too, which was done, in her sick way, to dig the knife in. Looking at all the facts, it is very clear what your intentions were. You would have left things as they were, your mother dead and cremated, with no comebacks to you, but this is where you messed up, Miss Bannon. You see curiosity can get to the best of us. There's a saying "curiosity killed the cat". When you received a call from the person you presumed was the carer, after you believed you had killed your mother, you were rattled. You mentioned to Stuart that the conversation had been eerie.'

He paused and looked at Stuart, who nodded to confirm the fact.

'I don't blame you for wanting to get to the bottom of it. I mean, there you are, Miss Bannon, believing your mother is dead, and out of the blue, you receive a call from your mother's phone asking about Justin. With everything that happened, you didn't have a chance to return that call until you were in prison, and that's when the same woman told you she was having Justin's baby. Of course, you wanted answers, and being in prison left you only one choice and that was to have Stuart investigate. On the face of it, it looked very probable that the person at the end of the phone, Lucy, *did* kill Joan. The evidence initially pointed that way. You are intellectually bright, Miss Bannon, there's no disputing that, but Lucy is deviously clever, and by unwittingly keeping a box full of evidence, she managed to prove her innocence.'

'But ...' It was over: reality hit her in the face. Yes, she was shrewd in the world of science but not so sharp when it came to technology. She had deleted the texts between her mother and herself, including the part that said, *It was so good to see you, my darling daughter, please visit again soon.* Lucy, however, kept the sent message on Joan's phone.

Kara, in her naivety and planning, had assumed her mother had passed away. But very cleverly, as she'd thought, she'd left messages that implied she still believed her mother was alive, so that at some point, if there was any suspicion, Kara wouldn't be implicated.

'After my conversation with Lucy, it was apparent that she had no idea you had visited and did assume it was just mad ramblings from a sick woman, but a while later, she saw the messages. Even in her devious mind, she never imagined that you, Miss Bannon, would have murdered Joan,' said Williams.

'No, but she is bad. Look what she did to me. She took Justin away from me, making me burn the house down.'

That devilish expression plastered across her face made Stuart almost wince. He pursed his lips, her voice now irritating him. 'You, Kara, killed your own mother before you even knew that Lucy had plans to steal him away from you,' he huffed. 'Don't get me wrong. We all know that Lucy is very manipulative and has an extensive criminal record, but it never included murder. She has already admitted that she took the solicitor's letter and copied the heading and typed out her own version that stated you needed to vacate the house, and so, yes, maybe she did have a part to play when you decided to burn the house down. However, the poor woman lost a baby of her own a few years ago. She is a product of circumstance, brought up by a father who worked long hours. With no mother in the house, she tried to find her own way in life and failed at every turn.'

He shook his head, sickened by the fact that Kara had managed to manipulate him. He had gone well beyond his role as a barrister to help Kara, strongly believing she was sincere and shouldn't be in prison – how wrong he was.

Kara leaned forward, placed her elbows on the table, and clasped her forehead with her hands, shielding her eyes.

DI Hamilton rolled the beige stone ring under Kara's nose. As her eyes fell to the object, she could see the inside and the name "Kara" engraved.

'My mother's ring.'

'Yes and no, Miss Bannon. The very sad thing is Joan was not your birth mother or Lucy's. She took you away from Lucy for your own safety. Les Fairmount, your father, couldn't handle both of you because Lucy was a danger. He was worried that Lucy would in some way hurt you. So, Joan unselfishly took you on as her own and adopted you, but, yes, this is her ring.'

With wide eyes and her mouth open, Kara glared in disbelief. 'So, where is my real mother, then?' she snapped.

Hamilton shook his head. 'Probably where you should be, in a mental institution because, Miss Bannon, we are also investigating the possible murder of Thomas Grey, which may very well implicate you!' He waited for a reaction, to give any clue or even a possible confession.

Her eyes widened and her body stiffened up. It was an expression of myriad elements they hadn't seen before. Her face darkened and she looked terrified, as if she was paralysed to the spot, staring at a ghost, her mouth locked in an oval shape.

'Lucy informs us that she found a letter from your mother addressed to you and attached was a solicitor's note. It acknowledges that she'd sadly let you down in your early teenage years and has sealed the truth behind the death of Thomas Grey. The letter is held with her lawyer in Australia. At this time, we are seeking a copy of the letter, since Lucy lost what was apparently a handwritten note. We will also be looking into his death. So, is there anything you wish to tell us on this matter?'

Her shoulders slumped and her head bowed in resignation. Her mind was now off to a safe place where no one could hurt her – it was in a book, a child's magical wonderland story, with fairies and pixies, not monsters and demons.

'Miss Kara Bannon, you are under arrest for the murder of Joan Bannon.'

Chapter 23

Six months later

Deni placed her arm around Kara's shoulders. 'Now you listen to me, my babe. Keep yourself together. This Stuart guy wouldn't be representing you, if he didn't believe in you. He ain't about to sell you down the river, it wouldn't do his reputation any good.'

'I know what you're saying, Deni, but you didn't see the look of hurt on his face, that day the detective charged me with murder.'

'Well, of course, he's gonna be knocked sideways. Bleedin' hell, I was, when I heard the news. I know you, Kara. I've spent many years inside to know the real nutters of this world, and I also know a genuine woman when I meet one. I get why you did what you did, and if the truth be known, anyone else would have done the bloody same, if they had the guts. That, my girl, is the difference. But you tried to be a little too clever about it, and that, I'm afraid, disturbs people and makes it a concern. Now, if you had knifed them both while they slept, everyone would be patting you on the back.'

Trust Deni to say it like it was. She was a shrewd one. With a half-smile, Kara replied, 'It's a shame you're not representing me in court. The jury would buy that defence.'

'Yeah, well, Stuart will be able to say it in the right way. Now then, brush ya hair, while I hold the baby.'

'I received a letter from Vic. She's working as a waitress in Rocky's bar. She sounds really happy, Deni.'

Deni looked at little Denise Rose's round chubby face and tickled her chin, as she held her. 'And Rocky? Have you heard from him?'

Kara placed the brush down on the sink unit and turned to face Deni. 'Yeah, we're still friends, and you were right. I *was* just carried away with the moment, and I guess he was too, but I have to say that Vic, Julie, and Rocky have been an enormous support.'

'Yeah, like family, eh? All for one and one for all!'

'I still feel bad for not letting you all know the truth, but I just couldn't tell you. I liked the way you treated me and it would have changed that. You would have seen me as a monster.'

Deni grinned. 'Like I said before, how could you trust anyone? We don't blame you. Besides, we all have secrets. I don't share my whole life story, ya know.'

Kara gave a generous smile and lowered her gaze. 'I'm so anxious about this meeting.'

Deni gently lowered the baby onto the playmat and gave Kara a hug. 'Now, you just get yourself off and see what he has to say.'

* * *

Nervously, Kara entered the legal visiting room. She avoided eye contact, embarrassed to look up.

Stuart stood and waited for Kara to take a seat. If she'd only known, he felt just as awkward as she did. 'Um ... would you like a tea before we start?'

She sensed the softness in his voice and peered up through her recently grown long fringe. He'd lost weight and his hair was now longer; instead of the short and neat look, his defined waves were tucked behind his ears.

'No, thank you, I'm okay.'

'But *are* you okay though, Kara?' His gentle words brought sudden tears to her eyes.

'Yes, but, Stuart, listen, I'm so sorry I lied. I saw your look of horror during the interview, the day you brought the detective to see me. I let you down, I know, especially as you were trying so hard to help me. I should have—'

He quickly raised his hand to interrupt her. 'Kara, I'm not surprised. How could you have ever trusted anyone, after all that you went through?'

'What are you saying? You don't actually believe me, do you?'

A compassionate smile adorned his face. 'Not only do I believe you, but we've tracked down the official letter that was held by your mother's solicitor, explaining everything. I'm afraid the letter Lucy was talking about was just a handwritten mock-up, but the actual letter is in this file.'

Stuart pulled from his briefcase a folder and gently placed it in front of her. As she opened it and removed the documentation, her eyes focused on the heading of a legal letter with a note attached and signed by Joan and countersigned by her lawyer. She frowned and looked across at Stuart.

'Joan had written a letter and had it sealed at her solicitor's office. The solicitor in question never knew what was in it, but your mother's express wish was that it was to be given to you on her death. The forms are just legal jargon, which confirm she had written the letter herself.'

With her hands shaking, she opened the letter and took a deep breath. She was well aware that this moment was likely to hold great significance for her.

Dearest Kara,
    I cannot ever forgive myself for what I have put you through.

I want you to know that I was totally to blame for what happened to you. Sadly, I was so in love with Thomas Grey that I couldn't bear the thought of him leaving me. I craved his affection like a drug addict, investing all of myself into the relationship, trying to satisfy my own needs and despicably ignoring yours.

I suspect you knew this because as young as you were you were also very astute. I allowed a man to abuse you for my own selfish compulsion. This may sound cold, but I intend it to be factual. I want you to know that not only did I believe you, but I also saw him molesting you. But, I lived in dread that this man would return to his wife, and in doing so, I saw my life was effectively over. It was him or nothing. But my selfish actions allowed him to take away your innocence. At first, I blamed you. I was so jealous because he obviously wanted you. Then, I thought I could turn a blind eye.

Why I allowed it to happen, I will never really understand, except I believe I had an addiction to his affection – a lame excuse, I know. Once you went to boarding school, his visits became fewer, and I somehow stepped back from the situation. It was then that the light went on and I realised what the hell I had done.

My darling Kara, if you are reading this, then I am dead, and I should imagine you will be dancing on my grave for what I did. Never once did you deserve it. You were always the sweetest, kindest girl who never saw bad in anyone. How cruel I have been to such a darling angel.

Hindsight is a wonderful thing, but if I could rewind my life experiences – if I could give you back a childhood that should have been happy and carefree with your dignity respected – I would do so in a heartbeat. I have taken that monster's life, not that it will give you back yours, but at least you will never live in fear that you may lay eyes on Thomas Grey again.

I will never blame you for hating me because I hate myself.

I only hope you find peace and happiness in your life.

Love

Your mother, Joan Bannon

Kara looked up at Stuart, her mind in a whirl and with a confused expression. 'What does this all mean?'

'Well, that letter is for you and the other document is for the courts. It's a confession to the murder of Thomas Grey.'

Kara was reeling in shock. 'My God, *Joan* killed Thomas? Will that confession be upheld in court?'

Stuart smiled. 'The CPS have dropped the investigation into the Thomas Grey murder. You are now not implicated. But, also, the good news is that this letter confirmed that you were sexually abused and that your mother, the one person who you should have been able to rely on, not only knew what was going on but watched it too, and that, my darling, is your ticket out of here.' His face flushed with embarrassment. He had just used a term of endearment. How unprofessional was that?

Still holding the letter, trying to take it all in, Kara broached the subject of Lucy. 'But won't Lucy contest all of this? She absolutely hates me.'

Stuart shook his head. 'No, not at all. We have taken a stack of statements from Lucy. I have interviewed her myself. In fact, Kara, she will be a witness in your defence.'

'But I don't understand it. She detests me.'

'No, Kara, she detested the *idea* of you. There is much that we don't know yet, but gradually, and with the agreement of Lucy and her psychiatrist, we are learning that Lucy's self-esteem was dealt a huge blow when Joan took you away. This was the start of her downward spiral. From the day she tried to suffocate you, she was unintentionally treated as a danger. She was not allowed

381

pets or close contact with smaller children. Unwittingly, Les had pinned her with a label and she became that person – a rebellious young child who turned into a completely unruly teenager with a real grudge to bear.

'Lucy decided that she was a horrible person, with a vindictive personality, and seeing herself as a loser in life with no future, certainly not one like her sister's. It was this that led to Lucy turning out the way she did. She felt she'd been robbed of a mother and wanted compensation in the form of stealing your life because she saw you as the person who stole her mother. So, voluntarily, Lucy is seeing her psychiatrist on a regular basis and is following a rehab programme.

'Once I told Lucy what you had been through and how you had suffered at the hands of a paedophile, she actually cried. You see, the handwritten letter she found didn't have all the details, and so she had no idea what your younger years were like. Joan only told her how well you were doing. She is willing to face the court and tell them exactly what she did to you, including falsifying the solicitor's letter that required you to leave the house and for taunting you whilst you were in prison.'

'Oh my gosh, I don't know what to think.'

Reaching across the table, Stuart placed his hand over hers. 'We got it so wrong, and not just with you either, Kara. Lucy was initially charged with the murder of a Lillian Blackwood because of an antique box containing an expensive bracelet with the name "Lilly" engraved on it. However, the coroner concluded that Lillian had in fact died of a heart attack and banged her head as she fell. So there was no foul play. On further investigation, it was found that Lucy bought the box and the bracelet for her daughter who sadly died. Her name was Lilly.'

Kara looked at his hand covering hers and felt safe. Maybe, one day, she could put her trust in others again. 'How are Lucy and her son?'

'She is doing very well, and Ben is coping just fine. She has shared custody with Justin, and by the way, she has a letter for you. I think she wants to visit you and apologise personally.'

Suddenly, Stuart gripped both her hands. 'I will do my best to get you out of here. I promise. Lucy's confession regarding her part in all of this will get you a lesser sentence when we go for an appeal, and when your new trial comes up, we have evidence to go for voluntary manslaughter, not murder. I will help you all I can.'

A tear trickled down her face – she knew he meant it. Perhaps she could trust again. A world without deceit would be perfect.

Acknowledgements

I never expected a complete stranger to come into my life and offer their help with my books for the love of it. I want to thank Robert Wood who has selflessly helped me along my journey. With so much patience and dedication, he has worked tirelessly to ensure my books are the best they can be.

Deryl Easton has been my go-to girl for advice and support which I will always cherish.

I want to thank Nia for believing in me and giving me the opportunity to be part of the HQ family.

Dear Reader,

Thank you so much for taking the time to read this book – we hope you enjoyed it! If you did, we'd be so appreciative if you left a review.

Here at HQ Digital we are dedicated to publishing fiction that will keep you turning the pages into the early hours. We publish a variety of genres, from heartwarming romance, to thrilling crime and sweeping historical fiction.

To find out more about our books, enter competitions and discover exclusive content, please join our community of readers by following us at:

@HQDigitalUK

facebook.com/HQDigitalUK

Are you a budding writer? We're also looking for authors to join the HQ Digital family! Please submit your manuscript to:

HQDigital@harpercollins.co.uk.

Hope to hear from you soon!

The next book from Kerry Barnes

is coming soon …

If you enjoyed *Deceit*, then why not try another gripping read from HQ Digital?

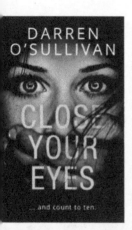